ONE LAST
BREATH

Books by Lisa Jackson

Stand-Alones
SEE HOW SHE DIES
FINAL SCREAM
RUNNING SCARED
WHISPERS
TWICE KISSED
UNSPOKEN
DEEP FREEZE
FATAL BURN
MOST LIKELY TO DIE
WICKED GAME
WICKED LIES
SOMETHING WICKED
WICKED WAYS
SINISTER
WITHOUT MERCY
YOU DON'T WANT TO KNOW
CLOSE TO HOME
AFTER SHE'S GONE
REVENGE
YOU WILL PAY
OMINOUS

Anthony Paterno/Cahill Family Novels
IF SHE ONLY KNEW
ALMOST DEAD

Rick Bentz/Reuben Montoya Novels
HOT BLOODED
COLD BLOODED
SHIVER
ABSOLUTE FEAR
LOST SOULS
MALICE
DEVIOUS
NEVER DIE ALONE

Pierce Reed/Nikki Gillette Novels
THE NIGHT BEFORE
THE MORNING AFTER
TELL ME

Selena Alvarez/Regan Pescoli Novels
LEFT TO DIE
CHOSEN TO DIE
BORN TO DIE
AFRAID TO DIE
READY TO DIE
DESERVES TO DIE
EXPECTING TO DIE

Books by Nancy Bush

CANDY APPLE RED
ELECTRIC BLUE
ULTRAVIOLET
WICKED GAME
WICKED LIES
SOMETHING WICKED
WICKED WAYS
UNSEEN
BLIND SPOT
HUSH
NOWHERE TO RUN
NOWHERE TO HIDE
NOWHERE SAFE
SINISTER
I'LL FIND YOU
YOU CAN'T ESCAPE
YOU DON'T KNOW ME
THE KILLING GAME
OMINOUS
DANGEROUS BEHAVIOR
NO TURNING BACK

Published by Kensington Publishing Corporation

LISA JACKSON
NANCY BUSH

ONE LAST BREATH

KENSINGTON BOOKS
www.kensingtonbooks.com

KENSINGTON BOOKS are published by

Kensington Publishing Corp.
119 West 40th Street
New York, NY 10018

Special book excerpts or customized printings can also be created to fit specific needs. For details, write or phone the office of the Kensington Special Sales Manager. Attn.: Special Sales Department. Kensington Publishing Corp. 119 West 40th Street, New York, NY 10018. Phone: 1-800-221-2647.

Kensington and the K logo Reg. U.S. Pat. & TM Off.

Library of Congress Card Catalogue Number: 2017959456

ISBN-13: 978-1-4967-0786-4
ISBN-10: 1-4967-0786-9
First Kensington Hardcover Edition: March 2018

10 9 8 7 6 5 4 3 2 1

Printed in the United States of America

ONE LAST BREATH

Prologue

It was all he could do not to wring her neck.

"We're both getting what we want," he bit out through his teeth, trying to hold on to his anger. "You're getting what you want. I'm getting what I want."

She was standing right in front of him, arms crossed, daring him, as she always did. "You'd better be right," she warned, inching up her chin defiantly. A sliver of light shot through the hotel room window from the sodium-vapor street lamp outside and glimmered in her hate-filled eyes.

He closed the gap between them and laid his hand against her throat.

She stiffened but she didn't back away, just glared at him. Her lips, so shiny as to appear wet, curled into a sneer. Almost challenging him.

The urge to crush her larynx was so great he trembled with the effort to stop himself and his back teeth gnashed with frustration.

With maddening calm, she said, "You're not that stupid."

She was right. He wasn't that stupid. But it damn near killed him to hold back. Instead of squeezing her windpipe closed, he let his hand move down her chest to her right breast, and caught a new gleam in her eye. Then he shifted up close to her, pushing her to the wall, seeing a slight intake of her breath as he thrust hard against her.

"You're disgusting," she muttered, as his mouth came down hard on those sneering lips.

She pushed her hands against his chest and yanked her mouth away, but he ground his hips into her and her breath started coming fast and shallow. Just as he knew it would. This, their game, always played out the same way. "We don't have time," she warned on a gasp.

"Oh, yeah, we do." He'd already found the zipper that ran down her back and was yanking on it.

"My dress!"

"Take it off," he ordered, but didn't wait. As she began to protest again, he yanked the gown over her head, mussing her hair, dropping the expensive designer creation to the floor. Then, using his weight, he forced her to the carpet as well. Her hands reached up, pushing off his suit jacket, working the buttons of his shirt, stripping him as he skimmed the slimming panties down her legs and kicked off his own binding pants.

And then he was on her, forcing himself into her, probing her hot, moist depths, her denials muted as she met each of his thrusts with her own moans and anxious movements, her fingers digging into his butt. He had to admit she was the best piece of ass he'd ever had, and he'd had scores.

In the midst of one hard plunge, she shuddered and gasped, "When the wedding's over—"

"We're strangers," he finished for her.

And then she threw back her head and let out a breathless scream, clinging to him. He came in a long groan of satisfaction.

God, he thought, a bit dazedly. *I could be with her forever. Too bad she's such a soulless bitch.*

Something's wrong.

In the garden of the hotel, Liam shifted his weight from one foot to the other, glancing down the grassy aisle to the arched arbor with its delicate pergola adorned in pink roses—the spot where his bride would appear. He felt a frisson of expectation and something else—fear?—as he waited to see Rory, glimmering in her wedding dress, waiting expectantly on the arm of her brother.

Never mind that Rory and he were already legally married and this ceremony, created at the behest of his mother, Stella, was really all for show. Still, he was tense. Nervous. And yes, expectant, his heart pounding as he waited to see her in the long white gown and veil, carrying a bridal bouquet . . .

Stupid, he chided himself, *she's your wife and has been for over two months. Get a grip.* Yet he tugged at the collar of his shirt, his gaze focused on the break in the greenery, his pulse jumping.

He checked his watch.

Again.

She sure as hell was taking her sweet time. He'd expected to see her five minutes ago, as had the whole group that had gathered for the event. Guests seated in white chairs spread across the expanse of lawn, nervous members of the wedding party, even some of the hotel staff—all seemed to be holding their collective breath.

Come on, Rory.

He heard a couple of tiny coughs. A soft whisper. The wind riffling leaves on overhead branches.

The organist was staring down the petal-strewn walkway, too. Her plump hands were poised over the keyboard, her brow furrowed. Behind rimless glasses her eyes were filled with concern, their expression just visible in the gathering twilight.

The weather hadn't been favorable, clouds gathering. The hotel, perched high on a cliff over Lake Washington, was already awash in exterior lights, evening rapidly approaching.

The preacher, bald and dressed in black, waited with an open Bible in hand. He caught Liam's eye, silently signaling his concern.

"What's the holdup?" his best man whispered as the preacher stepped over to the organist, said something under his breath, and the woman at the keys began playing softly again, the same familiar strains of *Pachelbel's Canon*, joyful, lilting music that just screamed "wedding" as the guests filtered in.

"Don't know."

"She'd better show up soon." Standing next to Liam, Derek, his half brother, shifted from one foot to the other, crushing the blades of grass beneath his weight. They were about the same size, Liam slightly taller, both trim, both having inherited their father's light brown eyes and thick, coffee-dark hair. Derek, older, sported his mother Karen's wide forehead and single dimple, while Liam's jaw was a little more square, his eyes deeper set. However, despite being born to different mothers, Geoff Bastian's sons did look like brothers. "The natives are getting restless," Derek added, and he wasn't wrong.

Guests were shifting in their chairs and craning their necks as they cast looks toward the empty arbor.

Derek frowned, surveying the crowd. "You want me to go looking for her?"

"No!" Liam said a little louder than he'd wanted, turning a few heads. He lowered his voice and added, "She's only a few minutes late."

"Maybe she wants to make a grand entrance," Derek said. "Well, I guess she already is."

"Right." Liam clenched his teeth, reminded himself to be patient. This, a "proper" and showy wedding, was created at his mother's insistence and would be over soon.

If and when it ever got started.

The gathering wasn't large by Bastian wedding standards, but more than a hundred people were waiting on the lawn in neat rows of white chairs, some festooned with bouquets of roses and baby's breath. Most of the guests were friends of his parents; some were of his own acquaintance. Very few were aligned with his wife, however; just her mother, and step-brother Aaron, the person she'd chosen to walk her down the aisle.

Liam didn't much like anyone in her family and the feeling was mutual. Her stepbrothers were definitely interested in the Bastian money, but they still felt more comfortable with Rory's previous boyfriends, none of whom Liam had ever met. But maybe the monetary interests were less than he thought and that was the holdup? Was Aaron involved in some eleventh-hour, last gasp effort to stop the wedding? Maybe thinking he could wrangle Rory out of her marriage if she didn't go through with this formal ceremony? He wasn't the most reli-able of guys at the best of times, though he did seem to have Rory's best interests at heart . . . No, Aaron didn't have that strength of conviction. Everett, Rory's elder stepbrother, now there was a guy who would stop the earth spinning on its axis if he thought it might gain him something. He was as wily and determined and full of bad choices as his father . . . who just happened to be doing five to ten in prison and therefore would not be attending his stepdaughter's wedding.

Liam shifted his stance. He was tense all over. Maybe Rory was the reason for the holdup. She hadn't been crazy about this big show of a wedding, nor had he, for that matter, but they'd both bent to Stella's wishes.

Almost of its own accord, his eye found his mother, who was sitting like a frozen mannequin, or maybe like a prisoner in front of a firing squad. Her swept-up blond hair seemed to defy the elements, while other women were swiping away errant strands from the bursts of a crisp and persistent breeze. Stella hadn't wanted the marriage at all, but since Liam and Rory had sealed the deal two months earlier in front of a judge, she'd had a near breakdown at the news, then had suddenly ramped up and decided to make the wedding the event of the season. Though the Bastians hailed from Portland, Rory's family lived in the Seattle area. When Stella found she could get a hotel on Lake Washington because some other unhappy couple had called it quits at the last moment, she'd grabbed the venue and leaped in with all the fervor of a new convert, ignoring the grumblings of Liam's father about cost, time, and work.

So, here they were.

He caught movement near the pergola and witnessed Darlene, Rory's mother and the matron of honor, peeking out from a space between the hedgerow and slats of the arbor. A concerned look was etched on Darlene's features, and she bit at her lower lip. As if she, too, was edgy, beginning to worry.

Great.

Liam willed his wife to appear. *Come on, come on.* His jaw tightened. Rory wouldn't stand him up, would she? Heaven knew she was as opposed to all the pomp and ceremony as he was, but she'd agreed to this spectacle and they *were* already married.

She'll be here. Have a little faith. She won't run out on you. What would be the point? This is just some wedding-day glitch. It happens all the time. The delay's probably because of Aaron. Between dope smoking, video games, and the occasional part-time job that invariably fizzled within the month, Rory's step-brother wasn't exactly a rock of responsibility.

Frowning, Liam pulled on the edge of his sleeve and noted the time. Not quite ten minutes had passed since Rory was supposed to have started her short walk from the arbor. Aaron was probably late to pick her up. As usual.

Just hold on. You and Rory will laugh about this later . . .

The minutes ticked by. Liam shifted his gaze from the decorated arch to the guests seated in two groupings of white chairs on either side of the pink rose-petal path. To his right, visible through a break in the hedge, were the gray-green waters of Lake Washington far below the cliff's edge. Though rain was pending, it was a beautiful evening. It should be a moment to remember . . .

The sea of expectant faces swam before his vision and he settled his gaze on his father, who was tense and looked almost angry. He could tell Geoff was beginning to wonder if the no-good, no-class, no-nothing girl Liam had brought home was about to stand him up. Unheard of! No one deliberately let down a Bastian.

Liam inwardly sighed. His father was a domineering patriarch and had been all his life. Stella leaned in and said something to Geoff and he brushed her off. Liam could tell he was getting antsy. The last thing he needed was for his father to make a scene.

Where was Rory? She knew what Liam's family thought of her, but she'd been stalwart in her decision to marry him. Maybe "stalwart" was too strong a word. More like she was as eager as he was to get past this hurdle, start their life together and damn the consequences.

Except she wasn't here.

The niggling worry dug farther into his brain and he felt himself start to sweat. Rory had not invited Everett Stemple— nor Harold Stemple, Rory's stepfather, who couldn't make the wedding for obvious reasons—but Everett hadn't taken the snub well. *You'll be sorry*, he'd told Rory in front of Liam, though Liam had thought it was petty anger at the time, not a serious threat. Could Everett be involved in this delay some-how? Maybe he'd coerced Aaron into some half-baked plan to stop the event, just to be an asshole. That would be just like him.

His mother was staring at him. He could read the set of her jaw, the burn of her gaze. She'd called the Stemples "the under-belly of society," and she didn't really differentiate Rory from her stepfamily. Stella was wrong about Rory, but she wasn't wrong about Harold Stemple. A year and a half earlier Harold had mounted a home invasion on a wealthy Seattle family, try-ing to steal their jewels, not realizing they were the kind of people who owned stocks and bonds and very little in the way of items that could be pawned. Harold tied them up and then took the husband to an ATM, where he got about three hun-dred dollars and his picture on the ATM camera. There was talk that Everett was involved, too, but nothing was ever proved. It was a mystery why Darlene stayed married to the man, but Rory had embarrassedly admitted that her mother felt she was somewhat psychic and believed the powers of the universe wanted her to stay in the union.

But Rory was different than all of them. A redheaded burst of sunlight who'd literally bumped into Liam on a crowded Seattle street and stolen his heart in fifteen minutes. His mother had practically contorted herself into a pretzel to get him to marry Bethany, whose family's social standing was in a range with the Bastians', and had been nearly apoplectic when he'd chosen Rory Abernathy.

"You can't do it," Stella had declared.

Watch me. He hadn't said the words, but the meaning was there. He hadn't told Stella that he and Rory were already mar-ried when he'd delivered the news that he was in love with her, but he'd had to soon after, as she suddenly appointed herself his matchmaker, throwing Bethany at him full bore along with a few other socially accepted women on her list for a special dinner that she began setting up immediately after hearing his plans. He'd wanted to tell her that he and Rory were already married, but his mother had pushed so hard he'd backed off. He'd called her the next day to let the ax fall. Stella had taken about a week off, at least she'd gone silent for that amount of time, only to resurface as the wedding planner who would not be challenged. By the time Liam got Rory down to Portland from Seattle and she met his family for the first time, Stella had already booked the venue.

"A few words in front of some judge are not going to suffice," she told them both. "If you want to be part of this family, you need to be recognized in the eyes of God."

Rory had been taken aback, torn between amusement and anger at Stella's high-handedness. Liam had been annoyed by the posturing because his mother didn't have any relationship with God, or at least she hadn't in all of his thirty-four years. Like Rory, he couldn't decide if he was pissed, or if it was funny, that Stella was throwing around edicts that had no substantive basis.

"We'll think about it," Liam told his mother, and in the end, laughing over a bottle of wine till they both cried, he and Rory had decided to go through with the ceremony.

"Whatever floats her boat," Rory said, smiling.

She was amused by his money and position, but not interested in it. In fact she'd shied away from any real relationship with him at first *because* of his family's social status. Unlike him, she hadn't believed their whirlwind romance had the strength to endure, and she'd been as slippery as an eel to pin down for a first date. Her elusiveness had forced him to pursue her, something new and unusual in his dealings with women. Her coolness had made him almost desperate to connect with her. He'd had to work damn hard to convince her to go out with him, and even then she'd kept him at arm's length for what had seemed way too long, when in actuality it had been less than a week.

"Jesus, where is she?" Derek wondered aloud, breaking into Liam's thoughts.

Liam didn't answer. Derek was probably eating this up. He considered Liam's relationship with Rory bad news, a stupid mistake. "You're obsessed, man. Thinking with your dick, and it's not going to turn out well," he'd said enough times for Liam to want to take him down to the ground and wrestle him like they'd done when they were kids, though Derek, being three years older and a whole lot tougher, had generally beaten the shit out of Liam.

Now he heard Derek snort softly in that *I told you so* way that made Liam, absurdly, want to wrestle him again. Wouldn't that be great. The Bastian brothers rolling around on the grass and rose petals, getting filthy and torn at Liam's wedding. Stella would have a shit fit and his father's face would turn brick red, the volcano building, about to erupt. The consequences from such a social faux pas would be dire, which made him want to grab Derek all the more.

With an effort, he brought himself back from the brink.

Rory, where the hell are you?

She was late.

To her own damned wedding.

Rory paced in the hotel room and wished she'd never agreed to go along with the farce. Worse yet, she'd asked Aaron to walk her down the aisle, though she'd put her foot down at the "giving away" part. Talk about an outdated male-dominated ritual. She was her own woman and she should never have even asked her stepbrother to escort her, but it was too late now.

Where was he?

She glanced at the clock on the bedside table. She was already ten minutes behind schedule and expected that if Aaron didn't appear soon, someone else would come knocking. Probably her own mother, Darlene, whom Rory had chosen as matron of honor. What a mistake. Darlene was less reliable than Aaron: flighty, easily influenced, convinced she was somewhat psychic . . . But Liam's stubborn, snobbish mother was even worse. Stella didn't even bother to mask her disapproval of her new daughter-in-law. Rory should have stopped this whole, awful charade before it ever got off the ground.

Well, to hell with it. She was here, for better or worse.

For richer, for poorer, in sickness and in health . . .

Rory scooped her bouquet from the bed, rose petals scattering, and started for the door. She'd walk herself to the makeshift altar. The sooner Stella's elaborate cere-*money*, as Geoff Bastian had called it, was over, the better.

She shook her head. Good God. Was she really doing this?

As she made her way toward the door, she caught a glimpse of herself in the mirror. Slim figure dressed in a long, white, shimmering gown, complete with train and a wispy veil pinned to her wild red curls. She hadn't bothered to drape the sheer fabric over her eyes. It wasn't as if she were some innocent virgin. She and Liam had been married for over two months, most of which had been taken up with wedding preparations.

She clamped her teeth together, saw the fury and determination on her own face, and immediately let out her breath. The whole aura of pretentiousness bugged her, but she'd agreed to this event in a misguided attempt to please Stella—though no one pleased Liam's mother unless she wanted to be pleased— and let's face it, she'd kind of been attracted to the idea of a real wedding, with real guests and a white dress and a tiered cake. She'd actually entertained the idea that it might be *fun*.

Now she groaned, and her green eyes watered a bit. Embarrassment? Fear? Anxiety? Maybe a little of each. She had to keep reminding herself that it would all be over soon, and that this wedding in a grand hotel with incredible views, liveried waitstaff and room charges that would make a normal woman faint, was all for show.

But this is what it's going to be like being a Bastian. All façades and hidden emotions. Can you do it, Rory, my girl? Can you?

She made a strangled sound. No. Not the way Stella ran the show.

"He married *you*," she told the anxious-eyed woman in the mirror, running a hand over her flat stomach and blinking away the wetness that starred her vision. Of their own accord, her eyes then sought out her overnight bag, sitting at the end of the king-sized bed with its ocean-blue comforter accented with crisp white sheets and pillows.

But . . . if things didn't work out?

She tore her gaze from the bag. She wouldn't think of all the problems hovering at the corners of her world. She loved Liam. He loved her. They were going to be together forever and have a happy life.

Rap. Rap. Rap!

"Thank you, God," she whispered, hurrying to answer the soft knocking on the door.

"About time, Aaron," Rory complained as she threw back the door. "We're already late and—"

But she didn't see Aaron. At least not his face, which was hidden by a huge bouquet of helium balloons—silver, white, and black—floating in the air in front of him.

"What're you doing?" she demanded and didn't bother keeping the anger from her voice. "I'm already supposed to be at the altar!" She batted at the balloons when he suddenly pushed his way into the room.

"Wait! Wait!"

Balloons fluttered about and she caught a glimpse of his face, his *masked* face. "Aaron? What are you doing?"

For a wild moment she thought it was Liam, planning to kidnap her and take her away from this madness. But as the man kicked the door closed and came at her, her anger gave way to fear.

"Stop this!" She tried not to sound panicked, but her heart was pounding wildly.

"Stop what?" The voice was high-pitched and whiney, a child's voice.

"Who are you? What—I—I have to go!" She sprang for the door, but his hand reached out and manacled her wrist.

Pop!

A white balloon shriveled and fell to the floor, its string snaking on the carpet.

What?

Pop! Pop!

Two more balloons died a quick and noisy death.

"Aaron, for God's sake. It's not funny." But she knew it wasn't Aaron. Gut instinct told her so.

Then her gaze caught on the knife gripped in his hand, a long, slim blade glinting wickedly as it poked yet one more balloon.

Pop!

Oh. God.

He let go of the rest of the balloons and they separated and floated lazily toward the ceiling. Everything turned to slow motion. His mouth was set inside the ski mask, red lips flattened in anger. This was no joke.

She opened her mouth to scream, but he was on her, a gloved hand smothering her mouth, the other fast and hard around her wrist.

"Don't even think about it," he ground out in that squeaky falsetto. He'd huffed helium from the balloons, she realized. "Do as I say, or you both die. I'll slit your throat and then I'll slit his."

His? Whose? Liam's?

She couldn't stop the shaking gasp that left her lips.

His gaze scraped down her body. "That's right. You'll never get away, and that baby of yours will die."

He knew? How? No one knew, not even Liam.

Reflexively, she struck him with her free hand, her fingers curling into a fist as she jabbed sharply upward, connecting with his nose, hearing the crunch of cartilage. He yelped in pain and pulled back the knife.

Panic spread through her.

His knife hand slashed downward as she propelled her knee to his groin. He twisted, mitigating the blow somewhat, doubling over with a gasp as the blade caught in her veil and ripped it from her head.

"I'll kill you!" he cried.

She swung her knee upward again and this time she connected fully. Hard. He cried out and his fingers loosened on her wrist, the knife dropping from his other hand, but his body still blocked the door. "That was a big mistake!" he spat out, crouching and holding his crotch.

Her gaze searched frantically for the knife. It was beneath his feet. Unreachable.

Knife . . .

She glanced toward the fruit tray on the table to her right. A small paring knife was wedged into the brick of cheese. She leapt to it, snatched it up, spinning around as he lunged at her, knocking them both into her overnight bag, toppling it to the carpet. His right hand was splayed on the table, and without hesitation she plunged the tiny blade deep into the flesh behind his ring finger.

He gave out a high-pitched, piggish squeal of shock and outrage. Rolling to his side, he clutched one hand with the other, blood showing on his fingers. She scrambled to her feet, breathing hard.

"Bitch!" he cried in disbelief. "I warned you! I warned you! You're all going to die!"

Rory didn't wait. She leapt over him, but his fingers caught in the train and he yanked her roughly backward, tearing the fabric with a sickening rip. Stumbling, she jerked her dress free, only to have her own feet tangle in the lengths of silk. She caught a glimpse of her reflection in the full-length mirror: flushed face, mussed hair, red stain on the bodice of her white dress where his blood had smeared. Her gaze dropped to the knife still gripped tightly in her hand. Bloodstained. "Oh, God." As if suddenly shocked, her fingers shot out straight, releasing it where it dropped to the ground next to the masked figure on the floor.

Run!

Her first instinct. Always.

Run!

Maybe she should race to the area where the guests were gathered, to Liam . . . to the police . . .

Run!

You have to leave. Now. How could you ever explain this? What happened here. About the past? The secrets? And . . . the baby?

Her assailant was writhing on the floor, blood on his neck darkening his black shirt. His own knife was only a few feet away. He wouldn't be down for long—

He started climbing to his feet, ready to attack again. She snatched up her overnight bag as he staggered toward her, growling unintelligible words. With a grunt she swung the case hard, right at his head.

Bam!

He fell backward, knocking over the table, his head hitting the floor with a loud thud. He gave out a sick moan and then lay still.

You killed him!

Oh, my God!

You killed him!

No . . . No. Don't go there. It was self-defense. He was attacking you!

Run! Save yourself. Save the baby! Liam and his family can't help you. Not now. You know it!

On quivering legs she took two steps toward the door. Her attacker groaned and shifted his legs. Panic surged. Whoever he was, he was still alive. She hadn't killed him. At least not yet.

She didn't stop. Buzzing with fear, she twisted the knob and pulled open the door. Searching both ends of the hallway before stepping outside the room, she gathered her dress and bag, softly closed the door behind her. Hurriedly, she headed for the stairs, one hand jammed into her overnight bag, fingers over her cell phone.

Cameras!

All hotels have cameras!

You're doomed, Rory. Doomed.

She kept her head turned downward, though anyone viewing a tape of her escape would know instantly who she was by her hotel room number and her damned bridal gown. As she reached the stairs, she heard voices and footsteps approaching from a floor below. Rather than risk meeting anyone, she flew down the hallway to the employee elevator, the one she'd seen used by a hotel maid earlier. Pounding on the call button she tried to think clearly. Could she abandon this mad escape and seek out Liam? She glanced at her cell phone, saw the text that had come in from him only moments earlier.

Where are you? Everything okay?

Her heart twisted.

Throat dry, hands shaking, she typed out: **Small glitch with dress. OK now. Be there in a sec.** Then for good measure: **Can't wait. Xoxo.**

Liar! He'll never forgive you.

Despite her hasty text she knew it was only minutes—seconds maybe—before someone came to her room and found her gone, the would-be killer lying on the floor possibly dying.

Who was he?

A bad dude. Someone connected to your stepfamily? You should have been more forthright with Liam. You should have told him everything instead of holding back..

The elevator doors parted and the car was thankfully empty. She pressed the button for the lowest level, and then silently prayed the car wouldn't stop on its way to sub-basement C. She wasn't so lucky. With a jolt the elevator halted on the first parking level and she wondered how she could explain herself to anyone getting on. Her ripped and bloodied bridal gown to start with and her obvious disarray and panic would invite speculations, questions, offers of help . . .

Her heart clutched!

With a whisper, the doors parted.

Rory braced herself.

But no one entered. The parking level seemed deserted.

Because everyone's already at the wedding.

Well, thank God! She pounded on the button and the elevator door closed again. As soon as the car landed at the lowest level and the doors opened again, she strode quickly into what appeared to be the darkened bowels of the hotel, the overnight parking.

Dusty pipes hung overhead, fluorescent lights sizzled, and tire marks blackened the concrete floor. She was nearly overcome with the scent of exhaust old enough to coat the gray walls. She didn't waste any time and made the call.

Holding her breath, she was afraid the wireless connection wouldn't work, but she was wrong.

Voice mail answered.

Damn!

"This is Rory. I'm in trouble. I need you," she said breathlessly. "I'm heading for the lake and the marina, just south of the hotel landing. Meet me there in ten minutes."

She clicked off and prayed he got the message. Then she went to work. In the shadow of the cement wall of the elevator shaft for privacy, she stripped off the expensive dress, kicked off the useless glittery heels, and pulled on her jeans, a sweatshirt, running shoes, and her favorite baseball cap. Despite the fact that the day was growing dark, she slipped on her sunglasses as well as an oversized jacket. She ditched the dress in a wastebasket and took off running, up the stairs to the ground level of the hotel and into the fresh air.

She heard the sound of a car's engine and flattened against the wall only to catch a glimpse of a gray sedan speeding in from the street. She glanced back and saw it racing up the spiral ramp, its tires squealing a little all the way around the turns.

She hesitated a moment, counting her heartbeats, then dashed around the front of the hotel, avoiding the wedding party, intent on reaching the stairwell to the lake. Music reached her ears, the rising notes of *Pachelbel's Canon* from the arbor behind the hotel.

Her music. *Her* wedding . . .

A soft cry of anguish squeezed past her lips, but she cut it off. *Don't go there. It's over. Just as you knew it would be.*

She headed away from the ceremony, ducking around fountains and across the courtyard, trying to avoid catching sight of anyone, which was impossible. She passed a couple pushing a stroller, and an older man in a sport coat and loosened tie, smoking a cigarette as he made his way to the parking area. Quickly, she slid around the building, past cars parked on the street. A woman was walking her dog, a terrier of some kind, and it came unglued, pulling and straining at its leash, barking loudly at the sight of her.

"Stop it! Jeeves, cut it out! *No* barking! Zero. Got it?" Dressed in a puffy coat, stocking cap, and leggings, the woman tugged on the leash to give Rory an apologetic half smile. "He won't bite, really. He's . . . he's a sweetheart. Just a little territorial on the leash."

Rory gave a quick nod and circumvented the dog to head down a service alley between two of the buildings on the hotel property. Around a corner she made her way past garbage bins and parked cars that nearly blocked the narrow lane. At the far end of the alley, she found her way to the side of the hotel property and hastened to the hundred-year-old staircase leading down to the shores of Lake Washington.

The last notes from the organ slowly faded away, the music seeming to hover on the breeze, leaving a gap of expectance.

Liam's throat was dry. He could hardly work up any spit. He checked his phone again, but there were no further texts from Rory. He'd been momentarily relieved at the last one. Problem with the dress? Okay. He could wait. But it sure had been a lot longer than "a sec" . . .

The tails of his tuxedo jacket whipped in a sudden gust of wind. Some of the guests ducked their heads or threw up a hand to catch escaping hair and hats, but no bride appeared through the wall of greenery.

Derek exhaled heavily through his nose.

"I'm getting to the bottom of this," Liam said as he caught a glimpse of Rory's mother, Darlene, the matron of honor, peering nervously from a crack near the arbor.

"Wait," Derek advised, his hand around Liam's upper arm.

"No."

"You're already married, man. It's not like she can get cold feet. Didn't she say she hit some kind of snag and was on her way?"

"I don't like it." Something was off. Really wrong.

"Give it five more minutes. What will that hurt?" Derek flashed a smile meant to be calming.

It wasn't.

"Trust me, you don't want to mess this up any more than it already is," Derek added.

"Fine. Two minutes. That's it."

"Chill out."

No way in hell. He didn't care if he mortified his mother by chasing after his wife. He didn't give a damn about this ceremony.

"More music," Derek suggested, and Liam, jaw set, nodded shortly to the organist, who drew a breath and started in once more.

The guests couldn't decide whether there was a problem or not. Liam's father, Geoff, was tight-lipped, and his mother stared straight ahead, forcing a tight smile, trying to hide the faintly triumphant look on her face. Stella had never liked Rory. And he could practically hear the *I told you so* swimming around in his mother's head. Now, standing at the altar, Liam turned his gaze to his ex-girlfriend. Bethany's blond hair was pinned up in some kind of knot that resisted the wind, similar to his mother's coif, and her face was serene. From her seat next to her new boyfriend, her plus-one, she caught Liam's gaze and lifted an eyebrow, questioning.

He let his gaze slide from Bethany to his sister, Vivian, who was easy to pick out in her canary-yellow dress and wide-brimmed hat. Vivian's choice had caused Stella to groan, but Liam had inwardly applauded her. Derek had looked at the hat and drawled, "You're not meeting the Queen of England."

Viv had snapped back in a dead-on British accent, "Shut up, fuck-face."

Now, he caught his sister's eye. In her swirl of yellow, she gazed at him, brows also lifting in the unspoken question. Viv was the one member of his family who'd accepted Rory. "Come on, it's obvious he loves her, what're you going to do?" she'd said to their mother. "Clamp a chastity belt around him, lock him up and throw away the key?" She'd grinned wickedly. "Ooops. Too late for that, isn't it? He's already married."

And then a smattering of rain hit the congregation.

"I'm not waiting any longer," Liam muttered to his brother.

"Huh. I thought you'd be the one to call it off first."

"I'm going to go find her."

Derek's hand clasped his upper arm. "She's not going to give up Bastian millions. She'll get here."

"You don't know a thing about her."

"Nor, it seems, do you."

Roughly, Liam jerked his arm back. *Damn it, Rory*, he thought, *what the hell's going on?*

Hurrying down the slippery wooden steps, she clung to the rail and shut out all thoughts of the wedding and forced herself to mentally check off all the items in her bag: *Phone, underwear, makeup bag, two thousand dollars in hundreds, my grandmother's silver locket, gold band Liam gave me at our marriage, our real marriage . . . phone, underwear, makeup bag, two thousand dollars in hundreds . . .*

At a landing, she turned her face to the rain, looked down at the water, drew a breath, and checked her phone. No more texts. No return call. "Come on," she said. At the bottom of the stairs she dialed again the number of the one person she thought could help her: Uncle Kent, "The Magician." Kent Daley wasn't a magician and he wasn't her uncle or any kind of relative, but he could do magical things, like bury dead bodies where they'd never be found, metaphorically speaking, and he treated her like a favorite child. She'd thought of him often during her whirlwind romance with Liam, sensing she might need him, as she'd feared the marriage would be doomed before it began. He'd warned her to be careful when he'd learned she was marrying a Bastian. "People with money don't play by our rules, princess," he'd said. "They don't understand us, and we don't understand them. Not fully. Not the way we need to. You understand?"

She'd answered that she did, but now she realized she hadn't. And The Magician's advice hadn't stopped her from marrying Liam. Nothing could have deterred her. She'd trusted from her soul, wanting something good so badly she was willing to risk ultimate heartbreak. Even so, she'd called Uncle Kent before the grandiose ceremony, jokingly asking if he was available just in case she decided she wanted his special kind of "magic."

"You need me, I'll be there," he assured her.

His serious tone had brought instant tears to her eyes. "No, I'm just kidding. You sure you can't come to the wedding?"

"Not a scene I'm comfortable with."

She'd nodded. Though it was left mostly unsaid, they both had known you didn't invite a man like The Magician to your wedding. At least not to a Bastian over-the-top society extravaganza. Uncle Kent lived on the edge of legal, and purposely kept to the shadows. Having some members of her own family attend created enough complications already.

"You take care with those people," was his final warning. "Remember, their money doesn't make them special. They're no better than the rest of us."

Now, though, his promises seemed thin as tissue paper as he hadn't called back. Damn it all. Frantically, she texted him again:

I need you. ASAP!

The phone rang in her hand. She looked down and nearly cried with relief. *Uncle Kent!*

"I'm in trouble," she blurted into the phone.

He didn't waste time. "I just heard your message. Where are you?"

"At the bottom of the stairs from the hotel to the lake. I'm—"

"I know it. I'll be there, but don't turn south. Not to the marina. Okay? Walk the path north to the private homes. Get to the first private dock."

"Oh, God."

Her lashes starred with tears.

She was leaving Liam.

Forever.

He would never forgive her.

The rain had drifted to a faint sprinkle. The organist looked at Liam as she folded her hands and the music faded away. An uncomfortable moment passed. This time it was Derek who nodded to her, and she immediately straightened and apparently took it as a signal to start once again. But instead of *Pachelbel's Canon*, she hit the first loud chords of "Here Comes the Bride."

Everyone rose to their feet. Liam jerked around to look at Derek as the guests stood up. Derek waggled his head and lifted his palms, as surprised as Liam, but then he shrugged and said, "Well, either she's coming or she's not."

Liam snapped his attention back to where Rory would first appear. He was very afraid that Rory wasn't going to show. What he saw was Rory's mother reluctantly starting down the aisle, but her smile was forced and she stared at Liam questioningly as she stepped over the strewn rose petals.

Everyone looked expectant and Liam straightened, hands clasped in front him, praying silently that Rory would appear, sensing deep down that something was terribly, horribly wrong.

But then the music ran on . . . and on . . . and on . . .

No bride.

No text.

He checked. For the dozenth time.

Come on, Rory. Come on.

His hands were clenched, his gaze riveted to the empty arbor.

When the organist got to the end of the song, Liam signaled her to stop. No need to go on. Murmurs of surprise broke out in the crowd and Liam's father stalked up to his sons, the fading sun touching his silver hair, making it seem to glow.

"Where the hell is she?" Geoff Bastian stated tightly.

"I don't know."

"You're going to have to call this off, son. You've disgraced your mother."

"Stella'll get over it," Derek drawled.

"That girl—" Geoff shook his head and bit off his remark, though he clearly had a lot more to say.

"I'll go find her. You should sit back down," Liam told his father.

Derek said, "No, Liam, you stay here. I'll find her and—"

"I'm going," Liam snapped.

"Liam," Derek said long-sufferingly, but Liam had already taken a few steps down the aisle after his father.

Aaron suddenly appeared from behind the hedge. Liam stopped short. *Thank God!* But Aaron's face was grim as he ran up the bridal path, crushing the petals. Liam's heart froze. What? *What?* "Where's—"

Blam! Blam! Blam!

He whipped around. The sharp reports were deafening. Had a car backfired?

"What?" he asked at the same moment a woman at the end of the row nearest him began screaming, followed by others.

Not a car. Shots!

The world seemed to spin in slow motion. He watched as Aaron went down in a sprawling heap, pink petals fluttering upward.

Where the hell were the shots coming from? Panic ensued, people screaming and crying, running and knocking over everything and everyone.

Liam started to move toward Aaron.

Blam! Blam! Blam! Blam! Blam!

His body jerked as the first bullet struck. He staggered, but the force knocked him off his feet. The side of his head slammed against the ground.

Screams had turned to shrieks. Glass shattered. Wood splintered.

Someone was barking orders. A security guard?

"Move it. Get inside. Move it!" he hollered.

Lifting his head slightly, Liam caught a weird, panoramic view, as if he were looking through a distorted wide-angle lens at what had been the wedding venue. His father collapsed a few feet from him. People sprawled on the ground, crawling frantically, staining their expensive clothes. Others running wildly. Overturned chairs. Collapsed tables. Upended wineglasses. Shards of glass glittering amongst the grass and rose petals.

Frantic people scrambling to their feet, trying to escape the rain of bullets.

An older woman edged across the ground, her silvery skirt hiked above mud-stained knees as she sought cover behind the pathetically narrow protection of the white folding chairs.

Rory?

Where was she?

A new terror gripped him and he forced himself to his knees.

His head swam. He was vaguely aware of his sister's canary-yellow hat blowing across the grounds beyond the chairs as if it were trying to escape. And in the corner of his eye he spied his mother staggering into a heap beside Vivian, who was curled around a chair in a yellow ball.

No! he thought disjointedly. *No, Viv! No, no!*

He heard a noise. A cry of agony, and turned to spy Aaron writhing on the path, chairs upended all around him, his face twisted in pain. Blood showed on his white shirt, blooming a bright red.

"Up there! On the roof!" someone yelled. "The parking garage! The shooter's there!"

"He's shooting us! He's shooting us!" someone else cried.

The security guard was barking into his cell phone, "The South Lake Inn, that's right! An active shooter. Shot the hell out of a wedding here. I've got people down . . . what? I don't know. Injured for sure. Possibly dead. For the love of God, get someone here now!"

Someone was running. Footsteps pounding. Pandemonium ensuing.

Groggily, Liam twisted his neck and caught a glimpse of the edge of the parking garage. He blinked . . . was there a man peering over the ledge?

"Get down!"

"Run!"

People ran past him.

He tried to stand. Pain speared through him.

He wobbled.

My leg, he thought in a detached way, looking down at his thigh where blood was soaking through a hole in his pant leg. A bullet to his femoral artery? The thought was fleeting, somehow seeming not related to the moment.

Everything in the surrounding chaos seemed surreal, as if in a distorted dream. The screaming, crying guests, the organist shivering behind the keyboard player, the minister leaning over a fallen man. The security guard, a gun in one hand, phone in the other, spitting out information to the phone, frantically waving people into the building.

Liam's right hand moved automatically to clutch at his gut and he mentally ordered himself to pull it away. When he saw the bloody fingers, he glanced at his once white, now red, shirt. Another bullet to his midsection.

This could be bad, he noted in wonder, distantly aware his reaction was all wrong.

He was on his feet now, swaying, managing one more step.

Derek was suddenly next to him, swearing viciously as he grabbed hold of his brother. "Shit, man!" Derek's face was white and drawn. "Lie down. Lie the fuck down! Do you want to bleed out?"

"Rory?" he asked. Did he hear sirens?

"She's not here!" his brother babbled in shock, taking Liam's weight as Liam felt himself falling. "She's in the wind!"

"Where is—?"

"Hell, I don't know. Her own damned wedding. Where is she? Don't you die on me, Liam. Oh, shit. Don't do this, man, don't you do this!" Derek's white face swam into his vision.

Liam struggled to hold on, but there was no escape from the blackness coming for him, the sensation of sweet oblivion calling.

"*Liam!*" A pause. "Help! I need medical help here! Liam . . . Liam! Jesus . . ."

Just before he passed out, slumped heavily into his brother's arms, Liam suffered a moment of terrible clarity: *Rory knew about the assault. Somehow, some way, Rory knew.*

Chapter 1

Portland, Oregon
Five years later . . .

Most every window of the storefronts on the street level had
been smashed or broken and the ones recently installed to the
apartments above, still sporting their manufacturing stickers,
weren't in much better shape. Though intact, all save for one
were starred and cracked, possibly from the small piece of concrete at Liam's feet.

Derek ripped off his hard hat and threw it on the ground.
"This keeps happening, we'll go broke!"

The sound of an electric saw buzzing on an upper floor was
a steady noise he had to shout over. Liam yelled, "Put that
back on."

"I don't give a damn what falls on my head."

"Don't be an asshole."

"What should I be, huh? Calm and frozen like you? This has
been going on too long and I know who's behind it."

"Random vandalism," Liam said.

"Everett Stemple," Derek spat back. "Blames you for his sister's death. Blames all of us."

"Stepsister. And she's not dead, she's MIA," Liam corrected, as he always did when dealing with Derek's insistence that Rory was deceased. It was easier for Derek to act like Rory was dead, because he wanted to blame all the Stemples all the time, including Rory.

Maybe she was dead. Maybe that's why no one had found a trace of her, apart from a bloodstained wedding dress. Not Rory's blood. Someone else's, a male's, still unidentified. Not that the Seattle police were actively looking for Rory anymore. She was on the back burner, a footnote to the shooting at the hotel by a man who had been traced to an abandoned vehicle, the fuzzy photograph from a faraway street camera little help in identifying him. The once hot trail was now covered in ice, though Seattle PD had never closed the case, and Detective Mickelson, a heavyset older man with a world-weary face, hadn't given up believing he'd be the one to close it. According to him, he never would, and though now retired from the force and working in private investigation, he periodically checked in with Liam to let him know he was still committed to working the case. It appeared to be the man's Great White Whale, and if his obsession turned up Rory, so much the better, though no concrete leads to her whereabouts had panned out thus far. The shooter's identity was still in question as well, though Mickelson had his theories.

In the beginning, Rory's disappearance had seemed connected to the shooting, yet there was no evidence to support that argument. But something had happened in her hotel room. A knife fight of some kind, as one knife was found with the same blood that was on the dress discovered during the search in a parking garage garbage can. The knife was believed to have come from the cheese-and-fruit tray whose contents had been scattered over the floor. Liam had been desperate to find her, but as time passed the investigation led in a different direction, and finding Rory became an adjunct to the main crime: an ambush by a male shooter who'd mowed down Aaron Stemple, killing him, and injuring several other wedding attendees. Liam's father, now confined to a wheelchair, had been among the wounded, as was Liam himself. His injuries had healed, but occasionally, when his mind drifted to that day, phantom pains emanated from the bullet scars.

Detective Mickelson believed the shooter was either dead or incarcerated for some other crime, since the trail just seemed to end. The authorities had gone through thousands of interviews, trying to ascertain a motive. There had been a flurry of interest in Harold Stemple, whose prison friends had ties to released criminals who could have been involved. But Stemple had lost his youngest son in the debacle, and he was still married to Darlene, the last Liam had checked, so it seemed unlikely he would risk their lives. The man had been convicted of home invasion and attempted robbery, but he'd been in prison at the time of the shooting, and there appeared to be no credible connection.

There was the thought that a disgruntled ex-employee or subcontractor who'd worked for Bastian-Flavel might be responsible. The authorities had even scrutinized Liam's father's ex–business partner, James Flavel, a man in his late seventies who was retired and living in Arizona and had declined the invitation to the wedding. Flavel had been entirely cooperative, and though he and Liam's father had suffered a falling-out years earlier, they still considered each other a friend, and there was no serious animosity. Flavel had moved on with his life and was having a romantic renaissance, of a sort. He was the most eligible single male in the retirement community where he resided, and he spent most of his time either golfing or dating some other woman in the complex, which created ongoing tensions amongst the female residents but appeared to have no bearing on the shooting.

Liam was sick to the back teeth of the whole thing. From being desperate to find Rory, yearning for answers, yearning for her, he'd slowly grown cold and remote, the memory of their love turning from a pulsing ember to a diamond-hard stone. The fact that Derek seemed determined to keep bringing up Everett Stemple as the vandal who was harassing their projects pissed him off. Stemple still lived in Seattle, the last Liam had checked, and it wasn't feasible that he would drive three or four hours each way to commit crimes against the Bastians. Sure, Everett had been crazed with grief and fury in the beginning. His brother was dead and Rory was missing and he somehow thought Liam was responsible. But that was a mad reaction, and even Everett had eventually recognized that that scenario made no sense.

Now, Derek was talking to their foreman, Les Steele, gesticulating toward the broken windows, his dark hair flying in the wind. The saw was still buzzing, making every word a shout, so Steele merely pointed to Derek's discarded hard hat. Liam bent down to pick it up. No need to get a citation about unsafe practices just because Derek was angry, frustrated, and stubborn.

Liam met up with Steele and Derek.

"We need more security," Steele said loudly, above the racket.

"We're like bleeding money," Derek moaned.

"I'll order it," Liam stated firmly.

Steele nodded and pointed to where he was needed in a confab with a couple of other workers who were talking with a crane operator. Liam elbowed Derek, whose gaze was following Les, and once he got his attention, Liam gestured to the parking lot and Derek's beat-up, green Ford F1 truck, the vehicle they had driven to the site in as they'd been at the company office together when they'd learned of the sabotage.

Derek swept off his protective headgear again as soon as they were away from the hard-hat area. "It's our building that keeps getting hit. It's not Barlow's." He pointed to an apartment building going up several blocks away in the same Sellwood district. It was new from the ground up, whereas the Bastians' Hallifax building was a complete gut job. Maintaining the building's original walls and façade, keeping its beautiful architecture and neighborhood flavor, the project was looked on as a model for the area.

"They should be hit, not us. Barlow razed that thing to the ground. We're trying to make everybody happy here. Keep the original design."

"You like the original design," Liam reminded him.

"Yeah, I do, and so does everybody else! Well, most people around here anyway . . . that's why this destructive shithead should be going after Barlow, not us! We're doing this the right way."

Though Liam saw Derek's point, agreed with it, even, he didn't say anything. Their father had wanted to blast the building to smithereens and go modern, just like Barlow Construction, and it had been Liam and Derek who'd talked him into hanging on to the old, citing the antique shops and general feel of the area. They'd believed, and Liam still believed, that their project would be welcomed by the neighborhood residents and shop owners, and that seemed to be the case . . . at least at first.

As for their father, he was far too embittered to care about a design that was organic to the community. Geoff Bastian was infuriated that he'd lost the use of his legs and had never become comfortable with the wheelchair. He still tried to run his company, but he relied on his two sons to be his legs because he refused to show up at the work site being wheeled around. In some ways this made it easier for Liam; he could see for himself what needed to be done and tell his father about it later rather than have Geoff second-guess him over every decision, no matter how small. Of course, Geoff always wanted a full accounting, but Liam, with Derek's help, kept to the basics. The less said, the better.

If Derek felt slighted by the fact that Geoff put his younger son in charge, he didn't say so. Maybe he understood that his own mercurial temperament, so much like Geoff's, was the very reason he'd been passed over. Liam, with his icy control, a learned behavior that had been honed to an even finer point by Rory's defection, was better at running the show.

"What are you doing tonight?" Derek asked once he was behind the wheel and Liam was in the passenger seat. By mutual unsaid agreement, they were heading back to the Bastian-Flavel corporate offices along Portland's South Waterfront.

"Meeting Beth for dinner."

"Where?"

"Why?" Liam hedged.

"Where are you going to dinner? Is it a state secret?"

"We don't know yet. I'm going to text her."

"Bullshit. You just don't want me to know because you're embarrassed. She's talked you into another expensive restaurant where you'll order foie gras and lobster and a bottle of wine that would cover my rent for a month."

"You're not poor," Liam reminded his brother, hiding his anger because Derek had hit a nerve. Bethany Van Horne was used to living high on the hog. She was a good partner, great lover, but she had an expectation about money and finances that was the one reason Liam hadn't asked her to marry him. Well, that, and the fact that he was still wedded to Rory Abernathy, a situation his whole family and his would-be fiancée wanted him to rectify. And he should, he knew. It was time to get on with his life. Make a plan. Everyone thought Bethany was better suited for him. Everyone assumed that Liam and Beth were about to take the plunge. Everyone knew it was Liam who was dragging his feet. None of it was fair to Beth.

"I might not be poor, but I'm not engaged to a Van Horne," Derek pointed out. "Although I've heard rumblings that things aren't quite as rosy as they were, financially speaking."

Liam didn't respond. He'd heard the rumblings about old man Van Horne's business losses, too. Profits down in their lumber company. A possible leak of sensitive company dealings that may have squelched a potential sale. Bethany hadn't said anything about it, but she may not be completely aware, as she was only peripherally involved in her father's company.

"I'm not engaged to a Van Horne, either," Liam said as he pulled into the lot.

"You should be married to her."

"Yeah, well, a few hurdles to jump first."

"Annul that marriage, bro. I mean, c'mon. A month or two of wedded un-bliss and then she scoots out?"

"I know your feelings about Rory, Derek."

"Well, know this, too. This isn't the first time she's run out on a guy. She was engaged once before, but took off before that walk down the aisle."

"I know, Derek," Liam said evenly. "She was scared of him. She ran because she didn't know what else to do."

"She told you?" He didn't bother to wait for Liam to reply. "What I heard was she ran because she figured out he was a loser who was never going to make enough money for her."

"Who told you that?"

"I've known it for years. It was all over the wedding. But nobody could talk to you about her. Still can't. I'm surprised we're even having this conversation. Maybe you're finally getting over her."

"I've been over her for years," Liam stated. "I just don't like talking about her and the wedding and Dad being in that wheelchair. It's turned him into a mean, frustrated old guy."

Derek made a face and looked past Liam. "He's always been a mean and frustrated old guy."

Liam heard something in Derek's tone, a wistfulness, maybe sadness. Derek had always been the "screw up." Except for his out-of-character marriage to Rory, Liam had been the more dutiful son.

For some reason that thought ate at him.

Derek climbed out of the truck and Liam followed suit. They headed back toward the corporate offices together, but as Liam punched the elevator call button, Derek hesitated. "Go eat fucking goose liver and fish eggs or whatever. I'm going to have a beer and ribs down at McCallum's."

"Now? It's three o'clock."

"Yeah, well, tell the old man I'm done for the day. I want to talk to some guys. See if anybody knows anything about what's going on down at the job site."

McCallum's was a favorite haunt down by the Willamette River. While it seemed like every establishment with a water view was an upscale, trendy hot spot, McCallum's stubbornly remained true to its working-man roots. A lot of the guys who were working on the Sellwood project ended up at Mc-Callum's.

"Let me know if you learn anything."

Derek waved him away as he headed outside to his truck. The green Ford might be beat-up, but it had every bell, whistle, and electronic device available. Derek might needle him about Beth and money, but he was used to having nice things himself. He just wasn't great with finances, and his relationships with women ran along the same lines.

Like you're an expert.

Liam took the elevator up to the tenth-floor offices of Bastian-Flavel Construction. Di, the receptionist, smiled at him and said, "Your fiancée's here."

He opened his mouth to correct her, but then stopped himself. Why bother. She might not be his fiancée yet, but he was on an inevitable track, one he'd willingly stepped onto, so there was no reason to jump off and deny it existed. Instead he gave her a small wave of acknowledgment and headed to his office.

Bethany was standing by the floor-to-ceiling windows that looked over the river, a small smile of pleasure on her face. She wore a taupe linen straight sheath and matching pumps, and her smooth tresses, once blond and now reddish, an affectation she'd adopted over the last few years, were pulled back and clipped at her nape by a dull, silvery hair clasp. A faint scent of something gingery and citrus wafted his way. She looked and smelled like money.

Liam had an instant flashback to Rory. Her wild red locks, holey jeans—from use rather than design—the flip-flops or slip-on sneakers, her array of colorful T-shirts that shrank after a good washing, ones she was always tugging down to hide the peekaboo line of smooth skin they offered up, her favorite fish-skeleton earrings that were more nickel than silver, the smell of coffee surrounding her as they'd met in one of the coffee shops of the company she'd worked for.

"Hi, there," Beth said, turning to meet his gaze, her smile widening.

Liam shook off the memory. How had he ever thought Rory would fit into his world? They'd been from totally different social strata, different economic levels, different everything. Those kinds of relationships only worked in fairy tales. He was lucky she'd taken off for God knew where. Lucky.

"Thought we were meeting at the restaurant." He headed toward his desk, but she intercepted him and gave him a quick hug and kiss on the cheek.

"I didn't know where you wanted to go, so I thought we could pick out a place together. Am I bothering you? Do you have a lot left to do?"

"It's fine. I'm pretty much done here." For a moment he considered telling her about the continued vandalism at the site, but that kind of information seemed to eat at her far more than it did him. He didn't like the vandalism. It completely pissed him off, even while he recognized some of that kind of thing happened during construction. Overall, the neighborhood was happy with the building's renovation, but there was always a faction against change, or maybe it was just random, like he'd told Derek. No matter what the root cause, Bethany wasn't the one to talk with about it. Bad things happening at his business made her uncomfortable and anxious, a product of her father's topsy-turvy years in business, he suspected. Beth had never felt safe. Whenever Liam mentioned any kind of problem, he had the sense she wanted to clap her hands over her ears and shake her head. She needed to believe everything was fine and good. Smooth. Easy. Perfect. She would always change the subject from business as soon as she could. Her interests lay elsewhere, and Liam had learned over the last few years to tell her as little as possible about his work.

"Then let's go early and have a drink," she suggested. "How about the Portland Grill?"

For a wild moment he thought about suggesting McCallum's. Instead, he pulled himself back and said, "Sounds good."

She linked her arm through his. "You have somewhere else in mind, I can tell."

He shrugged. "There's a sushi place in Sellwood, not far from the construction site. It's a hole in the wall, but it's supposed to have great food. There's always a line."

"A line?" She lifted the toe of one taupe pump. "I can't stand too long in these."

"Ah."

"Sorry." She looked at him beseechingly.

"No problem. You're right. We'll go to the Portland Grill."

An hour later Liam pushed aside his plate, a delicious salmon meal that he couldn't do justice, and reached for his wineglass.

"Something wrong?" Beth asked.

"No."

"I swear I ate more than you did." She, too, had ordered the salmon and was nearly finished with it, and had made a dent in the accompanying risotto. Now she put down her fork and looked around, as if she couldn't bear to be seen out-eating him.

He wasn't really hungry. He was . . . dissatisfied. With life, at some level, he recognized, draining the glass of cabernet. It felt like he'd been holding his breath, waiting for something to happen, ever since Rory took off from their wedding and a gunman rained bullets upon his friends and family.

"I have something I want to talk about," she said, sliding her hands across the table and lifting her fingers, wanting him to entwine his with hers. He set down his glass and indulged her, though it sort of bugged him.

"What is it?"

"Well, you know we're going to Napa next weekend."

Liam nodded. He didn't want to go. He should. He'd promised. But the friends they were meeting were hers, and he always found himself watching the clock when they were together, which wasn't often, as he tended to find ways to beg off.

"I just thought maybe . . . well . . ." She flushed. "I know this is unorthodox, but you kind of like the unorthodox, so I thought, what the hell."

Her fingers had clenched around his, surprisingly strong. He thought he knew what was coming and his heart started beating hard. No. He didn't want to hurt her, but he wasn't ready.

"Liam Bastian, would you—"

"Uh, no, Beth. Wait. Time isn't right. I'm sorry. I don't want to be a bastard, but—"

"—be my boyfriend?"

Her face suffused with color as she let go of his fingers and reached into her purse, pulling out a small blue velvet ring case, opening it to reveal a green ring with Yoda's image stamped into the plastic.

"I saw it at a novelty shop and just thought . . . Oh, I don't know. It's dumb." She snapped the case closed and shoved it back in her purse.

"No, it's great. I'm sorry," he said lamely.

"It's okay."

"No, it's not. I know it's not. I'm not trying to be a bastard, you know. I'm just trying to figure stuff out."

"I know. I also know you're still not over her."

"That's not true."

"Isn't it?" She lifted her chin.

"I'm not over what happened at the wedding," he said. "But I'm over her."

"Really? Then why did you ask Brian Jacoby to find her?" she asked.

"How did you know?" he burst out, unable to hide his surprise. Jacoby was a private investigator who'd done some work for Beth's father, and yes, he'd put the man on a retainer a while back and asked him to see if he could learn anything more. But as before, there was no trail. Rory had disappeared into thin air.

"I wish it wasn't true, but you're still in love with her, no matter what you say. Your actions prove it. I thought you would forget her. That time would erase her from your memory, but every year, I swear to God, it's worse! You and I are moving further apart and it's because of her."

"No, no . . ." Liam searched for a defense, uncomfortable hearing his own thoughts coming out of her mouth. "But I am still married to her. I'd like to get that settled."

"You could have your marriage annulled just like that if you tried!" She snapped her fingers. Her angry eyes glittered with unshed tears. "You just don't want to. You'd rather chase after her to the ends of the earth than marry me."

"That's not true, Beth."

"Isn't it? What did you think? That I was going to propose to you? I have some pride left, you know."

"Let's not fight."

"Oh, sure. Let's not fight. I know, I know." She lifted a hand to forestall anything he was about to say. "Fighting in public is not the Bastian or Van Horne way. And I agree. It's just that I feel like fighting. I feel like screaming," she said intensely in a lowered voice. "You don't want to go to Napa. You just want to go to work and numb out in front of the television."

"That's not really true."

"I want to start a life together, Liam. I want to buy a house together. We've talked about it. We've looked. Kind of. It doesn't have to be today, but sometime. Can't we take a few steps in the right direction? Something? You haven't even asked me to move into the apartment with you!"

She was hammering him with words, logic, the length and breadth of her dreams. And she was right. He'd been stuck in idle for five years.

"Will you . . . move into my place with me?" he asked, feeling as if his chest was clamped in a vise. It pissed him off at himself. *What's wrong with you, you dick? This woman is everything you want. Why can't you commit?*

She laughed, shaking her head. Swiping at the tears in her eyes. "Sure. Yeah. Let's do that." Her voice was defeated.

He almost said he was sorry a third time, but managed to clench his teeth and keep the words from coming.

She heaved a sigh and looked around the restaurant. "As long as you're looking for her, I don't stand a chance."

"Jacoby hasn't found anything. I'll call him off."

"Don't do me any favors," she said bitterly.

"I'm sorry, Beth," he said, unable to stop himself. "I mean that."

Tell her you love her. She's waiting for it.

The moment spun out but he couldn't say the words. Couldn't make himself.

She inhaled and exhaled, not looking at him. Finally, she slid him a look out of the corner of her eye. "You'll really call Jacoby off?"

"Yes."

She nodded.

Liam sensed the moment of crisis had passed, but he still felt like a complete heel. "Could I see that ring again?"

"Don't, Liam."

"Oh, come on. Please? I'm kind of a Spider-Man fan myself. Maybe I just didn't give it the proper respect it deserved."

"You like Spider-Man?" She finally turned fully toward him, swallowing hard, putting on a brave smile. "How come I didn't know that?"

"I guess you don't know everything about me." Actually, he'd just made that up on the spot to make her feel better. He hadn't seen a Spider-Man movie since Tobey Maguire played the lead.

"There was a red Spider-Man ring at the shop."

"Yoda's fine. I like Yoda. I could be a Jedi Master."

She chuckled, though she shook her head some more. "God, Liam, I'm sorry. I don't mean to be impatient, but I am. I love you. You know I do, and I know you love me, too."

"Yes," he said. Even that was hard, but he did love her . . . just maybe not as deeply, romantically, as he'd loved Rory.

They managed to get through the rest of the evening without bringing up anything about their relationship, and when he dropped Bethany at her parents' home, where she was staying since she'd released her apartment in the hopes of moving in with Liam, he wrested the Yoda ring from her and put it on his little finger. He kissed her goodbye with more tenderness than his usual quick peck on the lips.

"Can't wait for Napa," she said.

"Me too."

"Liar." She smiled. "But I'll take it. And we are going to have fun, Liam. And maybe we can start thinking about moving in together, like you said."

He nodded.

"Maybe next month? Or September?"

"September," he said, seeing her face shutter at the delay, though she threw him a quick smile of goodbye as she turned away.

That last exchange left him with a bad feeling about his condo, and he drove instead to his parents' home in Portland's West Hills, pulling into the drive and parking in one of the four garage bays, then heading back outside and walking along the stone pathway to the backyard and the illuminated outdoor pool, a crazy indulgence as Oregon's weather made swimming a challenge except for the dead of summer. The surface of the turquoise water riffled in an evening breeze. Far below, Portland twinkled and pulsed in a million lights.

He stood there for a long time, drinking in the view, his thoughts churning. Finally he pulled out his cell phone and called Jacoby's cell number, expecting the man's voice mail. He was surprised when the gruff-voiced private investigator answered on the second ring, as if he'd been waiting for a call.

"Speak of the devil. I was just thinking about you," Jacoby said.

"I'm giving up the search. Send me the final bill."

"That right? You still got a little left on your retainer. Sure you want to give up?"

"Yeah."

"Well, how about I use up the rest of the money and just see what I see."

Liam smiled faintly. "Unless you've found her already, I think I'll call it quits." There was a studied silence on the other end of the line and the smile on Liam's face slowly dissolved. "Jacoby?"

"I got a lead. That's all I'm saying. Give me a week and maybe I'll have a different answer for you."

"Bullshit." His heart was pounding again—deep, painful beats that nearly suffocated him.

"One week," Jacoby said.

Chapter 2

Point Roberts, Washington

"You okay, sweetie?" Heather Johnson asked, bending down to her daughter outside the weather-beaten front door of the ABC and Me preschool. The wind was high and it felt like rain was in the air. Heather's hair whipped in front of her eyes and she anchored it at her nape with one hand.

Charlotte tilted her curly head to one side, the reddish curls bouncing around her face. Normally she would probably shake her head and laugh, but today she was sober. "Uh-huh."

"You sure?"

The four-year-old wasn't even close to her usually ebullient self.

"Pretty sure," the little girl said, imitating her mother's tone, Heather realized, which made her almost smile.

"If you still don't feel good in a while, tell your teacher. She'll call me, and I'll come get you, okay? Mommy's gotta go to work."

Charlotte didn't react. She seemed almost lost in thought, which was sometimes her way, though mostly she bubbled on about the very active inner world where her "friends" lived in trees, or caves, or under toadstools and who had lots of brothers and sisters, friends only Charlotte could see.

Heather and her daughter walked into the older, single-story brick building that housed the year-round preschool.

"You call me if you don't feel better, okay?" Heather said as she signed her daughter in at the secretary's desk. "You tell Miss Evers."

"Kay."

In Charlotte's room Heather made eye contact with the preschool teacher and released her daughter's hand. She tried to ease away, but Charlotte clutched her hand and followed Heather back to the secretary's desk, her tiny face drawn into a pout. "I don't want to stay."

"Come on, Charlotte!" Miss Evers called, walking quickly to the door of her room. In jeans, a T-shirt, ponytail, and perpetual apron, she stayed just inside, guarding the entry to her classroom, her attention on the other four-year-olds happily drawing or molding Play-Doh even as she reached an arm toward Charlotte. Heather brought her daughter back and placed Charlotte's hand in Miss Evers's. Miss Evers dragged her attention from the kids in the classroom to smile down at Charlotte. "Don't forget, it's your day to take care of Winston, right?" Winston was the class lizard, a bearded dragon and a favorite of the children.

Charlotte nodded, looking at the floor.

"She's been a little off this morning. No temp, though," Heather said.

"No worries. I'll watch her. Come on, honey."

But Charlotte stood stock-still and lifted her eyes to stare stubbornly at her mother as if she were being left in the care of a prison matron.

Heather gave her daughter a quick hug, then said to the teacher, "Call me if she seems worse."

"I will." Miss Evers herded Charlotte into the room, toward the other children, but Charlotte kept looking back at her mother. Heather winked at her and gave her a thumbs-up, then hurried outside. A chill had taken hold of her and she shivered. The whole morning had started wrong. Charlotte, usually bouncing into the bedroom, had not wanted to get up, no matter what Heather tried. The little girl usually loved preschool, but she'd been listless and disinterested in breakfast, getting dressed, having her hair combed and teeth brushed—the whole nine yards. Getting her shoes on her feet seemed to take hours. Then Heather had spilled the milk while pouring it over her daughter's cereal and the coffeemaker had refused to turn on. The red light had remained dark. No juice getting to it.

Sigh. Ah, well. Just life.

Your life.

She climbed into her ten-year-old Honda Accord, the one old Mr. Wharton had sold to her for a song, though even then Heather had owed him money.

Money.

With one last glance at the preschool, she climbed behind the wheel and switched on the ignition. It was summer, but surprisingly cold this July morning. She ratcheted up the heat, glad for its sporadic warmth.

If you'd stayed and married Liam, money wouldn't be a problem . . . no alternative life as Heather Johnson. Married . . . wealthy . . . Rory Abernathy Bastian.

Well, screw that.

She didn't want to think of that day, of what had happened

in the wake of her departure that had left her inundated with would've and could've.

But the *attack*! Not only a knife-wielding, masked assailant coming at her before the ceremony, but the subsequent assault by a sniper who had targeted the whole wedding party! People had been injured, her stepbrother, Aaron, killed.

Because of her?

Could that be true?

Heather's heart twisted at that thought. Had her assailant survived his wounds and somehow made his way to the roof of the parking structure, letting loose a barrage of bullets on the wedding party? It didn't seem possible, time-wise, but maybe . . . ? Or did he have an accomplice? Were there two would-be killers? Were they in collusion, or could they have worked independently? That seemed too far-fetched, but the whole scenario had been horribly, fatally disastrous.

She hadn't known about the attack till she was safely away, and when she learned what had happened, she almost high-tailed it back to Liam. But she stopped herself on the brink of that bad decision, fully aware that she might have inadvertently been the cause of all of it. And Liam was alive. Injured, but alive. If she went back, would that be the case?

The killer was after me.

She exhaled heavily, coming back once more to that inescapable conclusion. She'd dwelled on the attack for months, years . . . and fought spurts of desire to return and explain her inexplicable actions. Talk to the police. She'd been miserable and guilt-riddled. If she'd stayed, would Aaron have lived? As it was, a gunman had mowed him down, wounded Liam and Geoffrey as well.

Her thoughts and worries about Liam had nearly driven her back to the U.S. mainland, until she'd heard that Liam had survived. She'd actually cried tears of relief to know that he'd been rushed to the hospital and his injuries hadn't been life-threatening. Aaron hadn't been so fortunate.

Oh. God.

Now she felt a welling sadness once again, a feeling that arose whenever she thought of her stepbrother who was supposed to walk her down that fateful aisle. "Rest in peace," she whispered, not for the first time.

She turned the key in the ignition and heard the Honda cough several times before the engine turned over. *Uh-oh*, she thought. That had been happening more and more frequently lately and she couldn't afford car repairs. She exhaled heavily, prayed the sedan would keep running for a little longer.

Then what? she asked herself, and had no answer.

You're a coward, Rory. You should have gone back.

"No," she whispered under her breath. At least here, Charlotte was safe. Besides, she was a new person. Rory Abernathy was the girl who'd been engaged to Liam Bastian, but Rory Abernathy no longer existed. She'd died an unlamented death when she became Heather Johnson. Maybe everyone back on the mainland who'd known Rory thought she was merely missing, but in Heather's mind, she was six feet under. She was Heather Johnson now; that was the name on her U.S. passport, that was the name that mattered.

But at what price?

"Stop it," she warned herself tightly. She tried to calm herself before the guilt became crippling. She had a daughter to care for. That was what was important. She was lucky to have her, so lucky. She'd suffered a miscarriage once, when she'd been with Cal Redmond, her previous fiancé, and she'd had a terrible feeling she would never have a child. That her one chance was over. Her relationship with Cal had been breaking up—he'd been part of her past, someone who knew the Stemples—but she'd wanted their child more than anything. When it was all said and done she'd felt like she would never find anyone again. Never have a relationship. Never have her own baby. She'd had no idea then that meeting Liam Bastian was right around the corner, and of course she also hadn't foreseen the tragedy that would occur.

But she got Charlotte out of it. Her little girl. That counted for everything.

She couldn't change the past and she knew nothing that would clear up the mystery of the shooter, so she stayed away. Thankfully, so far no one, not even the police, had come knocking.

Hitting the gas, she switched on the radio to a hard-rock station to drive all thoughts of her old life from her mind, then drove the half mile to her job at the Point Bob Buzz, one of the few coffee shops in Point Roberts.

To the driving beat of Metallica, she checked her mirrors and the traffic on the cross streets, a habit she hadn't been able to shake in all the years she'd lived here, though there were few cars. As ever, she saw nothing unusual and pulled into the uneven gravel lot, parking toward the back, wedging her Honda between her boss's car, Connie's blue Subaru Outback, and a battered old pickup that hadn't moved in six months. It was parked where it had died. The truck was owned by Connie's uncle and was beginning to grow moss. Connie had complained more than once to him, but the old guy had yet to put in a new battery, or whatever it needed, nor had he taken heed when Connie threatened that she'd have the old "bucket of bolts" towed.

"If he weren't my blood, I'd push that thing right into the ocean," Connie had declared more than once, though it hadn't happened yet. In her early sixties, with straight, graying hair, Connie Fellows had a soft spot for cranky relatives, stray cats, and, as in Heather's case, a single woman who claimed to be escaping a bad relationship.

Connie had accepted Heather's hard-luck story involving an abusive ex; and though it had been a lie, Heather had been desperate enough to spin it believably. She felt a little bad about deceiving Connie, but she would do whatever it took to care for her child.

Now, Heather dashed into the back door of the shop and was greeted with a wall of warmth and the smells of bacon sizzling on the griddle, cinnamon from the batch of rolls Connie had already taken from the oven, and, as ever, the welcoming scent of brewing coffee.

In the small nook between the dining room and the back exit, she locked her purse in a cubby, then put on a clean apron, wrapping the strings twice around her waist. "Morning," she called through the swinging saloon doors separating the employee area from the hallway to the dining area and kitchen.

"Mornin'," was the reply. Connie.

Pushing her way through the doors, Heather spied Connie in the kitchen. While Gustaf, the chef, was grilling bacon, Connie, her face red, apple cheeks shining with perspiration from dealing with the hot oven, was already slicing apart the wide sheet of cinnamon rolls. With a huge butcher knife she was separating each monster pastry and placing each roll on an individual plate. She smiled and nodded at Heather as she went about her work.

Connie had opened the coffee shop twenty-five years earlier in this northern Washington town, and in the four-plus years Heather had worked here, she hadn't seen Connie even take one vacation. Her business had boomed, at least by Point Roberts standards, enough so that she'd expanded with an additional dining area added to the small coffee shop with its vintage flair. Until Starbucks or some other franchise opened shop in the area, an unlikely proposition in this remote U.S. outpost, the Buzz had cornered the market on the coffee and breakfast crowd. Point Roberts is a quiet little town situated on the tip of the Tsawwassen Peninsula, a piece of land that juts down from British Columbia, Canada. As the area is below the 49th parallel, Point Roberts is part of the good old U.S. of A., though a person couldn't reach it by car without going through two border crossings, one into Canada, the other out of Canada to land on this scrap of American soil. A person could boat here from the U.S. mainland, as Heather had nearly five years earlier after her horrifying escape from her own wedding. Luckily, she'd had The Magician on her side and he'd produced the Heather Johnson passport with her picture on it, though he'd let her enter Customs alone.

"Better I'm not with you," he'd told her, and she'd understood that Uncle Kent preferred to stay deep in the background. He might be a magician, but his business practices were . . . edgy . . . and he made a point of avoiding entanglements with the authorities.

Still, she'd asked him to take her "to the ends of the earth," and where she'd landed was Point Roberts. With his thinning white hair flying in the wind, Uncle Kent had steered his Bayliner across the choppy waters of Lake Washington, racing past the floating bridges, the small craft bouncing as it sped. Later, he'd slowed the boat, guiding it carefully through adjacent waters to the Ballard Locks and eventually to Puget Sound. Rory's heart had knocked feverishly the whole trip, and especially as they'd passed through the locks. Despite her baggy jacket, jeans, and oversized sunglasses, she'd felt that everyone in the nearby boats had been staring at her as if they could read from her expression that she was on the run.

She'd told herself she was just being paranoid, that no one was pointing fingers, that they couldn't know she was a runaway bride escaping from what had turned out to be the scene of a deadly assault. Her admonitions had only partially worked as she'd fought tears and seasickness while Uncle Kent had steered steadily northward, skirting the San Juan Islands through pelting rain, eventually landing here in the dark. White-knuckled and scared to death, Rory had miraculously managed to get through Customs with the fake ID she'd had Uncle Kent create for her two years before she'd ever met Liam Bastian.

Just in case, she'd told herself.

Rory had known from the time she was thirteen that she would likely need an escape plan, and a new identity if and when things ever went sideways. Sadly, she'd been right.

As it had turned out, Point Roberts had been perfect and now, settled in this small town on a scrap of the United States that dangled from the Canadian peninsula, Heather had no intention of leaving until Charlotte was too old for school in this U.S. enclave, and until she was certain that her past would never catch up to her.

Still, she checked. All the time.

The short hallway opened to the area behind a long counter that separated the work area from the dining section. Seated at tables and in booths, a few customers had collected in groups of twos and threes and were deep in discussion or reading the paper or on their smartphones as they sipped coffee and picked at scones or dug into breakfast.

Hearing the soft ding of a bell that indicated a car was inside the Buzz's drive-up lane, Heather stepped forward to the window just as Joanna called, "Incoming!" and tossed a glance over her shoulder to make certain Heather had heard.

Joanna, who was all of thirty, sometimes acted like a mother hen. Tall and lean from years of running, she had a brush of blond hair that she knotted up to the top of her head, messy strands forever escaping.

"I'm on it." Heather assured her, putting a smile on her face as she spoke into the microphone, her eye on the camera mounted over the sign where customers placed their orders. She could see the driver, a woman, as she turned toward the microphone. Tammi Forsythe. One of the Buzz's regulars.

"Good morning, Tammi," Heather greeted her. "What can I get started for you?"

"Medium double mocha, no whip, just foam," she said succinctly into the microphone. As ever, Tammi was in pajamas and a coat, a baseball cap low over her eyes, studying the menu through owlish glasses. "Add a bagel, would you? Cut in half. Jam and cream cheese?" She turned in the seat to talk to the two preschoolers strapped into their car seats and her voice was a little muffled. "Bagel, okay?" Looking back to the camera, she confirmed. "Yeah, make it strawberry jam and a couple of apple juices. God, what's that gonna cost me?"

"You got it," Heather said, hitting the appropriate buttons on the register, tallying the total bill in Canadian dollars. Tammi was one of the customers who always paid in Canadian currency, though the Buzz had two tills, one right above the other, one with U.S. dollars and one with Canadian.

"That'll be—" she began, rattling off the cost of the order, but Tammi was already driving forward, the nose of her older model Toyota becoming visible in the garden window that allowed Heather a view of the lane.

Joanna was already placing a warmed bagel into a sack with packets of cream cheese and jam while Heather started the coffee drink. Soon, cash was exchanged for breakfast and Tammi rolled away, her kids yelling from the back seat as Heather went into full barista mode. A second car rolled in after the first. The early risers had been arriving for a few hours now, Joanna catching the earliest ones as Heather's shift always started after school drop-off.

Between customers, Heather cleaned the station, stocking supplies and checking her phone. No text from the day care center. Maybe her baby was doing better. She sure hoped so. Another ding indicated an approaching customer as the cars began stacking up, a line forming. She and Joanna worked in tandem: Joanna, tall and gaunt, pulled together the orders while Heather, a few inches shorter with natural red hair, the dark dye she'd used when she'd first arrived in Point Roberts having grown out over the course of the last two years, dealt directly with the customers.

"Mutt and Jeff," Connie had called them on more than one occasion. "Complete opposites, you two." Today, though, she had no time for observations as the surprisingly robust morning crowd arrived.

Joanna started working double duty, making drinks for both the drive-up and the inside counter, while Connie was busy both in the kitchen and with customers in the dining area. Carlos, who also worked in the kitchen, was handling one of the registers this morning. His quick smile, dimples, and flashing eyes were a welcome relief from Joanna's dour expression. The customers loved him and the dining room worked better whenever he was at the register; at least in Heather's opinion.

"A well-oiled machine," Connie had often said of the operation, though usually sarcastically whenever there was a glitch in the system and someone got the wrong order or was left waiting for their food.

Every day by noon the Buzz ran out of Connie's cinnamon rolls, but Connie refused to budge when it came to baking any more. The ovens could only handle two dozen at a time and that, she figured, was plenty. "I'm not coming in earlier than four a.m., no siree," Connie had said whenever the idea was posed to her. "I know that Jake, over at the inn, starts work at two or something ridiculous. That's just nuts."

"Five thirty in the morning is nuts," Joanna agreed, and Heather always felt a little jab of guilt that she didn't have to be at her station until seven fifteen bcause she was single and had a preschooler. Everyone else's shift started earlier to tend to the early risers and set up for the day. But she knew no one really minded. Even Joanna understood. She just liked to grumble.

As there was a break in the drive-through line she took another moment to check her phone, but there was still no text from Miss Evers.

That was good, but she sent a quick message: **How's Charlotte?**

When there was no answer, she decided not to wait. She called the pediatrician's office and explained Charlotte's symptoms to a nurse who told her to keep her eye on her daughter, but if she wasn't feverish, showing signs of infection or not unusually listless, to wait for twenty-four hours.

"Call back and make an appointment if she doesn't get better or if her temperature rises," she added just before they ended their call. Heather had just clicked off her phone as the next customer, an elderly man, pulled up in a dented pickup. Mr. Selby. The old guy drove in about three times a week, always complained about the price of coffee but ordered a double mocha and left Heather a quarter in the tip jar sitting on the window ledge.

She started his drink before he started to either order or complain.

The next three hours she had a fairly steady stream of cars at the to-go window while other customers gathered inside. Between the rattle of silverware, hum of conversation, bursts of laughter, squawking over the speaker for the drive-up, and hiss of the espresso machine, Heather was lost in white noise. Only after the last car, a van with four kids, a harried mom, and now, five iced drinks, rolled to the exit, did Heather have a chance to check on Charlotte again. She blew a strand of hair from her eyes and caught a glimpse of Connie approaching. The inside crush had disbursed and Connie had just finished wiping down a table after a lingering group of five men—regulars who thought the Buzz was their private club—finally packed up their hats, canes, newspapers, jackets. and filed out.

"So what's up?" Connie asked as Heather fished in the pocket of her apron for her phone and rapidly texted Miss Evers again. Connie leaned heavily against the counter as Heather placed the phone back in her pocket. Behind her rimless glasses, her brown eyes showed a touch of worry. "You have to be somewhere?"

"No, why?" Heather began refilling paper cups and lids in a dispenser and called to Joanna, "We have a pot of decaf going?"

"Ready in two minutes," was the response. Joanna was wiping down the machines as she was about finished with her shift. When the green light switched on, indicating the pot of coffee was ready, she added, "All set." She whipped off her apron, tossing the soiled towel and apron toward the bin.

Heather heard the ding of an incoming text and grabbed up her phone again. It was Miss Evers: **Not her best. Hard to scare up a smile.**

Heather felt a pang of worry.

"It's just you keep checking your phone. And looking worried."

"Oh. No. Charlotte was just a little off today and when I dropped her off she seemed kind of out of sorts. No fever. No runny nose, but . . . she just wasn't herself. That's all. I don't want to miss a call from the preschool."

"Ahh. Got it." Connie, who had raised two sons, nodded. "Hope she's okay." Worry creased her forehead.

"Me, too."

"But?"

She showed Connie the phone.

"Oh, too bad. She's a little imp, that one," Connie said with genuine fondness. "Maybe you want to pick her up early? Joanna can take over."

"I heard that!" Joanna said and poked her head from the

back hallway. She was throwing her jacket over her arm as three men in full beards strolled in.

Connie grabbed some menus. "Let me know," she said to Heather.

"Hey, I'm outta here!" Joanna started for the door.

The inside bell dinged, indicating another drive-up customer had arrived.

Catching a glimpse of a black SUV pulling into the drive-up lane, Heather stepped into her station and switched on the microphone. "What can I get started for you?" she asked, then looked at the image from the camera mounted in the drive-up lane.

She froze.

Good God! *Liam?* No! Couldn't be.

Her heart missed a beat and she blinked, telling herself she'd made a mistake. Her thoughts of Liam must have conjured up his image in her mind. Swallowing hard, she stared at the screen. He was looking right at the camera and she recognized his deep-set eyes, sharp features, and rumpled near-black hair. His jaw, still strong, was shadowed by stubble and his lips were as blade thin as she remembered.

It was Liam. It was.

Liam is here. In Point Roberts? How? Why? Why now?

She couldn't think. Couldn't breathe. This couldn't be a coincidence. He'd found her.

"Just a regular coffee. A small. Black," he said, and his voice resonated in her ears. Oh, God, oh, God, oh, God. It was Liam! No . . . God no! When she couldn't find her voice, he repeated the order.

"Yes. Uh, got it . . . please drive forward." She automatically lowered her voice, an instinct of self-preservation, as she killed the microphone and stepped speedily out of her glassed-in work area. Trying not to sound frantic, she yelled to Joanna, who was just stepping outside through the back exit. "Hey! Before you go, could you get this customer?" Heather was already heading to the restroom. "I've got kind of an emergency." She didn't wait for an answer but pushed open the door and stepped into the tiled room. Fortunately it was empty. Without thinking about it, she walked into one of the two stalls, drew a deep breath, locked it behind her. She was shaking all over.

Liam couldn't be here.

It's not him. Can't be. Not after all this time.

Your paranoia got the better of you. That's all. Pull yourself together.

Her hands were clenched so tightly she could feel her pulse in her palms. Or was that because her heart was pounding so heavily in her chest? As if it were trying to jump from her rib cage? This was all just her wild imagination playing tricks on her. Had to be.

She gasped sharply when she heard the door to the restroom whoosh open.

"Heather?" Connie's worried voice reached her. "Are you all right?"

"Yes . . . yes . . . I-I will be . . ." She didn't bother trying to keep the anxiety from her voice.

"You're sure?"

"Yeah . . . just give me a few minutes."

"Okay." Connie sounded hesitant and it was nearly another full minute before Heather heard the door open and close again. As soon as it did, she leaned down to peer under the lower edge of the stall, checking to see if she could view Connie's white, heavy-soled shoes. Satisfied she was truly alone, she stood, then immediately sank against the stall door.

Liam?

Here?
After all these years?
How? *How?*

But the image she'd seen in the camera's eye kept her rooted to the spot.

How had he found her? She'd known he'd survived the attack, of course. The Internet had kept her well informed. But there had been mention of an injury, and she hadn't discovered, despite repeated searches, how serious it was. She shuddered and placed her hands over her face, wondering for the millionth time if somehow the horrific attack at the wedding was her fault, if her marriage to Liam had somehow prompted the violence and bloodshed.

She let out a long breath and checked her phone. Three minutes or four minutes had passed since she'd spied him in the camera's lens. Surely that was long enough for him to pick up his order, pay the bill, and drive off.

Right?

But what if he came inside? Decided he wanted a late breakfast? What if he is even now ordering a cup of coffee and settling in?

She glanced around the stall as if an emergency exit would miraculously appear, which was pointless. She knew this tiny restroom, and the only exit was the door to the dining area. There was a narrow window mounted on the back wall, but it was so small a child couldn't slip through, even if it hadn't been painted shut, which it had been, several times.

It's not *him. He probably never even thinks of you. It's been five years. Rory Abernathy is part of a distant, painful past that he'd rather forget and probably has.*

Calmer, she walked to the sink, and worried because her disguise was no longer intact. She threw a bit of water over her face, but was careful not to smudge her makeup or dislodge her false eyelashes. Just in case.

What about Charlotte?

What if Liam found out that he has a daughter?

Her heart tumbled. A new fear gripped her.

What if he's here in Point Roberts not because of you, but because of Charlotte*!*

At that moment the door opened again.

Chapter 3

Something was up. Connie Fellows could feel it—sense it. She hadn't worked with the public for damned near forty years and not learned a thing or two. About people. Friends, customers, coworkers, even strangers; she could read them. Despite their outward attempts to appear "normal" or "calm," most of the people gave off little hints to their emotions, be it internal turmoil, happiness, fear, or indifference. Connie had become adept at deciphering the truth. She recognized people's fears and worries, unmasked as they were by body language, tics, eye contact or lack thereof, or general tension.

She was rarely wrong.

And right now she was willing to bet the Buzz's income for the day, that Heather Johnson was scared out of her mind. But why? If she was freaking out over Charlotte, she would share that with her. So, this had to be because of the man who had pulled into the drive-up window. Heather had left her station in a panic and hightailed it to the bathroom about that same time. It was as if Heather had seen a damned ghost.

"What's going on?" she asked, finding Heather at the sink in the restroom.

Heather had frozen at the sight of her, the water running, her newly, and overly, made-up face tense. But now she feigned nonchalance as she reached for a paper towel from its dispenser, dabbed at her cheeks, and met Connie's gaze in the mirror.

"Nothing," she said, trying for a smile.

"This isn't about Charlotte?"

She seemed about to say it was, but Connie could tell there was more, and maybe Heather understood that, because she said instead, "I just felt sick, you know, like a sudden attack of cramps."

Connie did know. But she wasn't buying it.

Heather wiped her hands. "Maybe . . . maybe whatever Charlotte's got, I've got a touch of, too."

"But, you're okay now?"

A bit of hesitation. "I . . . don't know. I'm still queasy. As I said, it might just be cramps . . ." She let her voice trail off. Beneath all that face makeup, she'd paled. But Connie guessed whatever was bothering her wasn't cramps. Nor the flu. No, it was something else.

"I was just wondering if the last customer you were dealing with was the problem," Connie suggested.

"The customer?"

"A man." Connie watched Heather's reaction as they walked back into the dining area together. "In a dark SUV of some kind. Good-looking guy. Probably in his midthirties. Strong jaw. Thick, brown hair. Grim expression."

Heather shook her head. "I think the last customer I dealt with was a woman. Yeah, Denise Cromley. She ordered her usual skinny latte."

"I saw a guy come through after that." Connie walked to the

register, touched the screen, then studied the list of recent receipts. "Here it is. He ordered a small regular coffee."

"Oooh. Right." As if suddenly remembering, she nodded slowly. "Uh-huh. You're right. That's about when it hit."

"He didn't bother you? Because the transaction is recorded, you know. Cameras at the sign where a customer orders, and here, in the workstation. Through the window."

Heather's lips parted. Obviously she'd forgotten that little fact.

"No. I barely remember taking his order."

Liar, Connie thought, but didn't make the accusation. Whatever the reason, Heather preferred to keep it to herself. She was a private person and Connie had been forced to pry to find out that Heather had been running from a bad dude, an abusive boyfriend who lived, Connie thought, somewhere in Alberta. But she wasn't sure. Heather had been evasive when questioned, except for admitting that the man from whom she was running wasn't her child's father.

Which was a story in and of itself.

Because Heather had been pregnant when she'd applied for the job, something she'd failed to mention until it had become very obvious.

Now, Connie wondered if the man in the SUV was Heather's abusive ex. A handsome son of a bitch, she'd give him that.

Heather licked her lips and glanced at the door. As if she expected the Grim Reaper to suddenly enter. "You know, I think I might have to leave early."

Connie wasn't surprised. Was ready for the request. The dining room was nearly empty, the lunch crowd only starting to dribble in. "Okay."

"You're sure?"

"We'll be fine," she said. "I already talked to Joanna."

As if on cue, Joanna appeared, flying through the swinging doors. She shot Heather a glare meant to cut through steel as she tied on her apron again and made her way to the drive-up station. Pointing an accusing finger in Heather's direction, she said, "You owe me," and there wasn't a bit of humor on her face.

"I do," Heather agreed, but she was already leaving.

Connie watched as she sped through the double doors, stripping off her own apron and locating her bag in her locker. Ashen faced, she was out the back door and inside her rattletrap of a car within the minute. Once behind the wheel, Heather tore out of the lot in a spray of gravel, as if Satan himself were giving chase.

Maybe he is.

As the car disappeared, Connie reached for her pack of cigarettes, then remembered the three bearded men who were still waiting for their orders. They sat at a table by the windows, but had watched the exchange. "Sorry about the delay," Connie said, forcing a smile. "I'm sure your order's up." She retrieved the sandwiches, placed them on the table, and as the trio dug in, found and heated the last three cinnamon rolls, drizzled them with butter, and carried the platter to the table.

As the men looked up she headed back to the kitchen, where Joanna, still in a bad mood, muttered under her breath, "Just for the record, I never trusted her."

"Who?" Connie asked but guessed.

"Heather." Joanna looked out the window and narrowed her eyes. "There's just something not quite right. She keeps secrets." With a glance at Connie, she added, "I wouldn't be surprised if she was in some kind of big trouble. I mean really big trouble."

"Like what?"

"I don't know, but she's running from something, something more than just some guy."

Connie wanted to argue but didn't. For once she agreed with Joanna, the Buzz's resident conspiracy theorist.

What was he doing here? For God's sake, *what the hell was Liam doing here?* Heather drove to the preschool in record time, all the while checking her rearview, certain a black SUV would be following.

None appeared.

In fact, the warm July afternoon seemed lazy and calm, not the least bit sinister.

Parking at the edge of the asphalt lot of ABC and Me, she spied no one lurking in the shadows, no dark vehicle parked across the street, nothing out of the ordinary. As she climbed out of her car, she heard seagulls calling as they flew overhead, and the quiet thrum of slowly passing cars.

It was summer. Children's voices floated on the air from the fenced play area and the windows of the brick building were cranked open to let in a soft, salt-laden breeze.

Nothing is out of the ordinary, she told herself, but her heart was knocking wildly in her chest as she hurried across the dry tarmac.

She found Miss Evers herding the children into the classroom from an outside door.

"You're here early," she said upon seeing Heather.

"I was worried about Charlotte, and since it was a slow day at work, I asked to get off early so that I could take her home." She caught sight of her daughter, the last in the line of the children filing inside. "How about that, honey?" she asked, hurrying to catch up to her child. When Charlotte raised her arms to be picked up she felt the unexpected burn of tears.

"She's been kind of quiet," the preschool teacher admitted, "but I checked her temp, like you did. She's been normal all day."

"Good." Heather had to ask, "Did anyone else stop by and ask about her or call about her?"

"No." Miss Evers stared at Heather hard, maybe picking up on her tension. "Why?"

"You would let me know, right?"

"Of course." There was security here. Anyone who came into the school had to sign in and sign out, the same with each of the children. A secretary was posted at the front door and all of the other exits opened to a huge fenced playground, which included a covered area. "Is something wrong?" she asked as one of the kids, a little boy with a buzz cut, tugged on the edge of her shirt.

"Tommy's being mean to me," he said, his lower lip protruding.

Miss Evers glanced toward the offender. "Tommy? We play nice."

"Silas started it!" Tommy, freckle-faced and stubborn, wasn't going to back down. Standing near the water table, he sneered at the smaller boy and splashed indignantly. "Anyways he's a baby. A big baby!"

"Am not," Silas wailed.

"We're fine," Heather said, and Miss Evers nodded.

"Sorry." She flashed a patient smile, then turned to face the petulant four-year-old. "Tommy, we've talked about this. Already twice today."

"It was my ball!" Tommy said.

"I found it." Silas wasn't backing down.

"Let's go home," Heather whispered into her daughter's hair and she felt Charlotte nod while still clinging tight. Which was unusual. Charlotte was an independent little girl who would run rather than walk and bounced on her feet rather than stand still. Today, she was sluggish and wanted to be held. Heather had to reach around her to grab her backpack and the papers from her assigned cubby.

But at least Charlotte was safe.

Heather carried her daughter outside, where the sun was peeking through high clouds. Again she scanned the parking lot. Again she saw nothing out of the ordinary.

What had she thought? That Liam would find out that he had a child, drive up here and, after grabbing a cup of to-go coffee, come here to steal Charlotte away? That Melissa Evers would just let the girl take off with a complete stranger? That Charlotte would willingly take off with a man she'd never met? "Let's get you buckled up," she said as she eased her daughter into her car seat.

"Can we get ice cream?" Charlotte asked.

"I suppose." Glad that she was interested in something, Heather clicked the buckle and made certain the straps were tight.

"Okay," Charlotte agreed and tried to smile, but the grin was fragile and fell off her face as quickly as it had appeared.

Double-checking that she wasn't being followed, Heather drove to the ice cream shop near the waterfront. She told herself that she hadn't seen Liam after all, that she'd panicked and overreacted, but despite her arguments to the contrary, she kept an eye out. At the ice cream store along the waterfront, its wooden cone-shaped sign swinging in the breeze, Charlotte perked up enough to order her favorite flavor, cookie dough with sprinkles and gummy worms. But she only took a couple of bites and then just sat holding the cone. She didn't even try for Heather's scoop of chocolate chip mint, which she usually marauded, though it was a game they often played. Charlotte would steal a bite and laugh uproariously as Heather feigned umbrage. The more Heather pretended to be angry, the more bites Charlotte would "steal."

Not so today. The ice cream was melting, the gummy worms looking as if they were drowning in a sea of vanilla. Heather pulled the plug on the afternoon's excursion. "Let's get you home," she said, and tossed the gooey remains of the treats into the trash.

She loaded Charlotte into the Honda again and by the time they got home to their little rental, Charlotte had fallen asleep in her car seat.

Heather hauled her inside the cottage, which had once been a separate garage for the larger house that faced the street. The owners of the main house, Bud and Maxine O'Brien, were in their late sixties and spent as much time traveling as they did at home. For a break on her rent, Heather watched the place for them and took care of their cat in their absence.

As her place was tucked behind the Cape Cod–style house and wasn't visible from the street, she felt somewhat secure, away from passing vehicles and prying eyes.

Bud and Maxine had never asked too many questions and offered Charlotte the grandparent figures she needed. Often Charlotte was in the "shop" with Bud, watching as he muttered under his breath while working on some project Maxine had cooked up for him. He was handy, could repair just about anything, and always took the time to show Charlotte what he was doing. Maxine did the same in the kitchen, allowing the little girl to stand on a chair and help as she baked pies, cookies, and cakes for a church bazaar, or test the sweetness of the various jams she canned every year. "Cherry is the best," Charlotte had confided to Heather on more than one occasion. "I no like blackberry." She would then twist her face into a frown to show her disgust of the fruit that grew wild along the roadsides.

Right now, the O'Briens were away on a trip to New York, and Heather was in charge.

Her living situation was nearly perfect.

Or had been.

As long as no one from her past life discovered her, she and Charlotte were safe. Right?

A little needle of guilt pricked her thoughts as she realized most of those who had once been close to her didn't know if she was dead or alive. She'd thought about righting that wrong, many times over, but had always decided to keep silent. She'd rationalized that the pain of their not knowing wasn't worth placing her child in jeopardy. Her would-be assassin's threat, hissed in that wheedling, thin pitch, still chilled her and lifted the hairs on the nape of her neck.

You'll never get away and that baby of yours will die!

"No!" she cried aloud and jumped at the sound of her own voice. Liam and his family would just have to wonder if she'd escaped.

She had a new life now and so did he. She'd dug around on the Internet and discovered that he was with Bethany Van Horne again, the beauty his mother had picked for him years ago.

She placed her daughter in her little bed. Charlotte immediately snuggled into her pillow, burrowing beneath the blankets. Satisfied the girl would sleep, Heather left the door ajar, then she walked the few steps to her living room, a small space with a white brick fireplace and view to the backyard. Attached by an eating bar to a tiny kitchen, the small communal area served multiple functions: playroom, den, guest room, and dining area. Fortunately, she never had much company, as the hand-me-down futon she used as an extra bed was on its last legs. Literally.

She made herself a glass of iced tea, checked once more to see that Charlotte was sleeping soundly, then carried her phone and drink through French doors to a deck that ran along the back of the small house. From one of the outdoor chairs, she could watch squirrels run through the fenced-in garden and hear Charlotte, should the girl stir. The yard wasn't very big but it was private and a secure place for Charlotte to play. She usually brought her dolls or stuffed animals out here. Even now, one naked baby doll was strapped in a little walker that Charlotte had played in herself before she'd learned to walk.

The second Heather sat down, she punched in The Magician's number.

"Hello?" Uncle Kent's familiar voice made fresh tears jump to her eyes.

"Is he here?" she demanded, setting free the worries that had eaten at her for the past two hours.

"What?" The rise in Uncle Kent's smooth tenor filled her with terror.

"Liam?" she asked, eyeing her fenced backyard with new suspicion. "Is he here in Point Roberts?"

So this is what a wild-goose chase feels like.

In the small dining area of the Point Bob Buzz, Liam finished his coffee and pushed aside his plate, including the uneaten portion of his BLT. He sat in a corner booth of the restaurant, which was little more than a coffee shop attached to a single dining room that now, in early afternoon, was almost empty. A group of three bearded men, friends who'd called to the owner about the "epic" cinnamon rolls, had left not long after he'd strolled in, and now, aside from a couple of teenagers sipping iced coffees while staring at their phones and laughing at what he thought were YouTube videos, and two women in deep conversation over a small table and coffee cups, he was the only customer in the establishment.

And Rory wasn't in sight. Not at the drive-up window where he'd ordered coffee earlier, and not in the dining area, nor, from what he could see through the service window behind the counter, in the kitchen. After she hadn't been at the window, he'd driven to the two other restaurants that served breakfast in town, neither of which offered drive-through service; she hadn't been working at either one. Besides, Jacoby had been insistent that she worked at the Buzz, specifically manning the drive-up window, on weekday mornings. The PI had even taken some pictures of a woman who resembled Rory, though the snapshots hadn't been conclusive, at least in Liam's opinion. The woman in the photo had straight, red locks and dark eyes, while Rory's were green. But those were easy changes, a simple disguise, he'd told himself. Maybe . . . just maybe. He'd like to know that at least she'd survived, and at most the reason she'd run. Was she involved in the attack that had taken her stepbrother's life and injured others? He hadn't believed it, had refused to listen to that line of thought, but now, five years in . . . he wasn't so sure.

He'd driven up here, across the border into Canada, and then across once more to enter this bit of U.S. land, the end of Tsawwassen Peninsula, because Jacoby believed he'd found Aurora "Rory" Abernathy Bastian, his wife. Soon to be ex, he reminded himself, as his attorney was working feverishly to ensure that Liam was single.

So he could get married again.

He frowned at that thought. Marrying Bethany when he still had so many questions about his first wife was the main reason he had yet to pop the question. As far as he knew, Rory could be a criminal, somehow involved in the attack at the wedding, but it just didn't make any sense. Where had she gone? Why? Was she alive? Dead? Why the hell had she run?

He made a sound of disgust. Beth was sure as hell mad at him now. She might never forgive him for flaking out on the trip to Napa. The color had drained from her face when he'd told her he had a lead on what had happened to Rory and was going to look into it. She'd recovered enough to announce she was going with him, but he'd turned her down, insisting she go on to Napa with her friends and maybe he would meet her later. That hadn't gone over well, and she'd canceled the trip rather than go alone. He'd half believed that might be the end of their relationship, and maybe it should have been, but Beth was nothing if not stalwart in her belief that they were meant to be together, Rory or no Rory. She'd swallowed back her anger and said she would be waiting for him when he got back. The hell of it was, he wasn't sure if that was a good thing or a bad thing. He almost wished she would lose her cool and call him out. That, he would understand. But Beth could control her emotions in a way that was awe-inspiring. It just wasn't conducive to a passionate relationship.

He noticed that he was drumming his fingers on the table, and he stopped himself just as he spotted the plump waitress watching him. Ostensibly she was wiping down tables, then carrying out trash, but he'd felt as if she, behind a pleasant smile and rimless glasses, had been observing him, even going so far as to take out a cell phone as if to check a text or something, but instead maybe to take his picture. There had been something awkward about how she held the phone. And he'd noticed that when she'd slipped through the kitchen for a few minutes, she'd appeared at the side of the building, her slim shadow and flapping apron visible in the corner of the window. From the shape of the shadow, she'd been holding her camera in a position to snap a shot of the parking lot, where his SUV was parked.

Why would this woman care?

It all smelled bad.

He frowned at that thought and saw the plump waitress heading his way again with a half-full glass pot of coffee in one hand and his bill in the other. Good. Time to get out of here.

Or was it?

He'd come all this way.

To a tiny spot on the map that did have an airstrip and marina, so, though there was international red tape to deal with, escape could be made quickly by land, air, or sea.

Placing his bill on the table, she let the pot of coffee hover

over his empty cup. "Can I get you anything else? More coffee?" The name tag pinned to her white blouse read CONNIE.

"Maybe." Before she could start pouring, he reached into his pocket, grabbed his phone, and flipping it deftly, hit a button to light the screen and showed her a couple of the shots Jacoby had taken. One was a close-up of the drive-through waitress, headset in place. "This woman, she works here?" he asked.

Connie hesitated. How could she deny the obvious, when the outdoor shot was obviously of the drive-up window at the Buzz?

"Who took this?" she demanded, still holding the coffeepot.

He ignored the question. "I'm looking for Aurora Bastian. She might call herself Rory Bastian or Rory Abernathy, or use some other alias."

"And who are you?"

"That's the thing." He tapped the small screen, drawing her attention back to the woman he believed to be Rory. "I'm her husband."

Chapter 4

At the mention of the word "husband" he thought she flinched the tiniest of bits. "No one by any of those names works here." Connie was shaking her head.

"But this woman." Liam held up the screen on his phone. "Who is she?"

"I don't give out the names of my staff or my customers to anyone." Connie was quickly losing patience, a tic near the corner of her eye visible despite her glasses.

"You own this place?"

"That's right. And there are privacy laws that I'm not going to break, so I think we're done here." She handed him his bill. "You can pay at the register." Then she turned and marched off, heading toward the counter and the kitchen beyond. No doubt to contact her employee—the woman in the photo on his phone—and warn her off.

He would have to move fast.

He'd overplayed his hand.

No surprise there, he thought as he scraped back his chair, tossed enough cash on the table to cover his meal and a healthy tip, then made his way out of the cozy little diner with its dark secrets.

At his SUV, he took off his jacket and tossed it into the back seat, then climbed behind the wheel where the interior was warming as the sun had peeked through the clouds, summer appearing after a cool morning.

He wasn't cut out for espionage, or chasing down women who had spurned him, even if he'd made the mistake of marrying this particular one.

Switching on the ignition, he heard the big engine of his Tahoe roar to life. For a split second he considered leaving this little town, driving back to the mainland and picking up the life he'd left to take off on this last-ditch effort to find his wife.

She was alive.

He knew it.

The picture didn't lie.

And the coffee shop's owner's attitude only fueled his suspicions that he was zeroing in on Rory. She couldn't be far. There wasn't anywhere to run.

Except the open sea.

If her MO hadn't changed over the years, and she found out from good old Connie that he was here, in Point Roberts, searching for her, Rory's first instinct would be to run. If so, she'd have to take a boat, plane, bus, or car. And he was betting on the car. It would be the easiest and quickest way to bolt. A private vehicle would be able to take her somewhere even more remote than Point Roberts and wouldn't require tickets or schedules.

Gravel crunched beneath his tires as he drove out of the lot, away from a wreck of a vehicle that seemed destined to die behind the kitchen of the Point Bob Buzz. One last look over his shoulder confirmed what he already suspected. He caught a glimpse through the window of Connie with a cell phone in her hand.

Would Rory return to pick up her final check?

Liam doubted it. If it turned out to be truly Rory in the picture, and she knew he was here, she'd run. He'd learned by experience: it was what she did.

Frustrated, he pulled into the parking lot of a minimart, yanked his cell phone from his pocket, and punched in the numbers of the private investigator who had brought him this far. Jacoby answered on the second ring and Liam, the engine of his Tahoe idling, said, "I need information on the employees of the Point Bob Buzz."

"You struck out?"

"She wasn't there."

"Christ, Bastian. Don't tell me you just bullied your way inside and she bolted."

"Something like that."

"What did I tell you? You need to dance the dance."

"I just need the information. Fast."

"Figured." Was there a touch of a smirk in the heavy-set man's voice? "I figured you just might blow it. That's the problem with you rich folks. Impatience. No finesse."

"So, what have you got?" Liam asked curtly.

With a snort that could have meant anything, Jacoby got down to business. "Three women currently work in the Point Bob Buzz," he said. "Connie Fellows, the owner."

"We've met. Not her."

"Joanna Travers, from Vancouver. But she's not your girl. It's the third one," he said, obviously enjoying the suspense. "Heather Johnson. I just got a copy of her driver's license. I'll send it along. She's the one."

"You have an address for her?"

"On the license. Unless she's moved: 107 Looking Glass Lane."

Repeating the address, he was already plugging the information into his GPS, waiting for the route to appear on the map of Point Roberts that showed his position on its screen.

He felt a sizzle of adrenaline flowing through his blood at the thought that finally, after five years, he'd see her again. Then, maybe, he could get some answers and get the hell on with his life.

The route appeared and he rammed his truck into gear and checked his mirrors as Jacoby said, "There is one other thing."

"Yeah?" He pulled into a side street and waited at a stop sign. "What's that?"

"She doesn't live alone."

"No?"

A husband. Or boyfriend. Another complication. He should have figured.

"She's got a kid, Liam. A daughter."

"Slow down, slow down," The Magician said from the other end of the wireless connection. "I can't understand you. You're talking too damned fast."

"But I have to tell you—" Heather started to argue.

"I'm serious. Okay? Just take a deep breath and start over. From the beginning." Uncle Kent was serious, and though Heather's heart was still jackhammering in panic, she did as she was told, drawing deeply of the fresh air, forcing a wave of calmness to wash over her.

The Magician continued, "All I got out of it was that you think Liam's in Point Roberts and you're worried about Charlotte."

Heather nodded, though he couldn't see her. She watched a robin hop through the grass of the backyard, searching for worms, while her heart seemed to be exploding in her chest.

"I saw him. Liam. At the Buzz this morning," she said after taking another prescribed deep breath. "I'm pretty sure of it and . . . yes, Charlotte isn't herself." She went on to describe the events of the morning, how she'd been certain Liam had found her, how she'd hidden out in the restroom before barreling to the preschool, gathering up her sick child, and landing back home.

"You're certain that it was Liam?"

"Yes . . . yes . . ." she insisted, then bit at a fingernail, her temporary sense of equanimity oozing away. "Look, I'm not *a hundred percent* sure. But . . . it sure looked like him through the screen and it sounded like him and—"

"So you only saw him on a screen?"

"While I was taking his order, but it was him."

There was hesitation.

She barreled on. "I know this is kind of crazy, y'know, after all this time and . . . but . . . wait." She heard a ding indicating that a text was coming in. The message was from Connie. "Hold on a sec," she said into the phone, then switched to the text screen. "Oh, no," she whispered as she saw that Connie had sent two pictures. One was of a black SUV with Oregon plates, parked close to Connie's uncle's wreck of a truck, and another was of Liam, sitting at a table in the dining room of the Buzz.

No, no, no!

Her worst fears had come true.

"Heather?" The Magician said when the silence had stretched.

"I-I'm here," she said shakily, her brain on overdrive, her fears mounting. "The text. It was pictures. Of Liam."

"*What?*"

"He's here." *Oh, God, oh, God.* "He's here, Kent. In Point Roberts." The panic that she'd tried to keep a rein on had burst free.

"You're sure?"

Another ping of the phone and she clicked to read the message, again from Connie. As she scanned the quick note, she said, "It's definitely Liam and he was at the Buzz. Asking about me. Look, Kent, I've got to get out of here." Her mind was already scrambling, wondering how she would leave with the O'Briens still out of town, not due back for another day. She'd promised she would watch over the place and Mr. Bones, the black cat currently sliding through the leafy branches of the shrubbery planted near the fence line.

"Let me think," he said. "Just because he's at the Buzz doesn't mean—"

"What's to think about? Didn't you hear what I said? He's here. *Looking for me.* He already knows my place of work, so he probably knows my name and where I live and Charlotte . . . oh, Lord, what about Charlotte?"

Her baby. The reason she ran in the first place. Someone at that wedding had been out to kill her and Liam and the baby and . . . "I'm coming to Maude's," she said. "Are you there? I mean, not still on the connection, but are you at Maude's house?" Maude Sutter was The Magician's girlfriend and had been for as long as Heather could remember. She lived in Vancouver, a few miles north in Canada, and was the reason that Heather had ended up here in the first place. It was through Maude's connections that Heather had found this home and her job at the Buzz.

"Yes, I'm here."

"I'll be there in . . . an hour or two, depending on how long it takes to close things up here, traffic and the border crossing." She was already mentally sweeping these few rooms, making a mental list of everything she would need to get out of town and leave little indication that she, or at least Rory Bastian, had ever set foot here.

"Okay. We'll strategize then."

"We'd better do more than that," she said and clicked off.

She fought down the welling panic that threatened to paralyze her. Liam probably knew her name? What about her address? That he had a daughter? Her heart squeezed. How had he found her? How? Had he been looking all this time? What about the police?

"Stop it!" she cried and sprang out of her chair, nearly toppling over the remains of her iced tea as she hit the table. Picking up the glass, she spun around to see Charlotte standing in the open doorway, her favorite blanket dangling from her fingers, her one-eyed stuffed bunny with the lopping ears tucked under her arm.

"What's wrong, Mama?" she asked, four-year-old eyes worried, dark smudges beneath them.

"Uh. Nothing. I, er, I was talking to Uncle Kent. We're going to visit him and Aunt Maude."

"We are?"

"Yep. Right now. We just have to feed Mr. Bones and make sure he has plenty of water."

"He drinks from the fountain."

"I know. But we'll fill his dish anyway."

The O'Briens had one of those feeders that was a dish attached to a dispenser that could hold a week's worth of food. The water dish was similar, so Mr. Bones would be good for at least a week and he did hang out at the fountain, mainly in hopes of pouncing on an unsuspecting bird.

"Come on," Heather said briskly. "Let's pack up. You can help."

"After we feed Mr. Bones?"

"Exactly," Heather said cheerily, though she was frantic. At least Charlotte was awake and, it seemed, not as listless as she had been.

"So, once we take care of the kitty, let's pack up, okay?" Heather leaned down to be able to look her daughter in the eye. "It's a game. The faster, the better. Grab all your favorite toys, and blanket. Ready?" Charlotte was staring at her intently with eyes so like her father's that Heather's heart twisted. "Okay. One, two, three . . . go!"

* * *

107 Looking Glass.

Liam parked across the street of the small house with its paned windows and flower boxes, a river-rock chimney beginning to crumble near the top of the smokestack, the door painted a bright red. The tidy little home was off the street, tucked between larger homes and a hedge, in this part of town that wasn't far from the waterfront.

An older model car was parked near the front door.

He drew a breath. Couldn't believe he was here. Couldn't believe he might see Rory again. He wasn't sure how he felt about that. Not really. And he wasn't certain he wanted to examine his feelings too deeply, dig into his own psyche, pull out his emotions and lay them out on the ground to be trampled down.

You just need to get this over with. Put it behind you.

He was mad at Rory. Seething and infuriated about what had happened at the wedding. Somehow she was involved. Not completely. He'd never believed that. But somehow . . . someway. Coincidences like her disappearance and the shoot-out at the wedding didn't happen independently. He'd said as much to Derek, who'd shrugged and answered, "Hey, her family's fucked up. A bunch of criminals."

"Her stepfamily," Liam had reminded him.

"Her mother's as screwed up as the rest of them. Psychic ability, my ass. How come she didn't see that attack if she's so in tune with the universe?"

Darlene, Rory's mother, had tearfully come to the hospital, clinging to Liam's arm before and after surgery. Vivian had screamed at her, "Let go of my brother and *get out.*" Stella and Derek had been dealing with his father's injuries and hadn't paid too much attention to Darlene, who'd begun keening in some indistinguishable tongue at one point, which had at first infuriated Vivian and then had struck her as funny. She'd doubled over in fits of hilarity, choking in air, she was laughing so hard. Stella had come in and looked as if she was going to give her a hard slap to bring her back, but Liam had yelled at her to leave her alone.

The wailing had slowly stopped and Darlene had come out of her trance to blink at Liam a few times, saying, "Aurora's safe now. I don't know where she is. We're not supposed to. But she's safe and she sends her love."

"Bullshit!" Vivian exploded, jumping forward, so Liam yelled at her and Stella grabbed her arm, yanking her back.

Darlene left a few moments later, but Vivian sicced the police on her, saying she knew where her daughter was. Apparently that wasn't true because Darlene passed every lie detector test, as did Everett Stemple, who swore he had nothing to do with the attack. Even Harold Stemple took the test. In fact he had insisted on it, to make sure somebody didn't "try to falsely pin another crime on him."

Jacoby suspected that Darlene did not know where her daughter was all these years. That wasn't the way he'd found Rory, though he'd been less than forthcoming about what his methods were. "You don't want to know, and I don't want you to know, in case people want to ask too many questions, you understand?" he'd finally told Liam.

Liam had nodded. He understood that too much scrutiny might bring up something no one wanted: a complaint about Jacoby's methodology. A question about why Liam hadn't immediately told the police. The hammer of the law down upon Rory's head before Liam had time to get at the truth.

And so now, here he was. In front of the place where she lived. Where she'd taken refuge. The sanctuary to which she'd escaped. The notion that she'd somehow found a better life, left him standing at the altar because she'd hooked up with someone who had offered her more, had been way off base. The waitress job at the Buzz was a fair indication that she wasn't exactly rolling in riches, and now this neat but tiny home.

Maybe it wasn't about money. Maybe she just found happiness elsewhere. Perhaps with someone else.

That idea still rankled but he reminded himself that she ran because she knew about the attack. Hadn't there been blood in the hotel room where she'd dressed in her wedding dress, the very lace-and-silk gown that had also been stained in splotchy dark stains?

The blood had been analyzed and hadn't been Rory's. The reports had proved the blood to be from a male. An unknown male. Probably the assailant who had opened fire on the ceremony, a murdering bastard who was still at large.

Her accomplice?

No. It still didn't make any sense that she was complicit in the murder. If she'd wanted out of the marriage, he'd have divorced her. There was no need for the violence of the attack, the sheer terror rained upon the group of guests. There had to be another motive, one he didn't understand, but one, he suspected, she understood. Somehow she'd been tipped off to the attack and had run. So who was behind it? How did she know the assailant? Why, why, why?

He rubbed his leg where the bullet had entered. He still bore a scar, of course, and felt pain at times where the muscle had torn and the bone had shattered. A series of surgeries involving pins and bone grafts had given him the ability to walk, but it had taken nearly a year for his strength and endurance to return. He'd been lucky the bullet to his gut hadn't hit his spine. It had passed through, nicking his intestines, but had done far less damage than anyone expected. A miracle, his mother had pronounced in tears. Everyone told him how lucky he was.

He didn't feel lucky.

He'd hate to count how many hours of physical therapy,

miles on a stationary bike, and steps on a treadmill he'd logged while recovering. With each effort, while sweating bullets and fighting through the lingering pain, Liam had silently vowed to find Rory and bring her to justice. One way or another he was going to clear up the mystery of the attack on the wedding party.

Of course Bethany had been at his side throughout. He'd woken up to her worried face in the hospital. Her eyes had filled with tears when he'd focused on her. "Thank God," she'd whispered, and grabbed his hand, then turned to avoid letting him see the tears drizzle down her cheek. When she'd faced him again, she was all brave smiles, and gave him words of encouragement. "Don't scare me like that," she'd scolded as she'd leaned down to kiss him. Then the doctor had come into the room and she'd been ushered out of the ICU only to return later in the afternoon. She'd resented everyone else surrounding him, especially Darlene, and she missed the scene between Darlene and Vivian, but she was his most steadfast companion. Slowly, day by day, as he'd recovered and been released to a private hospital in Portland, then a rehabilitation center and finally to his condominium, she'd been rock steady. Liam had recently asked about the boyfriend who had been her plus-one at the wedding, to which she'd just shrugged. "He was just a date," she said.

Liam had been standing at the floor-to-ceiling windows that looked over the Willamette River. As he leaned on his crutches, he could see Bethany's ghostlike reflection in the glass and her wistful smile. "You're still married to her, you know," she'd said, never speaking Rory's name.

"I know."

"What're you going to do about it?"

"Go back to work."

"That's not what I'm talking about."

"I know," he said again and caught a tightening of her jaw in the reflection as her mouth bowed into a sad frown. "I haven't decided yet. It's only been three months."

She'd wanted to argue, he'd seen it in the image of her eye, but she'd just slipped her hand over his as it rested on the handhold of the crutches, and when he'd rotated his head to meet her eyes, she'd managed a bright smile. "Just don't take too long," she'd said lightly. "You could lose me."

But he hadn't. Not in five years.

Training his gaze on the cottage, he climbed out of the SUV and headed for the front door. As he passed the Honda he noticed a child's car seat strapped into the back. Just as the private investigator had said. He felt a pang of regret. A kid complicated things. Big-time. What would happen to the child if the police were called in?

It doesn't matter. A person was killed in the attack.

And Rory had answers. If not all, then some.

"Showtime," he muttered under his breath and was surprised that he didn't feel an immediate sense of satisfaction, that after all these years there was little triumph in knowing he'd finally run her to the ground. Well, too bad. Pocketing his keys, he jogged across the empty street and up a broken concrete path to the front door. He pounded on the door, heard a child crying and a sharp, "Hush," before the door was swung open and a woman of no more than twenty, with a girl of two balanced on one hip, stood on the threshold. She shaded her eyes with one hand. "Can I help you?" she asked, squinting. The little girl with brown hair that looked as if it had been combed with a Mixmaster stared suspiciously at him.

"I'm looking for Rory, no, Heather Johnson."

"Well, make up your mind." Her voice was tinny and her expression perturbed.

"Does she live here?"

"Nuh-uh." She was shaking her head and heavy footsteps approached. From the interior, a burly man of about twenty-five, tattoos running up both meaty arms, appeared. A beard covered the lower half of his face, a baseball cap was pulled low on his forehead, and his eyes, beneath the bill, cut like lasers as he stared at Liam.

"Somethin' I can help you with?" he asked.

"He says he's lookin' for a woman," the woman clarified. "Heather somethin' or other."

Liam said, "Johnson."

The guy frowned. "What you want with her?"

"Old friends."

The trio in the doorway didn't say a word.

"I heard she lived here."

"Where you hear that?" the man asked as he stepped in front of his small family protectively, wedging his heavy body between Liam and his wife.

"Mutual friend."

"Well, the friend got it wrong. Ain't no one here but us. Me and my family."

"How long have you been here?" Liam asked.

"Not quite two years," the woman said. "Right before Emmy here was born."

"Who the hell are you?" the man demanded.

"Liam Bastian."

"If you're so friendly with this Heather person, why don't you know where she lives? Huh? Why don't you, y'know, tweet her or somethin'? Whoever gave you this address sent you barkin' up the wrong tree. Me and Mona here, like she said, we been here nearly two years and we don't know nothin' about Heather anybody."

The man was adamant. He crossed his arms and waited. Obviously expecting Liam to take the very broad hint to leave.

"Well, maybe she lived here before you moved in."

"I said I didn't know her, didn't I?" The man was insistent. Liam saw Mona's mouth open as if to disagree, but she closed it again quickly. This was a small town. Everyone probably knew everyone. "Mona, here, she never met whoever lived here before us, neither."

Next to him, Mona lifted her chin a bit and her eyes flashed with resentment.

Liam said, "Heather works at the Point Bob Buzz."

Almost imperceptibly Mona nodded and again caught herself, looking away quickly and pushing some of her child's wild hair from her face.

"Then maybe you should check with Connie. She owns the place. She can probly send you to the right address," he said.

This guy wasn't about to budge. His jaw was set, his feet planted, his lips thin. And he was lying through his not-so-straight teeth.

Liam wasn't going to get anywhere with him or the wife, Mona, as long as he was around. "Thanks for your time," he said and walked away. From the corner of his eye he saw Mona punch the guy in the arm, not hard, but enough to have him swivel his gaze so she could get his attention and, it seemed, chew him out.

Liam filed that bit of information and he punched the number of his PI into his phone and drove to the place that he'd rented. As was usually the case, he had to leave a message, which was simply, "Call me." Obviously Rory, now Heather, had moved since obtaining her driver's license, but it should be a simple matter for Jacoby to find her new address. Hell, she could've moved several times since residing on Looking Glass, keeping herself under the radar.

Except for the job.

Which she might never return to, now that she was warned off. He thought about calling the police as he pulled into the gravel parking area and stopped near the cedar-shingled cottage tucked into the woods. He locked his car and took the stairs to the porch that skirted the building that was little more than one of those fashionable "tiny houses." As he was stepping into the living area his cell phone rang. The caller ID was Jacoby's cell number. Liam dropped his keys on the small kitchen counter and answered. "The address was wrong."

"What?"

"The Looking Glass address on Heather Johnson's driver's license? Bogus. If she ever lived there, she split. The couple who greeted me at the door had been there nearly two years."

"Huh."

Liam leaned a hip against a wooden counter with a minuscule sink and half refrigerator tucked beneath it. A microwave was cut into the back wall beneath a flight of stairs leading to the bedroom loft.

"I'll dig a little deeper," Jacoby decided.

"Do that." Liam hung up and tamped his rising temper down. All wasn't lost. Yet. He noticed a few calls that had come in, three from the foreman he'd left on the apartment construction job. He called the foreman back and was relieved to learn the problem was with the city and the permits instead of more vandalism, a small glitch that was already being taken care of since the foreman had made the calls.

Thank God for small favors.

He put in a call to Derek, too, who thought he was on a business trip to Vancouver, looking for Canadian investors. Derek never had much interest in the Bastian-Flavel Construction deal-making, though his father was a far different story. Geoff Bastian had been a little harder to fob off, but Liam was bound and determined not to let anyone in his family know what he was doing. Bethany had to know the truth, since he'd blown off the Napa trip, but she was as interested as he was in keeping the nature of his trip under wraps. She wanted him to just take care of it. No muss, no fuss. She, too, had left several messages on his phone, but he wasn't ready to call her back yet.

So where was Rory?

Still in Point Roberts? Hiding out in this small town, right under his nose?

Or had she already taken off? Afraid of confronting him? Scared that her neat little life was about to unravel?

Well, he wasn't giving up. Not yet. He'd come too far. He planned on finding her, contacting the authorities so that she could be interrogated if not arrested, and if nothing else, demand the divorce he so desperately needed.

His jaw tightened as it always did when he thought of Rory, his marriage, her disappearance, and the dissolution of their short union.

He decided his mother had been right. Stella had warned him not to get involved with Rory when she'd first learned of the seriousness of their romance. "Nothing good will come of it," she'd said on a sigh as she'd climbed out of the heated pool. She'd toweled off, her body trim and tanned in a sleek navy one-piece, and Liam noticed that surprisingly not one strand of her short hair had gotten wet while she'd stroked through her ten laps. "I'm sorry, Liam," she'd added, dabbing at her face before dropping the towel onto a striped chaise longue flanked by huge pots of geraniums and some cascading white flower he couldn't name. "But it's just the way it is when people of different . . . stations . . . get involved romantically." She'd shrugged. "There's just too much inequity."

His father clarified, "Your mother thinks Rory is a gold digger." Shirt sleeves pushed up, Geoff Bastian had been seated at an outside table in the shade of the porch, newspapers spread in front of him, a sweating glass of scotch anchoring one corner of the business section.

This was hardly news to Liam, but Stella felt compelled to defend herself. "Not exactly," she said, sending her husband a sharp glare. She turned to her son. "I'm just saying you're setting yourself up for heartache, honey. That's all."

Over the tops of his reading glasses, Geoff had raised his eyebrows while mouthing, "Gold digger."

"I heard that," Stella said as she walked behind her husband and through the open French doors to the family room.

"I don't know how she does that," his father had grumbled, picking up his newspaper and snapping it open.

Liam didn't either, but Stella Bastian had always made it her business to know exactly what all the members of her family were doing at any given time. It was uncanny and a gift. And it bugged the hell out of Liam. His mother should just butt out.

And yet, hadn't some of her predictions come true? Hadn't she been nearly apoplectic at hearing the news he and Rory had gotten married in a civil ceremony, without his family's blessing? Hadn't she said, "Marriage is about commitment, Liam, not lust, for the love of God. You two have barely known each other a month, and now you're married? I can't believe it." At that point she'd nearly swooned into her favorite wingback chair positioned near the fireplace in the family room. "This . . . this . . ." She'd waved a long-fingered hand in the air as she searched for the right word. ". . . this foolish mistake needs to be undone."

Rory, standing next to Liam, her hand in his, had glanced up at him with the *I told you so* look in her eyes that had bored into his soul. She'd warned him this utter dismay would be his parents' reaction. Meanwhile, her larcenous family had insisted that the Bastians would receive the news of the union with the same warmth the Montagues had felt upon hearing that Romeo had married a Capulet. And they'd been so, so right. At the time, Liam had waved off Rory's concerns with a blithe, "My folks will come around."

Rory hadn't been convinced, even bringing up the obvious fact that Stella had wanted Bethany Van Horne, a beautiful and socially acceptable choice for a daughter-in-law. Liam had laughed off her worries and told her he was going to marry who he chose and he'd chosen Aurora Abernathy, for better or worse.

He'd never anticipated that the worst could be a rifle assault on the wedding, a horrifying murder and a missing bride.

The irony was that now he was, indeed, planning to marry Bethany, the girl of his mother's dreams. Which was a good thing. He just needed to find Rory, serve her with divorce papers, meet her face to face and get some answers.

His phone chirped again.

A message from Jacoby.

With an address in Point Roberts.

Not ten minutes away.

Liam felt his resolve harden as he headed for the door.

Jacoby wouldn't make the same mistake twice.

Chapter 5

Heather was sweating bullets by the time she drove through the border crossing and headed into Vancouver, British Columbia.

With Charlotte strapped into the back seat and a good share of her worldly possessions stuffed into every available space in her small car, she headed directly to Uncle Kent's condo. Heather knew she'd have to return, to feed the cat if nothing else, and to grab the last of her belongings, but for now she just needed to keep Charlotte safe.

Her daughter was still not her usually ebullient self, but part of her mood could probably be attributed to Heather's freakout. She'd made a game of gathering up toys, clothes, electronics, and toiletries, but Charlotte was astute, a kid who saw beyond the surface and no doubt she'd read the tension beneath Heather's forced smile and recognized panic in her mother's eyes.

Even now, though quiet for the most part, Charlotte had asked, "What about Mr. Bones? Does Uncle Kent know we're coming? Why are we leaving so fast?" Heather had made up quick answers. "The cat will be fine. I'll be back tomorrow," she had answered. "It's kind of a surprise. Uncle Kent will be thrilled to see you, honey." None of the answers had rung true and Charlotte, big-eyed and suspicious, was holding tight to her stuffed rabbit and staring at the back of Heather's head as if silently willing her mother to spout out the truth.

No way.

Not yet.

Her "Heather Johnson" passport still worked, thank God, at least as far as getting into Canada and back to Point Roberts. Entering the U.S. mainland again hadn't been an issue until she'd seen Liam in the monitor of her station at the Buzz.

Throat tight, she kept checking her mirrors to see if she was being followed. So far, no black SUV was in sight and traffic was light enough that she could track the vehicles within a hundred yards behind her Honda. Even so, her heart was pounding, her hands sweaty, though she'd cracked the window and the summer day was cool.

As she glanced into the reflective glass, she zeroed in on her red hair. She wished she'd had time to dye it dark again, become a brunette.

Why? What's the point? He's found you, hasn't he?

Not yet.

Heather maneuvered through the increasingly heavy traffic through the outskirts of Vancouver and tried to distract her daughter with a game of "Who can spy the next red car," to no avail. At last she pulled into the driveway of the townhouse and watched the cars driving past. No vehicle slowed. No black SUV slid into the open parking spaces on the street, nothing looked out of place. A jogger sped past, wireless earphones visible, ponytail swinging, and an elderly couple, both wearing hats, walked a dog on the sidewalk along the narrow street that headed into the park. Another neighbor was watering the flowers in her front-porch planters that exploded with pink and purple petunias.

Liam, if he'd been in Point Roberts, hadn't followed her to Vancouver. Still, her pulse raced as she helped Charlotte from her car seat.

"I can do it," her daughter told her while struggling with the buckles and holding her one-eyed stuffed bunny in a death grip. Heather waited while her daughter asserted her independence, releasing the buckle, climbing out of her car seat and through the sedan's open door, slipping her free hand into Heather's as they headed up the steps to the front porch.

Heather leaned on the bell, but the glass door was opened immediately and Maude Sutter stood in the hallway. "Well, holy sh—moley. What in the world's going on?" She reached for Charlotte but her sharp, blue-eyed gaze was firmly focused on Heather.

"I wish I knew."

"It's a game," Charlotte said sagely. "See how fast we can get here."

"Well, I hope you didn't break any speeding laws on the way. Come on in."

"My things—"

"Kent's on his way. Let him unpack for you. I'm hoping you're staying for a while." In a lingering cloud of expensive perfume mingled with cigarette smoke, she nuzzled Charlotte's cheek. "Now, you, Charlotte, my love, tell me everything that's going on, will you?"

Charlotte immediately brightened and began chatting.

"There's iced tea on the counter in the kitchen, something a little stronger in the cabinet in the den. Whatever you want or need." Still holding Charlotte, she closed the door behind Heather and led the way along a narrow hall to the back of the house, where the kitchen looked over a small garden. "I've got a new birdhouse," she murmured into the child's ear. "Let me show you." Without another word to Heather she took Charlotte through a back door to the yard, where hummingbirds and bumblebees were buzzing over a riot of blooms. After dropping her purse and computer bag onto the table, Heather poured herself a glass of iced tea from the glass pitcher on the table and considered adding a splash of vodka, but decided to save the alcohol for later. She needed a clear head, now more than ever.

How had he found her?

Why had he tracked her down?

What was she going to do?

She stood in the open back door and watched Maude walk her daughter along flagstone paths through the shrubbery, loving the image of a sixtyish woman in a flowing white caftan holding the hand of a little girl in clothes still splotched with preschool finger paint and wrinkled from her nap. Charlotte had never met either one of her biological grandmothers—neither ice-queen, snobby Stella Bastian nor easily influenced Darlene Stemple who thought she was a little psychic and yet had married the unscrupulous Harold Stemple. Rory's own father, Uncle Kent's good friend, had died suddenly of a heart attack when Rory was about Charlotte's age. Rory sensed that Pat Abernathy hadn't completely walked the straight and narrow, much like The Magician, but overall he'd been a good man. Darlene had been lost after his death, completely undone. Rory could vaguely remember the different men her mother had been attracted to, ones she suspected Uncle Kent had somehow managed to dissuade from pursuing her. But he hadn't been able to stop Darlene from falling for the handsome and slick Harold Stemple, a man who was little more than a common criminal. A thug who married Darlene and brought his teenage sons, Everett and Aaron, into the household when Rory was thirteen. Aaron, the younger son, hadn't been so bad. He'd become friends with Rory, and that friendship was why she'd asked him to walk her down the aisle. But Everett was a different case entirely. He'd learned at his father's knee, apparently, and was aggressive and very aware of his good looks. The Stemple and Abernathy households had barely come together when he began making lewd remarks to Rory, suggesting that she really should let him show her the sexual ropes, inviting her to touch him and even going so far as to not only try to kiss her, but feel her up. Once he'd even slipped into her bedroom and climbed into the single bed that had been pushed up against the wall. Only a knee to his groin and her scream had forced him out of the room. After that, she'd installed a lock on her door, especially when Darlene didn't take seriously her daughter's claims of being nearly raped.

"He would never have really done anything," Darlene said the next morning when she and Rory were alone. "He was just teasing. Giving you a scare."

"He's a sexual predator!"

Darlene raised her hands on either side of her head, as if she wanted to cover her ears. "Everett wouldn't do that."

"He tried to rape me, Mom!"

"Oh, the drama. Come on. He likes you."

"I don't think he does!" she'd cried, tears standing in her eyes. "Rape's about power, Mom! That's what it is!"

Darlene had blinked back her own tears. "I know . . . I know. He shouldn't have come into your room. That's a violation. But nothing happened, so we're all okay. And I know things are going to get better. I talked with Laurie yesterday, and she sees great changes in the future. I can already feel them happening."

Rory had wanted to scream. Laurie was one of her mother's "psychic" friends.

"Don't tell Harold," Darlene added in an undertone. "I'll talk to Everett."

"Oh, sure. That'll do a lot of good."

Her mother had missed the sarcasm and tried to cuddle her then, but Rory had shaken her off. Together they'd gone to the hardware store, installed a dead bolt on the bedroom door, and Rory had made it her mission to get out of that shabby little house with its secrets and lies the second she turned eighteen. Which she had. Never looking back except to ask her mother to be her matron of honor at Rory and Liam's second wedding and, with no one else to turn to, she'd chosen Aaron to walk her down the aisle. Her stepfather was in prison and Everett wasn't invited. Period. Despite Darlene's desperate pleas that he was part of her family and Rory should get over her negative thoughts.

"Pervert," she muttered now, draining the last of her tea, biting down on an ice cube just as she heard the front door open and Uncle Kent's footsteps sounded in the hallway.

The Magician had returned.

No one was home.

Liam knew it the moment he pulled into the drive, past a larger house to what appeared to be a guest house, probably a garage that had been converted to living quarters.

No vehicle was visible and all the shades were drawn in the little cottage that shared the address of the main house, the only difference being that a B had been attached to the numerical address.

Nonetheless he climbed out of his Tahoe and walked along a short path to the front door, where he rapped firmly.

No answer.

No sign of life.

And yet he felt as if he was being watched.

The hairs at the back of his neck lifted and he turned to find a black cat seated on a fence post near the back of the large home, gold eyes staring at him curiously. "What're you lookin' at?" he asked in frustration. The cat didn't move, aside from the slight twitch of its tail.

He banged again, then headed to the main house, where he leaned on the doorbell, heard the peal of chimes, but no answering footsteps. He wasn't surprised; the place felt deserted, though a quick look in the mailboxes indicated that either the mail had been stopped or had been recently picked up and the cat . . . either belonged to a neighbor or to the tenants.

If so, they wouldn't be gone long.

Rubbing the back of his neck and feeling like a burglar, he wandered to the rear of the cottage, to the small backyard with a deck. He tested the slider to the back of the tiny home, but it was locked tight, again the shades drawn.

Her boss had probably tipped her off. Connie, he suspected, was the only person who might have a clue as to where she'd gone. Unless the owners of the larger home, the O'Briens, had been filled in. He expected Rory, aka Heather, would lie low now, at least for a while. She could've taken off indefinitely.

But someone would have to know.

She'd have to have a forwarding mailing address, yes?

"Hell," he muttered. What he needed was the number of her cell phone, assuming she had one. Everyone did these days. Even runaways.

On the edge of the deck he saw one of those walker things, all bright colors of plastic with lights, music, and mirrors to keep a baby entertained. He'd seen one before at his sister's house and he tried to imagine it now with Rory's child inside. The kid would be younger than a year to fit the device, fifteen months at the most, not old enough to walk on its own. A baby that young suggested that there was a man in Rory's life, the father of this kid, and for an insane moment he felt a spurt of jealousy. When he'd first heard about the kid, the fleeting idea that it might be his had crossed his mind, but at the time of the wedding Rory had been reed thin; and even if she had been pregnant, a child of their union would be at least four years old by now, far too old for the walker.

So where was the father, he wondered, then decided it didn't really matter. The problem at hand was that he was locked out, couldn't get inside to try to determine where she'd gone.

His option was to attempt a break-in, and he considered it. No one was around. He tried the door again and it didn't budge, so he circled the house. No windows unlatched. Nope, locked up tight as a drum.

He hadn't come this far to go home empty-handed, without answers. He'd worked on enough job sites that he knew how to get into any locked building, but, as luck would have it, at that moment a police car cruised past the end of the drive, slowing as the officer swept her gaze over the drive. She didn't pull in, but inched by after giving Liam the once-over, so he couldn't risk a break-in. Not with his Tahoe's license plate visible, as he was parked in front of the cottage. Besides, he didn't know when the neighbors would return or what kind of security system was in place.

His cell phone vibrated in his pocket. He pulled it out and saw that Bethany was calling him. He stared at the phone as it buzzed in his palm, but he didn't press to connect. When it finally stopped ringing, he put it down by his side, frustrated, lost in thought.

After a few moments he decided to call her back. He owed her that much. What the hell was he doing here, chasing ghosts? Beth was his future.

He saw that she'd left him a text: **When are you coming home?**

Home.

Giving up for the day, he made his way to his SUV, took one final look at the house where he suspected Rory resided, or *had* until this morning, then he drove off. He was done for the day, though he wasn't about to give up. It didn't really matter if Rory had a new man or a child. That was her future. Liam was here to seal off her past. She needed to return to the mainland and grant him the damned divorce as well as come clean to the police so that he could go back to Portland and pick up his new life.

As The Magician stepped onto the back porch, Heather flung herself into his arms. "You have to help me. Help us," she whispered as his arms wrapped around her and she fought like hell not to break down completely.

"What's going on?"

"Unca Kent!" Charlotte's voice rang out, and as Heather turned in the older man's arms, she saw her daughter running up the gravel path toward the porch. She started coughing as she neared him, something Heather realized had been happening more often. Charlotte was still paler than usual, but the spark had returned to her eyes and she threw out her arms as she hurried up the steps. The cough worried Rory, but Charlotte was giggling as she neared them. Maybe it was nothing . . . maybe . . .

Kent released Heather and scooped her daughter into his arms. "How's my girl?" he asked, pressing his nose against her face so that she giggled and wriggled when his white whiskers brushed her cheeks.

"Better, obviously," Heather said.

At a slower pace, Maude joined them and turned her face to allow Kent to buss her cheek. "Looks like you're just what the doctor ordered," she observed.

"Always." He responded with a deep chuckle and Heather saw that when they looked into each other's eyes there was affection, yes, but something more, a deeper connection.

Her heart twisted. This is what she'd thought, what she'd hoped she would share with Liam forever. Before she'd met him, she'd had her share of boyfriends, none particularly serious, and they'd always disappointed her. Her high school boyfriend, Josh Langley, had left for college and dumped her after the first weekend. When he'd finally come home to visit his family, he'd made it clear that he was long past high-schoolers or teenagers, or more specifically, Rory Abernathy. There had been a couple of other boys she'd dated before she graduated, but those flirtations had been short-lived and unmemorable and had ended when she hadn't seen fit to put out. Those boys had reminded her of her stepbrother, Everett, with his belief that if he just talked to her the right way or kissed her gently at first, she would really like sleeping with him.

Her only relationship post-junior college had been Cal, who'd been more into weed than into her, a perpetual "student" who never seemed to attend class. When he wasn't high, he was decent enough for the most part, but decent wasn't good enough. Too much dependence on marijuana wasn't what she wanted for the man in her life, though she hadn't recognized that fact until after they'd become engaged. She'd tried to break off their engagement several times, but Cal didn't take the news well. When she found out she was pregnant, she'd been torn, knowing it wasn't going to work with Cal. She kept the secret to herself and then the whole thing became a moot point after she miscarried. She never told him about the baby, she just left Seattle for a while. She ran. When she returned, she ran into Liam Bastian—literally—walking down a Seattle street. Though Liam hailed from Portland, his mother, Stella, happened to be a Seattle native. Seattle was also Uncle Kent's home base, when he wasn't with Maude in Vancouver, and later, as Rory grew more anxious about marrying Liam, saying as much to Uncle Kent, she'd been glad The Magician would be nearby in case anything went wrong.

She should never have married him. She'd known it wasn't going to work. She'd even tried to thwart the relationship in the beginning, knowing her own history with unreliable men. She'd laughed when he told her he loved her. Wouldn't believe it. It was too crazy! She was no Cinderella to his Prince Charming.

Looking back, she should have stuck by her guns and refused to fall in love with him.

But then you wouldn't have Charlotte. It's still all for the best.

She glanced at her little girl being led into the kitchen with the promise of warm cookies and being able to "glitter paint" on the table. Maude was already spreading newspapers and finding the paint set.

Uncle Kent waved her out to the porch, and she fell gratefully onto the outdoor couch and picked up her tea, now mostly melting ice cubes. The kitchen window slid open noisily.

"Iced tea?" Maude said through the screen to Uncle Kent.

"Got anything stronger, luv?"

"I just might."

The window snapped shut again.

"Tell me," Kent said, sitting opposite Heather.

And she did. While Maude brought out a plate of cookies from the local bakery and a tall glass of amber liquid over ice for The Magician, and Charlotte drew unicorns and princesses on plain computer paper, Heather brought Kent up-to-date. She started by telling him about seeing Liam in the screen for the drive-up window at the café, explained about running home and Connie calling to confirm that a man who looked like Liam had been asking about her, and how she'd gathered Charlotte and raced here. She handed Kent her phone, where Connie's pictures confirmed her story and ended with her worries about Charlotte, as the little girl hadn't been herself.

"She seems all right now," he said, casting a look through the open doorway to the chair where Charlotte, on her knees, was leaning over the table and dabbing at her art.

"Maybe it's a cold developing. She's been coughing some," Heather said, hoping it was some minor illness.

"So why do you think Liam would show up now? What's it been? Five years? Why all of a sudden?"

"Maybe it took that long to hunt me down. I don't know. Maybe because he's getting married again and needs a divorce?"

Kent's eyebrows raised.

"You think I don't keep track of him?" she asked, feeling a little foolish. "And it's not what you think. Not that I'm in love with him or anything like that," she said, wondering if she was lying. "But I have to know if he's going to come looking. Because of Charlotte."

"He has a right to know about her."

This was old territory. "I know you think I should go back and face the music and you're right, I should. But I can't. I'd lose my daughter." She took a swallow of her nearly forgotten iced tea and leaned back on the cushions. "Trust me, I've beaten myself up over this, over and over again."

He drank in silence for a second as Heather heard the quiet conversation between Charlotte and Maude emanating from the kitchen, the sound of traffic from the main street a few blocks away, and the caw of a crow who was perched in an apple tree in the backyard.

"I've gone over what would happen to me if I returned. First off, I'd probably be interrogated by the police for, oh, I don't know . . . days? And probably held in jail, as a flight risk. After that, if they determined I was involved, I might be arrested, and what would happen to Charlotte?"

"Maude and I would step in."

"You mean, Maude would. You'd be in trouble for helping me escape, if that's even the right term for it. Aiding and abetting a fugitive from justice. No one will believe we didn't know about the shooting, even if they think we weren't directly involved. And I'm guessing you might have more than one outstanding warrant against you."

He gazed toward the window where Maude had appeared. "It's complicated."

She closed her eyes. "Do you know how awful I feel? I . . . I left Liam at the altar where he got shot, his father, too, and poor, poor Aaron." She felt close to tears again, her eyes burning. Liam had survived, and his wounds, a bullet through the leg and another through his torso, had healed, if what she'd read was to be believed. She didn't know the extent of the damage, of course, but he was alive and well enough to run a company and squire Bethany Van Horne around.

Geoffrey Bastian had been hit as well, two bullets lodging in his spine, one severing his spinal cord, so that he was confined to a wheelchair. She'd seen pictures of him in some motorized contraption, though he was still a force to be reckoned with, still a figurehead in Bastian-Flavel Construction, though his two sons, Liam and Derek, ran the business on a day-to-day basis.

Some of the guests had been injured. One took a bullet to her arm; one the victim of broken glass in her knees and palms. The third, his sister, Vivian, had been knocked to the ground by another fleeing attendee, breaking her ankle. As Heather understood it, from accounts on the Internet and in newspapers and a snippet on cable news, it was a miracle more people hadn't been seriously injured.

She'd wondered often enough who had been the intended target. One or more of the Bastians? But Aaron had been the one who'd lost his life. She felt deep sorrow for his life being snuffed out so violently and early. He had been the kinder of her two stepbrothers. No prince, of course, but still. Dead. Long before his time. Because he was at *her* farce of a wedding. Had Aaron just gotten in the way of the bullets? Or had he been the mark? His father, after all, was a criminal. But . . . why the attack on her? By an assailant with a *knife*? Who *was* he? Why hadn't he been apprehended? He'd threatened her. Known she was pregnant. Was he the man who'd rained bullets on the wedding guests? These were the same questions that haunted her sleep.

"I haven't even visited Aaron's grave," she said, her throat thick.

"He'll forgive you." Kent tried to make a joke. It fell flat and he added, "You just have to find a way to forgive yourself."

She snorted.

"It takes time." He smiled kindly. "You've got it."

"I suppose."

"So try not to freak out. It was bound to happen that you'd run into someone from the Bastian family at some point."

"Maybe."

"And you've been lucky, right? You haven't seen anyone associated with Liam until now?"

"I guess."

"You know."

She let out a sigh as she opened her eyes and stared into the yard with its riot of blooms and stately trees. "Not exactly associated with Liam, maybe. But a couple of times I was half convinced that I saw Everett."

"What?" Kent's face tensed. His lips within the neat goatee compressed. "You never said."

"But then I'm always seeing someone," she said dismissively. "I wasn't certain. It was just a glimpse or two." *And it turned my blood to ice.*

"In Point *Roberts*?"

"Yes. The first time, I was coming out of the grocery store, and I thought he passed me on the street. He was driving a pickup of some kind, but he was wearing a baseball cap and sunglasses, so I told myself I was jumping at shadows."

"When was this?"

"A month ago? Maybe six weeks?"

"And the second time?" he asked.

"Maybe a couple of weeks ago. On the docks." She made a face, lips tense. "I'd taken Charlotte down to look at the boats, and there was this guy on a cabin cruiser. He was leaning down over a coil of rope, I think, again with the hat and sunglasses, and when he saw me looking at him, he turned around quickly and disappeared down a hatch. The sun was out, bright against the water, spangling, y'know, and I just wasn't sure."

"Not like you are about spotting Liam today."

"Exactly. This time, I knew immediately, then Connie confirmed it. The other man, the one on the dock and by the grocery store? I'm pretty sure he was just someone who reminded me of Everett." At least that's what she'd told herself. "I haven't seen him since."

"So what do you want to do now?"

"I don't know. Hide out here, I guess. For the night at least. The O'Briens are coming back tomorrow. Once they're home and can check things out to make sure Liam's not hanging around, I'll go back and pack up my things and move, if my car holds out."

"What's wrong with your car?"

"It has trouble starting sometimes. It's okay."

"Maybe I should take a look at it."

Heather shrugged. She didn't want to be more of a burden than she already was.

"Where are you planning to go?" he asked.

"That's the million-dollar question," she admitted, her shoulders sagging with the weight of a decision she didn't want to make. "But away from Point Roberts. I think my time there is done." Her heart grew heavy when she considered pulling up stakes and taking Charlotte from the only community and friends she'd ever known. No more ABC and Me preschool or Miss Evers, or even Tommy the bully. No longer would she see Connie, or Joanna, or Carlos. Heather drained her glass, looked at The Magician and hoped to God he could pull the proverbial rabbit out of his hat.

Chapter 6

Charlotte had perked up. After a day of art, card games, and "dress up" in some of Maude's old gowns, they'd had an early dinner and watched some television before the little girl had tumbled into the double bed tucked into an L-shaped room on the second floor.

Heather had indulged in two glasses of wine with a salmon dinner that Kent and Maude had put together, which included Maude's "famous" scalloped potatoes. They seemed happy together and when Heather, helping with the dishes, asked again why they'd never married, Maude had smiled and said, "We'd kill each other if we were married. This way, the romance never dies." She'd dropped a saucepan into the dishwasher, then touched Heather's arm with wet fingers. "I know it sounds crazy, but I've been married before. Three times." She held up three beringed fingers to prove her point. "I was mad about each of my husbands and then once we were married, I was mad *at* each of them. Being single and having Kent part-time suits me just fine."

Kent had come in from the dining area, carrying two plates that he slipped into the sink. "Trust me, I've been after her all these years to let me make an honest woman of her, but, as I said before, there are complications."

She rolled her eyes and snorted. "A man of mystery."

Heather smiled. They all knew that The Magician skated a bit with the law. They also knew he was loyal to a fault.

"I'm just after her money," he said.

Maude chortled and he wrapped his arms around her middle, standing behind her while she rinsed plates before stacking them in the dishwasher.

"I adore you despite your poverty," he proclaimed, and they both laughed.

Heather's heart twisted as she thought about her own life, how she'd vowed after the debacle with Liam to never risk love again. Wistfully she wished somehow she could reclaim that which she'd lost, then mentally chided herself. She and Liam had never had this kind of relationship.

She left them bickering playfully in the kitchen and walked into the living area, where she'd contacted the O'Briens and spoken with Maxine, who'd let her know that they had already decided to cut their trip a little short. When Heather mentioned that she'd left the cat for the night, Maxine had assured her that Mr. Bones would be fine. He did have a pet door, and despite his nocturnal feline instincts, generally stayed inside at night. She seemed unconcerned that anything bad might happen to him, but told Heather that they'd have their neighbors make certain that he was all right and "in for the night."

She'd just hung up when Kent came into the living room and sat in his favorite striped recliner. "A disgusting piece of furniture if you ask me," Maude had said behind The Magician's back, "but he loves it and it fits him and"—she'd shrugged—"what're ya gonna do?"

Kent leaned forward. "Let's figure out a plan," he suggested, and Heather nodded.

"I think I need to be in the States," she said. "Charlotte will be going to elementary school, not this year, but next. So maybe it's time to move."

"Oh, dear. I hate to think of you far away," Maude said.

"Me too."

"You know," Uncle Kent said and Heather braced herself. "If we could just clear up what happened, maybe you wouldn't have to be on the run. If you told the police what you told me, about the attack on you, they might be lenient. You left a wedding. That's not a crime."

"You don't believe that. And I'm worried you'll be charged with aiding and abetting. The Seattle police sure questioned you after I disappeared, and you never told them where I was. You thought it was a good idea for me to stay hidden then, and even though they've circled back to you a few times, at least that one detective has, you've stayed mum. Are you saying you've changed your mind?" she challenged.

He didn't immediately respond. After a few moments, he said, "You might be able to offer them some evidence. You told me you thought you knew your attacker, this guy who huffed the helium."

She'd mentioned it once and Kent had never let it go. "I can't prove anything and I don't know who he was, or even if he lived. I stabbed him," she said, swallowing.

"There were no other deaths reported, and you stabbed him in self-defense."

"How can I prove that now? After all this time?" She shook her head. "I'm the runaway bride, and worse than that, I left the scene of a vicious, murderous assault, so why would anyone believe me?"

"Maybe the man in the hotel room was someone from the

wedding party? Or . . . Everett, your stepbrother," he said, running over old territory. "Or maybe someone else? Didn't you say that you thought you saw Cal Redmond there?"

"I said I saw someone who looked like him," she reminded him. She'd been hurrying through the lobby of the hotel on her way to the room where she was to get dressed, and thought for a half second that she'd spied her ex-boyfriend in the bar. It had just been a glimpse of a man standing at the edge of the long bar, close to the door of the kitchen, and there had been something familiar in his bearing, the way he carried himself in the dark pants and white shirt that the waiters wore, that had reminded her of Cal.

She'd taken two steps backward as she'd passed, but the man was gone, the door to the kitchen swinging as if someone had just slipped through, and she'd told herself the sighting had been her imagination, nothing more. Wedding-day jitters. After all, she'd run out on Cal and it had not gone well.

During the choppy boat ride through the Strait of Georgia she'd told Uncle Kent about possibly sighting Cal, and just recently she thought she'd seen Everett. The truth was, she was always thinking she saw someone. It was part of her paranoia. Once she'd been sure she'd spied Liam's half brother, Derek, and another time a customer at the drive-through looked so much like Aaron that she'd scalded her hand pouring coffee.

"Okay, let's leave it for now," Kent said, exhaling heavily. "Think about it in the morning."

Heather was only too happy to let it go.

Later, in the small bedroom upstairs with Charlotte sleeping next to her, Heather stared out the open window. Over the shimmering lights of the city, she saw the night sky, only a few stars visible. The house was quiet, only the tinny sounds of a muted television reaching her ears as Uncle Kent watched some late show downstairs.

Charlotte let out a sigh, smacked her little lips, and turned over. Heather's heart cracked a bit. She'd never known unconditional love until Charlotte had been born, in this very house with the aid of Narna, a midwife. Heather was grateful that she didn't have to birth her child in a hospital, under glaring lights, with dozens of nurses and a doctor and too many government forms to be executed, documents that might give her away.

She'd taken a risk, she thought now, but Kent's rented row house was only five blocks from a major hospital. If complications with the birth had occurred and she needed to deliver her baby at a hospital, Heather would have done so.

As it was, the birth had gone well. Her water had broken at midnight and within four hours, she was holding a slippery and squalling newborn whom she'd immediately christened Charlotte Jane, the names coming from favorite books she'd read.

Charlotte's birth felt like nothing short of a miracle. Maybe she was born to be a mother, maybe because her relationship with her own mother, Darlene, was iffy at best, maybe because she'd never felt so complete in her life, whatever the case, she was enjoying motherhood to the fullest. Despite her guilt and culpability over leaving on the day of the wedding, at least she had Charlotte, and until today they'd been safe living a quiet, simple life.

Now that had changed.

Because somehow Liam had found her.

Had she done something that had tipped him off?

Did someone she knew in Point Roberts contact him?

Could he have hired a private investigator to track her down?

"Doesn't matter," she whispered into the darkness. The fact was that he was on the peninsula and, after locating her place of work, had probably found her home. No telling who he'd talked to.

Worse yet, if he didn't know already, he was soon to find out about Charlotte. Point Roberts was small, and when he asked about Heather Johnson at the market, or bank, or bakery, he'd learn she had a child of about four or five, a girl. And then it was just a matter of simple math.

He'd *know.*

His whole family would know.

The secret would be out.

She had recently confided in Darlene, but had sworn her to secrecy. Her mother was the only person other than Uncle Kent who knew she was alive, though she hadn't told Darlene where she'd landed and, of course, The Magician had kept his mouth shut. Heather had always used a burner cell to phone her mother, and when Darlene had pressed her for pictures of her only grandchild, Heather had gone against her better judgment and relented, having Uncle Kent send the photographs from a Seattle post office. It had been risky, but could she really deny her own mother a glimpse of the girl? Wasn't it bad enough that Charlotte knew no one in her family other than Heather, "Uncle" Kent, and Maude?

But then recently, because she'd begun to feel relatively safe, she'd given up the burner cell and had started calling her mother on her regular phone. A risky move, she knew. One she was now regretting.

Her heart suddenly somersaulted. Had Darlene told Liam? Is that how he'd found her? Did he know about *Charlotte?*

You're putting the cart before the horse. You don't know that he has any clue that he's a father . . . yet.

"Only a matter of time," she thought aloud.

And then she'd have to face Liam. Her heart twisted at the thought. The ironic thing was that she was the one who had fought the attraction. She'd been filled with trepidation and tried to avoid a relationship with him, but it sure hadn't worked.

They'd met by running into each other. Literally. They'd bumped into each other on a windy day in Seattle. Liam had been in Washington on family business, where Rory's dysfunctional—oh, let's call it what it was and is, criminal—family called home. She'd been hurrying down a narrow, steep sidewalk near Pioneer Square. It wasn't dark yet, not really, but the oppressive clouds and rain had made twilight come early.

The week before she'd felt as if someone was watching her, which she told herself was ridiculous, more of her own paranoia, but nonetheless, she'd sensed a presence whenever she was alone, unseen eyes hidden in the shadows.

"Don't be a fool," she'd warned herself that day after a particularly nasty run-in with her boss, she'd left the office and was heading to the bus stop. The wet street was crowded, the city teeming with pedestrians and vehicles, the view of Puget Sound obscured by the thickening mist, when she'd felt it again, that uncanny sensation that she was being watched, possibly followed. She'd looked over her shoulder and seen no one focused on her, just other commuters and workers hurrying along the streets, some with umbrellas, others in hoods or hats, others bareheaded against the steady drizzle.

She saw no one following her, no one avoiding her eyes, no one staring at her. She was imagining it, that was all. She'd had a bad day at work and—

Bam!

Her shoulder slammed into someone and she started to fall, purse flying, the wet concrete racing up at her. A strong hand grabbed for her shoulder and the man she'd run into—or who had run into her—caught her just as she landed, one knee banging painfully into the sidewalk. People on the street quickly stepped around her.

"Sorry!" the guy said, and in his free hand she saw his phone and the text he'd been typing. Obviously he hadn't been paying attention to where he was walking.

"You should be." Her tights had ripped, her skin visible through the torn fabric. She stood, pushed off his arm, then found her purse on the curb, wet from the rain that was running down the street. When she bent over to pick it up along with a few items that had poured from it, a pen, mirror, lipstick, and her wallet having skittered partway down the hillside, she staggered a bit. But when his hand reached for her again, she shook him off. She retrieved everything quickly, then straightened to find him standing next to a parking meter.

"Are you okay?" he asked.

"Do I look okay?" she snapped. Flushed with embarrassment and anger, her frustration with the horrid day erupting, she added icily, "Do you think you could watch where you're going?" Tossing her hair from her face she muttered, "Forget it."

Thank God she wasn't bleeding, only her tights and her pride damaged.

"I'm sorry."

"Well, fine," she said tightly.

"I'll take that as 'apology accepted.'"

She glared at him. Who was this guy and why did she care?

"Believe it or not, I just told my brother I can't stand anyone who won't look up from their phone. That's what I was texting about, and then . . ." He rolled one palm toward the leaden sky and offered a self-deprecating grin. "I am really sorry and you're right. I should be looking where I'm going, too."

Somewhat mollified, she turned away. Her skinned knee throbbed and she still wanted to light into him, but he seemed sincere, his head bent against the rain, his light brown eyes glinting with amusement and embarrassment.

"Okay, let's just forget it." She started down the hill again.

"No, wait." He caught up with her.

She stopped short, and whatever he saw on her face had him lifting his hands in surrender and laughing, a deep rumbling sound that made other pedestrians turn and smile as they passed. "Let me make it up to you."

She was immediately suspicious. "No need."

He glanced at the name of the bistro on the flapping green awning above their heads: RENDEZVOUS. "Let me buy you a cup of coffee, or a drink?"

"Truly. It's all right. I'm fine." He didn't seem convinced so she said it again, sincerely, and started walking.

He fell in step beside her. "It would make me feel better."

"It would make *you* feel better? Oh, well, that changes everything. By all means, buy me a coffee and make yourself feel better."

He laughed again, a really infectious sound that raised goose bumps on her arms. He was finding the whole scenario funny, while her knee was aching and she was getting wet. She nearly snapped at him again, when she felt that same sensation that had been with her earlier, that someone was observing her every move. Someone malevolent. Someone nearby. Someone who meant her harm.

"Okay," she said quickly, changing her mind. "Fine. If it'll make *you* feel better, by all means." What was she doing, anyway? Besides sensing some malicious force in the air, she'd just had a fight with her boss at the office where she was employed and expected that when she returned to work in the morning, she might find herself out of a job. Ned Castrell didn't take kindly to being shown up, and she'd made the mistake of pointing out his accounting error in front of *his* boss. Worse yet, he was always saying something slightly lewd, as if he expected her to find him funny, and he looked at her in a way that reminded her too much of her stepbrother Everett's lewd gazes when she was in high school. Castrell asked her out once, despite the fact that he'd been married at the time, even suggesting he could "show her things she'd never experienced before." She'd threatened him with sexual harassment and he'd backed off, except for the ogling stares. She figured her days at Java Jive, a Seattle-based coffee company, were doomed.

So be it.

It wasn't as if she planned on spending the rest of her life there.

The job was just to make ends meet. She was seriously thinking about taking more business courses, finishing her degree, working toward a job with more career potential.

So why not take this guy with the phone up on his offer?

He was definitely handsome, with his dark, now wet hair, those intense eyes and a strong chin with a day's growth of beard. Yeah, definitely on the hunky side of the male-o-meter. There were crinkles near the corners of his eyes, as if he either spent hours in the sun squinting, or laughed a lot. What would it hurt to spend half an hour with him in this very busy bistro?

It's just coffee. And you'll get out of the rain, away from the hidden eyes and maybe even forget Ned Castrell for a while. You'll never see him again. This is just to make him feel better, so what does it hurt? Where do you have to be?

The sad answer was "nowhere." She didn't even have a cat waiting for her in her walk-up. Even so, she'd meant to turn him down. She really had. But the kicky April breeze was turning into an all-out gale, and she didn't really have anywhere to be, other than her empty apartment. She offered him a cool smile. "A place called Rendezvous wouldn't be my first choice to go with a complete stranger, but okay."

He thrust out his hand. "Liam Bastian. Not a stranger anymore."

"Rory Abernathy," she replied cautiously, shaking his hand. His grip was strong, but not crushing, his eyes warm.

And that was the beginning of their whirlwind romance, one that still had the ability to turn her throat dry and make her heart beat a little faster. He'd swept an arm toward Rendezvous's front door and Rory had led him inside the bistro.

Chapter 7

Heather stared out the window of the bedroom she was sharing with Charlotte, watching the sway of black leaves against a sky which was only a few shades lighter. Rendezvous. From the onset of her relationship with Liam she'd told herself she was making a mistake—hadn't she learned anything from running out on Cal?—but she hadn't really listened. Looking around the restaurant, she chose a place in the rear, a recently vacated booth with high backs that was near a hooded fireplace and a comfortable fire. She and Liam waited as a busboy swept away the glasses from the previous occupants, then wiped the table clean. There were people on either side of them, the conversation was a continual hum, the waitstaff slipping in and out among the tables. The place was anything but a secluded, intimate rendezvous.

Good, she'd thought at the time.

She sat across from him as they'd glanced over the menus and then ordered coffee drinks, hers a mix of coconut and cream with a shot of Baileys for good measure, and his black.

As they sipped, her insides warmed with the drink. She told herself not to be fascinated by his blade-thin lips or just the hint of a dimple on one side of his face. When he ordered her a second drink, she wanted to argue, but had glanced out at the slanting rain and decided sitting near the fire and talking to a handsome man wasn't all that bad. He was bright and witty and never once pulled out his cell phone again. Nor did she. As the gas flames licked the logs and she sipped the rich drink, she learned that he was in construction and worked for his father's Portland company. He was visiting Washington with his brother, Derek, and while Liam was attending a conference in the heart of Seattle, Derek was scouting out real estate for potential expansion into the area. Derek was heading back to Portland that evening, Liam staying on a few more days.

She found out he was single, a lifelong Portland resident, liked the great outdoors of the Pacific Northwest, and worked for the family business that had been in Oregon for over a quarter of a century. He hiked and biked, fished, and even windsurfed along the windy beaches of the northern Oregon coast. He mentioned getting a pilot's license and seemed comfortable in his own skin. She had to admit, she liked his self-confidence, and she began to thaw in spite of herself.

But when the conversation turned toward her, she became uncomfortable. She always kept talk of her own family to a minimum, the fewer answers the better, she reasoned. And as this was only a quickie coffee date, really some kind of penance for knocking her down on the street, there was no reason to divulge too much.

"You've lived here all your life, then," he said as the waitress refilled his cup.

"Around here. Not in the city, really." She wasn't about to explain that her small family had never settled anywhere for more than six or eight months at a time. She'd been enrolled in six different elementary schools. She'd never made any friends that had lasted more than a year, two at the max. And then there were the problems with her older stepbrothers.

At eighteen, she'd struck out on her own, working during the day, taking classes at night. She'd put up with a series of flaky roommates, two of whom had skipped out on the rent, just like her own mother and stepfather had done on more than one occasion, hauling the kids out of bed in the middle of the night, hustling them into a rattletrap car and driving to an unknown destination. That always meant a brand-new school for Rory, along with a different curriculum, a stranger for a teacher, and a classroom of kids who stared at her for what seemed like weeks until she'd settled into a desk and eventually made friends with a small group of girls whom she never brought home.

She'd been told her stepfather's hunt for a job was what had uprooted the small family from one battered apartment to the next, but eventually she realized that Harold was always keeping one step ahead of the law.

But on their "date," she didn't confide any of this to Liam Bastian, who, she'd gathered, had been born to money. He hadn't said as much, not outright, but she could tell by the cut of his clothes, the way he spoke and held his head, his body language. Liam Bastian knew his place in the world.

Finally, she set the glass mug on the table and said, "Thank you. But I have to run." She stood up, her knee aching a little.

"Too bad." He said it as if he meant it and pulled out his credit card to pay. The waiter scooped it up as he added, "I thought you might show me the city."

"Seattle?" she said, her eyebrows rising. "Even though you live in Portland, a couple of hours away, you want a tour of Seattle?"

"More than a couple," he clarified. "With traffic—"

"Come on. Haven't you ever taken the train up here for a Mariners or Seahawks game?"

"Well, maybe . . ."

"So I'm guessing you know the city."

He grinned. "Okay, ya got me. I just wanted to spend a little more time with you."

She shook her head, tempted but firm. "I don't do 'tours.'"

"What does that mean?" He smiled as the waiter put the bill down and he signed it in a fast scrawl.

"Just what it sounds like." She smiled back as she shrugged into her coat. The man was way too attractive.

"Make an exception."

She shook her head as she walked around other tables to the door, Liam following behind. Why not take him up on his offer? she argued with herself. He was smart and interesting and certainly good-looking. Why not spend a day with him? But she added a lie instead. "And I've got plans."

"Cancel them."

"Pretty bold, the way you keep ordering me around," she said.

"Not ordering. Suggesting," he said easily. "These plans . . . are they life-or-death?"

"Not really."

"So . . . they're maybe changeable?"

"I don't know you." She flipped up the hood of her coat and glanced up at him through a fringe of faux fur.

"How do you think you ever will if you don't spend more time with me?" His eyes glinted. "Come on, Rory, take a chance. You seem like a risk-taker." They were walking toward the waterfront now and the sidewalk was more crowded with pedestrians, while traffic was clogging the streets. Cars, SUVs, trucks, and buses jammed together.

She smiled back at him, cautiously. "You don't know anything about me."

"Yet," he said as the wind battered her face, raindrops peppering the ground. "You said you were single, so I'm guessing no serious boyfriend's in the picture."

That much was true. She'd broken it off with Cal two months earlier, the last straw coming when she'd learned he was supplementing his wages as a waiter by stealing food from the kitchen of the upscale restaurant and reselling it. She'd begun to think she only attracted the wrong kind of man.

She let Liam walk her to the bus stop, where a bus that would take her to the University District was just pulling up. "Gotta run," she said and picked up her pace. "That's mine."

"I could drive you."

She almost hesitated. Almost, but instead, turning her head to call over her shoulder, she said, "Thanks for the coffee!" She waved and, following a lumbering man in a tweed overcoat straight out of the 1940s, she climbed aboard. As she was wedging herself into a seat, she glanced out the window and saw Liam standing at the stop, his phone already in his hand, as if he was picking up from the very call he'd dropped over two hours earlier when he'd bumped into her.

That should have been the end of it. And she'd expected to never see him again.

But she'd been wrong.

The next day at work she found out she was still hanging on to her job, though Ned warned her, leaning over her desk in the accounting department, his nose pressed so close to hers she could view his pores, "Another outburst like yesterday's, Abernathy, and you'll find yourself looking for work."

"And if you don't quit leaning over my desk and staring at me, I'll file a formal complaint with HR."

"I know people in Human Resources."

"So do I, and I've got some of your little jokes recorded on my cell phone," she'd blustered, lying through her teeth but satisfied to see him pale beneath his fake tan.

"You're lying."

She pulled out her phone then, and scanned the small screen.

"You're a stone-cold bitch, Abernathy, and trust me, you're gonna pay for this."

"Compliments won't work," she said tightly, and as he sent her another murderous glare, added, "Have a nice day."

Ned nearly ran into one of the office gofers, a young woman with a killer figure who was carrying a white bag with markings from a local bakery and a cup of Java Jive coffee. "Whew," she said as she brought her bounty to her desk.

"Don't let him ever get to you," Rory warned. "He's a bully. Always stand up to him."

"Maybe he has a small penis," she suggested.

"Maybe." Rory smiled.

She thought about just leaving work. Getting the hell out. Not giving any notice, just never showing up again.

But then you'd be running again. Like you always do. Like your whole damned family does—fleeing in the middle of the night. And this time you wouldn't get a reference to get another job.

Gritting her teeth, she stuck out the rest of the day, avoided Castrell, and walked out of the building at five p.m., where she'd spotted Liam Bastian, big as life. In jeans, an open-collared shirt and his ubiquitous jacket, he was waiting under a portico from the building that housed the central offices of Java Jive.

Having spent the afternoon ignoring the hard-edged stare of Castrell, she was in no mood for anything other than a long, hot bath, glass of wine, and a good book. She'd planned on grabbing takeout Thai food on the way home, but it looked like her plans for eating chicken *panang* curry out of the carton were about to be scrapped.

Liam was phone-free, at least for the moment, one shoulder propped against a concrete pillar holding up the portico. She walked straight up to him. "What?"

"I had some time to kill, so I thought I'd wait around till you got off work."

"You a stalker, Mr. Bastian?"

"It's Liam. And I've never been a stalker before, but I don't know. Maybe it's a new affliction."

"I should've never told you where I work."

He nodded. "That might've been a mistake." He was staring at her with those slightly bemused eyes, the irises of which were a light brown color, almost gold.

She couldn't help but smile. She wanted to go with him, but she couldn't trust her instincts. They'd let her down too many times before. And really, Liam Bastian, damn him, seemed to be too good to be true. Which she also didn't trust. She'd learned that lesson the hard way. Over and over.

"I could take you to dinner," he suggested.

"Or I could go home and put my feet up."

His crooked smile touched his eyes. "I could go with you. Takeout, or in this case, take-in pizza? We could pick up a bottle of wine."

The thought was enticing. But dangerous. She knew little about him other than what he'd told her, though she had Googled him and confirmed the facts: thirty-four, unmarried, graduate of Oregon State University, currently working for the company his father founded, Bastian-Flavel Construction in Portland, Oregon.

"I don't think that would be a good idea," she said, even though she'd come up with much the same plan earlier, with one big exception, of course. In her envisioned evening there had been no Liam.

She started walking down the hill to the bus stop, to the spot where she'd run into him the previous day, and once more she felt as if she was being followed, though of course she wasn't, not that she could see.

"Then let's grab something together," he said. "You pick the place. You're the native."

She probably should have said a firm no, but she hadn't, and they'd spent the night on the town with dinner at a funky Italian dive off the waterfront and drinks at an Irish bar a few doors down. She'd let him walk her to the bus, and as she'd turned to catch the big, rumbling vehicle, he'd grabbed her elbow. "Let me drive you," he'd insisted as rain fell from the night sky and the lights and noise of the city had surrounded them. She'd been about to argue, but he'd leaned forward quickly and kissed her upturned face. His lips were warm in the cool evening and she felt them mold over hers as raindrops fell onto her cheeks and starred her lashes.

Though she fought her emotions, she leaned toward him, like a plant bending toward the sun. She longed for someone, something, that had completely escaped her all her life. She gave herself up to the thrill and warmth that invaded her body as his arms were surrounding her. Human touch. She was desperate for it, and she became oblivious to the hustle of the city surrounding them. Only when she heard, "Get a room!" did she pull back, surprised at her reaction, and made her way on weakened legs to the bus.

"Rory, I can drive you," she heard Liam call after her as she climbed aboard, but she shook her head. She stumbled to one of the last seats available. As the bus chugged away from the stop, she craned her neck, looking out the window, feeling a little buzz from the drinks and a surge of lingering excitement from his kiss. She watched him walk away. Oh. Lord. One kiss and she'd nearly melted against him. What was wrong with her?

Still basking from the glow of that one kiss, she touched the glass and looked out the window to a side street, where she was certain she caught a glimpse of a dark figure staring at her.

Her throat tightened and she blinked, but the bus rolled past, the image disappeared, and she exhaled and told herself she was imagining things, the ghosts of her past chasing through her mind, forcing her to feel things that weren't there. She was away from her family now, the horror that she'd lived through for those years was over. No need to worry.

Nerves jangled, she took a sweeping gaze of the other passengers and decided she was safe. She settled back into the seat. Thoughts of Liam came rushing back, crushing her worries. The hours with him had been magical and exciting, but their night together was at an end, though she replayed it over and over again as she made her way to her apartment, one of the cheapest ones in the U District, which she'd sublet, probably illegally, from a student who had dropped out of college before the term was over. She slept on the pull-out couch, the bedroom belonging to a roommate she'd barely seen, a girl who spent all of her time at her boyfriend's place. Rory and Ashley were passing ships, only seeing each other in their shared bathroom and kitchen and then only sparingly. Ashley was set to be married in the summer, and then Rory would have to move.

Again.

Crawling into her couch-turned-bed, she wondered what it would be like to put down deep roots, to find a home that she could call her own for more than a few months at a stretch, to feel as if she belonged. As she stared at the blue luminescent face of her digital clock, she replayed the scenes of the past few days in her mind, how she'd wanted to run away from her lousy job and Ned Castrell, how she'd hoped to spend a quiet, boring evening at home, and how Liam Bastian had changed all that.

He was staying at a hotel downtown and had told her the name and room number as some kind of not-so-subtle invitation, but she'd declined either visiting him there or inviting him here. Now she wondered if it had been a mistake, especially after her reaction to him.

She did believe he was interested in her. But what would happen when he found out about her family, how they were all just one step away from the law? Worse yet, what happened when *they* found out she was dating a wealthy man, someone who would be immediately perceived as a mark? She shuddered inwardly at the thought. No, better to let things be. She sensed Liam might just be the kind of man she could fall for—big-time, and that would be a mistake of colossal proportions. She needed to get her own life on track before she complicated it with anyone else.

Oh. God. What was she thinking? Was she seriously contemplating a *relationship* with him?

That would never happen.

And yet, that's exactly what happened.

The following Friday, he met her after work and spent the weekend with her, blowing off the last of his conferences and walking through Pike Place Market, which was teeming with customers browsing the fresh fish, homemade wares, and art, then down to the waterfront where seagulls wheeled through the gray skies and ferries churned through the water. They headed to Pioneer Square for the underground tour, where there were remains of the city as it once had been. And then, to cap off the "total tourist experience," he insisted on dinner at the Space Needle, where, despite the rain, they viewed the shimmering lights of the city.

As they were leaving, he took her arm and said, "I'm not taking no for an answer. I'm driving you home."

The wind was stiff, buffeting their bodies, the rain a fine mist. She thought about returning to her empty apartment, as her roommate was again a ghost, so she considered. What would it hurt? She didn't have to invite him in, or if she did, she could insist he leave when she wanted him to, *if* she wanted him to. But in the end she didn't give in. She was too unsure. Instead, she caught a bus that would drop her off only blocks from her apartment.

As she stared at the night scape of the city, through the raindrops on the windows of the bus, she wondered why she resisted.

Because Liam is dangerous. She sensed he was a man to whom she might lose her heart, a heart she guarded ferociously.

Usually impulsive, ready to cut and run, Rory had learned to protect herself, as well as land on her feet, to rely on no one but herself. Maybe that was what this was all about. Since Liam Bastian was different from the other men she'd dated, she sensed he could hurt her. It would be best if she got on the bus tonight, then avoided him, thus ending the "relationship" before it really began.

"You're an idiot," she muttered to herself as the bus screeched up to the stop near her apartment building. She stepped onto the curb, into the lonely night, feeling the dampness of the night pressing against her face.

As the bus rumbled away, she dashed across the street to the front door of the older building with its brick-and-glass façade. As she did, she heard footsteps behind her. The street was nearly deserted, the vapor from the street lamps causing an eerie glow.

Her heart froze.

A glance over her shoulder confirmed that a dark figure was hurrying forward, emerging from the alley she passed. Oh. *God.*

Fear propelled her. Blood cold, she ran for the door, all the while reaching into her purse, her fingers fumbling as she located her keys.

Move, Rory!

She splashed through a puddle on the sidewalk, heard the

rush of traffic speeding past. Would someone stop if she was assaulted? Maybe she should call for help now. From the corner of her eye, she saw him, a tall man in dark clothes approaching rapidly.

She opened her mouth to scream just as the door opened and he stepped into the pool of light cast by the bulbs set deep into the ceiling of the portico.

"Rory!" he called. She recognized Liam and her knees gave way. He swept her up, wrapped his arms around her and pulled her against him, then pressed cool lips against hers.

"Oh, God," she gulped out.

"You all right? I didn't mean to scare you."

"Well, you did!" She sounded so breathless. Fear, or something else? Something more treacherous, sliding through her, a wanting she knew would only cause her pain . . . yet . . .

Standing in the puddle of light, feeling the strength of him, she made the irretrievable mistake of kissing him back. Automatically she opened her mouth and felt his tongue touch hers. A shot of pure sensation sizzled through her, and she knew, despite all her protests, she was lost to him.

Without a word, she led him to the elevator and the upper story apartment. They didn't bother with the lights, or a lock on the door, just tumbled together on the futon that was her bed and struggled out of their clothes, always touching, ever kissing. Rory felt the warmth of his tongue glide down her body, leaving a trail on her bare skin. Blood thundered in her ears and she felt an instant warmth growing deep within her when the tip of his tongue found her nipple and toyed with it.

I'm in trouble, she silently told herself in her one last moment of sanity, then her body arched, he took her breast into his mouth and her body arched to meet him. Her fingers traced the sinewy muscles beneath his skin as she felt him slide into her, his eyes locking with hers as they began to move together.

Then her throat was tight, her entire body pulsing with need. She met his thrusts with a sweet rhythm of her own. The moment built and built. She couldn't breathe. It was better than anything. The totality of feeling. All beyond her experience. Everything intensified, faster and faster, hotter and hotter, the crescendo building until she was screaming silently, her fingers digging into his flesh. She wanted to drag him into her core, feel him inside her as deep and connected as she could. Her thoughts splintered and she suddenly came in a breathless spasm, crying out in surprise. He groaned as he met her at the apex. When he fell against her, she held on to his perspiring, heaving body, full of joy and a kind of disbelief. So, this was what it was all about. Beautiful.

She never wanted the night to end.

But she couldn't tell him, not then, not for a while. She was too afraid. It took weeks of lovemaking before she could be completely honest about her feelings, and then once the words were out—*I love you*—she mentally braced herself for the rejection. It was too soon. Too soon! A part of her feared he would vanish like smoke.

He took a long moment to answer her, long enough for her to crawl inside herself and die a thousand deaths. It was about a month into their relationship and they were back at Rendezvous—his suggestion—and somehow she'd just popped out with her feelings, blurted those three little words over another coffee with Baileys. She saw everything in sharp relief, though the noise retreated to the background, deafened by her panicked heartbeat.

And then, in all seriousness, he asked, "What are you doing the rest of your life?"

And she answered without thinking, "Spending it with you?"

His slow smile was all the answer she needed.

Now, turning away from the window, Rory climbed in bed with her daughter, who was mumbling in her sleep, plagued by restless dreams. She touched Charlotte's forehead—a little warm, maybe?

She watched her daughter for a while, and Charlotte finally fell into deep, rhythmic breathing.

Rory pressed her face into her little girl's red tresses and blotted out any further thought about Liam Bastian.

The hotel room was dark except for what filtered in through the crack in the curtain from Portland's city lights, a strip of illumination that hurried over the end of the bed, striping their bare legs as it ran across the room and up the wall.

The woman lying naked on the bed felt like having a cigarette, though she didn't smoke, never had. She just felt like she should be doing something, and smoking was what they did in old movies after coitus.

Coitus . . . that term sounded quaint and old-fashioned, not anything that had just transpired between her and . . . her bedmate. She threw him a look. Also naked, on his stomach, too damn relaxed. What they'd just done was less than romantic. It was base, emotionless fucking. Period. And it was starting to sort of piss her off.

It had been a long while since they'd gotten together. You'd think that would have whetted his male juices—absence making the prick grow harder—but instead she'd just been subjected to a kind of rote thrusting that had left her thinking about all the problems she needed to take care of instead of a hopefully impending climax. (She hadn't felt anything close to that in months.) No, her mind had wandered to the same problems of five years ago. Problems that hadn't been resolved in the least at that fiasco of a wedding, although she'd thought for a short while that she'd gotten lucky and a few of the people she couldn't stand would die. But no! And that lunatic's rain of bullets had damn near hit *her*.

What had happened? She still didn't know. Nobody did, apparently.

And now . . .

Jesus Christ, here she was, lying naked in this three-star hotel room with a man she didn't even really like. Their affair had raged like a firestorm at the time of the wedding, but now . . . well, let's face it, he *smelled*. Sure, the odor could be called musky, male, maybe even sensual, but to her these days it was just plain old BO.

She was icked out by practically everything he did, though an honest part of herself, something buried deep in her female brain that rarely saw the light of day, had to admit she'd become rather particular as the years rolled by. Drop food on the floor and abide by the three-second rule? No way. That shit needs to go straight in the garbage. Let an animal lick you with its tongue? God, no. They were fine at a distance, but keep them away from her.

So, okay, here she was . . . tied to this sweaty male because of decisions made that she now wished she'd thought through a little more carefully at the time. What to do now?

She stared up at the darkened ceiling. She could lift her head and look past him to the clock on his side of the bed, or she could get up and find her phone to learn the time, but she did neither. She toyed with the idea of pretending to smoke as she looked down at her naked body, admiring her own smooth stomach and toned legs. She was a fine-looking woman. Who had said that to her? Or was it something from the days of coitus and old movies? *She's a fine-looking woman.*

For some reason that thought pissed her off, too. Like she was made for some man's pleasure.

She exhaled noisily, then decided to try the pretend-smoking thing. She brought her fingers up to her lips, sucked in a lungful of air, then blew out a fake stream that she could almost see. She kind of liked the feeling, so she did it a few more times before she tired of the artifice. What was the point, anyway?

He made some kind of noise with his lips that made her think about his breath. Garlicky smell. She wrinkled her nose. She had to get out of this rut she was in. And it also pissed her off that he'd fallen asleep almost instantly after he'd rolled off her.

"What time is it?" she asked in a loud voice.

He didn't move and she glanced over at him. One eye was open, dark and liquid, looking her way.

"Would you look at the time? Okay? *Please?*" she asked, jabbing an elbow into his ribs for good measure.

With a grunt of exaggerated effort, he lifted himself up and looked over. "Midnight," he pronounced.

"Oh, my God." She scrambled off the bed and searched for her clothes.

He turned over and watched her step into her scrap of panties and snap on her bra.

"Stop looking at me," she ordered, shimmying her dress over her head.

"C'mere."

"Fuck you."

"No, c'mere."

When she ignored him, sliding her purse from the nightstand, making sure her cell phone was tucked inside, he jumped off the bed and grabbed her around the waist, tumbling them both back onto the bed. She shrieked and immediately began slapping at him. He roughly clasped her hands together, manacled them over her head, held her there hard.

"Stop it," he ordered.

"You stop it," she spat back, squirming. "I've got to leave!"

His other hand was marauding over her body and she twisted

and fought and gnashed her teeth. But then he thrust one knee between her legs and dry-humped against her and goddamn it, she suddenly wanted him SO BAD.

"You better do it right this time, asshole," she whispered in his ear before clamping her small, white teeth onto it with vigor.

"Ouch! Bitch. I'll do it right."

His free hand yanked at her dress, hiking it up over her hips. She heard a rip.

"Damn you! I paid—"

She cut herself off on a gasp as he yanked off her panties with hard fingers and then was on her, driving into her so fast, thrusting with such force that she had to lift her palms to the headboard to keep from crashing her skull into it.

"I—hate—you," she gasped in time to his thrusts. "I—hate—YOU."

He came with a groan and a collapse that left her furious, still moving beneath him to ensure she came, too. She was so mad she could scream. He'd taken his pleasure and left her hanging!

But no . . . the furious rubbing was working anyway and his half-hearted attempts to aid her with a few desultory hip thrusts helped bring her to a climax. Not as good as it should have been, but at least she got there.

"Ooooh, oooh," she moaned on a deep exhalation of air.

"Good for you, huh," he said, self-satisfied.

That did it.

She slapped him across the face, hard.

Immediately he clasped her hands over her head again, and she could feel him harden.

"You can't do it again," she goaded. "You don't have it in you."

"Careful, bitch," he whispered.

She was getting really turned on. "Yeah, yeah . . . you're not man enough. Can't even pleasure a woman."

It was a game they'd played in the past. The distant past. She was thrilled the game was resurrected. She was moving beneath him, inviting him, even while she insulted him.

But then, instead of taking her like he should have, she sensed his cock start to shrivel. He rolled away from her.

"What?" she demanded. This was it. She couldn't stand for this any longer. She had to finish this affair tonight. Right now.

"We gotta talk about something."

Now he was sitting up. She could only see his back. Her excitement was quickly turning to anger. "Talk all you want," she snarled. "It's o—"

"He's getting out of prison. This week."

The rest of the word remained unsaid. She almost asked who, but the words turned to dust in her mouth and she felt a stab of fear. "No."

"I'll take care of it."

"What are you talking about?"

"I'll take care of him," he amended.

She started laughing, quietly, hysterically. He turned around swiftly and glared her down.

"What are you going to do?" she managed on a hiccup.

"I'll take care of it," he said again, biting off each word. "Now get the hell out of here."

That was a second shock. "You don't tell me what to do!"

"I said I'LL TAKE CARE OF IT! Just give me some room to breathe!"

She threw herself off the bed, straightened her dress, slipped into her shoes, swept up her purse, and stomped out of the room. She would have slammed the door behind her, but it was too late to bring that kind of attention to herself.

Take care of it, my ass. She was the one who always handled things.

She marched down the hallway, aware she was missing one piece of her outfit.

Well, screw him. He could just figure out what to do with her panties. She hoped to God they drove him crazy with lust, but more than likely he wouldn't even pick them up.

And THAT pissed her off, too.

Chapter 8

At the Buzz, Connie cut the engine, the headlights of her Outback catching the abandoned pickup before dimming in the dark parking lot. Under her breath she muttered an oath about her uncle's damned truck, one that she knew, deep in her heart, she would eventually have to towed to an auto salvage yard. The rusting, useless vehicle and Uncle Ira's disinterest in moving it was a constant source of irritation. She had a feeling she was going to have to take matters into her own hands.

Sighing, she hankered for a cigarette for the first time in two weeks. She ignored the craving, grabbed some groceries from the back seat, and made her way into the little coffee shop. Without Heather, she would have to double-up on her shifts.

Heather . . . What was her secret? And why did Connie feel the need to protect her? Probably because of the kid. No matter what kind of trouble Heather had gotten herself caught up in, it wasn't little Charlotte's fault and Connie, married three times herself, knew about lousy, and at the very least emotionally abusive, ex-husbands. "Losers," she muttered. Every last one of them.

This morning, against her better judgment, she'd called in her backup barista for the early shift. Debbie was her niece, her brother Bob's youngest child, who at thirty-two had yet to launch and leave home and oftentimes smelled of marijuana smoke, seeming to be drifting through life. Debbie couldn't hold a steady job, was forever late, was rarely able to make correct change, but was friendly enough and sweet, if that counted for anything in today's world.

Half an hour later Debbie rolled up in her canary-yellow Volkswagen Beetle and, dark braids swinging, hurried into the shop. "Hey!" she called cheerily and went about finding a clean apron as Connie switched on the lights to indicate the shop was open.

"You've got the drive-up," she yelled, and Debbie nodded as she emerged from the small alcove where the supplies were kept. Head bent, Debbie was tying the apron strings around her slim waist and yes, there was a distinct odor of Mary Jane hanging around her. At five thirty in the morning? Hadn't she heard about coffee and caffeine to get the day started? Hell, she was coming to work in a coffee shop!

But Connie held her tongue as she drizzled icing over warm cinnamon rolls. She didn't care what Debbie did, not really, as long as it didn't affect her job.

Debbie smiled at her. "The window? Oh. Sure. Whatever."

Connie had already set up the computer and made certain the till was loaded. All Debbie had to do was hand over the drinks and collect the money or debit or credit cards. And, oh yeah, make change. It wasn't rocket science.

The door opened and Carlos swung in. He greeted them all with a smile just as the bell sounded and the first customer rolled through the drive-in lane. "Here we go," Connie called out. "Remember, the amount of change is listed on the screen."

"I know, I know." Debbie was already turning on the mic.

"Welcome to the Buzz, what can I get started for you this morning?"

"Medium coffee, black," was the response.

Connie glanced at the screen to see a black SUV. The man placing the order through the open window of his vehicle was the same person who'd come through yesterday, the one who'd made Heather flee in panic. Obviously he was back, checking for her. Connie's heart pounded, and while Debbie prepared the order, Connie said to Carlos, "Take over the cinnamon rolls, will ya? I forgot something at the house."

"Sure," Carlos said with a quick nod, his dark, netted hair glinting under the bright lights illuminating the back of the counter.

Connie was already stripping off her apron and heading for the back door to the parking lot. Her plan was half-baked; she didn't even know exactly what she was doing, but she hurried outside where the sky was starting to lighten. She didn't think twice, just jumped into her little car, flicked on the ignition, and threw it into gear. Then she waited until the Tahoe nosed its way from the lane used specifically for the drive-through and turned onto the nearly deserted street. She followed, at a distance, just like in the movies. With so little traffic in this small town it would be easy for the driver to spot a tail, but then a strange thing happened. As she slowed, another car sped around her, then backed off, as if it was following the same vehicle. She considered that it was someone on his way to work, but when the black Tahoe stopped for gas, the gray car slid into a spot against the curb where the driver waited, not turning off his engine.

Connie did the same, three blocks farther back.

Was this a coincidence? It sure didn't read that way.

She wished again for a cigarette and nearly drove to the mini-mart at the gas station for a pack of Salem Lights, but was afraid the driver of the Tahoe would recognize her, so she held back until he'd filled up and pulled out of the station. The gray sedan with Washington plates held off for a beat, allowed another car to enter the road, then pulled away from the curb. She did the same, lagging back, wondering what the hell she was witnessing.

At a distance, still following, she watched both vehicles pass through the border crossing into Canada. She followed them, nervous, feeling as if she were in some made-for-TV mystery, as she waited impatiently for the guard to let her pass. It felt like forever, but was in reality only a few minutes, until she drove into British Columbia, too.

She expected the two cars she was following to take the road into the U.S. as soon as they were off the peninsula, but instead of heading east onto the highway that would eventually curve south toward the U.S. and Washington State, the SUV with the gray car behind it continued northward.

"Uh-oh," Connie said aloud. The man in the Tahoe, Heather's louse of an ex-husband, must have located her. Still driving, ignoring all safety laws regarding cell phones, she snatched up hers and punched in Heather's number, hoping the call would go through without problems, a dicey proposition whenever you crossed the border. She heard it ringing, which was a good sign, but Heather wasn't picking up. "Come on, come on," Connie muttered, squinting a little as the sun crested the eastern horizon. Frustrated, she hung up, waited two minutes, dialed again.

"Hello?" Heather answered, sounding groggy.

"Heather, it's Connie," she said tersely. "That guy who's looking for you? He's heading north into Canada right now, doesn't appear to be going back to the States."

Heather inhaled on a gasp. "You're sure?"

"Yep. And I think he's going to Vancouver."

"Oh, no!"

"I figured you'd want to know." Connie had guessed that

Heather would head into the large city. "Look, I don't know where you are and I don't want to know, but if you're in that area, he's probably not just driving blind. Someone or something must've tipped him off."

"I think you're right."

"And there's something more. I think maybe he's being followed. Another car, a gray sedan with Washington plates that were obscured with mud, kept a tail on him."

"He's being tailed?" she asked, sounding incredulous.

Connie nodded, though Heather couldn't see her. "That's what it looks like."

There was a long pause, then Heather seemed to rouse herself. "Thank you, Connie."

"No problem. You be careful and take care of that little girl," Connie said as she looked for a place to turn around.

"I will." Heather promised. Then she was gone.

As the sun rose, Liam drove northward. The word he'd gotten from Jacoby, just after he'd stopped by the Point Bob Buzz in hopes of spying Rory, was that she was indeed in Canada, and possibly Vancouver. Jacoby had said he'd found out through some relative of Rory's that a man named Kent Daley was a close personal friend of the family's and that Rory, as a teenager, had considered him more of a father figure than Harold Stemple. Daley spent a lot of his time in Vancouver, B.C., and because of the city's proximity to Point Roberts, it seemed a connection, if a weak one. But since Liam was this close, he'd decided to check it out.

And if you actually find her?

He tried to imagine that meeting and couldn't.

"I'm going to ask her for a divorce," he said aloud. "Clean that up. Move on."

He heard his own words. They hung in the air over the hum of the SUV's engine, mocking him.

You're so full of shit, Bastian. You want to see her again, to find out why she fled the wedding, if she was involved in the shooting. You want to see her face again, see if she conned you. And deep down you want to wring her neck ... or make love to her.

He took a corner too fast, braked hard, and brought the vehicle under control. The car behind him nearly rear-ended the Tahoe. He slowed down, raked a hand through his hair, and wondered why it had always been this way with Rory, why she'd always gotten so deeply under his skin. From that first moment when he'd nearly knocked her down on the rainy streets of Seattle, she'd affected him way more than he liked.

Traffic was increasing, commuters driving into the city of Vancouver. He glanced at his phone, hoping Jacoby would call with a definitive address. When the cell didn't ring, he saw the sign for a diner advertising breakfast and pulled into the lot. Rather than drive without direction in the unfamiliar city, he would order breakfast and do a little research himself. He'd start by Googling this Kent Daley guy, then do Internet searches of all of the members of Rory's family, double-checking if any one of them had links to Canada, British Columbia, or Vancouver.

Briefly he thought again of the retired detective who'd been so on top of the investigation immediately following the wedding shooting. Mickelson had been after a single perpetrator, hot on the man's trail, at least in the beginning, but that trail had gone cold very quickly. The detective had not been particularly focused on Rory's disappearance, believing it to be separate from the shooting, which had both frustrated and relieved Liam. He didn't want Rory to be involved, so he was glad the investigation seemed to lead away from her. Still, he'd wanted to be kept abreast of every twist and turn, but Mickelson wasn't interested in keeping him that well informed. It hadn't helped that Stella and Geoff had seemed more than glad to be left out. They'd wanted to sweep the whole thing under the rug, embarrassed and fearful as the terrible attack had splashed across the papers and every news cycle for days and weeks on end. The shooting that had taken his father's legs, and Aaron Stemple's life, had played hell with his parents' status with their rich, so-called friends, and though they'd given lip service to wanting to find the killer, the larger truth was they just wanted to put it in their rearview and move on. It was only recently that Geoff occasionally spoke of the incident that had changed his life and showed some interest in pursuing justice.

Part of the reason Mickelson had left the police force was because of his single-minded pursuit of one man, Pete DeGrere, when others in his department weren't as convinced. DeGrere was currently serving a term in prison for an unrelated crime, a convenience store robbery, and Mickelson's superiors felt the crimes were too disparate to point to DeGrere as the shooter. At least that was the gist of what Liam had learned. Mickelson had become a private detective and Liam had briefly considered using him in his search for Rory. The man was already obsessed with the case and it seemed that if anyone could find her, he could. Except he was an ex-cop, and Liam sensed that there could be unforeseen complications if he actually ran Rory to ground. Mickelson might want to "do the right thing" in that by-the-book cop way, and Liam wasn't sure that's what he wanted. So, he'd gone with the Van Horne's investigator, Jacoby, and the man had delivered.

Now, Liam exhaled heavily, his pulse racing a little as he got out of the car and headed into the diner, wondering if the pies the place advertised as the best around could compete with Connie's cinnamon rolls. He'd eaten one on the way over, and it had been pretty terrific.

He wondered idly if Rory had ever helped with the baking at the coffee shop, wondering also if today could be the day he actually met up with his runaway, soon-to-be-ex-wife.

Rory stared into space, frozen where she stood. Her pulse had skyrocketed, her anxiety level to the max. Even though she didn't want to believe what was so blatantly obvious, she had to. Liam was here. Looking for her. She'd seen him with her own eyes.

Finding her feet, she stepped to the window at the front of the town house and peeked through the blinds. At this hour there was little traffic, dawn's light creeping through the streets, the buildings still lying in night-shadow. Swallowing hard, she studied the landscape. Was there someone lurking in the shrubbery near the sidewalk, hidden eyes staring up at her from the crevices between apartment houses? Her heart rate ticked up a beat as she noticed movement, a shadowy figure. Oh. God. He was here!

Then the figure moved into the light and she saw it was only a man in his late twenties walking a small dog.

She exhaled heavily. *Get a grip, Rory.*

How had Liam found her? Why now? What had changed?

She threw on fresh clothes and wondered if he'd sent someone else, a private investigator of some kind, to locate her. Was that why she'd experienced such cold certainty that someone was following her? Because they had been? She'd thought she'd seen Everett, but maybe it was someone else, someone on Liam's payroll all along.

It didn't matter how he'd located her. He had. This was happening.

Galvanized by a sense of urgency, she started packing while Charlotte lay snuggled beneath the rumpled covers on the bed. Heart thudding, Rory carried one bag down the stairs and found Uncle Kent at the kitchen table, reading glasses propped on his nose, the morning paper strewn over the tabletop.

"Coffee's on," he said without looking up.

She smelled the warm scent of a fresh brew. "Liam's on his way here."

Kent looked up in surprise, crumpling the paper. "What?"

"Connie called me. She followed him and he's heading this way."

Kent was on his feet. "You're certain? How did he find you?"

"I don't know. He came to the drive-through at the Buzz this morning, just after Connie opened the shop." She gave him a quick rundown of her short conversation with Connie.

"Oh, dear." Maude appeared in the doorway to the kitchen. She'd obviously heard most of what Rory had said. "You can't stay here then." She was shaking her head sadly as she walked to the coffeepot gurgling on the counter, pulled out a couple of mugs from the cupboard and filled them both. Handing a ceramic cup to Rory, she asked, "You're sure about this?"

"Yes." It was a lie. She wasn't sure about anything. Not one solitary thing.

"Why now?" Maude asked, voicing Rory's thoughts as she laid a hand on her arm.

Rory shook her head.

Kent said, "If he found you, he probably found us. Or vice versa."

Rory took a swallow of coffee, not really tasting it. Her mind was already spinning ahead, plotting her escape. "I have to wake Charlotte and leave. Now. He could show up at any second. I just needed you to know what was going on."

"We'll handle it if he shows up here," Kent said. "If Liam asks about you, I'll say I haven't heard a word."

"What if he *knows* you were the one who helped me get away from the wedding?"

Within his goatee, Kent's lips twisted into a wry smile. "Don't worry about it. I'll stonewall or something." He was always up for a challenge, a chance to match wits with an opponent or, if necessary, elude the authorities. He hadn't been dubbed The Magician by Rory's family for nothing. Her mother had joked once that "Kent could make bodies disappear if he wanted to." Rory had remembered that line when she'd called him in desperation at the wedding.

"Okay, then. Thank you." She had to trust him.

Maude slid into one of the chairs at the table, her eyes troubled. "So where are you going?"

"Good question . . ." Rory hadn't thought that far ahead. All she knew was that she had to flee immediately.

Kent took off his glasses and regarded the lenses critically, looking for smudges. "I know you don't want to hear this, but—"

"Don't tell me to talk to the police, okay?" Rory interjected, even though she'd suffered the same thought. "I just need to get somewhere safe."

"And where is that?" Kent asked.

There's nowhere safe. "I don't know yet, but I can't stay here. I've involved you both enough." She took another swallow of coffee, felt it burn in her stomach, and left the cup on the counter. "I've got to go."

Where? Where? The question followed her up the stairs and into the bedroom, where she found Charlotte had roused. "Hey, sweetheart," Rory said in a strained voice. She sat down next to her on the rumpled bedclothes. "How're you feeling?"

Her daughter's lower lip extended. "Not good."

"No?" Worriedly, Rory eyed her daughter closely, pushing the girl's mussed hair from her face. "How about breakfast?"

Charlotte shook her head. "Not hungry." This, in and of itself, wasn't unusual. It took Charlotte a little while after she woke up to want food.

"Okay, we'll take something with us."

"Where are we going?" Charlotte asked, perking up a bit.

I wish I knew, Rory thought, but said, "Somewhere interesting. It's . . . a surprise." *For both of us.*

"Disneyland!" her daughter guessed, and Rory's heart sank. "Silas was there! He saw Mickey!"

"Nooo, not Disneyland this time."

"Where?" Charlotte demanded, her little brows slamming together, disappointment radiating from her.

"You'll see. Come on, get dressed, and you can help me pack." Rory was already off the bed and retrieving a pair of shorts and a T-shirt for her daughter from their hastily packed bag.

"Are we going home?" Charlotte pulled off her nightgown and picked up the shirt.

"Not right now." Rory felt a pang of regret. Point Roberts was the only home Charlotte remembered, the place Rory had once considered a sanctuary.

She'd been wrong.

Does he know he has a daughter?

The question made her go cold. Had he somehow learned about Charlotte? If a PI had tracked her down, wouldn't he have discovered that she had a child? Oh. God. Would he try to take Charlotte away? And what about the would-be assassin? The man who had attacked her at the hotel and had whispered terrible threats in her ear. The one who may have shot and killed her stepbrother.

Those thoughts propelled her. Throat dry, she scooped up her daughter's stuffed rabbit and handed it to her. "Come on, Charlotte. We're outta here."

Chapter 9

"So Pete DeGrere is scheduled to be released today," Shanice Clayburgh announced as she shouldered open the door of Mickelson's office. Balancing a cup of coffee in one hand and her phone in the other, she plopped into one of the two worn chairs facing the battle-scarred desk.

"Today?" Mickelson repeated, scowling. The senior partner of Mickelson and Hernandez, Private Investigations LLC, Roger "Mick" Mickelson was a big bear of a man. He'd once played college football, a lineman for Washington State, though that had been thirty years and as many pounds earlier. After marrying his college sweetheart, he'd joined the Seattle Police Department where he'd become a detective, before his marriage and career had blown up. He'd started his own small investigative firm four years earlier. Now he was huddled over the scarred top of his desk, papers strewn haphazardly before him, an ever-present oversized soda cup placed within arm's reach. The office was sparse, a few pieces of battered, used furniture in a suite of three rooms, Mickelson's being the largest, the one with a view of the dusty concrete building that stood not twenty feet away. "I thought tomorrow or . . ." He glanced at the calendar tacked on the wall near an ancient file cabinet.

"Nope. Today's his lucky day. As of today, Pete DeGrere is a private U.S. citizen." She forced a humorless smile and ignored the excitement coursing through her veins. Finally. She had the opportunity to nail the sick dick-wad. "Ain't we lucky?"

"We sure are." Mick returned the grin. He leaned back in his chair, rubbed his chin where reddish stubble was visible. "Scumbag," he said with a frown. "No, wait. Sack of shit is more appropriate." Mickelson was never one to mince words or keep an opinion to himself. He'd retired from the force to open his own PI firm, but even as a cop, his mouth had gotten him into trouble. Hence, his early retirement. "Let's find him."

"One step ahead of you," Shanice said. Her phone vibrated in her hand and with a quick glance she saw a text had come in from Deon, her on-again, off-again boyfriend. She'd thought they were in "off" mode. Apparently not. She ignored the text and said, "I figure DeGrere will find the nearest bar and strip club, spend whatever cash he's got, then, once he sobers up and realizes he's broke, he'll land at his sister's place, just outside of Tacoma."

"Why there?" Mick raised an eyebrow, encouraging her. He knew a lot about DeGrere, had made it a personal quest, but he liked it when Shanice got her teeth into a case.

"Because she's always got his back. One of the few. His best friend, Ralph Stutz? Remember him? Went to high school with Pete back in the seventies? He's dead. Embolism last May. Out of the blue." She snapped her fingers. "Just like that. DeGrere's only real friend. He's got no one else to turn to. He'll look up Sally and she won't be able to turn her only brother away."

Mick agreed, but asked, "You know this . . . how?"

"Oh, come on. You know I keep up."

"Good."

"DeGrere's a loser. A braggart as well as a snitch. It's what got him into trouble."

Mick grunted his agreement. "He boasted about the Bastian job."

She took a sip of coffee. "Told his cell mate, who passed it on. Police questioned him but he denied it, and the guy who spilled the beans reneged. Said he was just jokin', tryin' to get DeGrere in trouble."

"I know."

In prison, Pete DeGrere had boasted about his part in the assault at the Bastian wedding five years earlier, and the man had been a marksman during his stint in the army. A little checking and the police had discovered DeGrere had indeed been in the area at the time. A known thief who had a previous assault charge on his record, DeGrere had been elevated from person of interest to suspect, but there just hadn't been enough evidence to nail him. Despite the department's best efforts, the DA wouldn't go to trial on a case that didn't look like it could be won. And then DeGrere had been caught on camera breaking into a convenience store and the rest was history: He was convicted and sent up the river, and Seattle PD hadn't been able to find another suspect, witness, or enough evidence to convict DeGrere of taking part in the Bastian wedding assault.

Mick refused to give up on DeGrere. And though others in the department thought DeGrere might be good for it, too, no one could get any traction. Mick had left the department for a lot of reasons, but his immediate superior's remarks about Mick's "bull-headed resistance to a full investigation," had been the icing on the cake. Bull-headed resistance? He'd been trying to nail the perp, for God's sake.

And now DeGrere was going to be set free. Even after bragging to a cell mate about his part in the attack. Not that the snitch was reliable. The man was a con who knew the system, having been in and out of jail. He was a guy who would do anything to get out of prison, a problem which was only complicated by the fact that DeGrere was known to stretch the truth more than a little himself. An argument had been made that it was just bravado talking, good old Petey DeGrere spewing yet another lie to elevate himself within the shady circles of the prison community. And that argument still stood.

"DeGrere's our man," Mick said.

"I agree," Shanice said. "No one wants to nail his skinny ass for this as much as I do." She'd been chasing leads on the assault ever since she'd learned of it, five years ago. She'd known Aaron Stemple, who had been killed at the wedding. He'd transferred to her high school their senior year and he'd been a shy kid in a dysfunctional family. His older brother had been a juvenile delinquent and petty thief, his father a criminal who'd been in and out of jail, his mother having bailed on the marriage when he was a kid, and he'd ended up murdered at his stepsister's wedding. Shanice had felt bad about that. Aaron hadn't deserved to die so young, so violently. Her heart still turned cold at the thought of it. She'd been his secret girlfriend in school and had willingly lost her virginity, well, really handed it over, to him one glorious summer night. She wanted to know who'd killed him. Maybe as badly as Mick wanted to find the assassin as well.

And DeGrere had been in the area when the assault on the wedding had gone down, but before a case could be built against him, he'd been picked up for another charge and sent to prison. Though Mick believed DeGrere was a hired gun for someone else, there was no evidence. If DeGrere had been paid for the shooting, he'd kept the money somewhere safe and hadn't had a chance to spend it before he ended up behind bars.

If, as Mick believed, DeGrere was the shooter, why had he chosen the Bastian wedding as the venue? Who was he really trying to kill? More than one person? DeGrere wasn't the most stable guy, but he had no personal motive to try to harm the Bastians that could be discovered. Mick's feeling about De-Grere was more gut instinct than dogged police work; he could admit that. But DeGrere had committed crimes for payment in the past, and he'd been near the wedding site on that day, and he'd bragged about the shooting to his cellmate, whether Seattle PD believed him or not . . . it all just fed Mick's and Shanice's suspicions.

But if DeGrere's motive was money, what was the person's who'd hired him? Who was the intended victim, or victims?

Mick and the other Seattle PD detectives had initially floated the idea that Rory Abernathy was the target since the shooting started soon after the first notes of the Bridal March, but nothing had ever materialized from that theory. They also considered that the bullets were meant for Aaron Stemple. Though there was no video footage outside Rory's room—it was learned afterwards that cameras weren't working on several of the hotel's floors—Aaron had been caught racing along the outside walkway toward the ceremony from the bride's room's general direction. It was postulated that he'd seen something or someone or knew of the shooter, but he was killed before he could explain why he was running, and to date no correlation to the theory had been found, either. Though Mick was sure the answer lay with Pete DeGrere, the lack of hard evidence had thwarted an indictment against DeGrere, and the investigation had subsequently stalled.

But now DeGrere was being set free.

"I'm going to find him, talk to him," Shanice said determinedly. "Maybe shake something loose."

Mickelson looked at her over the tops of his readers and fixed her with an icy glare. "Be smart," he said, as if he'd ever followed that advice himself when it came to DeGrere. "Go easy."

"Always."

He gave her that I-know-better stare. "I'm serious. We want to put him away forever."

Shanice's smile was cold. Mick was warning her to rein in her emotions, to think with her head, not her heart, to tread lightly so they could take the jerk-face down and not make the same mistakes he had.

Yeah, right.

"I got this," she said, standing. Then with a sly grin added, "Trust me."

As she breezed out of the room she was half-certain she heard, "I wish I could," muttered under Mickelson's breath, but for once, she let it go.

The address Jacoby had provided belonged to Maude Sutter, and when Liam introduced himself, she was nothing but gracious, even asking him in and offering him iced tea, which he'd declined. She'd smoked a cigarette on the back porch and admitted to not only knowing Kent Daley but confiding that they'd been "a couple," for years. But that was as far as Liam had gotten. As for Daley, he didn't appear to be around. No sign of him, at least not that Liam could discern.

Maude said not one word about Rory Abernathy or Heather Johnson, and no matter how many ways he'd asked about her, the answer had always been the same. "I don't know anything about her, other than what I read in the papers. What was it? Five years ago or so?"

Nor would she say much about Kent either. When Liam had pressed, she'd stubbed her cigarette out in a tray positioned on a wicker outdoor table and leaned in close enough that he could smell the lingering smoke that clung to her. "My relationship with Kent is very private and we both have pasts that . . . well, we just don't talk about. You don't reach our age without accumulating baggage. But we feel, or at least I do, that the past is in the past and that's where it's going to stay. Now, I don't think I can help you anymore." She'd stood and waited.

"I'd like to speak to Mr. Daley."

"I would, too. When you see him, let him know." She'd smiled at him and he'd reluctantly gotten to his feet and followed her as she'd led him through the house to the front door. But as they passed by the stairs, he'd spied a tiny pink sock on the landing.

"You have any visitors lately?" he asked, plucking the cotton stocking from the stair at his eye height and holding it out to her.

She didn't so much as blink, just held his gaze as her fingers curled over the tiny scrap of clothing. "Always someone, it seems," she said enigmatically. "Now, if you'll excuse me . . ."

He could have been rude and pushed it, but he'd sensed she wasn't a woman who could be bullied. She'd been steadfast in her denials. And she'd been alone; he'd sensed the house was empty. Kent Daley obviously hadn't been in the house, nor had Rory, but the little sock was a clue. Liam would bet that Rory had been there with her kid—probably a daughter—but had been spooked and taken off. Daley, too, maybe.

So he was back to square one, and as he drove south toward the border on his way back to Portland, he felt more than a little bit of disappointment. He'd really thought he might see Rory again, that this would be it, his quest at an end. That he'd finally be able to confront her. Demand answers for questions that had festered for five years. But as the miles rolled beneath the tires of his Tahoe, he realized it wasn't going to happen now, maybe ever. He could chase down Kent Daley but wasn't sure that would help, either. Rory clearly wanted to stay missing. That was something he'd learned years ago, though he still persisted for reasons that seemed less clear-cut as time went on.

It was time to forget her. Go through the legal motions of divorcing a missing person. Give up this endless chase.

He'd told himself the same thing countless times.

He needed to heed his own advice.

"Forget her," he said aloud, yet his hands tightened on the steering wheel, almost of their own accord. He needed to know what had happened. What was the shooting about at the wedding? Why? Why had someone opened fire on his family? And what did it have to do with Rory?

He switched lanes and increased his speed, plagued by the same questions that had dogged him since that terrible day.

Stella had always insisted he was the target, that Aaron had just gotten in the way. In his mother's twisted mind, she was certain that Rory had only married him for his money, then had tried to kill him off so that she could inherit his share of the family fortune as well as collect on a healthy insurance policy in which she was named Liam's beneficiary.

Liam had dismissed that theory immediately. If Rory had really wanted to kill him, which he didn't believe for a second, why go to all the trouble and risk of hiring an assassin like De-Grere for a very public and bizarre shooting? Why not just quietly take him out sometime later into their marriage?

Stella, bullheaded as always, had stuck to her guns, telling him often enough that the only reason Rory hadn't collected on the insurance was because her plans had gone awry and Liam had survived.

He shook his head and twisted on the radio, trying to find a decent station, giving up when all he could find was country music or rap. As he snapped off the radio, he thought of the terror of those heart-stopping moments when bullets rained down on them. Automatically, he rubbed his thigh, thinking of the wounds he'd sustained in the attack, as if the pain still persisted. It didn't. At least for the most part.

Was it possible, after all, that Aaron Stemple had been the target? Liam had floated that idea at a family barbecue around his parents' swimming pool, and his mother had snorted her disgust. "Why?" she'd demanded, pouring herself a glass of wine from a chilling bottle of chardonnay on the serving cart parked near the arborvitae hedge, a living, green wall that offered privacy. "Why go to all the trouble and danger to attack him at the wedding?" Liam had been seated at the table a few yards away from his mother, his gaze on the aqua water and his sister's young children, Landon and Estella, as they'd splashed around and laughed and shrieked, their arms in floaties. "Did he have any enemies?" Stella had asked, eyebrows arching as she sipped from her glass.

Liam admitted, "I don't know."

"We all have enemies," his father had cut in. "I didn't get rich making only friends." Geoffrey had been seated in his wheelchair, which he'd rolled to the table, positioning himself in the shade offered by the striped umbrella. Sunglasses covering his eyes, he'd stared out at the pool and the splashing children. Vivian, stretched on a lounge chair beside her husband, Javier, had flapped a bored hand at them.

"Don't talk about it," she called.

"Well, I don't think they were after Aaron Stemple," his mother had said in that freezing way of hers that cut off all conversation.

Bethany had been there that day, and she reached under the table to link her fingers with Liam's, as if to somehow reassure him, while Stella, in that Stella take-control way of hers, changed the topic of conversation and began nattering on about a new variety of roses she wanted to plant in the coming year, a subject that had bored the hell out of everyone there but had effectively shut down all talk of the assault at the wedding.

Now, at the border crossing into Washington, the cars were idling and Liam suddenly wanted the trip over, to get back to his life—his job, his upcoming marriage to Bethany and a future with children, where the tentacles of the past couldn't reach him.

Of course, that was unlikely until the mystery of who had attacked the wedding party was solved. Maybe Pete DeGrere, maybe not. Whoever he was, the shooter had fled, leaving his rifle behind, an unregistered weapon that, as far as the police had been able to determine, had never been used in another crime. An older model, it could have been bought and sold a dozen times. Untraceable. Not a fingerprint on it—wiped clean. Nary a hair caught in it. And there had been no cameras in the parking garage, or any on the hotel property that had caught a clear image of the perpetrator. Though the police had been careful about everything they said, Liam thought they were working on the theory that Aaron had been the target, too, or perhaps Rory, who was supposed to be on his arm. That theory had initially gained credence from the bloody wedding dress left at the scene and the fact that Rory had disappeared. Maybe the shooter, waiting for Rory, had developed an itchy trigger finger and had shot Aaron before she appeared. But why hadn't she shown up? Had she been tipped off? Waylaid by the killer? Why was there blood on her dress? It was too bad the hotel cameras hadn't all been working. She'd just disappeared. Escaped the bloody scene and never returned. Not a text, phone call, or any goodbye. She'd just vanished.

His lips tightened. She had to have had an accomplice to escape so completely, and if so, then logically she had to be guilty. But why? Stella assumed Rory had been after the Bastian fortune. Had she hired a sniper to . . . what? Take out his entire family? His father, mother, brother, sister, and himself, so that she could inherit? That idea had been posed enough by his own family to surface again in his mind, but it was ridiculous.

"Is it?" he could almost hear his mother say as he was allowed to cross back onto U.S. soil. "What if everything went wrong? The shooter missed and Rory, realizing she would be a suspect, quickly covered her tracks and ran? She had to have an accomplice, of course. How else would she get away without a trace? Hmmm? And if she had an accomplice, she had to be guilty."

His fingers gripped the steering wheel more tightly as he drove into Washington and envisioned his mother, sipping from her stemmed glass, the expensive chardonnay catching in the sunlight, Stella's eyebrows arching over the tops of her sunglasses as she made her well-honed point.

He didn't believe Rory was guilty. Didn't want her to be guilty. But his mother's insinuations lived beneath his skin, making it impossible for him to completely dismiss them. There was a reason for the shooting. And maybe it did have something to do with Rory. That much he would allow.

"Charlotte?" Rory said, glancing over her shoulder to the car seat where her daughter was nodding off. "Are you hungry?"

No response.

Maybe that was good.

Charlotte was sleeping and had been since before the border crossing. Now they'd driven halfway across the state of Washington, heading toward Oregon. She would have liked to stay in Seattle, but there was a chance someone would recognize her, someone from her past. The chances were slim, but she needed to drive as far south as she dared, to put distance between herself and Point Roberts. Fleeing to Oregon wasn't safe in that Portland was Liam's hometown, a place where his family lived, but few of them would recognize her on the off chance she was spotted. She didn't intend to stop. No, she would sweep through the city and continue south to Salem, where her mother had ended up. Fifty miles south of Liam's home, it would be a safe haven for a few hours before she continued toward California. San Francisco sounded good, or even farther to Los Angeles or some smaller city in between.

"How about McDonalds?" she said over her shoulder, trying to rouse her child. "For breakfast . . . or, I guess, lunch?" Since they'd escaped from Maude's town house in a hurry, Charlotte hadn't had a bite. Nor had she eaten much the night before. Rory bit her lip and waited, casting glances into the rearview mirror. The little girl just wasn't like herself. "I can run through the drive-through and get you a McMuffin?"

No response.

"Sausage? Or maybe pancakes? You like those."

Still nothing. Not so much as a flicker of an eyelid.

"Charlotte?" she said a little more sharply.

The girl's little lips moved, but she didn't wake.

With one eye on the mirror, Rory glanced ahead and saw the signpost indicating she was within thirty miles of Portland. Good. Or was it? Her phone buzzed and she answered quickly, expecting her mother as, just after crossing into the U.S., Rory had called and hung up rather than leave a message. Darlene knew the number.

"Hey, finally," she said and switched into the slower lane.

"You called me?" Darlene asked, and there was always that hint of worry in her voice. It brought tears to Rory's eyes, but she blinked them back quickly as she held the phone to her ear and scanned for cops. She couldn't afford a ticket now, and being on a cell phone was like waving a red flag if she passed any police cruisers tucked into their hidey-holes along the freeway. Wouldn't that just be the worst? Forced to try to explain herself, to either lie and use her fake ID, or admit that she was Rory Bastian, the missing bride whose disappearance was connected to a murderous assault on the wedding party?

She put the cell on speaker and set it in the cup holder. "I'm in the U.S., darn near the Oregon border. Heading your way," she said. "I think Liam found me."

"What?" Darlene asked, shocked.

Quickly Rory filled her in, talking fast as she realized the damned phone was nearly out of juice. ". . . so I need a place to lie low." The Columbia, a huge river that separated Washington from Oregon, came into view and traffic thickened.

"You could stay with me—"

"No, no. Not your house. God, no. That's the first place he'd come looking, but maybe a nearby motel? Or something, I don't know, about ten or twenty miles from your place?" The more she thought about it, the more she thought some distance would be a good idea. "Like maybe in Albany? Or Eugene—"

"That's a long ways from me."

"I know, but I won't be staying long anyway." She switched into the middle lane, a semi on her right, cars whipping past her on the left.

"I'm sure Liam thinks I'm still in the Seattle area. I only moved this past year and, well, I'd thought he'd moved on." Darlene added tentatively, "He's with Bethany Van Horne, you know."

"Yeah, I know," Rory snapped, hoping she didn't sound as if she cared. "I heard. But he did come looking for me. Somehow. So he might know where you are, too." As much as she wanted to believe differently, she couldn't take that chance. Meeting Darlene was a little risky, but staying at her home would be downright dangerous. She eyed the upcoming span across the river, then glanced at her kid again. Still sleeping. "I think I'll go through Portland and stop somewhere south, maybe around Woodburn."

"I'll meet you there," Darlene said with uncharacteristic decisiveness. "I can be out the door in five. I'll keep my cell on. Call me when you're through Portland."

"Will do." Rory hung up, dropped the phone in the cup holder, and tried to rouse Charlotte again. No luck. She drove across the Glenn Jackson Bridge that connected Washington and Oregon and felt a chill down her spine.

Welcome to Oregon, the state of the Bastian empire. Her jaw tightened as, still in the center lane, she drove just under the speed limit and past the exit to the airport, its control tower visible to the west while Mount Hood loomed to the east, miles up the river. Biting her lip, she intended to skirt Portland, hoping to stay on I-205 until she saw the backup of cars through her bug-spattered windshield.

No good.

She didn't like the prospect of sitting in traffic. No, no, no, she needed to get past Portland and fast. The quickest route seemed to merge onto I-84 and go right through the heart of the city to I-5. "Great," she muttered and eased into the exit lane where she at least could keep moving.

Even if it was through what she thought of as Liam's territory. She touched her toe to the accelerator, then eased back moments later when she realized she was traveling fast enough to alert a cop. No. No mistakes. She had to be careful, especially now.

Rory held her breath as the traffic clogged again as she neared Portland's city center. She crossed the Marquam Bridge, which spanned the Willamette River that divided East from West Portland. The bridge curved downward onto I-5, heading south and offering a display of the skyscrapers standing like windowed sentinels on the banks of the river, the forested cliffs of the West Hills rising behind them. "Oh, God," she whispered and thought of the Portland attractions: Pittock Mansion and the Rose Garden on the upper hills, Voodoo Doughnut, a favorite visitors' haunt in Old Town, the Eastbank Esplanade on the east side of the Willamette. Her heart twisted at the thought of the places she and Liam had planned to explore in this, his town, and she cleared her throat, telling herself that she would be through Portland within minutes.

Good!

Liam might be chasing her in Canada, but being so close to where he lived gave her the heebie-jeebies.

As she began to merge with other traffic on the west side of the bridge, Charlotte cried out, "Mommeeee!"

Glancing into the rearview, Rory spied Charlotte heaved forward against the restraints of her car seat. Her face was white, her eyes wide, her mouth rounded. In a rush, vomit spewed from her mouth.

"Oh, God! Sweetie!" Rory gasped. Frantically, she looked for an exit. "Hang on!" Charlotte was sobbing between bouts of coughing and vomiting.

No, no, no! This can't be happening.

"Mommee—oh!" She threw up again.

Rory was frantic as she cut through traffic, easing past a small white sedan, while the driver, an older man in a baseball cap, laid on his horn. "Sorry!" she said as if the jerk could hear her, and sped off the freeway.

Now what?

She knew little about the city, but saw a sign for Barbur Boulevard and headed in that direction. Now, Charlotte was sobbing hysterically.

"It's gonna be okay," Rory said.

"No it's not!!! Oooh."

Spying a taco shop, Rory sped into the parking lot and hit the brakes, parking at one edge where there were no other cars. Cutting the engine, she threw open the door and jumped out, then disengaged the car seat and gathered her crying, scared daughter close, rocking her from side to side, smelling the sour odor of vomit. "Shh, honey. Shh. You're okay."

But was she?

Oh, God, why hadn't she taken Charlotte to a doctor in Vancouver?

"Shhh." She kept rocking and hugging her daughter, as slowly her daughter's shaking shoulders finally quit quivering and her gasping sobs became brittle, foul-smelling hiccups.

"It's going to be all right," she said, barely conscious of a man and woman stepping from a nearby battered pickup. In their seventies, they cast concerned glances in Rory's direction, glancing over their shoulders as they slowly made their way up to the brightly painted door of the restaurant.

What was wrong with Charlotte? Half a dozen illnesses flew through her brain, all of them horrible. Meningitis? Severe flu? Lyme disease? Something horrible she couldn't even name?

A warm breeze scattered pebbles, dry leaves, and a bit of trash across the dull asphalt. Charlotte sighed heavily against her. This was all so wrong. As much as she needed to escape, to run fast and far, she had to put Charlotte first. And second and third and so on. "Come on, sweetheart," she whispered into her daughter's curly hair. "We're going to see the doctor."

Charlotte protested without much enthusiasm. "No."

"It'll be quick. I promise," she said, setting Charlotte back into her seat.

"Nooooo!" Charlotte wailed more loudly as Rory opened the passenger door and, grabbing some napkins from the stash in her glove box, cleaned off the little amount of vomit that had caught in her daughter's hair. "No doctor!" the little girl cried.

"We need to get you well."

"No!"

Rory tossed the napkin down on the floor with the rest of the mess, then pressed a kiss to her daughter's sweaty forehead. "It's going to be fine. You're going to be fine," she said, buckling Charlotte into her car seat.

The little girl began whimpering and tears streamed down her cheeks.

Rory climbed back into the driver's seat and checked her cell phone for the nearest hospital. She was heading toward the city of Laurelton, which had its own hospital.

For the moment she didn't care about the fact that she was running from the law, that all of her ID was fake, that Liam would find out that he had a child, even if the assassin found her and Charlotte. Not now. All that mattered was that a doctor made sure Charlotte was going to be all right.

Laurelton General was a couple of miles southwest. She aimed her vehicle in that direction.

Nothing tasted sweeter than freedom, Pete DeGrere thought as he tossed back a double bourbon neat and savored the warmth of the alcohol sliding down his throat to hit his welcoming belly. It had been far too long since he'd had a shot . . . make that several . . . but those days and prison were now in the rearview mirror. As he'd heard the gates clang shut behind him, he'd offered a mock salute to the final guard and thought, *Fuck you all, suckas. Pete DeGrere is on the outside. For goddamned good!*

Now, as he contemplated another drink, he eyed the dancer who was going through the motions of making love to a long, shiny pole. Her heart wasn't in it. She wiggled and stripped, acted as if she were really getting off as the music pounded— some kind of tribal beat overlaid with something kind of techno, but she, a bleached blonde, gyrated without much enthusiasm. Her painted-on smile looked as phony as a three-dollar bill, but she had great tits, and, well, Pete didn't much care anyway. He was just grateful to be here, watching her, drinking bourbon, being on the *fucking outside. Yeah!*

The place was pretty empty in the middle of the day. Just a few losers, regulars he guessed, wetting their whistles and maybe privately jerking off in the darkened room. Yup, some of 'em had that glassy-eyed stare that comes with self-stimulation.

Then again, maybe they were all just wasted on bad drugs and weak drinks.

But who cared? He was free. *Free* after nearly five years, which was over eighteen hundred days. What a waste in that shit hole! And for what? They hadn't even got him for the really big stuff.

Holy shit, he thought with a grin he couldn't quite swallow. He glanced around the cavernous room. Yeah, just a few sorry souls, though he felt as if there was something off about the place, got a creepy sensation that he was being watched. But hey, they were all watchers here, right?

Probably just jangled nerves. He'd been on tenterhooks, hoping for, living for, this day.

Less than three hours earlier, he'd boarded a bus and sat in the back, his knee bouncing, his blood singing, anticipation making him sweat. He hadn't made it all the way to Seattle. Instead, somewhere south of Sea-Tac Airport, he'd spied a titty bar, one of those long, low, dark buildings with a bright yellow neon sign of a curvy woman over arched, foreign-looking lettering: The Nile. Yeah, like they were talkin' about that damned river somewhere in Egypt. Over the yellow panels were silhouettes, not just of the girl with the big tits, but some alligators—or were they crocs over in Africa? didn't matter—and some palm trees and a pyramid. Like you were in fuckin' Egypt instead of the good old U.S. of A. Well, everybody had to have a theme, he supposed. So the Nile it was. As long as inside there was strong drinks and a lot of hot women, he didn't give a rat's ass what you called the place.

He hadn't been disappointed. Okay, some of the dancers looked like they'd been around the block more than a few times, but they still looked good to him, horny as he was. And the liquor was smoky and gave him an immediate buzz that he liked. He liked a lot. He'd forgotten how good it felt. Only trouble was, a guy had to go outside for a damned smoke, and

that bugged him. Was nothing sacred anymore? He loved looking at naked boobs through the haze of smoke. Loved letting
the cigarette dangle from his lip and just draw on it and squint
at a twentysomething chick making love to the pole. Got him
hard and aching for a good fuck.

Shit, he'd settle for a bad one right now. As long as he'd been
away, what did it matter, good or bad? As long as it was pussy,
he was in.

He motioned for another drink and a waitress in heels that
elevated her at least four more inches quick-stepped his way.
One eye still on his surroundings, Pete said, "Another," mo-
tioning with a finger to his drained glass.

"Sure." She smiled brightly and he almost thought she was
coming on to him, then realized it was because she was hoping
for a healthy tip. Forget it. If he was giving out some of his few
dollars, it was going to be to stuff them into that tiny scrap covering her twat. Yeah, that G-string was a little bit of nothin',
but it did manage to conceal her most private of parts. He wondered, knowing she was shaved or waxed or whatever, if the
thatch of curls that had once been at the juncture of those long
legs was anywhere close to the pale blond color of the mane of
curls surrounding her Kewpie-doll face.

He figured not.

As his fresh drink arrived, he saw a shadow move in the back
corner, behind the stage. Probably the manager or a stagehand
of sorts. Right.

So why did he feel as if he was being watched?

*Shit, you probably are. This place is probably crawling with
hidden cameras.*

So what?

He was keeping his nose clean.

At least so far. His sister had said she'd lined up employment
of sorts for him, something about being a neighborhood handy-
man. That was good. He liked it. What better way to case a

joint than to be hired to clean up the yard, or fix a fence, or un-
plug a toilet? He chortled, low in his throat. Yeah, it would
work out just fine.

Blondie's music stopped and she sashayed her tired but tight
butt off the stage. While there was a break in the action, he decided to go out for a smoke. After an hour and a half of staring
and drinking, he definitely felt a buzz. More than a buzz. He
was on the verge of being shit-canned drunk, but he slid off his
stool, hiked up his pants, patted his breast pocket to assure
himself that his trusty pack of Winstons was still tucked safely
away, then eased his way outside. He had to be careful about
how he walked through the tables, didn't want anyone to know
he couldn't hold his liquor like he used to.

Shit, he already needed to take a piss.

"Candy ass," he muttered under his breath at himself and
stepped outside to the cool of the evening. Maybe he'd just pee
outside. If no one was around . . .

He felt a presence, the same kind of tingling against the back
of his neck that he would feel on the inside when Fuck-Face
Frank used to troll through the cells at night. Fuck-Face,
named due to the fact that his features were messed up from a
knife fight and botched surgery, was a favorite of the guards
and had his freedom to wander the corridors but had never
taken an interest in Pete, thank the gods.

A glance around showed that he was alone in the back lot
where the asphalt was a crumbling layer of dust over the potholes. A solitary tree grew on the other side of a high fence of
rotting boards. The fir offered some shade and two Dumpsters
gave him a little privacy, so he lit up, took a deep drag, and with
the Winston still between his lips, sauntered over to the man-
sized space between the two huge, smelly bins and unzipped
his fly. Sighing, smoke filtering from his nostrils, the end of his
cig burning, he let his bladder release. He still had a good stream,
he was thinking when he heard something—a footfall?—be-

hind him. Oh, shit. He'd be caught for indecent exposure or some other penny ante—

And then breath against his nape.

Warm.

He started to turn, to look over his shoulder, when he felt the blade. Swift and sharp, slipped smoothly between his ribs.

What?

"'Bye, asshole," a harsh voice whispered as he started to shriek and the knife, pulled out of his back, was slashed across his throat and blood—oh, shit, *his* blood—sprayed the rusted, graffiti-marred Dumpster in a vibrant red splatter.

He tried to scream but failed. He caught a glimpse of dark sunglasses and his own horrified reflection in the gogglelike lenses. Then he fell forward, his body sliding down one of the Dumpster's metal sides, his cigarette expelled, his life ebbing as he hit the dirty, crumbling asphalt with a bone-jarring thud.

Chapter 10

The hospital ER was half full when Rory ran inside, holding her listless child in her arms. Cold tears of fear had collected on her cheeks, and it was all she could do to remain calm as she cradled Charlotte in shaking arms and related her symptoms.

"She's unconscious," Rory choked out in a waiting area half filled with patients and relatives hanging out on the worn sofas and chairs.

"We'll get her in a room," the woman at the desk assured Rory as she swept her gaze to the listless child. Pert, in her fifties, with short, gray hair and oversized glasses, the receptionist exuded efficiency. Good.

"When? *Now?* You're not going to make me wait, are you?" She heard the rising hysteria in her voice but didn't care.

"There's a lot of summer flu going around this year," a woman from somewhere behind her in the waiting room said loud enough in a nasal tone for all to hear. Rory expected the remark was intended for her, something in the woman's tone implying "wait your damned turn."

Rory blocked her ears to it. She needed help and now. She

was scared she would be left to wait with the others. Should she leave? Find an urgent care clinic? Somewhere that would provide a quicker service? What if she were stuck here for hours and Charlotte got worse, only double-doors away from medical help but left to wait for hours as others, perhaps trauma cases or accident victims, were rushed in ahead of her.

Stick it out. This will be faster than trying to locate another facility. And though you're loathe to give up any indication of where you are, you'll have to offer up your insurance and your credit card. This is Charlotte's health, maybe even her life. You can't mess this up. No matter what the consequences.

"My daughter needs help now," she said to the woman at the desk, and she was ushered to a desk where she sat down and another hospital worker, a petite Asian woman with kind eyes and fingers that typed at the speed of light took her information.

She gave the woman Charlotte's name and said hers was Heather Johnson. Her heart was hammering as she watched her type in her Point Roberts address and then take her insurance card from an American carrier and her credit card for copying. She rocked Charlotte gently, half expecting the police or some member of the Bastian family to burst through the emergency room doors, throw her to the carpeted floor, and cuff her in a wild, guns-drawn arrest.

Dear. God.

She silently counted to ten and took a deep breath.

Remember: You're Heather Johnson now. Heather Johnson. Not Aurora Abernathy Bastian. All your ID and Charlotte's are Johnson.

"You can fill out the rest later," the woman said, handing Rory back her information, which Rory slipped into her purse.

"Thanks," Rory said as a male nurse appeared from behind the very doors and the inner sanctum Rory had thought would be barred to her. Bristling with determination and speed, he was thin and tan, with freckles and neatly shorn brown hair. He spied Rory, still holding limp, unresponsive Charlotte.

"I'm getting a gurney," he said, bustling down the hall, only to return in a very short time, transferring Charlotte from Rory's arms to the collapsible bed. He pushed Charlotte back through the automatically opening double doors with Rory following behind.

From somewhere behind her that same woman's shrill voice said, "Now wait a darned second—"

But Rory didn't look over her shoulder as the doors swung shut. She was relieved and worried. No one would have responded so quickly, or put Charlotte at the head of the line, unless there was a reason to worry. Oh. Dear. Jesus. Again all those horrible childhood illnesses loomed and whistled through her head. Charlotte had been immunized, yes, but . . . what about serious influenza, or some other deadly virus, or God only knew. Inside she went cold as death. The nurse swept aside the curtain to a cubicle. "I'm Nurse Tom," he said to Charlotte, then glanced at Rory. "And you're Heather Johnson. This is Charlotte Johnson, yes?"

"Yes."

"What is your daughter's date of birth?" He was standing at the computer monitor that swung from an arm attached to a pole placed near the hospital bed. On the screen Rory read her daughter's name.

As Charlotte was transferred to the bed, Rory told him Charlotte's birth date, the most wonderful day of her life, she thought.

"Got it." He double-checked a small ID bracelet that he wrapped over Charlotte's tiny wrist, then started taking her vital signs while Rory silently watched and mentally climbed the walls. *Please let her be okay*, she prayed.

"Hey, Charlotte, can you hear me, honey?" the nurse said, bending over her. Dear Lord, she appeared so little. So frail.

Talking softly, explaining what he was doing, he started the exam as Charlotte lay on the bed. The curtain whispered, billowing as another patient was admitted to a nearby stall.

"Char-baby?" Rory said. "Sweetheart? We're at the hospital now. This is Nurse Tom. Honey?"

Charlotte's eyelids fluttered and she mewled, "Mommy?"

"Right here, sweetheart. I'm right here." She clasped Charlotte's little hand, wanting to cry for joy that her daughter was coming round.

"Hey, Charlotte. How're ya feeling?" he asked as the little girl regarded him warily. He plucked a chart of faces from the wall. "See these? This is about pain. The smiling face, she doesn't feel any pain at all, but these other guys—" He touched each successive visage where the expressions turned a little grimmer and more pained with each representation.

"That one," she said, indicating the last grimacing face with a teardrop sliding down its flat countenance. "That one." Rory hoped not.

"Okay." He made another note on the computer. "Just sit tight. The doctor will be right here," he said briskly as a horrid racking cough erupted from the other side of the curtain.

"Wait a minute. What do you think it is?" Rory asked as Nurse Tom started for the exit.

"Dr. McMannis can make that determination."

"Is it the flu, or . . . ?"

At that moment the doctor arrived, sweeping the curtain back as she stepped toward Charlotte. She wore silver-framed glasses and her hair was in a messy bun. Her face was long with a very prominent nose, but her eyes were sharp with intelligence. "You the mother?"

"Yes."

"There's a little more paperwork to fill out at the front desk."

What? No! In her mind's eye she saw the police, en masse,

weapons drawn, waiting for her on the other side of those formidable double doors. Her heart started to pound. "I've got papers to fill out in my purse."

"Ah. Did they give you the HIPAA form?"

Rory was already searching through the papers. "I don't see it."

"Mommy, don't go."

"I'm right here, baby," she said as the nurse gave a quick report about Charlotte's vitals, then after a quick bevy of questions, left. Dr. McMannis was holding a stethoscope to Charlotte's chest. The little girl's eyes had closed again, her breathing shallow. She looked so sick. So damned sick. Rory's throat closed. She said to the doctor, "She just started throwing up. And now she's . . . asleep, again, or . . . unconscious . . ."

"Was the vomiting the first symptom?"

"No . . . she's been fighting this for a few days."

The doctor turned her attention on Rory. Sharp eyes narrowed a bit behind her lenses. "I thought it was the flu, I guess." Rory felt put on the spot.

"We'll run tests. I want to make sure this isn't bacterial."

Bacterial . . . Rory didn't like the sound of that. "You mean like . . . meningitis?" she asked faintly.

"And strep throat, among others. But it could be viral. Could be influenza. We'll give her a swab test, but I'm going to admit her."

She regarded Charlotte once more, her face tight. "I'm going to admit her. Keep her under observation for a while. You need to fill out the HIPAA."

That thought stopped her cold. Overnight? Charlotte was that bad. "I don't want to leave her."

"I'll have it brought to you."

Then she was gone in a whoosh of curtains and Rory sat in the plastic chair beside Charlotte's bed, only letting go of her hand to finish filling out the forms she'd been given. She wanted to believe this was nothing more than a bad case of the flu, and that Charlotte was going to be her bouncy self by morning.

She looked at Charlotte, alarmed at her face that was now, after being wan and pale as she'd thrown up, red. Hot-looking.

The Asian woman who had helped her at the admissions desk threw back the curtains and shot Rory a brief smile as she brought her the HIPAA form and collected the other pages Rory had filled out. Rory got as far as *Aur* when she caught herself up short. What trick of the brain had caused her to almost write her real name? She quickly scribbled out those letters and wrote *Heather Johnson* on the HIPAA form, then exhaled slowly as the woman swept the page up, adding it to the others as she disappeared back through the curtain.

Holy moley. It was as if being in the Portland area, so near the Bastians, had scrambled her brain.

A few minutes later Nurse Tom was back with Charlotte, giving her a nose swab.

"Do you think it's flu?" Rory asked anxiously.

"We'll know in about thirty minutes."

"Okay."

Dr. McMannis returned as Nurse Tom left with the swab. The doctor stared down at Charlotte who was unresponsive again. After a few minutes, McMannis said, "We're going to take her to the ICU."

An icicle of fear stabbed Rory's heart. "What?" she asked faintly.

"We've had a particularly bad strain of influenza going around. I just want to see her through these next few hours."

"Okay . . ."

Charlotte was whisked away and Rory followed after her in a daze. Charlotte was taken into the ICU and Rory was asked to remain behind while she was being initially admitted. A gaggle of different nurses and doctors kept passing through and Rory stood outside the doors, numb with fear. She walked over to an alcove with two chairs and a small table with several dog-eared magazines, but she couldn't read. Was unable to concentrate on the two-month-old woman's magazine she picked up and flipped through. Words swam in front of her vision. The celebrity interviews, diet secrets, "summer" recipes, and guaranteed ways to sexually satisfy your man, held no interest. She saw a word puzzle, something she used to do. With shaking hands, she searched in her purse for a pen to try and work the crossword puzzle. But her brain was disengaged and she had to open every compartment within her bag. That's when she saw the packet. A thick envelope she didn't remember stashing in a zippered pocket. She pulled it out and slipped open the flap to spy dozens of hundred-dollar bills, some U.S., some Canadian. There had to be five thousand dollars in the packet, maybe more.

Her heart nearly stopped.

How in the world . . .

Uncle Kent. And probably Maude, too. They had always been her support from the moment Charlotte had arrived, and they'd paid all of her maternity bills. Tears suddenly swam in her eyes and she stuffed the thick envelope back into her purse, then looked up and saw that no one in the waiting area appeared to be watching her.

But then she'd thought she'd been safe in Port Roberts, and look how that had turned out.

Not that it mattered. Nothing did. Nothing but Charlotte. The whisper of a thought glided through her brain and it cut deep.

You should tell Liam about Charlotte. He's her father. He deserves to know. What if the unthinkable happens? You have to call him.

Opening her bag again, she intended to reach inside and pluck out her phone, dial Liam, and tell him to hurry to Laurelton General.

But then sanity took hold and she dropped the burner phone back into the depths of her purse.

Not yet.

She bit her lip.

Maybe not ever.

Mick was just calling it a day, standing up from his desk, stretching the kinks from his back and wondering how his partner, Gabe Hernandez, was doing on that divorce case he was working on. Hernandez had damn near gotten smacked in the head by a cast-iron skillet thrown by his client's wife, the last Mick had heard.

He twisted his neck and heard a satisfying pop as the tension that had gathered all day released. He was about to grab his jacket when the door to his office burst open and Shanice came blasting inside, all skinny jeans and fury. Her eyes were wild, about twice their normal size, and she was holding her cell phone away from her as if it were poisoned.

"What?" Mick asked sharply, rounding the desk, ready for battle. He didn't know where it was coming from, but something was definitely wrong and he wasn't a man to wait like a sitting duck while it unfolded.

"That was my friend Jenny at Seattle PD," she said in a strangled voice, then threw up her hands in despair. "I can't believe it. I just . . . can't believe it!" She was beyond upset. Waaay beyond.

"What?"

"Jesus, Mick . . ." She struggled for a moment. Stared at the ceiling tiles and shook her head for a long second, then calmed slightly, leveled her gaze on him. "Pete DeGrere is dead."

"*What?* No." He thought he hadn't heard right, but her expression said it all.

"Dead? How?"

"Murdered! Someone got to him first." Her fist balled and he thought she might punch the desk, the window, or him.

"Who?"

"Don't know. He went to a strip club, The Nile—it's a strip club not far from Sea-Tac. He must've gone straight there, as soon as he was out. I thought he might do that, but didn't know where he would land." She was punishing herself, angry that she hadn't followed him from the prison; Mickelson could read it in her eyes. "Anyway, he had a few drinks, watched the show, then he went outside for a smoke or to relieve himself behind the building and there, with his damned pants down, literally, somebody took him out. Slit his throat. The owner found him when he went out for a smoke. Body was still warm."

Mick returned to the far side of his desk to sink back into his chair, the springs shrieking in protest under his weight.

"He couldn't have been out more than a few hours." He could see she was having a hell of a time processing as she shoved her cell into the pocket of her gray jacket, a favorite she'd tossed over a black T-shirt.

"Jesus." Mick thought about it. "Was he rolled? Someone thought he had money?"

"Jenny didn't say. Probably hasn't figured that out yet. Maybe he spent everything he had on Boopsy, or Ginger, or whoever the hell was hugging that damned strip pole."

Mick's cop sense was kicking in—that, and logic. He answered his own question. "No, they were waiting for him. Somebody didn't want him talking."

"But he talks all the time. That's what he does ... did. He doesn't know enough to keep his mouth shut ... didn't know ... aww, shit." She finally dropped into her favorite chair facing his desk, and some of the color had returned to her face. "I shoulda planted myself outside that gate today. Got to Pete first. I knew it. Damn. But, you know, I thought I had time to catch up with him."

"I know. At his sister's."

She threw herself to her feet and walked to the window to stare through the dirty panes at the building next door.

"Don't beat yourself up. I agreed. And believe me, I wanted to nail his ass so bad I could taste it." That was true. He'd been savoring the thought of grilling Pete "Mr. Big Talk" DeGrere. Now it was too late. He scratched at his chin and thought. He couldn't just kick himself; he had to find another way to get the information he needed. "No asking him about the assault on the Bastian wedding anymore."

"Damn."

Mick opened his bottom drawer and dug out the information he'd copied from the police files on the Bastian case. Not strictly by the rules, but he'd done it anyway. He never planned to quit trying to solve the crime, so he'd taken his notes on the case with him when he'd left the force. "We need to grill everyone in DeGrere's cell block; see what they know. Pete could have given up more info than we've already learned."

"Most of it BS."

"We'll have to sift through it." It would have been so much easier and more interesting to interrogate DeGrere, to find out how much was boast or bravado and how much was just plain bullshit. "Somebody knows something. Not all information began and ended with DeGrere."

"Okay. Right. It's not as good as the horse's mouth, but I'm gonna check with his cell mate again and Frankie Rubino. He said he knew something before, then shut down in the interview."

"Rubino," he repeated, recalling the lifer. "Fuck-face."

"The very same."

"I don't know. It's hard to trust a guy with a nickname like that." The con wasn't known to be accurate, not all the time. "He just likes to dick around with police."

"I hate to tell ya, but we're not cops anymore."

He nodded. Glancing over at the dying African violet located on a file cabinet near the window—a gift from a potential girlfriend who hadn't panned out—he studied its withering leaves. Like this case, he thought, dying no matter how many times he tossed the dregs of his coffee on the damned thing.

He didn't have much faith that Shanice would learn anything more than last time the man with the horrible scars was interviewed, but he said anyway, "What the hell. Give it a try. Pete did love to talk, and Rubino always has his ears open. If Pete didn't confide in him, maybe Frankie overheard him bragging to another con." Mick gave Shanice a slight smile. "And Frankie does like the ladies. Maybe you can pry something close to the truth out of him."

She snorted.

"Somebody on the inside must know if he shot up the wedding and killed Aaron Stemple. Pete couldn't keep that to himself."

"If?" she asked, catching the small admission as she turned away from the ugly view to face him. "*If* he shot up the wedding?"

"I think he's good for it, but we still haven't established any kind of motive. But I'm willing to bet my favorite dog that somebody knows how Pete was involved, why he was in the area. Pete was always after other people's money, so it's a good bet he struck up a deal with somebody else, the man behind the man."

"So it comes down to who was the target. The bride? Aaron? Liam Bastian? Maybe all three." She gave him a sidelong look. "Think Harold Stemple had anything to do with this?"

Mick didn't immediately respond. When he'd first been dogging DeGrere, he'd thought there was something in the fact that Pete and Stemple had wound up in the same prison. Mick had floated the idea that DeGrere's life could be at risk because Harold Stemple might want to avenge his son Aaron's death, and Pete was certainly a suspect in the killing. But there had never been a trace of animosity between the two men, as far as was reported, so more credence was added to the theory that DeGrere was not the shooter, that he'd just been around the wrong area at the wrong time, a theory Mick had dismissed. He *wanted* DeGrere to be the doer, hated the braggart, and it would have just made things easier. As for Harold Stemple? He was a penny ante crook whose foray into home invasion was a complete bungle, costing him twenty years. His gun had gone off and taken a chunk out of the woman of the house's thigh, and the husband had gotten the drop on him. There was talk that Stemple had come with another man who'd never entered the house or been seen—speculation running high that the second man was his son Everett—but that had never been proven. Neither Stemple nor DeGrere was the brightest bulb in the fixture, but Harold had managed to keep his mouth shut about his accomplice, if there was one, a trick Pete DeGrere had never managed.

"Seattle PD'll be talking to Stemple," Mick said. "If Stemple had Pete killed because of Aaron, they'll figure it out." That bugged him more than a little. He still thought of the Bastian wedding assault as *his* case.

"Who would Stemple hire to get that done?" She was walking now, back to her chair and thinking aloud. "His surviving son? Everett?"

Mick grunted an assent. His thoughts touched on Aurora Abernathy Bastian, visualizing Everett Stemple's stepsister, the runaway bride with the lush red hair and lovely smile. He'd only seen her in pictures, ones he'd gotten off the Internet and from the Bastian family while he was still with the department.

Still, he understood the attraction, all right. The girl just had a face that made you want to know her, a beauty that was more about character than facial structure.

Shanice said, "We need to know if Stemple's involved and this is about Aaron, or if it's something else entirely. It's not random that Pete DeGrere's dead on his first day out of prison. I won't believe that."

"Even Pete didn't have that bad of luck."

"If he killed Aaron . . ."

She didn't finish the thought, just tightened her lips. She'd always taken Aaron Stemple's death hard, a personal connection she'd never quite explained to him. Mick said, "You can bet whoever killed Pete did it to keep the truth from coming out or for revenge, or both. Bastian and his son Liam are lucky to be alive. Maybe one of them was the target, or both of them, and maybe they're holding a grudge."

"Or maybe the target was someone else, someone who was missed." She was resting a jean-clad hip against the corner of his desk.

"Maybe, but let's stick with the three that were in the bullets' first trajectory. They were all in the aisle."

"So were Derek Bastian and the officiant. And Aurora should have been there."

"But Geoffrey shouldn't have been. He was seated next to his wife and had just walked up to talk to Liam and find out what was going on because the bride was late."

They'd been over it a thousand times. Mick was inclined to knock out Derek, Geoffrey, and the officiant from the list of targets. The preacher and Derek had been farther back when the shooting began, Geoffrey just walking up the aisle. The crime scene techs had proven what had been obvious, that the shooter had aimed for the aisle area, before the spray had widened in an arc into the guests seated at the ceremony. It had been the police department's theory that the arc of bullets was an afterthought, that the shooter had only moved the gun after he'd hit his target, trying to make it seem more like a wild, random attack. Or that someone or something had made him change direction. Had his arm been hit? Had he found another target? Was the fact that the bride hadn't appeared the reason the attack wasn't more focused? Or did he want to kill or maim as many as possible?

No one knew.

The idea that Rory Abernathy Bastian was the target still had some merit. Everyone had expected her to come in on Aaron's arm when the Bridal March began. Maybe the shooter just had a premature ejaculation of his firearm, saw Aaron and assumed she was there, though a calm assassin wouldn't have been fooled. A billowing white gown would have been hard to miss. He scratched behind his ear in frustration. And then there was the fact that she'd run . . . after a struggle where someone had been wounded, possibly seriously wounded, though no one had shown up at any of the local hospitals requiring stitches that couldn't be explained. "The blood on Rory Abernathy's wedding dress wasn't hers," Mick mused.

"And it wasn't Pete DeGrere's. He was picked up after the convenience store robbery and had no injuries, and it wasn't a match anyway."

He didn't know where Rory Abernathy Bastian fit in to the picture. What had she run into that had stopped her walking down the aisle? Had it saved her from death? Or was Aaron the target, or one of the Bastians?

"Maybe Geoff Bastian was the target," Mick said. "He didn't want that do-over wedding. It was all his wife's idea. Keeping up with the Joneses. Bastian damn near blamed her for what happened to him. Like it was her fault he got hit."

"It put him in a wheelchair, so he lashed out. But he sure got over it."

"How do you know?"

"They're still married, aren't they?"

Mick grunted. There was no accounting for why people stayed together. "All right. DeGrere's dead and that's a fact, so what have we got? Harold Stemple as a prison inmate, the guy whose son was killed during the shooting. Aurora Abernathy still missing, Stemple's stepdaughter, blood on her wedding gown that she ditched before disappearing. Somebody waiting for DeGrere to get out so he could kill him. Picking him off at a nearby strip club, one of the first places he would go as soon as he was out."

Shanice shifted, reached into her pocket to retrieve her phone and glance at its small screen. A text, he guessed. She slipped the cell back into her pocket. "Deon," she explained. "Supposed to meet him in half an hour."

Mick was still rolling the case over in his mind. "It sure as hell would make sense that Harold Stemple's somehow involved with DeGrere and the wedding shooting. There are connections there. Maybe the police'll figure it out and finally lay it on Pete." *Or not.*

"That what you want?" Shanice asked.

"Sure."

"Bullshit, Mick. You want this collar yourself. You know you do."

"I'm no longer a cop. You just made that very fine point."

"But being a cop isn't about just wearing a badge. You're still one. Yes, you are. Where it counts." She pointed to her heart as she opened the door. "I'm gonna head back to my place and meet Deon. If you get hit by the answer, you let me know." She sketched a wave, then headed into the reception area where her desk was located, but she didn't stop there and made her way to the hall, where the door banged closed behind her.

Mick sat at his desk for another hour, staring into space, thinking about Pete DeGrere. Poor dumb ass. Sure, he'd wanted to nail the man for the Bastian wedding shooting, but someone had ended his life first, which really pissed Mick off. Now, he was going to have to come at the crime from another angle, but the only thing he knew for sure was that this morning he'd had one unsolved crime that kept him awake at night.

Now it looked like he was going to have two.

"Rory."

From her chair in the hospital waiting area near the ICU, Rory glanced up and saw her mother hurrying down the hall toward her, Darlene's Birkenstocks hardly making a sound. Mom's latest style was apparently Earth Mother as she wore a flowing, printed dress that fell to her ankles, her hair having grown out long and gray and currently clipped away from her face. It was much better than the spiky heels and skintight dresses she'd worn when she'd first started dating Harold Stemple, but, as ever, Rory thought it would be nice to have a mother who just fit in with everyone else's dress code for once.

"How's our girl?" Darlene asked, hazarding a quick look toward the closed doors to the ICU.

"It's the flu."

"Well, that's good, isn't it?" Darlene asked cautiously.

"A bad strain. I don't know. I just saw Charlotte and she's . . . the same," Rory choked out. As she tried to appear calm, to hide the fear in her heart, she added as much for herself as Darlene, "Charlotte's okay. She's going to be okay."

With worried eyes, Darlene settled into the chair next to Rory's. "Of course she is." She clasped Rory's hand and squeezed hard.

The action brought tears to Rory's eyes. She'd learned from listening to the nurses that another Portland hospital had lost a three-year-old boy to the flu that morning. And two elderly adults, a man and a woman, had passed as well. In the last twenty-four hours.

"You need to come stay with me," Darlene said briskly, and blinked behind the lenses of her glasses.

"I won't leave Charlotte."

"Yes. I know. What I meant is that you both need to come stay with me as soon as Charlotte's ready."

"I just want her well."

"Yes, of course." She patted their clasped hands, then looked around and finally stood up, releasing her grip. "We need to talk to someone."

As if on cue, the door to the Intensive Care Unit opened mechanically and one of the nurses, a petite woman with large doe-like eyes and a quick smile, slipped through. Her gaze found Rory as she stood. As she approached, her smile brightened. "Ms. Johnson?" she said, as they'd been introduced earlier, "Charlotte's awake and asking for you."

Rory was already on her way to the doors, but when Darlene tried to come in with Rory, she was detained. "Just her mother for now." The nurse was polite but firm.

Inside the unit, patients' beds spread out in a semicircle around a nurses' station, privacy curtains separating each case, but each bed visible to the attending staff.

Rory hastened to her daughter's side. Oh, God, again she was struck with how small her daughter was. There had been talk of moving her to the children's wing, but so far, that hadn't happened. Hopefully she would be released before being transferred.

"Hey, honey," she said softly as she neared.

Charlotte's flushed face scared Rory, but her daughter was awake enough to track her mother's approach and complain that she didn't feel good. "I want to go home."

"Me, too, honey, and we will," Rory lied. Where the hell was "home" now? Certainly not in Point Roberts, the only home Charlotte had ever known. But the fact that Charlotte was thinking about leaving and could voice her complaints was an improvement.

"When?"

"As soon as the doctors say so. Since you're getting better, it will be sooner."

"Now," Charlotte said a little crossly, but Rory was able to placate the little girl, and as she smoothed her daughter's hair and held back tears, she watched Charlotte start to nod off again. She was allowed to stay until Charlotte fell back asleep. "She's stable," the nurse said, when Rory pressed her. "We're just not taking any chances." The pinned-on smile had become smaller, the nurse's dark eyes more serious.

"I know others have died of the flu," Rory said, her throat hot.

The nurse sighed, her face suddenly a mask of empathy. "But your daughter's doing well."

"Can I stay in here with her?"

"Yes"—the nurse was nodding—"but your other guest isn't allowed."

Rory had dropped Darlene from her mind. Now she looked at Charlotte, then at the nurse. "I'll be right back."

Outside the doors, Darlene was pacing. When they opened and Rory appeared, Darlene shot to her daughter's side. "How is she?"

"Better."

"I want to see her."

"I know, Mom, but right now it's impossible." Rory explained that no one but Rory could visit at this time.

"Are they keeping her? How long? Why is she in the ICU? Shouldn't she be in a children's ward or something? Don't I count as a family member, for God's sake?" Darlene barraged Rory with questions she couldn't answer, and then as if finally realizing her daughter had told her as much information as there was, she suddenly stopped. "When was the last time you ate or slept? You look like hell."

"Thanks, Mom. And last night. For both."

"For the love of Saint . . . come on! Let's get some food in you," Darlene said. "There's gotta be a cafeteria somewhere."

"I'm not hungry."

"Well, you need to eat. We'll share something. Come on. Then you can go back to Charlotte and I'll head home." She paused at the desk in front of the double doors, explained where they were headed, and after getting sketchy directions, shepherded Rory toward a bank of elevators situated near floor-to-ceiling windows overlooking the parking lot.

Rory let herself be dragged to the cafeteria, where she picked up a tray and, following her mother along the counter of offered selections, she picked up a salad and ordered a bowl of soup from a bored-looking cafeteria woman who ladled the chowder without any expression. Darlene, shunning Rory's choices, picked up a processed turkey sandwich on wheat toast. Darlene paid for both their meals at a register.

Rory had argued about Darlene paying the bill, but gave up when her mother inserted her debit card before Rory could utter any further protest. Nonetheless, Rory couldn't help feeling guilty when she thought of the neat stack of bills Uncle Kent had slipped into her purse. She just didn't have the heart or gumption to argue.

"If I can't feed my own daughter, what kind of mother am I?"

After they sat at a semiprivate table with a window view of the hospital's ER portico, Darlene wolfed down every last bite of her sandwich while Rory picked at her meal. The soup and salad proved to be mediocre at best. And truthfully, she had little appetite, while Darlene tore into the pickle that had come with her turkey-on-wheat.

"I just wish I could get my eyes on that little girl."

"It's not going to happen, Mom. Hospital policy."

"Oh, drat. Fine." Darlene pushed crumbs around the plate

and shot Rory a look from under her lashes. "You gonna tell Liam?"

"Mom. You know what the situation is! No." But hadn't she considered letting him know?

"Okay. Okay. Well, really not okay." Her eyes met Rory's. "It's just that Charlotte is his daughter and, well . . . how are you going to pay for this?"

Oh. God. Rory felt the back of her neck tighten. "I'm not dropping this news on him so he can pay for it!"

"Oh, goodness. So dramatic." Darlene rolled her eyes.

"You know what happened at the wedding! I have to keep Charlotte away from them!"

"The Bastians? Darling, you don't know that. I've gone along with your secret all these years, but I've never really understood it. Maybe it's time to rethink this. You're here in Portland already. Maybe you should stay, start a life here."

"I have to protect Charlotte. That man who attacked me specifically threatened her." She pushed her bowl aside, remains of the soup slopping onto the table. "I *can't* let them know about her. Someone threatened her life and she hadn't even been born yet!" She'd kept her voice down, aware of people at other tables nearby, but her hands were flat on the table, anger and fear tensing every muscle. "I just wish I knew who the hell he was."

"We don't. But we know who he *wasn't*. Right? Harold was in prison at the time." Her lips pinched. "And . . . and it wasn't Everett—"

"We don't know that," she put in quickly.

Darlene rambled over her. "—nor Aaron, poor boy." She shook her head sadly. "It's not Everett. He's turned over a new leaf. Married a good woman. I told you that."

Rory snorted. "Married a good woman," she repeated sarcastically.

"And of course it wasn't any of the Bastians, either," Darlene went on. "They were the ones under fire, for God's sake." She fussed in her purse for a tissue and dabbed at the perspiration that had gathered on her forehead. Darlene never liked to talk about the wedding. No matter how she defended the Stemples, Rory knew she worried that the events had somehow been caused by their family. "So, let's talk about something else. You know I can sense things, that I have good instincts. I know you're skeptical, but sometimes I can feel what's going to happen. You've seen it. So I went to Laurie and she said—"

"Mom, please. No psycho bullshit right now."

"You always say that, Rory." She sighed.

"I can't listen to it. I've got to think of what's best for Charlotte and I don't want the Bastians involved."

"Well, they would help you financially, that's all I'm saying. And, as I said, Liam *is* Charlotte's father."

"I know, Mom! Believe me, I know." Rory wanted to press her hands to her temples. "You said you were going to help me. This is not the help I was looking for."

Darlene tossed her hands up and then back down again in annoyance.

Rory added, "If you really want to help me, then make Charlotte well, right now. Let her be her usual bubbly self. Abracadabra and then we can go!"

"Rory," she muttered, disgusted.

"Then, Mom, don't take this the wrong way, but please, *please*, shut up with the psycho stuff. Okay?"

Darlene pressed her lips together, looked at her daughter, then snapped her head in a nod. She'd never liked it when Rory used "psycho" instead of "psychic."

Rory looked away from her mother, pulling herself out of her anger. It was no good getting mad at Darlene for her foibles.

At the cash register, a thin, fortysomething man with longish hair was buying a cup of coffee. He reminded her of someone, and that in turn reminded her of her sightings of Everett in

Point Roberts. "When was the last time you saw Everett?" she asked.

"I don't know."

"I told you, I thought I saw him once or twice, like he was following me."

"I know," she said again. "And Rory, he shouldn't have come into your room, that is true. But it was never as bad as you made it out in high school."

"Mom . . ." Rory warned.

"I'm just saying. People change. Everett is traveling his true path now. He's a Scorpio, and scorpions sometimes have to sting themselves to death before they—"

"Mom!"

"—see what to do."

"I don't think people do change," Rory muttered, pushing back her chair. "I think Everett was in Point Roberts. And I'm sick of being scared."

"You're not going to confront him, are you?" She looked horrified.

"I don't know. I don't even know where he is, and no . . . I mean, I just want Charlotte well!"

She headed out of the cafeteria and heard Darlene's rushed, muffled footsteps hurrying to catch up. As Rory slammed her palm on the elevator call button, her mother said, "I guess I'd better go," and scrounged through her purse for her keys. "I do have some errands to run . . . an appointment I shouldn't miss, and since I can't see Charlotte . . ." Retrieving her keys, she sighed loudly, then said, "Listen, I'll call you later. Don't be mad. Please."

"I'm not mad. I'm . . . scared," Rory admitted and sagged against the wall.

Darlene blinked rapidly and bit her lip, then suddenly as the elevator dinged, announcing the car's arrival, she blurted, "Charlotte's going to be fine. I know you don't want to hear it, but

Laurie read your horoscope and everything's going to be straightened out, and . . . and good. Yes, good. By August seventeenth."

"I won't hold my breath."

"Oh, darling, you'll see."

Then, blowing a kiss as the elevator doors whooshed open, Darlene bustled away, pushing open a side door while Rory stepped inside the waiting elevator car. She couldn't worry about her mother with her whacked-out psychic mumbo jumbo. All she could be concerned with at the moment was Charlotte.

And then there was the problem with Liam.

Darlene's words, like the haunting moans of a ghost, swept through her mind over and over: *It's just that Charlotte is his daughter . . .*

Chapter 11

Thursday morning Liam wheeled his Tahoe into the circular drive outside his parents' house. He felt a little clearer about the future despite his disappointment at not finding Rory. A good night's sleep at his condo, six hours straight after he'd thrown himself onto the bed, then a quick shower this morning, had put things right. He'd then met with Les Steele at the Hallifax work site. They were moving ahead with the project but hadn't replaced the broken windows yet, though all the replacement panes had been ordered. "Kids," Steele had said, staring at the vandalism.

"Let's hope." A random attack was less complicated than some kind of coordinated neighborhood uprising, or worse.

Now Liam was on his way to meet with his father, checking in because Geoff chafed if he wasn't kept abreast of every detail of all the Bastian businesses. Normally, Liam dreaded these meetings. His father's seething anger was just below the surface at all times, but today Liam figured he could handle the old man. He felt better than he had in a while. Rory could run away from here to eternity for all he cared. He would divorce her in absentia and get on with his life.

Time to move on.

As he neared the house, he spotted a dark green Mercedes SUV parked across the drive in such a way that no other car was able to get past it. "Great." His sister's wheels. He glanced at his watch and frowned. It was pretty early in the day for Viv to be here. Liam was the early riser in the family. Viv tended to roll out of bed sometime after ten.

Usually.

Before he could even climb from the Tahoe, Vivian herself came flying out the front door, as if she'd been waiting for him. "There you are!" she cried, stopping about a yard in front of him. She was in black running gear with a teal stripe up the side of her leggings, her blond-brown hair banded into a ponytail, her blue eyes full of accusations, her mouth sullen. "We've been waiting for you."

"We?"

"Where've you been?"

"At work," he said, stepping around her and striding toward the house.

She hurried to catch up to him. "I mean before this morning, asshole. You were out there looking for *her*. That's what Derek said, and I, of course, defended you, and said 'Oh, no. Liam's too smart for that.' But look who was wrong. And then Dad went off on his usual tirade about her."

"You mean Mom." Stella was the one who'd struggled most with Liam's choice in marrying Rory. The one who had pointed out that she *had* to be a gold digger.

"No, I mean Dad. You know how he is." Her face was earnest, her lips compressed.

Liam didn't answer. Yes, he knew how his father was. Geoff Bastian acted like he had little to no interest in his children's romantic affairs. He let Stella play the heavy, which left him able to complain about all the drama, but in truth he was often more ironfisted than his wife when it came to family matters. He just handled himself differently. Liam had also learned that all his father's proclamations about Liam taking over the company had been just to hear himself talk, until the shooting. Then he hadn't been able to scramble around construction sites any longer in the same way, so he'd allowed Liam to finally take the reins. But that didn't mean Geoff had given up control. He used Liam for his eyes and ears, and to a lesser extent Derek, who professed loud and long that he didn't want any part of running Bastian-Flavel Construction, that he just preferred his paycheck with no strings attached.

"When the workday's over, so am I," Derek had said on many occasions, which Geoff tried to ignore, though Liam could see it stuck in the old man's craw. Geoff's relationship with his eldest son was full of dark swirls and eddies that Liam had spent the better part of his life trying not to get sucked into. Who knew how deep or muddy those fast currents ran?

"So?" Vivian asked now, bringing him back to the moment.

"So?" he repeated, lost.

"You didn't find her. Obviously. *So* what are you going to do now?"

He hadn't expected everyone including Viv to know all about his trip north before he had a chance to tell the tale himself, but he supposed the family grapevine was twisted and fast-growing enough that it had been bound to pick up the news and spread it.

Vivian grew impatient waiting for his answer and now stood in front of him on the brick steps, as if in so doing she could block his entrance to the family home. As if. "Liam, dear brother, you know I love you, but you've made this one really massive mistake, and you seem bound and determined to ignore fixing it. Time to get over it. Past time, actually. She's gone, and good riddance. Divorce her already." Then, as if she realized how harsh she sounded, Viv amended her words. "Hey, I liked her, you know I liked her, but she was a doe in the headlights when it came to our family. And mother's right about *her* family. Thugs, thieves, and criminals, every one."

Liam grimaced. They'd all learned a lot about the Stemples in the wake of Rory's disappearance after the wedding debacle. There was a lot Rory had held back, and it irked him to have his sister remind him of that fact.

"Excuse me," he said, gently pushing her aside. It wasn't often that Vivian offered her advice, but when she did he never heeded it, and he didn't feel like letting her know that he'd already decided to give up the search for Rory.

"You know I'm living here now," she said, following him inside the foyer. He glanced at her, seeing the shifting spots of light across her face from the huge crystal chandelier hanging high above their heads.

"You and Javier?" he asked.

"Me and *Landon* and *Estella*. No Javier. Just me and the kids. We're in the south wing."

"Okay." He didn't want to go there.

"Javier and I are separated, as you well know. Why do you even ask?"

"You and Javier separate all the time, get back together, separate again. I can't keep up with where you are in the cycle." He headed through the foyer toward the back of the house and the den, where he figured his father would be. Through a bank of windows, he caught a glimpse of the swimming pool, sparking blue beneath morning sunlight, and beyond, past a thin row of spotty hedges, Portland spread out along the shores of the Willamette River, as he turned down the short hallway to the den. Stella, in shorts and a boat-necked T-shirt, was seated beneath an umbrella, head and shoulders shaded, long legs stretched out on a chaise longue in the sunlight, as if she hoped they would tan. She was drinking coffee and looking sourly at the view, as if whatever she saw displeased her.

Vivian's footsteps clattered after him. "When did you get to be such a bastard? Javier and I have separated exactly twice . . . except for this time."

"So, that's three," he threw over his shoulder.

"Fine! Three!"

Her angry tone made him slow down.

"We're divorcing. We really are this time," she said in a small voice.

This from the woman who had so callously suggested he fill out the paperwork and end his marriage to Rory? Feeling a bit of a heel, he turned to see that her face was troubled, actually fighting tears. "Okay. Sorry."

She flapped a hand at him. "It's all right. There's apparently . . . someone else."

"Oh."

She blinked bravely, showing some of that Bastian spirit. Clearing her throat, she admitted, "Javier's fighting me for custody, can you believe that? Even though he's the one with the affair, he still makes all the money . . . and he knows people. He could win, Liam."

"You're the mother. You win."

"It's supposed to work that way, but what if he . . . has something on me."

"Like what?"

"I don't know. Some lie." She avoided her brother's eyes. "And . . . and what if he makes it stick."

This was a new wrinkle. "Is there something to have on you?" he asked, peering at her closely, hearing something she wasn't quite saying.

"No. Good God. No . . ."

"Vivian."

"No, Liam. Except for the DUIs, but that was two years ago, just after I had Estella. The kids weren't in the car. It was just me, and I'd only had a couple of drinks. I don't even drink anymore. Not much, anyway."

"That you, Liam?" Geoff bellowed from inside the den.

His insides tightened as they always did when he knew the old man was in one of his foul moods, which these days was more often than not. "Yeah," he called back.

Vivian grabbed him by the arm and pulled him aside. She stood on tiptoe and whispered in his ear, "I need an income of my own, Liam. I've been taking care of the kids. I haven't been focused on a career, and it's going to hurt me."

"You're still their mother—"

"Stop that. It's not enough."

"Yes, it is. It counts for a lot. You're being paranoid, Viv."

"I need a job. That's all. I want to work for the company."

"You?" he said before he could stop himself. The last thing he wanted was another relative on the payroll. Derek and his flakiness was more than enough, and although Vivian was more stable than their eldest sibling, she'd never really held a job.

"Yes, me," she snapped, inching her pointed chin upward, as if daring him to deny her some kind of birthright.

He couldn't imagine what she would do, but it was a moot point anyway. "Dad's the one to make that decision," he told her.

"He put you in charge."

More like he didn't put Derek in charge. Liam knew his father hadn't wanted any of them to hold the reins, and that he'd chosen his middle child because Liam was more responsible than his older brother. Also, Liam was Stella's child, whereas Derek was the product of Geoff's marriage to his first wife, Karen. If the old man had chosen Derek for a position of authority, Stella would have had a fit, would have seen it as a personal slight against *her*. That's just how twisted she was; always thinking every decision, every idea, every joke, every *any*thing was about her.

"Still, Dad makes those kinds of decisions. You know that."

"But you have influence. I need this job, Liam. Make sure he understands that."

"Talk to him yourself."

Her snort was answer enough, as she stood back on her heels. The truth was Geoff Bastian was old-fashioned and a bit misogynistic. He'd never considered Vivian for a job within Bastian-Flavel because she was a woman, and a woman's job wasn't in construction. Not that he'd said as much aloud, but his actions spoke louder than words. And the lack of diversity in all the Bastian-Flavel administrative positions said something about Geoff's feelings about that, as well. Geoff Bastian was a product of his generation, and he was slow to accept that the world had changed.

"Okay. Fine. I'll tell him you want a job. But you'll have to hammer out the details."

"Or not. That's what you're inferring."

"Just deal with him, okay. I'll bring it up, but it's up to you to close the deal." With that he continued down the hallway and left Vivian staring after him.

"Close that," his father said, making a shooing motion as soon as Liam entered the den. Liam softly shut the dark paneled door and turned toward his father, who was seated behind a large walnut desk covered by today's newspaper. Rimless reading glasses were perched on the end of his nose, and he still wore the neck brace he'd earned by insisting on going to the Hallifax renovation site and toppling out of his chair, nearly down the stairs. It had been Liam who'd scrambled past his shocked brother and saved Geoff. Even so, there was no talking him out of visiting the various Bastian-Flavel Construction work sites from time to time.

"So, you went after her, huh?" his father said as he folded the pages of the *Oregonian*. "To Canada. That's where you've been."

"Among other places. How did you know?"

"That PI? The one Van Horne used? What was his name?"

"Jacoby," Liam said, feeling himself tighten up.

"Yeah, him."

"He wouldn't have told you."

Geoffrey shook his head, his scalp showing in his thinning hair. Obviously the old man was in an argumentative mood. No big surprise. He slowly removed his glasses, folded them and laid them on the paper.

Liam said, "Jacoby signed a confidentiality agreement."

"Well, he did tell me."

"Then he's in breach of contract, because there's a discretion clause. One that he pointed out to me. His own personal credo."

"Okay." Geoffrey frowned, as if second-guessing himself. "Maybe I heard it somewhere else." That seemed a bald-faced lie. "What do you care, anyway? The point is, you're still chasing after her."

Liam's cell phone buzzed and he pulled it from his pocket. Normally he would let it go to voice mail when he was in a meeting, but he could feel his temper rising and almost welcomed the distraction.

"Don't answer that," Geoff said sharply.

Liam stared at the name in surprise. Mickelson. He'd entered the name in his contact list, but he and the detective hadn't been in touch much since Mickelson left Seattle PD. Ignoring his father, he answered, "Liam Bastian."

"Mr. Bastian, it's Roger Mickelson." Then without preamble said, "I don't know if you've heard, but it's been on the news.

Pete DeGrere was murdered yesterday afternoon, just after his release from prison."

DeGrere? Dead? "What? Dead?" Sweet Jesus! "No. I, um, didn't know he'd been released or that . . ." Liam's mind was racing and he turned his back on his father, who was watching him from the wheelchair at his desk.

"What is it?" Geoff demanded, his eyes narrowing on his son. "Who's dead?"

Liam didn't answer. Needed to concentrate.

Mickelson was still talking, "I've got my own detective agency, and I haven't yet spoken to the authorities about DeGrere since his death, but I still believe he was involved with the attack on your wedding."

"I remember." Now that the initial shock had passed, Liam had a million questions. "So, what happened? Where was he? Who did it?" He was killed yesterday afternoon? While Liam had been searching for Rory? Coincidence?

"Happened at a strip club not far from Sea-Tac, only hours after his release from prison. Attacked in the parking lot. That's about all I know."

"Man." Liam exhaled. He didn't care a whit for DeGrere, had never met the man, but if he was somehow connected to the attack that had killed Rory's brother, wounded him, and put Geoff in a wheelchair, then this was maybe connected. "You think his death is related to the sniper attack at the wedding?"

"That's the theory I'm going on."

And Rory, Liam thought. Jesus. He'd flushed Rory out of Point Roberts and now Pete DeGrere was dead. Was that coincidence? Had to be. Because DeGrere's release date had nothing to do with Liam's trip to Point Roberts.

"Whose death?" Geoff demanded again as he backed up his chair and rolled it around the corner of his desk.

"You think there's a link between the two events? Two . . . homicides?"

"Yes."

"You still think DeGrere was the shooter."

"DeGrere? That little shit? Is he dead?" Geoffrey demanded loudly, though he'd rammed his wheelchair within inches of his son, nearly toppling a lamp that was positioned near the French doors that opened to the back patio and the pool area beyond. "What the hell are you talking about? Who's dead? For the love of Christ, put your damned phone on speaker!"

"I'm doing some follow up. Just wanted to let you know about DeGrere."

"Has someone hired you?" Liam asked.

Mickelson paused. "Sometimes a case gets under your skin, y'know? This one did that."

Liam believed him. The guy sounded sincere. More interested in getting to the truth than Liam's own damned family. The very victims. How was that for ironic.

"I'll be in touch," Mickelson promised.

"Good."

Just the slightest pause, then, "And you let me know if you hear from that ex-wife of yours."

Wife, Liam thought as Mickelson hung up, *she's still my wife.*

"What the hell was that all about?" Geoff was glaring up at him, a position he detested, Liam knew. It made the old man feel smaller, less powerful to be relegated to a sitting position. He wheeled back to his spot behind the desk, reclaiming his place of dominance. "Who was that?" he demanded.

Liam explained about ex-police detective Roger Mickelson and Pete DeGrere's murder.

His father didn't waste time on false sympathy. "From what I remember, they all said DeGrere was a low-life thug. What happened?" He unfolded the paper again as if he hadn't just heard that the man who had probably put him in a wheelchair, wounded others, and ended a man's life, had been killed himself. "He could barely have been out of prison."

"He was attacked within hours of his release."

Behind his rimless glasses, Geoffrey's old eyes glittered. "Is this detective on the case?" he asked, scanning the business section.

"Yeah, somewhat."

"Somewhat?"

"Like I said, he's in private practice. I'd really like to talk to the Seattle police."

"Huh." Geoffrey snorted, then dropped his attention to the newspaper.

Liam studied him for a moment, certain his father was just feigning interest. "Jacoby didn't tell you where I was, so how did you know?"

Geoffrey kept on reading.

"Dad?"

"All right, your brother told me." He finally looked up again.

"Derek didn't know—"

"He deduced it. Derek saw Jacoby's bill. Gas receipts. Charged to the company. They go through fast these days. From Vancouver, B.C."

"Not that fast."

The old man didn't miss a beat, continued spinning his tale. "So he figured you were chasing after your missing wife."

Liam realized his brother hadn't seen the receipts go through the company books. No, there wasn't enough time for that despite the speed of Internet banking. No, he must have seen the PI's bill that had been in his suit-coat pocket. The suit coat that he hadn't taken on his own trip to Canada and Point Roberts, but was still hanging in his office. "Derek looked at my personal mail."

Geoffrey let out a huff of disgust and gave up the lie. Instead of deception, he went on the attack. Typical. "Don't look so goddamn affronted. We all wondered where the hell you blasted off to."

"You got him to do it," Liam realized with sudden clarity. "You told him to find out and he lifted the bill from my coat pocket. And you told Vivian and probably Mom, too, that I was off chasing Rory."

Geoff lifted his chin and once again pushed the paper aside. This time he didn't bother folding the pages. His expression was perturbed, bordering on anger. "Next time maybe you'll realize you just can't take off from the job without telling anyone where you're going."

"You knew I'd be back in a few days. I had my cell phone. You could have asked." Liam's temper was escalating.

"You didn't say you were leaving the country. So, where is she? Why did she run? Did she admit to being part of this?" He slapped a hand down on his thigh, hard, his face mottling with red.

"No."

"She tell you that her family was in on it? Harold Stemple's hanging out in prison, maybe acting the model prisoner. But his fingers are all over this. He probably hired someone to kill De-Grere to keep him from talking!"

"With all that money he's making in prison, working in the laundry or whatever?"

"He could have some cash tucked away. He is a thief, y'know. Suspected in dozens of burglaries."

"That's a pretty big leap, Dad. To think Stemple used all his secreted cash to pay a hired assassin to kill DeGrere on the first day he's out—"

"Well, what did she say?" Geoffrey demanded, waving away Liam's argument with a wide arc of one hand. "Huh? Your *wife*? What did she say?"

Back to Rory. "I never found her. She was gone by the time I got there."

"Jesus Christ." He shook his head and moved his wheelchair back and forth two inches, the way he always did when he was agitated, a nervous display that bugged the hell out of Liam. "I thought at least you'd get something done. Learn something from her."

Liam held on to his temper with an effort. "Mickelson's still on the case. It's the one that got away from him. He's doing it on his own."

"Well, that's something," Geoff allowed.

They heard a commotion in the hall and then a familiar male voice, calling aloud, "Hallloooo!" as the den door was yanked open and Derek appeared, wearing a construction vest. "Hey, brother!" His face broke into a wide smile. "Saw your car. On my way to work."

It was all Liam could do not to glance at the clock.

Geoff said, "Then you probably guessed we were in a meeting."

"I'll leave if you want," Derek answered, unperturbed at his father's icy tone.

"No need," said Liam. "We were finished anyway."

"Do I detect some tension?" Derek asked, looking from Geoff to Liam, brows lifted.

"You read my mail," Liam said.

Derek's eyes widened, then he shrugged a little. "Oops."

Geoff said a bit belligerently, "There aren't any secrets in this family. We all work together, and I still run the company."

"I beg to differ, Dad. Brother Liam's the one who's in charge. And he's doing a good job, right? The Hallifax building still has months before its renovation is complete and the apartments are renting at warp speed. And they're fucking expensive."

"None of that talk." Geoff glowered, and Liam wondered

for a moment if he was referring to Derek's swearing or the fact that Liam's idea had been successful, especially when both Geoff and Derek had been lukewarm about the project from the get-go.

"I'm just sayin' that Liam's got the touch. Good job in putting him in charge, Dad." He walked to the glass doors and stared out at the pool where Stella was sipping a mimosa, sunbathing and flipping through a magazine.

Liam gazed at Derek, wondering what his brother was up to, needling their father that way. However, Geoff remained stoic as he ignored Derek and said to Liam, "I don't care how you get rid of your problem, just don't let it get in the way. Hallifax is on time, the last I heard, which was last week. I need daily reports."

"I'm not sidelining you," Liam told him, facing his father once more.

"I didn't say you were. I just want the business to run efficiently. And I'm not sure about those last hires. Les Steele and Jarrod Uller? Never heard of 'em."

Liam said, not for the first time, "They came from Barlow Development and—"

"Those fuckers at Barlow," Derek growled.

Geoff snapped, "Derek!"

"Steele's built apartments all over the city," Liam went on, ignoring them both. "Uller's worked with him on every one. To get Steele to move and become our foreman and project manager required Uller. They're a package deal and they're doing a good job."

"Except for the vandalism," Derek pointed out.

"Yes, except for that," Liam said evenly.

"Well, don't hire anyone else," Geoff grumbled. "Eats up all our profits."

Liam thought of Vivian's job request and grimaced to himself. Or, at least he thought he'd hidden his expression until his father asked, "What's wrong?"

After a moment of indecision where both Derek and Geoff were looking at him expectantly, Liam decided on honesty. "Your daughter would like a job with the company."

"My—? Vivian?" Geoff's look was almost comical. "She hasn't worked a day in her life!"

"That's not true," Liam began, but Derek barked out a laugh and overrode him. "Viv wants a job at the company? Because she's divorcing Javier and needs some dough?" He let out a deprecating snort. "Perfect."

"What would she do?" Geoff asked in disbelief.

Liam said, "I don't know. Before I walked in here, she just asked if she could work for the company."

"Well, there's nothing for her to do," Derek put in.

Geoff shot his eldest son a dark look. "She doesn't deserve a job, but you do? Is that what you're saying?" He turned back to Liam. "She asked you, not me?"

"She asked me to ask you. Does it matter?"

"Yes, it matters!" He pointed both of his thumbs at himself and demanded, "What have I been saying? This is my company and these are my decisions!"

"Well, she's living here now. And she's right outside that door." Liam pointed to it. "Call her in here and tell her what you just told me. Now, I'm going to check on Hallifax and then I've got a meeting with the city planner."

"The city planner," Geoff echoed.

"About the parking issue on the east side."

His father grunted. "At Flavel? Those homeless people still in the way?"

"Yep," Derek said with a nod.

Liam responded a bit tensely, "I'll say it again. Their camp is sanctioned by the city. The problem is with our tenants."

"Those losers we're trying to boot out of there," Derek agreed. He shrugged as if there wasn't anything much to do. "Don't worry. I'm on it."

The old Flavel building on the east side of the Willamette River had been purchased from Geoff's ex–business partner, James Flavel, and then taken on by Derek, who'd made bad choice after bad choice, back when he'd still been interested in management. The result was the building had deteriorated to the point of almost being condemned. It was the biggest bone of contention between father and son because it was one of the main reasons, if not the only reason, Geoff had bypassed his elder son completely in favor of his younger, to head Bastian-Flavel Construction. Derek had used some less than legal tactics to remove the tenants who were behind in their rent. The result was that lawsuits had abounded and it had taken them to this point, years later, before the path was clear to move forward in renovations, though there were a number of groups in the area opposed to gentrification, so the project had gone fallow. Currently Bastian-Flavel Construction's main project was the Hallifax building, another older apartment project which was in a more centrally located neighborhood and considered to be a hot property.

"They can lawyer up all they want. Their leases and their lawsuits are done," Derek said darkly. "Assholes."

Liam didn't wait to hear any more. He had enough on his plate without playing referee for his family or revisiting old gripes about company decisions. "I'm outta here," he said, then walked out of the door and spied Viv still hovering in the hallway.

"You're on deck," he said. "I told Dad you wanted a job."

"And—?"

"And you need to talk to him yourself. Consider the ice broken."

He made his way to the front of the house, backed his SUV out of the circular drive because Viv hadn't moved her damned Mercedes squatting like an oversized toad and still blocking the drive. Then he drove away from the house, leaving the estate on the riverfront in his rearview.

Just another day in the life of the Bastian family—*his* family, he reminded himself. Did he really blame Rory for running the first chance she got? The answer: Yes. She was his wife, or had been, and would be for a few more days. Until he could finish the divorce papers.

If that's still viable. Now you know she's alive, the lawyer may have to take a different tack.

His cell phone, which he'd left in the car, made a noise and at the first traffic light he checked it. Bethany. Two messages asking that he call her. He would. Just not now. He drove to the south waterfront and the Bastian-Flavel offices, and when he stepped onto the street, he saw Rory walking down the street, away from him.

Rory . . . !

Liam's intake of breath was harsh, and his heart seemed to stop as he saw the long, dark red curls bouncing against her shoulders, the smooth gait of her steps. He strode forward rapidly, intent on grabbing her by the arm, darkly furious. After all the running away, she was *here*? *Now*?

"Where the hell have you been?" he demanded, holding back the roar of fury that threatened to engulf him as he spun her around.

She nearly stumbled, staring at him in surprise, her eyes wide, her mouth an O of shock. It wasn't Rory, he realized instantly, just someone with her same hair and body type.

"I'm sorry. I'm truly sorry," he stammered, feeling the fool. The past few days, being caught up looking for her, had obviously affected him and his judgment more than he'd realized.

As he released the startled woman's arm, he remembered the first time he'd met Rory, when he'd bumped into her and she'd stumbled on that steep Seattle street years before . . . "Thought you were someone else."

"I guess," she said sardonically, recovering herself. He half expected her to scream for the police, but she merely gave him a long look from head to toe, as if memorizing what the crazy man looked like, and twisted on her heel away from him.

"Jesus," he muttered, irked at himself. He headed in the opposite direction, glancing back once to see her enter an office building several blocks down the waterfront. She really looked nothing like Rory, he realized.

He was chasing shadows. Had been for five years.

Definitely time to move on.

Definitely.

It was late night, a strip of moonlight barely illuminating anything in the older building that was under a major, major redo, as Teri Mulvaney stumbled up the stairs, trying to avoid the broken glass and pieces of material that made an obstacle course in this dim light. It was a real bitch trying to see where the hell she was. And from the outside the building looked like this huge monster with smashed-out eyes. The windows were a mess. Lots of spiderwebs crisscrossing those panes. Somebody had bashed them up but good.

"I—ooh!" She sucked in a breath as her ankle twisted. Fought back a shriek of pain that came out as a moan. *Holy shit.*

"Shhh," her guide admonished in a whisper. "Can't have anyone see us."

"I know," she whispered back, trying to sound upbeat, though her teeth were clenched.

She shouldn't have worn her strappy heels, Manolo Blahniks, no less! The ones her ultra rich, ultra snobby bitch of an ex-sister-in-law had tossed her way in a lackluster show of generosity. Sure, they weren't exactly her size, a little pinchy around the toes, and therefore her heel hung over a little, but so what. They were *Manolo Blahniks*. Cost a fortune that she didn't possess! But they just weren't made for this dead-of-night outing. If she'd had any sense at all she would have called off this "date" before it began.

But he was handsome, in that way she liked. Not too handsome. Just kind of bad-boy, *ride a motorcycle and do a little slap and tickle to get the juices going* handsome. The kind of guy that could get you into a lot of trouble. Just like she liked. She'd met him at Waterfront Park. He was just standing, watching the river, and she'd left a nearby bar and was walking, well, okay, stumbling a little, toward the street, intent on getting an Uber and hoping her credit card wasn't maxed out. You know how those things go. Make a payment, gain a little breathing room.

He'd seemed like a ghost in the dark and she'd come up on him suddenly. "Hey," she said.

"Hey," he replied, turning to look at her. That's all it had taken. One look. She'd felt herself go hot and melty in her core, and he'd sensed it and simply moved a hand forward, catching her arm, dragging her to him. He'd started exploring her body immediately, taking all kinds of liberties. She'd pretended to be affronted, but, well, she had been kind of drunk, and it had felt a little good, and she'd been so lonely since her breakup with that asshole Karl. Still, when he'd wriggled his hand up her short skirt and stuck his fingers inside her, she'd slapped at him and told him to stop. Her mother had raised her right. He'd skipped first and second base and slid straight into third, and that just wasn't right.

"Oh, baby," he'd breathed in her ear, his fingers caressing hard, and Lord if she hadn't almost climaxed standing on her tippytoes in those heels that wanted to sink into the soft earth.

Had she whimpered? She was pretty sure she had.

"You want me to stop?" he groaned, his fingers stilling.

God, no. No! But nice girls would ask for a kiss first, so she'd turned her lips toward him.

"Say it," he ordered, his own lips a hairbreadth from hers.

"Say what?"

"Say you want me to stop."

"I want you to . . . ooohhh . . . !"

She'd come right then and there, pressing herself to his marauding hand, holding on to his shoulders, knees weak, body quivering, desperate for more contact. "Harder," she'd begged, pressing her hand on top of his, squirming against his hard fingers. He'd laughed and complied, rubbing her like she was a magic lamp, and she'd felt like one, bursting through to a shimmering climax, releasing a genie of desire, screaming silently in her throat.

Well, at least she'd thought it was silent, until his hands came around her neck and he whispered, "Quiet, beautiful."

Beautiful. He'd called her "Beautiful."

She'd been in lust like never before. He wouldn't tell her his name, which drove her insane, and caused her to masturbate when they weren't together, just thinking about him. She called him Duke in her mind, which was her boyfriend's name from two years ago, a real asshole, but she was still kind of habanero-hot for him.

From that first meeting, they'd met by the water every night for two weeks, kissing and rubbing and getting each other off. Though she'd certainly given as good as she'd got, he'd never fully climaxed, though she did on a regular basis with barely a tease to the clitoris. Crazy!

Then last night he'd said, "Wanna have some real fun?"

"Sure."

So, he'd told her to go to the bar and toss back a few cocktails, just to get the juices flowing. No problem there. Alcohol was her favorite sexual lubricant.

Then he'd come around for her in a pickup. Said he knew a guy who worked for a construction company and was borrowing it for a while. He got her off as they were driving along, and by the time they got to their destination, she was clinging to his shoulder while his right hand idly played with her in a way that made her want to shriek and claw and bite.

But now they were here, and she was picking her way through what had to be a hard-hat zone. Some old building under serious renovation.

"I wanna fuck on the top level," he said.

"Yeah? I don't see any elevator," she quipped, finding herself really funny. Those huckleberry-and-lemon martinis had gone down icy cold. She reminded herself to thank him for the extra dollars he'd given her to help get her drink on.

"We gotta go up five flights," he said.

Well, she was kidding about the elevator. Surely he knew that. She hurried up the first flight, missed a step near the top, and came down hard on her knee. She yowled with pain, but his hand swiftly came over her mouth.

"Shhh. Gotta be cool, baby, or they'll come for us. Gotta be real quiet."

They? The building owners? *The police?* She whimpered, but managed to shake off most of the pain as they climbed what felt like more than five stairways, finally reaching the top floor. The moon put a white spotlight on them.

"There we go," he said, turning her to face him.

Finally, they were going to get down to business. Enough with all this handsy stuff. She wanted him inside her right now! Sure, she would have preferred a bed. The last time she'd screwed in the great outdoors was on a beach, and she'd gotten sand up her crack and it chafed and felt like forever to get it all cleaned out.

She saw him take off his backpack, dropping it to the ground. He took a couple steps forward, looking over the edge of the building. "You can see the river," he said, pointing to the dark waters of the Willamette a number of blocks away.

She tiptoed closer, to stand beside him. She didn't do well with heights and it was a long way down.

He came up behind her and tickled her, scaring her. "Stop it!" she cried, hanging on to his arm with a death grip.

"What, you're afraid of heights?"

"Yeah, I am! Gawd . . ."

He turned her around to look at him. Now her back was to the edge of the building and that didn't sit well with her, either. The moon was to her right now, leaving them in darkness.

"I've never heard you like this," he said, amused. "Kind of bitchy . . . naggy."

"Come on," she said, trying to drag him away from the edge.

"I want to do it right here. Standing up."

"I want to lie down."

"It's filthy. No way. We'd need a blanket."

"Well, what's in your backpack?" she asked.

"A hammer. Some gloves."

"A hammer?" she repeated. "What for?"

"A little extracurricular activity." She could hear the suppressed laughter in his voice, though she couldn't read his expression.

"No blanket? Nothing?" she asked.

"Nope."

There was another note in his voice, one she hadn't heard before, one of excitement, anticipation. Well, good. Unlike most of the women she knew who moaned about their boyfriends getting right to the *wham, bam, thank you, ma'am* with barely a kiss, she was sick of foreplay.

"We're gonna have ourselves a gooooood time," he said, suddenly unbuttoning his pants and freeing a woody that sprang straight up, cocked and ready. Well, all right! She broke into a smile and ran a tentative hand over it. She'd felt him before, but he'd never been quite this hard. "What are you gonna do with the hammer, big boy?" she teased, catching his excitement.

"Smash a few windows." He laughed beneath his breath. "Beat you to death."

Teri's heart lurched. He was the one who'd broken the windows? But then he was pulling down her pants and panties, stepping closer to wedge his cock between her legs. She tried to bend over to free her feet from her pants—her best ones, that she'd gotten on sale at Nordstrom but still cost a fortune—but he wouldn't let her. He lifted her upward and settled her upon him, her knees bent outward, her feet still caught by the pants.

"Oh, my God, give me a break. I'll get them off," she whispered, giggling.

"Nah." He pushed his cock hard up inside her, hurting her a little because it was such an awkward position. "It's good, baby, huh."

"Real good," she lied. If he'd just give her a minute . . .

But then he began lifting her up and down on his cock, slowly, excruciatingly slowly, and she forgot her worries, her hands clinging to his shoulders. He held her with his arms, suspending her in the air, up and down, until she was squirming for him to go faster, harder. She wasn't a big woman, but she marveled at his strength. "You must work out," she panted.

"Some . . ." He spoke through gritted teeth, concentrating.

Before long she was close to coming. She tried to hold back, wanted the moment to continue, but he was strong, sure, and slamming into her in a way that sent her wild.

"You . . . you . . . oh . . . *ohhhh . . . oh, God!*" Her arms were wrapped around his shoulders, her eyes squeezed shut. She opened them, looked at the white orb in the sky, threw back her head, and wailed like a banshee.

He came on a groan right after she did. Moments later he pulled out and set her down on shaky legs. "Wow . . ." she whispered.

"No shit," he agreed, sounding as happy as she felt. He tucked his cock away and bent down to his backpack as she pulled up her pants and panties. The claw hammer appeared in his hand and she saw him swing it around, testing it. It whistled by her ear and she ducked away.

"Hey!" she cried fearfully.

"Don't worry. I got one for you, too." He pulled another hammer out of the pack and handed it to her.

"I'm not sure I want to destroy stuff," she said.

"I love destroying stuff."

He grabbed her by the hand and took her back down a flight. They walked to the windows. One was already cracked and he swung the hammer and smashed the still intact window next to it. The crash was deafening. Somewhere a dog started barking.

"You said to be quiet! Oh, my God." She was both horrified and thrilled.

"Here, you smash one and we'll get the hell out."

"O . . . kay." She aimed the hammer at the window with the spider cracks. Lifted the hammer.

"Wait," he ordered.

She stopped and looked at him. To her surprise, he yanked the hammer out of her hand.

"Change of plans," he said, and then he swung the hammer at her head, dropping her with one hit.

Pain exploded in her brain and dully, she cried out, heard him . . . oh, God, whistling. Her mind was disjointed. Pain screaming and slashing at her. Her body convulsing as she felt her aching body being lifted. Then he threw her, hard, slamming her back into the broken window, sharp shards tearing at her flesh.

She saw him smile in satisfaction at the tinkling of glass far below. One extra push and she was outside, in the air, gravity pulling at her as she free-fell through the night. She opened her mouth to scream and *bam!* Her body hit hard. Jolting. Bones breaking. She blinked in one last moment of consciousness, saw him staring down at her, grinning like the devil, as if he reveled in the image of blood mixing with her red hair.

Then his head disappeared back inside the building, his footsteps clamoring down the stairs, as gratefully the blackness swallowed her on this, her last, warm summer night.

Chapter 12

Liam's cell buzzed and rattled on his nightstand. He reached for it, opening one eye, seeing the lightening July sky outside the floor-to-ceiling window in his master bedroom, read the time: 5:37 a.m.

He saw the number: Jacoby.

He groaned inside. He was through chasing after Rory.

"Whad is it?" Bethany mumbled from her side of his bed as he picked up the phone and answered. Her hair was a tumbled mass on the extra pillow, and from beneath its curtain she opened an eye to stare at him.

He hadn't asked her to come over. She just had. And he hadn't said no. He'd half expected her to bring up the plans to move in with him in September, but she hadn't. She'd always been good at strategy and seemed to realize this was not the time to push him about their future.

"It's Jacoby," the private investigator identified himself as soon as Liam unplugged the phone from its charger and clicked it on. "Called you three times last night and you didn't answer."

"Phone was dead. I didn't start charging it till late."

"I've got some news for you about your wife."

Your wife. The words were a splash of cold water, bringing him fully awake. "Yeah?"

"She's here. In Portland. At Laurelton General with a sick child."

"*Here?*"

"Yessirree. Big as life."

"You saw her?"

"That's what you pay me for," the PI said, self-satisfied. "You shoulda picked up last night. I damn near called you at two a.m."

Bethany had lifted herself up on one elbow, staring at him. She brushed her hair from her face and Liam wished to high heaven he'd turned her down the night before.

"Was there an accident?"

"Don't think so."

"Is the kid okay?"

"Not sure." That sent a bolt of panic through him. "Okay, I'm heading there now," he growled, adding before he clicked off, "Thirty minutes, max."

"Where are you going?" Beth asked, her eyes wide as Liam headed for the connecting bathroom and kicked off his boxers. "You're getting up? Now? It's not even six yet." Then, worried, "What happened?"

He wanted to lie. To keep what he knew to himself, but Beth was already rising from the bed, stripping off her lacy nightgown, and as he opened the shower door and twisted on the taps, stepping beneath hot, sharp spray, she met him in the bathroom, naked. She reached for the shower door handle, but he grabbed it from his side, holding it in place so that it couldn't swing either way.

"No, wait. I have to get going," he said as steam began to rise.

"You don't want me to shower with you?" she asked in disbelief. "You're stopping me?" Her thin body, too thin, really, was stiff with outrage.

Sharp needles of hot water were bouncing off his skin, running down his face, plastering his hair to his head. He just wanted Bethany to disappear, didn't want this inevitable argument, then felt a guilty pang when he remembered the pain of having a lover really disappear. Still, Beth, if he didn't really want her to vanish, should at least go home.

She was staring through the rapidly fogging glass, "That was Jacoby, wasn't it?" she charged, her eyes wide, her color high. "You asked if he'd seen *her*, meaning Rory, right? That's what you asked him. You said, 'You saw *her*?' "

"Yes . . ." Liam admitted, swiping at the water on his face as she glared at him, her face almost ghostlike through the film.

"Great, Liam. Just . . . great!" Her jaw was tighter than he'd ever seen it, her lipstick-free lips compressed.

He almost explained that he needed to see Rory to get her signature on the divorce papers he'd had drawn up months earlier, but it felt too much like an excuse. Rory was a topic he and Bethany both avoided. She hadn't even asked him about his trip north, which led him to believe she must know something about it, possibly from Derek, or someone else in his family.

"What about a kid and an accident?" she demanded.

"Don't know."

"Does she have a child?"

He repeated: "Don't know."

"But you're racing to be with her. A hero."

Before he could even think about explaining, Beth turned on her heel and headed back into the bedroom. Liam, pissed and frustrated, just went through the motions of showering. His mind raced as he turned off the taps, wrapped a towel around his waist, and padded back into the master bedroom of his top floor condominium on Portland's west side. He had a view much like his parents', straight up the Willamette toward the Fremont Bridge, its arched span glowing heavenly white, touched by morning sunlight.

Beth was sitting on the bed, dressed in the white blouse, black skirt, and black wedge sandals she'd appeared in the night before. She'd even added the string of pearls, a gift from him, and they lay like a white promise at her throat. She'd pulled a brush from her purse and was slowly dragging it through her hair, not meeting his eyes. She was, in fact, staring at the green plastic Yoda ring lying forgotten on his dresser.

"I'll call you as soon as I know if it's Rory," he said.

"Thank you."

Her tone was serious, her words clipped. He sensed she'd regained control of herself and was once again holding her emotions in, as she always did. Beth was careful, a characteristic he'd thought he valued, but right now he wished she would just lose it. Yell and scream and make an ugly scene. Show some gumption. Anger. He'd witnessed just a glimpse of it in the shower, thought she might break down the damned glass, but here she was, pretending to be unperturbed. Fake.

He spent less than five minutes back in the bathroom, stepping into clean clothes and running a brush through his hair, not bothering to shave. He felt as if time was slipping through his fingers.

If you don't get there soon, she'll vanish. And the sick child. What was that all about?

Back in the bedroom, he buttoned his shirt and scanned the carpet for his shoes. Beth was still sitting on the edge of the bed, waiting, her gaze now on him. Her mouth was turned down at the corners, her lips newly glossed. For the first time in months, he felt no urge to kiss her, not even goodbye, and he felt a jab of guilt pierce his brain. The truth was, he was focused on finally facing off with Rory. And what about the sick child? Her baby, most likely. So where was the father? With her? In absentia?

"Okay?" he asked Beth, still feeling as if sand were slipping through an unseen hourglass. If he didn't get to Laurelton, and soon, Rory would vanish again.

Beth slowly rose, collected her clutch bag, shoved the brush inside. She'd managed some light makeup, but was paler than her usual self.

"Okay," she answered, which could mean anything, he thought. Nothing good, it seemed. She hesitated by his dresser and then deliberately picked up the Yoda ring, slipping it into her purse before preceding him out of the apartment. A strange gesture of repressed anger. It was all he could do not to run to his Tahoe.

But when he reached his rig, he caught a glimpse of Beth in a nearby parking spot. Steadfastly not looking at him, she was checking out her face in her mirror, touching the edge of her lips as if her lipstick had smeared, then messing with her cell phone.

Fine. Let her dawdle.

He couldn't wait. He backed out of his spot in the underground garage, drove to the exit, scanned the street for vehicles and pedestrians, then hit the gas.

Jaw set, he drove like a madman, speeding down the highway, disbelieving that he was actually going to see his *wife* face-to-face after all these years. Traffic was light as it was still early, the sun rising over Mount Hood on the eastern horizon. It was all he could do to stay within ten miles of the speed limit and his heart was beating like the proverbial drum. Dozens of questions, the same old queries, sped through his mind as the Tahoe's engine raced and its tires hummed over the pavement.

What happened?

Where did you go?

Why didn't you contact me?

What about your family?

How'd you end up with the kid?

Jesus, why did you leave? Were you forced? Or . . .

He rolled down the window to clear his mind, taking a page from Beth's book and forcing his raging emotions under control again. He didn't completely believe that after all these years he'd finally see her again.

There were too many almosts, too many dead ends.

But if the fates were with him and she was here, in Portland, in the flesh, he wanted to be ready, so he forced himself to be sharp, clear and calm. He wanted a clean divorce from her. Needed to cut all ties from her. But first, of course, he had to have some answers to his questions, the foremost being: Why did she run?

And he wanted to hear those answers from her, face-to-face, before she started talking to the police or the press or a lawyer . . . God, what a mess!

He squinted, the sun catching in his side mirrors, and out of the blue a memory found him and caught hold. In his mind's eye he saw Rory, laughing, her red hair tossed by the wind that had rippled across the water as they walked, arm in arm, along the shoreline of a lake in Washington. The sky had been cloud covered, dove gray, reflecting its somber color on the water. She'd snatched at her tresses, trying to corral them with one hand, which she finally succeeded in doing. He'd leaned in to kiss her and she'd pushed him away, only to grab him by his shirt and pull him into a real smacker, her lips hot and slick on the cool day.

"Love you," she said, then skipped away, teasing him, and hurrying along the lakefront.

His heart had clutched as she'd glanced back with an impish look, silently daring him to chase her. Which he had. Eagerly. Along the shoreline as the water had lapped the shore and a few fishermen had cast their lines.

When he caught up with her she giggled and half screamed. He'd wrapped his arms around her, kissed her soundly, and finally ended the embrace and tugged at her arm, pulling her into a small lakeside café known for its Dutch-baby pancakes, raspberry syrup, and strong coffee. They'd landed at a small table with a checked tablecloth and, while the heavyset waitress had hovered and offered suggestions, they'd been so caught up in each other and the promise of a long weekend alone that they'd barely had time to order. To this day Liam didn't remember what he'd eaten, only that he'd been completely and foolishly besotted with his bride.

He swore softly under his breath as the memory floated away and he found himself tearing along the highway, driving by rote, passing a semi at a good fifteen miles-an-hour over the speed limit. He slipped into the slower lane, tucking the Tahoe in front of the huge truck, and eased up on the gas pedal. God, what was he thinking?

"You trying to get a ticket?" he muttered, running a hand through his still-damp hair. His heart rate had slowed to a little above normal, but it was accelerating again. He could feel himself start to shift, sensed excitement begin to course through his veins, and he mentally cursed himself for being a fool for a woman who had so publicly spurned him, a woman who had run not only from him, but from tragedy, who had . . . well, he'd gone over the same curse a thousand times over. Yet still, he felt a kind of anticipation mixed with hard anger at the thought of finally confronting her.

He'd thought, no, he'd *hoped* he might skip that particular feeling, but here it was. Kinda pissed him off. How many times was he supposed to feel this way, only to be slammed down again?

He almost wished for a distraction. Something to throw him off course. Something to stop him from going after Rory one more time.

His cell phone rang at that moment. He'd placed it in the cup holder in the console. "Ask and ye shall receive," he muttered, glancing down at the phone impatiently. He saw it was his foreman. Les Steele.

He clicked on and pushed the speakerphone button so he didn't have to put the cell to his ear while driving. "Pretty early at the job site, Les, if that's where you are."

"Liam . . . yes . . . Here at Hallifax. I've called the police," Steele said, his voice a tight squeak. "Oh, shit, there's no easy way to tell you this, but there's a dead woman on the job site."

"What?" He swerved slightly. "A dead—?"

Steele was nearly babbling, which wasn't like him at all. "Ah, Jesus, it . . . it looks like she fell. Maybe from the roof. I don't know. Redhead. She's all messed up . . . Holy Christ . . . I mean she must've fallen."

Liam's heart jolted. His normally taciturn foreman was clearly shaken to his boots. "You're sure—?"

"Oh, yeah, I'm sure she's dead. Holy—"

"I'll be right there." Liam was already looking for a spot to pull a one-eighty. "You said you've already called the police?"

"Yeah."

"Don't do anything. Just stay there." He wheeled into the parking lot of a strip mall and rounded a few parked cars, heading back to the highway, where he waited for the same damned semi he'd passed earlier to whip past.

"Damn," he muttered as soon as he'd clicked off. A dead woman?

A redhead.

Rory!

"No. Shit . . . no . . . it's not . . . it's not." He shook his head, angry for even thinking that. He was consumed by Rory. "Goddammit . . ."

He sped through a yellow light, found the Sunset Highway and headed east, managing to find his sunglasses in the visor and slip them on. Threading his way through the thickening traffic, he headed through the canyon and tunnel, skimmed by the downtown area and over the river. The view of Mount Hood was spectacular, the sun rising over its jagged silhouette, but his mind was on the job site and the dead woman. Who the hell was she? Why was she there? His foot was heavy on the accelerator, and he had to remind himself over and over that there was no reason to go at breakneck speed. He just needed to arrive in one piece, without being slapped with a speeding ticket by some cop hiding in the alleyways between the buildings.

A dead woman.

On Bastian property.

Maybe it was one of the homeless people who'd wandered onto the site and discovered a way inside?

He turned off the main road, found the gravel entrance to the job site, a temporary gate in the wire fencing that ran the perimeter of the property. The gate was wide-open and his Tahoe bounced over several potholes.

He arrived just ahead of the police and found Les, white-faced and drawing hard on a cigarette, standing at the southeastern corner of the building. Liam slammed out of the Tahoe as the police cruiser skidded to a stop, effectively blocking the entrance to the Hallifax site. Two uniformed officers stepped from the vehicle, only steps behind Liam.

"Where?" Liam asked Les as he reached the shorter man.

"Right there." Les hitched his chin to a spot behind him, then tossed the butt of his cigarette into the dry dirt and gravel, squashing what was left of it with the heel of a work boot.

Liam held up, peering into the shadows where a body lay. He could just see a woman's leg, bent at an odd angle, her foot encased in a black, heeled sandal, and a tangled matt of red hair. Red . . .

Stumbling past Les, his vision blurred as he thought of Rory, that she could be the victim, her visage pale, her eyes staring blankly in death, he blinked hard. He stopped a few feet from the dead woman and forced himself to stare at the pooling blood beneath her head.

"No," he whispered hoarsely. "Please . . . God, no . . ." So caught up in the horrifying imagery in his head, he was unaware that the officers had joined him until one spoke.

"Officer Donnelly, Portland Police." The words brought him back. "Sir? Do you know the victim?"

He couldn't answer for a moment.

It wasn't Rory. It couldn't be. He let out his breath slowly and studied the body from a distance. *Come on, you know this woman* can't *be Rory. You know it, man. You're just caught up in her because of Jacoby. Pull yourself together.*

The police officer—Donnelly, did he say his name was?—asked him, "Sir. Are you okay?"

Donnelly's partner, the shorter of the two cops, inched forward to bend down and ascertain what was patently obvious: The woman, whoever she was, had died. Horrifically. From a fall. He then looked up to the half-renovated building and its six floors.

Swallowing hard, Liam was pretty sure it wasn't Rory. It didn't make sense. There was just no reason for this poor, broken, *dead* woman to be Rory.

But he didn't know for certain . . .

"Sir?" Again the serious baritone voice of the taller officer.

"I'm fine," he lied, and knew everyone there was aware that he was far from being anywhere near "fine."

Rory was at the hospital, he told himself. Jacoby had said she was there with a sick kid.

Barely registering what the sound was, he heard the roar of an engine, a screech of tires, and the slam of a vehicle's door. He glanced over his shoulder, still lost in thought. His brother, unshaven, dark sunglasses in place, serious set to his jaw, in jeans and a T-shirt, was striding toward them.

"I called Derek, too," Les explained, scrabbling in the pocket of his shirt beneath a neon vest, obviously in search of another cigarette.

"What the hell," Derek said, brushing past Les to where Liam was standing with the police. He gazed down at the body and his intake of breath was a gasp. "*Rory?*" he said in a strangled voice.

"No," Liam snapped.

"Jesus, same color hair."

"You know this woman?" Donnelly asked Derek.

"No ... I don't think so." Derek stared at the corpse in shock.

"Are you the owners of this property?" the shorter officer asked. Liam read his name tag. Dvorak.

Liam managed to pull himself back to the present. "Yes, I'm Liam Bastian. This is my brother, Derek Bastian. The Hallifax apartment building is a Bastian-Flavel Construction renovation project." He turned to Steele and added, "Les Steele is project manager. He called us as well as the police."

"Could I get a closer look?" Derek asked.

Donnelly said, "Just don't touch her."

"Don't worry. Not happening."

"Call it in," Donnelly said to Dvorak, and the shorter officer double-timed it back to the cruiser. By now a small crowd had started to collect on the other side of the street at a coffee shop. Three people were huddled together, all with white coffee cups, eyeing them with concern. The woman was holding the leash of a bouncing Jack Russell terrier in her free hand; the kid of nineteen or so in a long-sleeved tee, baggy jeans, and stocking cap, was drinking from his cup while balanced on a skateboard; and the third person, an older black guy in glasses and a Blazers' cap, was slowly shaking his head, as if making some kind of judgment call. "We'll need the coroner and crime scene," Donnelly called after Dvorak.

"Got it," the shorter cop yelled back.

When Derek moved toward the body, Liam did as well. He wanted to know. Dreaded to know. Had to know.

The dead woman's head was twisted, facing away from them. The left side of her face looked normal and her eyes were open. Brown eyes. Dark roots. Dyed hair. Not Rory.

Liam felt something give inside him. The invisible steel rod that had been holding up his backbone. It wasn't Rory. The dead woman wasn't Rory.

Derek verbalized his thoughts. "I don't know her. I thought it might be . . . well, but it's not. It's not anyone we know. Or . . . you don't know her, do you?" he asked Liam.

"No."

"Shit. She's a mess."

Les, smoking and keeping his distance, grunted his agreement.

Dvorak returned to stay with the body, his cell phone in his hand while Donnelly trooped to the front of the building. Derek and Liam followed after him and Les brought up the rear. "Front door's open," Donnelly observed. "Lock broken. Jamb splintered."

"It was a crappy lock," Derek muttered, shooting Les a look of accusation.

Les said, "Temporary door. We're putting the steel one on today. Just a couple more hours and she wouldn't have gotten in." He looked shattered, as if he might break down completely. "This homeless problem . . ."

"She doesn't look like a homeless woman," Liam pointed out, still slightly dazed.

"Uh-uh," Derek agreed. "Nice clothes and shoes."

Donnelly headed inside the building, ducking a little even though there was plenty of headroom. Liam, Derek, and Les were requested to stay outside until the coroner's wagon arrived. The three of them collected near the guarding officer who'd returned from the cruiser to stand by the body.

"Did she jump?" Derek asked.

Les squinted up at the top floor of the building and shrugged.

Liam was lost in thought. He was undone. The image of the dead girl seemingly imprinted on his retina. Still, he was relieved she wasn't Rory. But she was someone. Someone's daughter, or sister, or wife, or even possibly mother. Though he'd escaped the particular agony of losing a loved one, someone—several people, no doubt—hadn't been so lucky.

A loved one.

To change the course of his thoughts, he eyed his brother. "Why did you call her Rory?"

"Don't know. Just reacted. Probably because we've been talking about her and, come on, you saw it too. That woman back there"—he turned his thumb toward the mangled body—"she looked like Rory."

"But Rory knows nothing about this project," Liam said. "She's been gone for years."

"Come on, man. That dead girl looks like her! Why couldn't it have been her? You were just chasing after her. I thought maybe she came back and . . . I don't know . . . followed you."

Donnelly cut in. "So none of you have any idea who the victim is?"

Derek and Liam and Les all shook their heads. Les let out a long stream of smoke. "You know, that lock was stiff. Hard to work. Even Charlie has trouble with it." Charlie Zenk was a framer, big, burly guy. "So I don't know how she broke it open by herself. You'd need a crowbar."

"Maybe she had one," Derek said. "Or found one on the job site. The subs are always leaving their tools around."

"Not if I catch 'em. Most are pretty careful. Their tools are their livelihood, but even if she had a tool, why? Just doesn't seem like she'd go to all the trouble, dressed like she was."

"You think someone was with her?" Liam asked Les, then checked the time on his phone. He'd gotten the call from Jacoby at five thirty and now it was just after seven.

"I don't know." Another contemplative drag on his Marlboro.

"If there was another person here, forensics might be able to find some trace of them," Dvorak said. His eyes seemed to assess the three of them with more suspicion than his taller partner.

Derek frowned and turned to Liam. "What do you think?"

"Huh?"

"Where's your head, man? We got a dead body here."

Liam looked away. He was having trouble focusing on the suicide victim, which was how he was viewing her, because of Rory. Her death would have to be investigated by the authorities, and if they determined it wasn't an accident or suicide, a homicide investigation would ensue.

Homicide?

Was it possible that she was murdered?

Liam glanced to the top of the building. Had there been a struggle? Was she pushed? Did she stumble and fall? Was she alone? Or . . . ?

Who knew?

Someone.

The crowd by the coffee shop entrance was growing. More lookie-loos staring, the skateboarder gliding across the street for a closer vantage point.

Cognizant of time ticking away, he glanced at his watch. He didn't know why this poor girl had come to the Bastian-Flavel Construction building, but she had. Maybe she'd been partying nearby and the party had transferred to the empty building. "If you don't need anything further from me, I've got to go," he said to Dvorak, then reached into his back pocket, pulled out his wallet, and retrieved a business card. "If you need me for anything else, you can reach me either at the office or on my cell."

Dvorak took his card. "We may have more questions. The detectives, you know."

"Have them call me."

"Where are you going?" Derek demanded.

"To work. At the office."

"I'll go with you."

"No." Liam was firm. "Stay and wait with them for the coroner."

Derek gazed in shock at his brother, who was usually the more responsible of the two. He appeared about to protest, but held himself back. Instead he explained to both Liam and the cops, "Look. We've been having some sabotage around here. Those broken windows? Those weren't accidental. And I know who did it, or I got a best guess anyway."

Donnelly looked from Derek to the building. "You want to make a report?"

"You bet I do. The perp, the guy who's been breaking in? His name is Everett Stemple."

"Derek," Liam snapped. "You can't just make accu—"

"That's right." Derek rolled right over him. "Everett Stemple. He's related to Liam's ex and his dad's in prison for a crime the two of them did together."

Liam's ex . . . Not yet, but soon. Annoyed, Liam yelled back at them as he walked away, "Derek, don't make conjecture sound like fact."

He heard the officer ask, "But this Everett wasn't arrested?"

"Skated somehow. But he's got a record. Probably a rap sheet a mile long." Derek was serious. The last thing Liam heard was his brother saying, "I don't know who this girl is, but check on Everett Stemple. I'd bet a trip to Las Vegas that he's involved in this somehow . . ."

*   *   *

Laurelton General was twenty minutes from the Hallifax building, but with morning traffic it took about double that time now. By the time Liam wheeled into the parking lot, he felt hot and anxious and angry. He hadn't gone to the office. He'd said that for Derek's benefit. Instead he'd driven straight here, pushing the speed limit when he could, his head wrapped in thoughts of Rory, her sick kid, and a mysterious redheaded woman who'd wound up dead at the Hallifax apartment project.

Inside the concrete-and-steel building on the west side of town, he strode to the information desk, asking for Rory Abernathy, a name which got him nowhere, so he tried Heather Johnson and mentioned that she was here with her child, who was ill and had been admitted.

"What's the patient's first name?" the helpful woman at the desk asked, smiling at him. He returned the smile, realizing he needed more information from Jacoby.

"I don't know. I know . . . Heather, she's the mother. I think they were admitted yesterday."

The welcoming glow was starting to drift from her face. "I'll check on them," she said, and Liam could tell he was being dismissed. Privacy laws. He realized the prim woman with the sharp, bespectacled eyes was on guard, ready to call security at the least little suspicious act. Damn it all to hell.

"Okay, I'll be back," he said congenially. "I'm going to hit the cafeteria."

"What's your name?" she asked.

But Liam had turned away and pretended not to hear. Hell, no, he wasn't going to announce his presence. He headed in the direction of the cafeteria, then finding an elevator, rang for it, having no idea where to go next.

His heart was pounding rapidly. Maybe he should wait out in the parking lot. Eventually she would come out, if she was here. But what if it was another wild-goose chase? Who could he call to get past the gatekeepers and find out if Rory was truly on site?

He fished his cell phone from his pocket and contacted Jacoby. The PI didn't pick up and Liam clicked off in frustration. He could text the man, and was in the process of thinking what to compose, when one of the elevators reached the main floor and its doors whispered open. He was turned slightly away, involved in his would-be call, but he looked over his shoulder and saw Darlene Stemple, dressed in some long, flowing dress, step out of the car and into the wide hallway.

He froze.

She saw him at the same moment and her mouth opened in an O of surprise. "Liam!" she shrieked as a red-haired woman stepped out of the elevator behind her, nearly colliding with her as Darlene had stopped short.

The woman's head snapped up. She stared at him and shock registered on her oh, so beautiful and familiar face.

His heart slammed into his rib cage but he didn't so much as crack a smile.

"Hi, Rory," Liam said calmly, his tone cold enough to start a new ice age.

Chapter 13

Rory stared at Liam in disbelief.

He was here? At Laurelton General Hospital?

Her stomach curled into a tight ball even as her heart did a tiny little flip at the sight of his face, older now, even more handsome, if possible. She was immediately infuriated with herself that his appearance was what she noticed first.

A part of her noticed he appeared as poleaxed as she felt, and that, at least, felt a little bit good.

"Liam," she said, swallowing, her voice a strangled whisper. "How—how did you—?" *Find me. Find us.* But it didn't matter. He was here and glaring at her, and she sensed the anger and fury and hatred he was trying to hold under control. She felt herself cringing inside. Her overriding need to flee, to escape, came to the fore, and she wanted to grab Charlotte and run as fast and faraway as possible. The condemnation on his face was nearly unbearable.

Of course she knew how he'd found her. He'd hired someone, a private investigator or ex-cop or someone who knew how to track a person. But she'd thought, she'd hoped, she'd lost him, shaken off whoever was following her.

No such luck.

"How did I . . . end up here? Locate you?" he asked, stepping closer.

It was all she could do to stand her ground. As the elevator dinged, its doors whooshing open, hospital staff, patients, and visitors all stepping in and out of the cars, she squared off with her husband, the man she hadn't laid eyes on since the day of their "wedding" five years earlier.

"It took a while." He ran a hand frustratedly through his still thick hair, a gesture she'd witnessed so many times before, in much, much happier days, that it caused her heart to ache. As if he realized that people were passing, some staring, he grabbed her arm and threaded her between two nurses deep in conversation and an aide pushing an elderly man in a wheelchair, all the while surreptitiously checking the cell phone he'd pulled from his pocket as he shepherded her along the hallway.

Rory yanked her arm away and her mother, who had been initially dumbstruck, came hurrying after them, saying, "You don't have to force her, Liam! If you want more privacy, come back up to the ICU. There's a couch in a little nook area where Rory spent the night."

"No!" Rory practically screamed. What was her mother thinking? She didn't want Liam anywhere near Charlotte. "I'm not going anywhere."

Not only was she stunned at the sight of him, she was worried sick about her kid, sleep-deprived from worry and her restless night. Hour upon hour she'd roused herself as the alarm on her cell phone had gone off. She'd then jump at the sound, force herself awake, rotate the kinks from her neck, stretch her back and legs a bit, then go to check on her sleeping child. Luckily, Charlotte always seemed to be sleeping fairly peacefully.

"I don't think you have a choice." Darlene was serious. "Just here," she added, pointing to another nook near a section of floor-to-ceiling windows, not far from the bank of elevator cars and the stairs but out of the path of doctors, nurses, patients, and visitors who passed by. It was similar to her sleeping area outside the ICU.

Rooted to the spot, Rory wanted nothing more than to take off at a sprint. To grab Charlotte and run far away to . . . anywhere. But she fought the urge. Charlotte was too sick to move, needed doctors' care and now . . . now . . . whether she wanted to admit it or not, she wasn't going to be able to avoid the truth. Liam had found her. If he didn't know about Charlotte yet, he would soon enough. "Fine," she stated flatly, even though the situation wasn't. Nothing was "fine." Not even close.

Darlene ushered her daughter and son–in–law to the alcove with its view of a parking area stretching between the hospital and a concrete-and-brick structure that housed several floors of clinics and labs. The nook was complete with two short sofas facing each other, and a coffee table—a forgotten paperback novel and several dog-eared magazines scattered across its top—wedged between them. There was barely enough room to sit down and not bang your shins on it.

Rory and Darlene sat on one sofa while Liam claimed the opposite. Rory imagined the hundreds of questions that must be racing through his brain. Bracing herself for the worst, she pressed herself into the sofa cushions as he leaned forward, his hands clasped so hard his knuckles blanched. It was almost anticlimactic when all he asked was, "Why, Rory?"

Her throat closed for a second and as she replayed those terrifying seconds when she was being attacked by the would-be killer with his otherworldly, helium-induced falsetto, when a knife slashed in the hotel room and balloons floated as if in slow motion to the ceiling. "To save . . ." She almost whispered, "Charlotte," but she stopped herself, unwilling to go there, to admit that she'd been pregnant with his child. This wasn't the time. Not here, in this public building with people wandering past and her mother sitting rigidly next to her. "I . . . I was being attacked. A man in a mask came into the room with balloons and the intent to kill me."

"With balloons?" he questioned, his brows a dark line.

"I thought it was a gift. An arrangement, you know, like flowers. Someone wishing me well before the wedding, but . . ." She struggled for the right words and couldn't find them. Every muscle in her body felt tight and her heart was beating a wild tattoo. "But . . . no. He was there because he wanted to kill me . . . and . . ." She choked on her daughter's name. This wasn't the way to tell him and yet . . . here he was, in the hospital, and soon he'd know that he'd fathered a wonderful baby girl . . . Maybe she should just spit out the truth. All of it: The good, the bad, the ugly, and the beautiful—that he had a gregarious imp of a daughter with laughing eyes and springy red curls, a girl whose sense of humor had already developed, a curious child filled with wonderment and promise, whose laugh could brighten any room. She had to tell him. "Liam, there's something you should—"

"Who?" he cut her off harshly. "Who was trying to kill you?"

"I don't know. He was disguised, wore a mask, and he threatened me with a knife and he spoke in a weird high voice, like he'd been sucking helium from the balloons. It was—terrifying." She inwardly shivered at the memory.

"Why would anybody attack you?"

"I have no idea."

"None?"

She shook her head, but was aware that it wasn't going to matter what she said. His mind was already made up. He'd lived in his own world for so long, no doubt his feelings for her souring as he slowly realized she'd duped him, that she'd let him think she might be dead. "I've asked myself that for five very long years."

"It's okay," Darlene whispered, and patted one of her hands.

"No, it's not," she said, forcing a smile that fell off her lips as soon as she managed it. "It will never be."

Liam seemed about to say something when his phone rang in his pocket. When he ignored it, Rory went on to Darlene, "Nothing's okay about this, about that terrible day and . . . and . . . Aaron." She could scarcely get out her stepbrother's name, her guilt was so huge. "He was killed in that attack. Why? I mean and you"—she focused on Liam again, his sharp features now harsh and condemning—"you were injured, could have been killed."

"I survived." Not a muscle moved on his face.

"Your father . . . he's . . . okay?"

"I don't count being confined to a wheelchair for the rest of his life being okay."

Rory squeezed her eyes shut, felt tears burn the back of her eyelids, and this time when Darlene patted her hand she didn't draw away. When she finally opened her eyes she was looking straight into Liam's. The absolute censure in his expression killed her. "I'm sorry. For everything that happened."

"Why did you vanish into thin air?" He abruptly got to his feet, banging his shin, not even registering it.

"I told you—"

"I heard. You took off from the guy who attacked you. But then you just stayed away."

She climbed to her feet as well, more carefully. "Someone did shoot at the guests. Was it him? I don't know. I just ran. And then later, when I heard what happened and it seemed like the police and everyone thought I was involved, somehow a part of the attack, it seemed safer for everyone to just not come back."

"You knew Rory was all right." His eyes bored into Darlene, who was watching the escalating argument with wide eyes.

Darlene nodded jerkily.

"And Kent Daley," he swept on. "He was in on it with that woman in Vancouver, Maude. And Connie whatever her name is, the owner of the Point Bob Buzz, she knew, too." He came around the coffee table, his face close to Rory's. "But me, your own husband, you couldn't trust with the truth. You left me to wonder what the hell happened, not knowing if you were dead or alive, if you were wounded or complicit."

It sounded so cowardly. "I thought, because of what *he* said—"

"The killer balloon man."

"Yes. I thought it would be better if I left. Safer."

"You thought the assault on the wedding was about you?"

He was jumping to conclusions, but maybe . . . yes . . . when she'd heard what happened, she'd thought she made the right choice, more than she'd even known when she first ran. "I was singled out before the ceremony, so . . ."

He'll never understand. It doesn't matter anyway.

"I have to go and check on Charlotte." She would have pushed him out of her way, but he stepped back quickly, as if full body contact was too intimate for him.

"Your daughter?" he asked.

She hesitated, saw that her mother was about to say something—Darlene, who had been mute during their argument. Rory's heart jolted as she understood. She wanted Rory to come clean about Charlotte's parentage, tell Liam that he was her father. Right now.

"Maybe this is the time," Darlene said with a little hopeful half smile, encouraging her.

Liam looked at Darlene, who'd slowly risen to her feet as well. "For what?" he asked.

Rory shook her head, trying to silently communicate with

her mother. Liam was just so damned angry. This was definitely *not* the moment, *not* the place.

"For what?" he repeated in a dangerous voice, understanding they were keeping something from him.

"Mom, I'll handle this." Rory stared hard at Darlene. "Maybe you should leave me and Liam to work things out."

"I understand, but now that you're here—"

"Mom, please. Let me handle this."

"Handle what?" Liam demanded.

"I . . . I'll go get some coffee," Darlene said, looking worriedly at Rory, clearly wanting to stay.

"I'll call you later." Rory prayed her mother would finally take the very broad hint, even though she realized she would probably have to tell Liam the truth soon anyway. After she checked on Charlotte.

"This has to do with your kid?" he deduced.

"Yes."

Suspicions were gathering in his eyes, and though she wanted to blurt out what was becoming so blatantly obvious, she just needed a few more minutes before hitting him with the fact that he was a father, had been for five years, that in essence she'd kept not only the knowledge of his paternity, but the chance to meet his baby, see her grow, watch with amusement as Charlotte developed, that she'd kept both of their whereabouts a deep secret from him.

Oh, man, this was going to be a nightmare. If he was angry now . . .

"What is it?" he demanded.

"I've got to check on Charlotte." She skimmed past him, not bothering with the elevator but heading for the stairs, passing her mother, who was taking her sweet time heading out of the building.

Liam started after Rory immediately.

Darlene called after them both. "Let her go. She's had a tremendous shock."

"*She's* shocked?" Liam's laugh was bitter, without a trace of humor. "If you haven't realized it, she's trying to run away again."

From the corner of her eye, just as she reached the door marked STAIRS, Rory saw Darlene make a quick U-turn to head back toward the elevators, following Liam. No . . . no . . . This was getting worse by the second!

"She's not running away," Darlene declared as Rory reached the stairs and yanked open the door. "Aurora would *never* leave Charlotte."

Oh, shit.

"Is that right? Because she *loves* her daughter so much?" Liam was blunt. "Don't kid yourself, Darlene, Rory would leave anyone to save her own skin."

Not true, Rory thought as the door slammed behind her. Her vision was blurred by angry, unshed tears as she climbed the carpeted steps, heading to the floor where Charlotte was situated in the ICU. She would defend Charlotte to the death, lay down her life for her child, even run away from the man she loved to protect her unborn baby. But Liam would never believe that major truth. Never. He'd painted his wife as a self-serving criminal who would flee any difficult situation. Well, fine, let him think what he wanted, she decided as she heard the door to the staircase open and bang shut below her. She and Charlotte had been on their own without Liam for over four years and they could damn well keep on as they had been, mother and child.

"Rory! Stop!" he yelled, his voice echoing through the stairwell.

Like hell. She caught a glimpse of him passing the landing of the floor below as he took the steps two at a time. Great. She kept moving, passing an intense man in scrubs and a thin goatee. He barely noticed the drama unfolding around him, his footsteps never faltering as he stared at the screen of his cell phone and headed downward. She had one more floor, but Liam was closing the gap, and as she reached the landing and took a swipe at the door handle, he caught her, his hands descending onto her shoulders.

"Wait!" he insisted.

She wanted to shake his fingers off, but stood stiff and resistant as he turned her toward him. They stared at each other. Though she felt wretched inside, her guts twisting with guilt, recrimination, and soul-blackening grief for Aaron, she refused to be intimidated. "It doesn't matter what I say to you, Liam. Whether it's the truth or some horrific lie, you won't believe me. You've already decided not to believe me. You've cast yourself as my judge and jury and, yeah, you have your reasons, but I'm not going to waste my breath and bare my soul just to hear from you how bad I am. I know what I did, and why I did it. I've beat myself up over it for five years. But I did what I thought was best at the time."

"And was it?"

"The jury's still out on that one, and I've second-guessed myself every day of my life since I ran out of that hotel and stuffed my wedding dress in a garbage can."

"And yet you had time to find another man and have a child."

She didn't answer for long moments. Was aware of the beating of her heart. The angry pulse visible at Liam's temple. Of course that's what he thought. The fact that he could be Charlotte's father hadn't crossed his mind yet.

His cell phone rang in his pocket. It momentarily distracted him and she slipped from his grasp and yanked open the door, stepping into the hallway near the ICU, where she nearly ran into one of the nurses from the unit near the elevator bank.

"Oh, Ms. Johnson," the nurse said as she punched a button to call a car. "The doctor wants to talk to you."

Her heart somersaulted. "Charlotte?"

"Your daughter's asking for you and she's much better. Dr. McMannis is going to release her to a private room in pediatrics. It should only be just a day, or a matter of hours, before she can go home . . . I can't say. You really need to talk to the doctor."

"Oh . . . thank God . . ." Rory was almost sick with relief as she hurried down the hall to the doors to the ICU, aware that Liam was right behind her.

"Wait," he called as she pounded on the buzzer and identified herself before being admitted into the unit. He was right on her heels.

The door swung open and Rory stepped through, turning back to him. "Don't try to follow me, because hospital security will throw you out. I'll make sure of it."

His face flushed. "What about the police? Will security throw them out, too? Because they've got questions for you. Lots of them."

Her stomach squeezed with fear, but she managed to hold up a hand, her index finger raised to hold him at bay. What he was saying was true. One word to the police and she'd be dragged away from this hospital, her child, and . . . "Just give me a minute with my daughter, okay?" she croaked out. "I'll be back, but first I have to make certain she's safe." The doors swung shut automatically behind her, cutting him out, and she hurried to Charlotte's bedside, where Dr. McMannis stood typing into a keyboard that swiveled out from the wall. Charlotte, a smile breaking across her face, held her arms up to her mom.

"She's going to be fine," the doctor said as Rory hugged her little girl, fighting the flood of tears that overwhelmed her. She sobbed once, then pressed her face to Charlotte's hair as the doctor explained that Charlotte was "over the hump" with this particularly virulent strain of influenza. "She's coughing less, breathing easier. We'll be moving her to the pediatric wing very soon."

"Thank you." Reluctantly Rory slowly released Charlotte.

"I want to go home, Mommy!" Charlotte cried.

"You will, very soon," the doctor assured her as Rory began to gather her daughter's things. *Home. Where was that? Not Point Roberts. Not Seattle. Not here, certainly.*

"But first you need to get better," Rory said with an encouraging smile.

"Her preschool will need to be informed," McMannis said. "To advise them of the case. There could be others."

"It's ABC and Me, in Point Roberts, Washington. I can call them."

"They are probably already all too aware, as this stuff is nasty, spreads like wildfire." She gave Charlotte a thumbs-up and said, "You do as the nurses in Pediatrics tell you, okay?"

"Okay," Charlotte responded, lifting up her thumb in response. She coughed once, but it wasn't with the same intensity. The difference between the listless girl Rory had carried into the hospital just yesterday and this bright-eyed little cherub was unbelievable.

"I'll call for an attendant to move her."

"Can I do it myself?" Rory asked. "There's someone waiting for her in the hallway."

"Well . . ." The doctor glanced at Charlotte, who was already holding up her hands for Rory to pick her up. "I'll let Pediatrics know you're coming. They'll have paperwork." To Charlotte, she added, "I'll see you in your new room."

Charlotte put her other thumb up as well and giggled, and Rory shook her head, amazed by the transformation.

The doctor said, "It's remarkable, isn't it, how they bounce back at this age." And then a shadow passed over her eyes.

"Unless they don't, that is," and Rory remembered the rumors of the child and older people who had recently died. "But with this strain, this is what happens. Either the patient suffers a few days of feeling achy and feverish, coughing and being off their food, sometimes vomiting, then makes a remarkable turn-around, or it develops into something worse." Eyeing Rory, she said, "Settle Charlotte in, then go home, Mom. You look like you could use some rest."

Amen to that, Rory thought as the doctor, glancing at the screen of her phone again, headed off. She slapped the button for the electronic doors to open, then hurried through, her lab coat billowing behind her.

Rory stifled a yawn. She'd had so little sleep in the past few days, last night being the worst, that Dr. McMannis's advice sounded like heaven. She'd asked the staff about motel rooms and had been given the name of a couple that were nearby. After making certain that Charlotte was comfortable, maybe she could check into one and get some sleep and . . .

Reality struck. Liam was waiting for her, threatening to call the police.

"Come on, sweetheart," she whispered, her throat tight. "There's someone I want you to meet. Someone special."

"Who?" Charlotte asked, her eyes bright. "Unca Kent?"

"No, honey, but it's someone who's . . . a good friend." *God help me*, Rory thought, hoping Liam's threat of the police hadn't been acted upon yet. Her heart nearly stopped at the thought of Liam surrounded by officers of the law the first time he met his daughter.

Wouldn't that just be the icing on the cake?

There was a wheelchair beside the nurses' station and Rory quickly brought it to Charlotte. The little girl was intrigued with riding and settled herself down, straightening her back like a queen.

Jaw clenched, telling herself she could do this, Rory wheeled

Charlotte back through the doors of the ICU. She spied Liam, just slipping his phone into his pocket. He'd found her little alcove where she'd spent the night. He was alone, thank God, and leaning on a pillar. His cold gaze met Rory's in a heart-stopping moment, and then fell to the girl in the chair.

Rory took a position beside Charlotte who was examining the father she'd never met, her little features—so like Liam's—pinched in confusion.

"Who are you?" she demanded, leaning toward Rory.

Here it is, Rory, thought. *The moment of truth.*

Rory put a steadying hand on her daughter's shoulder and said through a dust-dry throat, "Charlotte, honey. This is Mr. Bastian."

Liam glanced at his phone as it rang again. Beth had been calling him and texting him since he'd left her. After being fairly passive when they'd parted at his apartment this morning, she'd done a complete about-face, apparently. He'd tried to ignore her, but this time he'd finally decided to answer, only to see that the call was from Derek.

"Hi, Derek."

"Where are you?" his brother demanded.

"Still at the hospital."

"The what?"

"The hospital." He drew a breath. "Rory's here. With her daughter."

"Wait. What? Rory's *here*? *Your* Rory?"

"Remember when you said you thought the woman who died at Hallifax was Rory? That you figured she might be back, and I laughed at you? Turns out you weren't far from the truth."

"Jesus."

"And she's got a kid. A sick daughter." Hearing the anger in his voice, he forced himself to be civil. None of this was Derek's fault. "I'm at Laurelton General."

Derek let out a long breath. "Holy shit, what a day."

"You called for a reason," Liam reminded him.

"The police, a couple of detectives, want to talk to you about the dead girl. I told them you were the one who found her."

"Les actually found her, but okay." A couple of detectives . . . "Do they think it was a homicide?"

"Don't know. You might want to call them. I have a number." He reeled it off to Liam, who told him to text it to him. Derek agreed and hung up.

Liam glanced at the window, the summer day was bright, the sun partially veiled by high clouds. His watch told him it was nearly eleven, but it felt even later. Hearing the faint beep of an incoming text, he saw the number on his screen, along with Beth's texts.

Where are you? Call me.

Are you still at the hospital? Was the woman Rory? Are you okay? CALL me.

The phone rang again and he saw it was Derek again. "Did you get it?" Derek asked when Liam answered.

"Yep, I'll call 'em."

"Jesus, Liam. Rory, huh? Just like . . . out of the blue?"

Just after Pete DeGrere's murder.

Was there something in that?

"I'll talk to you later," Liam said, clicking off as the doors to the ICU began to swing open and Rory came through, pushing a wheelchair whose occupant was a girl a little older than a toddler.

As she approached his heart stuttered a little. No infant. This child was three or four. Her hair was a riot of red curls, her little nose freckled, but her eyes and the shape of her face . . . *Viv*, he thought wildly. *She looks like Vivian as a child!*

Ashen-faced, looking as if she might take the kid and bolt at any second, Rory took a place beside the girl's chair and made introductions, though he barely heard them.

His throat closed and he felt his eyes burn. *His* child. *His.* Charlotte had to be his. He'd thought about it when he'd first learned she had a kid, but had instantly tossed the idea aside, never believing that for a second she would actually take his unborn child from him and then hide the fact.

He couldn't take his eyes off the little girl. "She's . . . mine . . ."

There was a long, long moment where he could hear Rory's stuttered breathing. He tore his gaze from Charlotte, risked a look at Rory. She didn't say anything, but her very silence was answer enough.

Chapter 14

"You . . . ran away *knowing she was mine!*" He heard himself, the shock and anger in his voice.

"I was attacked, Liam. *Attacked.* And he, whoever he was, threatened the life of my baby!"

That's not enough! he wanted to roar.

"And he . . . he seemed to know I was pregnant," she was saying through a shaking voice. "He said something about that."

"This attacker? *He* knew?"

"Or . . . guessed, I don't know! I was scared, scared for all of us. I—"

"Mommy?" Charlotte asked anxiously.

Rory cut off what she was about to say, casting an uncertain glance at her daughter. She drew an unsteady breath, pulled herself together and stated softly, "Hey, pumpkin, I bet you're hungry and Doctor McMannis said we've got to keep you full of liquids, so . . ."

"A milkshake?" Charlotte asked, lifting her head. "Chock-lit!"

"I don't see why not. I'll talk to the nurses when we get to your new room." She pressed a kiss onto her daughter's forehead and it seemed a natural expression of affection, one she'd done automatically and probably thousands of times before. She inhaled and exhaled several times, never looking at him, then said in an aside, "I'm taking Charlotte to Pediatrics. She's better, thank God. Probably be released tomorrow. Once I'm sure she's okay, then we'll talk . . . I'll explain . . ."

There was a thundering surf inside Liam's head. Threatening to drag him under. Drowning him. A tidal wave of disbelief, even though he believed . . . *he believed.*

From a distance he heard, "I'll tell you whatever it is you want to know then, and we can sort things out."

All the words he wanted to say were jammed in his mind. He felt an urgency to hold the little girl, but it scared him, too. His daughter . . . *his daughter.* One Rory kept from him all these years!

He would demand a paternity test, of course, but the timing, and Charlotte's facial features . . . Jesus, he *knew.*

He had a child? A daughter? Oddly, he felt a burst of elation at the idea. Ludicrous, given the situation. Rory was a fugitive and a liar and possibly involved in murder and . . . "She's going to be okay?" he managed to get out.

"Yes, it was the flu. Extreme case. Scary and can be dead—dangerous. But the doctor thinks Charlotte is going to be okay and—"

"What doctor?" He glanced at the doors from which Rory and Charlotte had emerged. "One in ICU?" The gravity of the situation slammed through him. What Rory was skirting, hinting at, was that his kid could have died from the virus? "Wait a second. She was released from Intensive Care?"

"Yes. Because she's so much better, thank God. Dr. McMannis—she's the doctor who took care of Charlotte—said that

Charlotte's improved enough that she could be released as early as tomorrow." Tears of relief shimmered in Rory's green eyes and Liam felt his chest tighten. The old emotions that he'd felt with Rory, those aching sensations of love and fascination that he'd tamped down for years, threatened to rise again, but he shoved them back down, buried them deep before they escaped. She was saying, "You can speak to Dr. McMannis yourself, but she assured me—"

"I will," he cut in, making a mental note to grill McMannis up one side and down the other. But first, since Charlotte seemed well enough, there were other pressing problems to deal with. The ICU doors opened again, and an orderly pushing a gurney with a pale, unresponsive teen connected to an attached IV pole slipped through.

The doors swung closed again as Rory made a sound of dismay. She was looking past him toward the bank of elevators. If possible her skin blanched even more, her eyes widening, her quick intake of breath a soft gasp. She blinked and swallowed, blinking away the tears as she visibly stiffened, as if readying for another confrontation.

For a second he thought the police had caught up with her. But twisting to glance over his shoulder he saw no uniformed officers fast approaching. It was Beth striding their way, her chin up, eyes focused on Liam and Rory. She stopped dead in her tracks not five feet away and, as if she'd overheard part of the conversation, she, too, had lost color, her lips compressed into a thin line.

"Beth," he greeted her. She shook her head at him, red-blond hair sweeping her shoulders, warning him not to say anything more. She was shorter than usual, not wearing her usual heels, and she'd dressed down from the clothes she'd put on at his apartment, into jeans and a long-sleeved T-shirt, her most casual. She tried to hide the wounded look that shadowed her eyes, a despair that should have touched him, should have made him feel guilty and yearn to fold her into his arms. The fact that it didn't said something he'd already known but hadn't wanted to face. He felt sorry for her, for finding out about Charlotte this way, and he felt the same about himself as he stood between the two women he'd once professed to love. But one he didn't, the other he did.

He knew it.

She knew it.

How had things gotten so twisted around?

Simple: Because Rory had lied. All of this pain, all of this confusion, all of these complicated emotions were because the woman he'd married had lied, run away and disappeared, leaving everyone else to pick up the pieces.

But it was to save her child. Your child.

If you believe her.

Clearing her throat, Beth broke the awkward silence. "I see you've come back finally," she said to Rory.

"Yes," Rory said tightly.

"What's going on?" Beth stepped closer to Liam. A proprietary gesture. "Liam?" she asked, but her gaze was on Rory and the little girl in her arms. Her jaw slid to one side. "Oh, let me guess. She's saying this child is . . . *yours*?" Obviously Beth didn't believe it for an instant and Liam couldn't blame her, except the resemblance to the Bastians was so damned evident it was hard to argue. Surely even Beth could recognize the distinctive hairline and chin.

Rory's grip tightened around Charlotte.

"We're not doing this here," Liam warned, seeing the storm clouds gathering in Bethany's eyes. Just this morning he was wishing for some outward emotion from her.

And now? He was pretty certain he didn't want to go there.

"We're engaged, did he tell you?" Beth challenged Rory. "Just this morning we talked about our plans and—"

"Beth! I said, not here. And we're not engaged."

"Not officially, yet," she answered, unruffled. "But we're moving in together this fall."

"Congratulations?" Rory said dryly, meeting Beth's eyes, her own green chips of ice.

"Nothing's been decided," Liam responded, his penetrating gaze on Beth, whose gaze was focused on Rory and Charlotte.

With a lift of her shoulders to indicate they were only talking semantics, she asked Liam softly, "You can't be defending her. The woman who literally left you standing at the altar? The one who ran out before the shooting?" She slid him a look of warning. "You and your father were nearly killed and her own brother . . . died."

Liam said tautly, "I can handle this, Beth."

"She's a *fugitive.*"

"I know what she is."

The elevator chimed, a light indicating a car on the nearest shaft had arrived. The doors opened and Stella, in white pants, heels, a peach silk top and a hard expression, charged out. On her heels was Vivian, who, similarly dressed, looked like the proverbial doe in headlights, as if she didn't know what was happening and why she was a part of it. Then Derek followed a few paces behind his stepmother. Only Geoff was missing.

Rory sighed and turned slightly away, protecting the daughter in her arms.

"What're you doing here?" Liam asked Stella.

"What're *you* doing here?" his mother repeated, casting a hard look at Rory. To Liam, she asked, "What's going on? Where are the police? Why hasn't she been arrested?" Her gaze flicked to Charlotte, then back to Liam, then immediately back to Charlotte. "Oh," she said, gulping. "Oh, Lord."

"Praying isn't going to help," Vivian said dryly, sounding more like her old self.

Liam turned on his brother. "You brought them? Why?" Before Derek could answer, he ordered, "Get them out of here." He gazed determinedly at his family and Beth. "All of you, I don't know why you're here, but this isn't the time or place."

Stella said, "For the love of God, Liam. I've been worried about you. I wanted to know where you were with all that's going on. Shouldn't I be worried? I forced Derek to tell me."

"With what's going on?" he repeated.

"The dead girl. On the job site. The redhead."

Liam saw Rory whip back around, zeroing in on Stella. Long-suffering, he said, "Mom. Not here. Not now."

Stella breezed past him just as a cell phone jangled and a passing hospital worker dressed in scrubs answered as he banged his hand hard against the elevator call button. She stared hard at Rory and Charlotte, but said to Liam, "I don't know what she's trying to pull here, but we'll let the authorities take care of it."

"We're not calling the police." Liam's voice was steel.

"What dead girl?" Rory asked.

"A woman jumped off the roof of one of our company's buildings, the Hallifax apartments," Stella said in a staccato voice, as if she were being forced. "A project managed by Liam."

"Jumped?" Rory repeated, aghast.

"What?" Beth stiffened. "Someone died? At Hallifax?"

"Swan-dived," Derek said.

Liam sent him a sharp look, but for once his brother was completely serious.

Stella said, "It's all very disturbing. Derek told us and your father before he brought us here." They had moved as a group to the far side of a hallway, gathered in front of unoccupied chairs and a couch flanked by two ficus trees that were leaning toward the light streaming through wide windows.

Viv said, "I came because I wanted to see that you were okay. I had to leave the children with Dad. The babysitter, who's turning out to be more unavailable than available, couldn't be reached *again* and we were in a hurry to get here because so much is going on." Her gaze was firmly set on Rory and Charlotte.

"Fine," Liam bit out.

Charlotte frowned. "Mommy?"

"Shhh. It's nothing, honey. Let's go." To Liam and the others, she said, "I'm taking my daughter to Pediatrics."

"I'll come with you," Liam said, to which she shot him a withering look, then turned on her heel toward the hallway where a sign read: CHARLES M. ROBINSON CHILDREN'S CENTER, and took off, pushing Charlotte's wheelchair ahead of her.

"What are you thinking?" Vivian asked him, her gaze still on Rory and Charlotte as they disappeared down the hallway . . .

Disappeared. What if Rory takes off again?

Panic scorched through him. She wouldn't leave again, would she? Not with the little girl still under doctor's care.

"I'm going down to Pediatrics," he said.

"So, she's yours?" Viv asked.

He didn't answer. His mind was on Rory. No. She would never risk harming her child.

"The kid," Derek clarified. "Viv wants to know if—"

"Yes!" He was 99 percent certain.

"God, he's hopeless," Viv declared on a sigh, then turned to Beth. "We Bastians all love each other, of course, but we're a pain in the ass. You'd be better off without him."

"I don't think so," Beth said, her gaze zeroing in on Liam. He didn't love her. He knew it, and he was certain she did, too. With Rory here, that realization had grown diamond hard.

"Can't believe Rory's back," Vivian said, checking her watch. "The last time I saw her was before the wedding, then we were all attacked and her stepbrother died and now this woman jumps off our building . . . ?"

Derek gave a short laugh. "You can't blame Rory for that."

Vivian asked, "You think it was suicide? Or something else?"

"What are you suggesting?" Liam questioned, counting the elapsing minutes in his head. Should he go? Now? Rory wouldn't want him there, but what the hell did he care? He didn't trust her. Couldn't.

"Maybe she was pushed," Viv suggested.

Derek laughed louder as Beth glared at Vivian and Stella warned, "For God's sake, don't let your imagination run away with you! We don't know anything yet."

"You said something about the police," Viv retorted.

Derek answered her, "They always investigate."

"Still, it's creepy." Viv drew a breath then exhaled, turning her gaze toward the hallway down which Rory had disappeared and where now an aide was pushing a boy of about ten in a wheelchair toward the pediatric wing.

Liam wasn't waiting around any longer. "Why don't you all go and let me handle this." To Beth, he added, "I'll catch up with you later."

"What are you going to handle?" she asked him sharply.

"I'm going to find out about Charlotte."

"Spoken like a dad already." Vivian turned to her mother. "I've got to get home anyway. Dad can't watch the kids for two long and that babysitter's flaked on me one too many times."

"Geoffrey can handle them," Stella snapped.

"Oh, sure. No, Mom, he can't. Liam wants us to leave, and I'm all for that." She inclined her head toward the elevators.

Stella suddenly turned to Liam. "You need to come by the

house and see your father. He's in a state about all this, you can imagine. As soon as you're through here, okay?"

"I'll see." Liam just wanted to get the hell away from all of them.

"Do it," Stella implored.

"You can't trust Rory," Beth warned.

"I know about Rory," he said tightly. He took off at a half run down the hallway, following the signs to the pediatric wing, thinking of all that he'd already missed, not only Charlotte's birth, but her growth from infant to toddler, to the girl she was now. He'd not witnessed her first smile, first tooth, first wobbly steps, first taste of ice cream . . .

But she was still very young.

He still had time. She was *his*. He had lots of time.

Depending on Rory.

Rory. His mouth tightened. He didn't know whether he wanted to strangle her or kiss her, to argue with her or make love to her, to turn her over to the police or to whisk her and Charlotte away and escape. Just as she had done five years earlier.

He spied the nurses' station just as another thought crossed his mind, one even darker: On the day Rory had disappeared, people had died. Now she was back, and there were two more unexplained deaths: the murder of Pete DeGrere and the accidental death or suicide of the girl at the Hallifax apartment building.

They couldn't be connected, especially the girl who'd fallen from the top floor of their building.

The red hair of the victim seemed to overtake his inner vision and he shook it away as his cell phone rang. "Hello?" he answered automatically.

"Liam Bastian?" a male voice asked.

"Yes," he said and his steps slowed. Rory was just ahead and deep in conversation with a heavyset nurse clad in neon pink scrubs as they disappeared through a doorway.

"This is Detective Willard Grant, Portland Police Department."

Oh. Jesus. He noted the room number into which Rory had stepped, then caught a glimpse of a doorway to an inner courtyard. One look suggested the garden was empty, more private than this hallway. Shouldering open the glass door, he stepped into a miniature garden, complete with concrete paths and child-sized benches. Characters from *Alice in Wonderland* peeked from beneath lacy fern fronds and thick-leaved hostas.

"I'm calling about the woman found dead on your property."

A frisson up his back. He'd just been thinking about her. At least it wasn't about Rory.

"Could you come to the office and make a statement?" the detective asked.

"Sure . . . about?"

"How you came upon the body. We're asking the same of Lester Steele and Derek Bastian."

"All right. How about later this afternoon? I'm tied up right now." His gaze moved down the row of windows surrounding the courtyard, and stopped at the one he thought was to Charlotte's room, the window directly above a series of brightly colored wooden toadstools, the perfect size for a toddler to perch upon.

"We know the identity of the victim, Teri Mulvaney."

"Never heard of her."

"Let me give you what we've got . . ."

As Liam stood in the sunlight in the miniature garden, the detective explained that Teri Mulvaney was a thirtysomething who had spent time at a bar near the Hallifax apartment project, and that her car and ID were located in the bar's parking lot. The police were trying to establish a connection, it seemed, between Teri Mulvaney and anyone who worked on the project at Hallifax or the Bastian company.

"Look, Detective Grant, I don't think I can help you," Liam said, feeling time ticking away. How long had he been out here already? Five minutes? Ten? Time enough for Rory to flee.

No, no, no. She won't leave Charlotte.

Still, he couldn't linger in this walled oasis. He glanced again at the window of the hospital room he thought was Charlotte's, the pane positioned above the toadstools. He even spied the heavyset nurse in her bright scrubs through the glass. "I've never heard of a Teri Mulvaney, and I don't think we've ever hired her. I saw her, you know, and didn't recognize her. You're welcome to check any of the employee records. I'll come down to the station as soon as I'm finished at the hospital."

"And when will that be?"

"An hour or so?"

The detective checked his schedule.

The White Rabbit near a fountain checked his watch.

Seconds in real time ticked away.

The July sun was relentless and Liam was already sweating.

"I'll be here," the detective said.

"All right, I'll meet you at the station." Liam finally clicked off, then twisted the kinks out of his neck and turned to head into the hospital again.

But the doorway was blocked. By Rory.

He didn't know how long she'd been standing there, but from the looks of her, long enough. Her expression carefully neutral, she asked, "You're going to the police station?"

"It's not about you," Liam answered her quickly.

"No?" Rory asked. The question had clearly caught him off guard, but his words had started her pulse pounding. The police, yes. She was going to have to face them sometime soon. She just wasn't ready yet!

You never will be.

"That was about a woman found dead at one of our properties, the Hallifax apartment reconstruction. That's why the police are contacting me."

"Teri Mulvaney."

"You heard that, too."

She nodded stiffly. Inside, she was falling apart. Seeing Liam again, dealing with him, was using up the small amount of energy she still had left.

"I don't have all the information, but it appears that she may have jumped," Liam said. "No one's telling me that for sure. Two homicide detectives have asked me to come down to the station and discuss her death." He paused, then added, "I would have been here sooner this morning, but her death took precedence. I came from Hallifax directly here."

"You never said how you knew to find me at this hospital."

"I got a call from the private investigator I hired to find you," he admitted.

She'd suspected that he'd hired a PI, but to hear him say it aloud made her go cold. The car that Connie had followed, which had been in turn following Liam? Was that whom he meant? "This investigator followed me from Point Roberts to Vancouver to *here*?"

"Yes," he said after a long moment.

She shivered, remembering how she'd thought Everett was following her. "What's his name? He found me at the hospital. He came to this hospital? He . . . oh!"

"What?"

Rory was remembering the man she'd seen in the cafeteria. The one who'd reminded her of Everett.

"His name's Brian Jacoby."

"I want to meet him," she demanded. "I want to meet him face-to-face."

Liam said slowly, "Okay. I understand . . ."

"Do you? *Do you?* I kept thinking I was being followed. I knew it! And I was scared and it was because of *him*! You did that."

Liam's face flushed. "You want to point blame at me for all of this?"

"I want to feel safe! That's what I want!"

Liam shook his head, angry. His gaze suddenly shifted past her, toward the door she'd just walked through. "Shit," he muttered.

She twisted around and there were Derek and Bethany, coming out to the garden where they stood. She knew exactly how Liam felt. *Shit.*

Derek was just pushing through, saying, "We took a vote. We're not leaving you alone with your . . . wife."

"We have a few more things to say before you banish us," Beth added, her gaze skating off Rory and landing belligerently on Liam.

Liam's face was tight. She could tell he was fighting to maintain his cool. Before he could explode, Derek turned to Rory, his eyes cool as he slowly looked her over, his gaze settling on her hair. "Hello, Rory. You're looking good. Long time, no see. Had a kid, huh?"

Beth interrupted, "I don't want to come off like a complete bitch, but I'm not going to let Rory ruin you again." She flicked a cold look at Rory. "He damn near *died*, and all you did was run away!"

"Beth," Liam warned.

"Don't tell me to stop," she snapped. "I have a right to say how I feel!"

"Later. Not here. Not now." Liam's lips were flat. "I asked you to let me handle this."

"Did you bring up Pete DeGrere?" Derek tossed out.

"I'm talking," Beth said tightly.

But Derek had the floor and he wasn't the kind to give it up. "You know about DeGrere? The guy the authorities thought did the shooting?"

He was asking Rory and she shook her head. She'd heard the name from The Magician, but there had never been an arrest, as far as she knew.

"He's the guy that did it," Derek proclaimed. "And he was killed on his first day out of prison. Just *two days ago*! Funny you show up, right on the heels of his murder."

"Derek!" Liam practically roared.

"Liam, can you give me just one minute?" Beth's voice could cut glass.

"Both of you need to just go!"

"She's influencing you already," Beth gasped. "You don't even see!"

"Your stepbrother, Everett, killed him," Derek stated with conviction, staring Rory down.

Liam moved forward swiftly, practically pushing them both back through the door into the hospital.

Rory sank down onto one of the toadstools. She felt almost dizzy, her head full of all the words and accusations swirling between her and Liam. His family hated her. Yet she couldn't take her eyes off Liam, aware how much she longed to be around him even now.

He returned alone a few minutes later.

"I don't want to talk anymore," she told him, distantly aware how defeated she sounded.

Long moments passed, then he nodded. "I'm going to go to the police station. Might as well get that behind me. Give me your cell phone number and I'll add it to my contact list."

Rory told him the number and watched him enter it into his phone.

"I'm sorry," he said. "For my family and Beth."

Rory shot him a look, a little surprised.

"I'll be back later." A pause and the faintest of smiles. "Don't go anywhere."

"I won't," she said, meaning it.

He nodded to her and left.

Chapter 15

Sitting on the sofa outside Pediatrics, Rory glanced at the screen of her phone, noting the low battery icon. She'd been living in the hospital for nearly two days and she was about out of juice, both with her electronics and herself. She was worn out and weary. Relieved Charlotte was on the mend, but nearly overwhelmed by everything else. Thank God Liam was gone for a while. She needed a respite. It was hell not having a good defense. All she knew was that she loved her daughter more than anything in this world and she was thankful, so thankful, Charlotte was going to be all right, and there was no way in hell that Liam, or any of the Bastians, for that matter, were going to get in the way of that. Their money would not make the difference. She would make sure of that.

You ran from the shooting. They could make a case using that alone.

"I didn't know about it at the time," she said aloud.

You have fake identification, no current job, a stepfather in prison, and a stepbrother who may be responsible for crimes which the authorities are working to prove. They could make a case using any of that.

"Liam won't try to take her from me," she answered, but her voice wavered a bit.

She didn't know what Liam would or wouldn't do. And his fiancée . . . even if it wasn't official, Bethany acted as if they were engaged, or as well as.

She sensed that Bethany, with her now more red than blond hair, was someone who would fight to the death for what she wanted . . . and she wanted Liam.

Rory set the cell phone on the table, squeezed her eyes closed, and ran her hands through her hair, tugging at the ends, purposely causing herself pain. She wanted to WAKE UP and have this all over. She'd known this day of reckoning would come with Liam. She'd just hoped Charlotte would be older.

Wishing wasn't going to make it happen, more's the pity.

Picking up her phone again, she considered calling The Magician. Uncle Kent and Maude had checked in with her, wanting to help, but she'd told them she was fine, that Charlotte had the flu but was improving, that she would soon be on her way south. She didn't mention the Bastians. Wanted to see how things went before getting them involved, which could be problematic for The Magician. It helped that she knew Maude and Kent were always there for her. She just wasn't sure what was going to happen next, and she didn't want to drag Kent into this battle with the Bastians until she understood what the rules of war were.

Her cell rang in her hand, sending a frisson of alarm up her spine. She looked at the screen and recognized her mother's number. She sensed anger mounting inside her, but she tamped it down. She wanted to be mad at someone, but none of this was Darlene's fault.

"Hi, Mom," she answered, pressing the cell to her ear.

"How's it going, Rory? Are you all right?"

"Just beat."

"You're still at the hospital," she realized. "Is Liam there?"

"He left a little while ago."

"Are you going to come stay with me?"

"I'm not driving to Salem, Mom. I don't want to be that far away from Charlotte."

"It's only an hour away," she argued.

"In good traffic. I've asked around. There's a motel not too far away that's pretty cheap. I'll just go crash there."

"I could come back, if you'd like," she offered.

Rory almost snapped that she didn't need her mother's help, but stopped herself. Darlene was hard to corral, but she was one of the pitifully few people on Rory's side. "I'm . . . fine. I'll call you later, okay?"

"Don't completely write off Liam," Darlene said quickly. "Charlotte's his, and blood wins out every time."

This was just the kind of thing Rory didn't want to hear and was why she couldn't lean on her mother. "What if he wants to take Charlotte away, Mom? If that's what you mean by blood wins, then yeah. It does, and I lose."

"I'm just saying that—"

"I don't want the Bastians' help. Any of it! They're having a DNA test done and God knows what will happen when it's totally proven that Charlotte is Liam's daughter. I just . . . I don't want to talk about it anymore."

"You're Charlotte's mother. It'll be okay."

Rory almost laughed. It was *not* going to be okay. "I've gotta go. I'll call later."

She clicked off and shoved the phone back in her purse. She was upset and scared, and Darlene's rationale didn't help. What chance did she have against Liam's family and their armada of high-priced lawyers? None! But she'd die before she let them separate her from her child.

You might have to run.

Her heart twisted at the thought. No . . . no . . . she was tired of running, and when had that ever helped her anyway? She'd run from the ruins of her relationship with Cal and all the pain that came with the miscarriage, a bit of her past she'd never told Liam about, and she'd run from Liam, too. To protect her unborn child and to just *get away*. Everett had scared her and she'd run from him. She didn't know whether Derek was right about him being involved in the sabotage, but she could believe anything when it came to her stepbrother. Her mother had acted like Everett had changed, was married and respectable now. Ha! A leopard didn't change his spots that much.

She got to her feet. Time to find that motel, maybe get a little bit of sleep, and think things over. She had enough cash to keep going for a while, but sooner or later she would need to start making plans for the future. What those plans would be, she didn't know.

But she wasn't going to rely on the Bastians. That would be playing right into their hands.

As she headed out of the hospital she realized she'd given Liam her number but she hadn't taken his. Well, she didn't need it, did she? She wanted nothing to do with him or his family, though that was a pipe dream on her part; they would be keeping in close contact with her and Charlotte whether she liked it or not.

She walked out through the main hospital front doors, standing for a moment in the late afternoon sun, trying to remember where she'd parked her car. Getting here with Charlotte was a blur. A moment passed and she recalled she'd left it on the lower level of the hospital's north side. She could either walk around the building and down some steps, or go back inside and find an elevator and the north-side exit.

It was then she noticed the van with its open door and the Channel 7 logo on the side. A news team. She momentarily wondered what the story was that they were reporting, and then realized the cameraman had spotted her and focused his lens right at her.

Her heart jumped.

Was *she* the story? Could they know about her already? *Would Liam tell them?* She saw a well-dressed woman in heels, the reporter, lean in to the cameraman and then turn her coiffed head Rory's way.

My red hair gives me away.

Rory ducked back into the building, yanking open the door, and stumbled into the main reception area. Anxiety driving her, she race-walked down the hall to the elevators, jumped into a waiting car, and punched the number for the next lowest floor. When she emerged into the correct parking lot, she glanced quickly right and left, but there was no one waiting for her, as far as she could tell.

She practically ran to her car and yanked open the door. Three minutes later, her heart rate still in the stratosphere, she eased out of the parking lot. Angry and scared, she kept checking her mirrors. If the media knew about her, how far behind were the authorities? Stella had said she should be arrested. Maybe she'd called the authorities, an arrest warrant had already been issued and what . . . leaked? Not that it mattered. Somehow the news team had found out about it and was following up.

Arriving before the cops.

Oh, geez. How long before the police get here?

She was shaking, her hands quivering on the wheel, sweat beading on her forehead and palms. Whoever had tipped off the cops or the news people or whoever, it was a first salvo in the battle for Charlotte.

Damn you, Liam!

She felt tears collect on her lashes and angrily brushed them away.

To hell with them all.

If they wanted a fight, they had one.

"There's no way that child's yours," Stella said for the umpteenth time, pouring a second glass of scotch for Geoff and setting it on the outdoor table in front of him. She poured one for herself as well and lifted her brows to Liam, who shook his head.

He was standing by a pillar a few feet away, sunlight bouncing off the surface of the pool, half blinding him. His niece and nephew were cavorting in the water, shrieking with delight, while his sister, in the shade of the umbrella, watched them closely. Liam had his phone to his ear, trying to reach Detective Grant, wanting to reschedule with him. He'd been given the update on Teri Mulvaney and, once he thought about it, he didn't believe it was urgent that he go down to the station immediately. On the other hand, Stella's imperative to stop by his parents', though he'd dismissed it at the time, had suddenly become more important. He knew them. Knew how his family planned and wrangled, and he didn't want them making decisions about Rory and Charlotte they had no right to.

And no matter what Stella thought, he sensed that Charlotte was his. He'd ordered a DNA test to prove to his family that he was her father. He was already convinced.

"What about you?" Stella asked, turning to Vivian, who was standing by the edge of the pool, lost in thought. Derek, who'd basically crashed this party, as Stella hadn't actually invited him, was sprawled in a chair. He was still in his work pants, but he'd taken his shirt off. Though his pose was relaxed, his face looked troubled and tense.

"No, thanks," Vivian said.

"I'll take a drink," Derek told Stella, who gave him a cool look. She had never made any bones about her feelings for Geoff's first wife's offspring, but she did get him the glass of scotch, plunking it down on the table beside him, earning her a "what gives?" look from Derek, which she ignored.

"We don't even know the child is a Bastian," Stella said again.

"I've ordered a DNA test," Liam said shortly. He'd mentioned it as soon as he'd entered the house, but no one had paid him much attention.

"She doesn't even look like you," Stella said.

"She looks like Vivian," Liam fired back.

He finally was put through to Detective Grant, and learned, to his surprise, that Desmond Grant was a classmate of his from high school. They hadn't been the closest of friends, but they'd been on the football team together. After a few moments of catching up, Grant told Liam it was fine if he came in the next day. The detective had warmed up considerably during their conversation and was uncommonly forthcoming with Liam. "We're getting some forensics. The victim was sexually active close to her death and we have a semen sample," he said. "We're checking into her whereabouts earlier in the evening, but her roommate says she had no current boyfriend. Should have more information by the time you come in."

"Okay," Liam said. After he hung up Liam almost rethought his refusal of the scotch before deciding he needed to keep his wits about him. Absently, he rubbed at his thigh, massaging the scar from the ravaging bullet, more a habit than from any real pain.

"I can't believe you have a child," Vivian muttered. Unlike

Stella, Viv had accepted that Charlotte was his, without the corroborating evidence sent to the private lab that promised fast results. Nonetheless Vivian's lips were pressed tight, her normal breeziness was absent.

"Worried about who inherits, sister, dear?" Derek asked with a sly grin.

"Oh, stop," she groaned.

Geoff grunted. "Leave it, Derek. Liam's right. DNA will prove who the sick girl's parents are."

"Her name's Charlotte," Liam reminded everyone.

Stella didn't hide her disgust. Hitching up her chin, she said, "Aurora got herself pregnant just to be part of the family."

"Thought you said there was no way the kid was a Bastian," Derek drawled.

"Goddamnit! Shut up, Derek!" Geoff shot back.

Liam looked at his father, who rarely let himself be baited, although he could faintly recall a long time earlier when Geoff would occasionally fall victim to the mercurial temper he kept under tight control and curl his fists as if he was going to hit something or someone. A vague memory flitted across Liam's consciousness—something about his father and Derek—hard to grasp, blown to smithereens when Vivian suddenly looked toward the house and her mouth dropped open in surprise.

"Shit," she said under her breath.

Liam followed her gaze and saw Javier Vega step from the interior of the house to the pool area. Vivian's soon-to-be ex-husband.

Geoff's brows knotted and Stella looked taken aback as well. "Brace yourself," Stella whispered.

"Hello," Javier said, and added quickly, "Sorry to show up unannounced, but . . ." Shrugging, leaving the apology in the air, he crossed beneath the shade of the umbrella to the spot where Vivian stood, then said softly, "I hope this is okay. You told me the door would be open."

Nodding, she said, "Yeah, I know. I made sure it was unlocked. I just didn't—I wasn't sure you'd come," she admitted. The naked hope on her face was painful to witness.

"You said it was important." Javier flicked a glance toward Geoff and Stella. "But . . . maybe I'm intruding."

Geoff shook his head stiffly, winced a bit, grumbling as he pulled at the neck brace. "Damn thing," he growled as he waved a hand at Javier to sit in one of the deck chairs.

Javier was a tall, fit man with dark coloring and a smooth, jungle-cat way of moving. In a white shirt and dark chinos, his near-black hair a bit longish, his feet in a pair of woven sandals, he looked the epitome of the macho Latin lover. Liam had never had a problem with the man, but he could sense the heightened awareness of the rest of his family at his unexpected appearance.

"Daddy!" Landon shrieked, swimming toward the edge of the pool, his arms held aloft by floaties.

"Hi, little man," Javier said, smiling and kneeling as his son splashed toward him.

"Daddy, Daddy!" Estella cried, jumping up and down. She was on the steps in the shallow end, also with floaties. She tumbled into the water from her excitement, and Vivian, springing to the edge of the pool, grabbed for her, bringing her back to the steps. Javier immediately straightened and asked if someone shouldn't be in the water with her.

"I've got my suit on under this." Vivian pointed to her shirt and shorts, flushing at being silently reprimanded by the man she was so patently trying to impress. Then, rather than get into an argument, it seemed, she turned the conversation back to his original statement. "It *is* important, Javier. Liam's little wifey showed up in Portland. And guess what? She's got a kid.

A girl. About four years old. When's her birthday, Liam? Did she tell you?"

Little wifey . . . Vivian had liked Rory once, or so she'd said.

"No, I don't know," he answered.

"Didn't ask her, did you?" Vivian's gaze slid from Liam to Javier. "Well, I did. Her birthday's about two months before Landon's."

Derek barked out a short laugh as he caught on. "You're worried about her being the eldest heir? Is that it? Well, don't be. Okay? Doesn't matter in this family." He spread his hands, then hooked his thumbs at himself. "Case in point."

Javier had turned to stare at Liam. "Your *wife's* here?"

Stella swooped in. "Yes, and her daughter is in the hospital with the flu. Getting better, but the girl's the reason Aurora showed up again, I'm going to guess. Aurora has no money, and she thinks we're all going to step up and take care of her and the girl."

"You don't know why she's here," Liam ground out.

"Oh, yes. Go ahead and defend her, Liam." Stella swirled her drink and seethed. "That woman's always been your blind spot. God knows why." Glaring at him imperiously, she took a sip.

"Well, if she's come here for money, she clearly doesn't know this family," Derek said. "You gotta earn your place in the Bastian hierarchy. Some of us just don't make the grade."

Geoff's eyes narrowed. "That's right," he said, his burst of anger replaced by his iron will once more.

Derek and Geoff had unresolved issues. They'd always treated each other carefully, as if one wrong step might start something neither wanted. But they'd never been so outright antagonistic as today. Rory's reappearance had triggered some latent emotion, one with an ugly side.

"You're not amusing," Stella told Derek sternly.

Liam had had enough. "I've got to go," he said to the group of them—his family—as he pushed away from the pillar. "So I'm going to head out."

"Oh, no, you're not leaving." Vivian stared pointedly at him from the other side of the pool. "We need to get some things straight in this family. I need a job, for one. No one's telling me anything about what's going on. Javier and I are getting ready to div . . ." She trailed off as Javier gazed pointedly at her, then at the kids. She finished with, "I need a job, that's all I'm saying. You all know it."

"I'm still here, in case you've all forgotten," Geoff growled, rolling his chair backward to find the shade again as the sun was inching across the sky. "You can have a damn job, Viv. Work it out with Liam. He'll find a place for you."

"Maybe you can work with me," Derek suggested, sitting up, his drink in one hand, his sarcastic smirk in place. He pretended to think for a second. "But I do more of the hard work, you know. More of a laborer. You might break a nail or two, working construction."

"Derek," Geoff warned through clenched teeth.

Derek met his father's gaze insouciantly. "I'm just saying, office work would suit her better."

Javier had wandered back toward the open slider door that led to the interior of the house, looking as if he longed to be anywhere but where he was. "Viv, I'd like to talk to you alone."

A frown flitted across her face at his serious tone, but she said, "Sure," and turned to Stella. "Can you watch the kids for a minute?"

Stella waved a hand of assent at her and took Viv's place by the pool steps as Vivian and Javier headed inside the house. She still had her drink in hand, and she didn't have a swimsuit on, as far as Liam could tell. Feeling her son's eyes on her, she seemed to read his mind and said, "If I need to, I'll just get wet!"

"I wasn't criticizing," Liam said.

Stella regarded him coolly. A doting mother she'd never been. But she was fiercely protective of her grandchildren, and Liam knew she would do anything for him and Viv, whether she acted like it or not. Derek, her stepson, was another story.

"Did you tell Liam what you did?" Derek asked her lazily.

Stella gave him a viperous look.

Uh-oh, Liam thought. No wonder there was no love lost between them. Derek did love to needle. "What did you do, Mom?" he asked.

When Stella didn't immediately respond, Geoff said, "Well, tell him."

"I—didn't do anything that I shouldn't have." She glanced away, as if she suddenly found the hummingbirds flitting near the fuchsia plants fascinating.

"She called in the reporters," his father said. "Told 'em about Rory's return."

Liam groaned.

"Don't give me that," Stella said, facing her son again. "She should be arrested! You know it. I know it. Everyone knows it. She left the country, for God's sake, used a false ID. That's a criminal offense!"

"Technically, she kinda didn't leave the country," Derek reminded her. "Point Roberts is—"

"She ran away from the wedding, while we were all being attacked. Attacked!" Stella interrupted. "And I'm not convinced she's not part of the shooting. I don't know why the police haven't arrested her already. You know why she didn't walk down the aisle that day. She knew someone was going to try to kill us all!" Stella's voice had climbed an octave and her color had heightened.

"Not true." Liam was firm. "Someone tried to kill her. She was running from him."

A short bark of laughter from his father. "You believe that bullshit?"

"Geoff," Stella admonished, nodding her head to the two young children still splashing in the shallow end of the pool.

"Yeah, I believe it," Liam responded hotly, heading for the open slider door himself. "I don't know what else I believe, but I believe that."

His father called after him, "She might've been in on it from the start, you know. You'd already married her. She was pregnant, if it's yours. Stella might be right on that, Charlotte might not be. We'll know soon enough. So, all Rory had to do was get rid of you and me, maybe Derek. Why not just rain some bullets on all of us and end up with a fortune? You didn't sign a prenup."

Liam stared at him. He was sick to the back teeth of this old, stale argument. "Yeah, maybe take out Viv and Mom, too. Have all the Bastian money for herself and her child since Viv didn't have any children yet."

His father shrugged, then finished his drink. "You got a better answer?"

"If you think she hired Pete DeGrere to mow down our family, and then killed him, too, I guess, since he didn't make it past his first hours out of prison, you're heading straight into conspiracy-theory land."

"Who's Pete DeGrere?" Stella asked, frowning.

"The guy that detective who got canned from the force was so hot to pin the crime on," Derek said. "Liam got a call from him . . . Mickelson. He said DeGrere was in prison for some stupid crime and he got out only to be murdered at some strip club somewhere around Seattle."

"That's horrible," Stella said, looking toward the children.

"He got what he deserved," Geoff said.

The sound of shattering glass in the house turned their heads. Liam went inside and headed in the direction of the kitchen, where Javier was talking low and angry. ". . . shouldn't have thrown that vase, if you want more money. What's wrong with you?" His voice cut off as soon as he heard Liam's footsteps. Moments later, Vivian appeared, her face white.

"Viv . . ." Liam said.

"Don't," she snapped, marching past him, swiping at the tears on her cheeks as she strode by.

Javier came out a moment later, nodded to Liam, his jaw tight, then headed toward the front door. Liam followed after him. Outside, Javier drew a breath, then turned his dark gaze on Liam. "She's lost her sense of self," he said as he headed for his car, a black Ford Explorer.

"What do you mean?"

"Does she seem the same to you?"

"Same—how?"

"She's not the girl I married." He climbed into his vehicle and fired it up, speeding around the curved drive out to the road. Javier supposedly did well at his job working for a large financial company, but he'd never been one to flash his money around. Vivian had joked once that he kept her on such a tight leash it was choking her. Liam grimaced. Maybe he'd had to. Maybe money was an issue. He watched his sister's SUV roar out of the driveway.

Money. The root of all evil, he'd heard somewhere. Certainly not from his parents, but it was true enough. He thought of Rory. Again.

She'd lived on a shoestring budget, from what he'd gleaned. Worked as a barista and taken care of herself and her daughter . . . his daughter . . .

He thought of the little girl he'd fought over with Rory. She was flesh and blood. *His* flesh and blood.

He registered the lump building in his throat, swallowed hard. He wanted the DNA test to come back and prove that she was his, wanted it so much it damn near hurt.

* * *

She called him on his cell phone, half expecting it to go to voice mail. He wasn't reliable with the phone, or maybe he just answered when he felt like it. But this time he picked up and said, "I've been thinking about you. Want to come to my place? Or, another hotel . . ."

"The dead girl . . . Did you do it?" she demanded.

"What?"

"The one at the construction site," she said icily.

"You want to fuck, I can tell."

She wanted to kill him! Wrap her hands around his throat and squeeze until his eyes bulged from their sockets. And yes, she did want to fuck him. Loud and long and hard. But she'd die before she'd tell him so. "She was a redhead," she pointed out through bared teeth. "The dead girl."

"So?"

"You have a thing for redheads."

"Oh, come on. Forget about her. Concentrate on the positive. You should be happy I took care of DeGrere. One less asshole in the world and no one to come back on us."

"Unless he talked before you took care of the problem," she reminded him tautly. "He was a blabbermouth."

"No one with any brains ever believed him. With him dead, there's no evidence that ties us to the crime."

"*You* to the crime. He never knew about me!"

"Come on over and let's talk," he whispered persuasively.

"No."

"I'm thinking about you right now, giving myself a little warm-up . . ."

She closed her eyes. She was so angry with him. She knew he'd been with that redhead. She knew it. But she wanted to feel him inside her. There was no reason to play this game with him. "All right," she said, tense. "But if I find out you were with that dead woman . . ."

"You'll have to punish me?"

She clicked off, her pulse racing. She was so wet between her legs, it was damn embarrassing!

She swept up her purse. They might've taken a long break where they didn't connect sexually, but they were back on now, and if he'd been screwing around, he was going to be very, very sorry . . .

Chapter 16

The Lamplighter Inn was a relic from the sixties with a faintly Victorian façade that couldn't disguise the fact that it was a beige, two-level motor court surrounded by an asphalt parking lot with painted lines and numbers designating the rooms. A couple of fake gaslights flanked a gingerbread peak with peeling paint, hence the name, but a flashing vacancy sign in the front window, with an arrow that pointed to the manager's office, killed any chance of one's feeling thrown back to a time of horse-drawn carriages and footmen.

Rory shouldered her way through a smudged glass door to the small lobby. At a battle-scarred reception desk she spoke to a balding man with bags under his eyes and explained that she wanted to pay in cash. She half expected him to deny her and demand a credit card, but it wasn't that kind of place, apparently. He took the money for the room and a twenty-dollar security deposit in case "you break something or something."

Ten minutes later she moved her car and parked in her designated spot. It was late afternoon and the sun was slanting down, gilding the fluttering leaves on the maple tree at the edge of the motel's parking lot. As she climbed out of the car, a soft breeze lifted Rory's hair off her neck and she breathed deeply before hauling her overnight bag from the back seat. A shiver ran up her back and she straightened quickly, feeling the hairs rise on her nape as she glanced around. That same old sense of being followed had caught her up. Her gaze darted from one shadowed corner to another, her pulse racing.

No one.

She told herself she was being ridiculous, and yet . . .

It felt like certain unseen eyes were following her every movement. She hurried up the stairs as fast as she dared, banging the bag into the rail several times as she headed to the second level, but she made it inside her room without incident. At the door to her room, she glanced down at the parking lot, thought she saw someone moving in the shrubbery surrounding the asphalt, but decided the shifting of the shadows was just a stray dog settling into a shady spot.

Nothing sinister.

She let herself inside the airless "suite," dropped her bag on the end of the bed, threw the lock, then made sure the curtains were tightly closed. She took a few steps back from the window and door and waited, pulse pounding, expecting . . . something.

Every nerve in her body was stretched thin.

She heard footsteps outside her doorway, but they didn't pause, and faded.

Then nothing.

God, how paranoid was she?

Pull yourself together.

Still she waited.

Seconds ticked by. From outside she heard a car engine turn over and the dog bark twice, then nothing.

She exhaled heavily and sank down on the bed. Was she imagining that someone was following her? Could it be Everett? *Could it?* Derek was blaming him for the sabotage at one of

Bastian-Flavel Construction work sites, even though there was no evidence that her stepbrother was now in Portland. This morning a dead woman had been discovered on that same site, and Derek seemed to believe Everett was involved in, if not completely responsible for, her demise as well. Liam seemed to disregard Derek's assertions, but then he'd been focused on his daughter and Rory and the past. Her mother had said Everett had turned over a new leaf, was married now, and that Rory's aversion to him was old information. Maybe Derek was doing the same, blaming Everett because he was a convenient bogeyman from long before. Maybe Everett hadn't been following her in Point Roberts. Maybe it was all in her imagination.

Maybe . . .

And Liam . . . She cringed, recalling how cold he'd been. She was pretty certain he wouldn't be able to forgive her, but then she wasn't asking for his forgiveness. She just wanted Charlotte. Unfortunately, now he might want his child as well.

She glanced at her overnight bag, feeling weariness overtake her. The long drive from Canada, the nearly sleepless nights at the hospital, and the worry over Charlotte had caught up with her. She could fall asleep on her feet.

Unfortunately there was much more to do. Picking up her bag again, she hauled it with her to the bathroom, locking the door behind her. Stripping off her clothes, she waited for the shower spray to heat, then stepped under the rush of water, feeling vulnerable.

Get over your freaked-out self. You're fine. Charlotte's better. This thing with Liam, you'll work it out.

Leaning against the tiles, she closed her eyes and forced herself to relax, to rotate her neck, to stretch her muscles as the warm water washed the grime and worry from her bones. Just a few minutes of soothing water. For just a little while.

Fifteen minutes later, she slowly lifted her bent head, turning her face to the spray of water, letting it run down over her eyes, nose, mouth, and down her chin. She just wanted to collapse in a heap, but she couldn't. She needed to return to Charlotte. She didn't trust the Bastians, any one of whom could head back to the hospital without her knowing it. She knew she could call Darlene back, but that came with its own problems. Her mother wanted her to throw in with the Bastians, accept their money, and though there was a temptation to do just that, it was too emotionally risky.

Rory finally twisted off the taps but didn't move from the shower. The motel's plumbing was noisy and temperamental, but she still just wanted to stay here. She felt almost frozen, zapped of strength. The idea of crawling between the sheets naked was so tempting that she almost did it. Almost.

Instead she resolutely toweled off and put on a clean pair of jeans and a light blue shirt. She then brushed the tangle of her hair, trying to tame the damp, unruly curls. When she gave up, she gazed at her reflection in the bathroom mirror, drew a breath, then headed back to the bedroom, picked up her cell, and saw that Connie had texted: **OK?**

"No—no, nothing's okay." But she couldn't say that; didn't want to go into lengthy explanations. She didn't want Connie to worry, and the last Connie knew, Liam was chasing after her and . . . someone was following him. Who was that? Everett? Someone else? Or was the car just a figment of Connie's overactive imagination? Rory didn't know, nor could she worry about it now.

She checked the time. Almost five o'clock.

She wrote Connie back, lying with each keystroke.

All good. Charlotte improving. Heading south. TTYL.

Sure? When? That nagging voice in her head kept gnawing at her. *When are you going to call Connie and talk to her?*

"Who knows?" She let out a sigh, hesitated for a moment, wavering about what she was about to do. In the end she checked the time and switched on the television, bracing herself for the local news. A daytime drama was just wrapping up. On the bubble-faced screen, a well-dressed woman dripping in jewels unexpectedly came upon another couple who were embracing. The woman stopped short and gasped in dismay. Shocked stares all around.

Rory thought her own face might have looked just as shocked as the woman's on the screen when she'd first encountered Liam again.

Liam.

If she'd thought seeing him again would chase him from her mind, if what she'd thought of as lingering curiosity about him would have been satisfied, she'd been wrong. Dead wrong. Kidding herself. Because, whether she wanted to admit it or not, she knew now that she'd never gotten over him, at least not completely.

"Perfect," she snarked at herself as she switched stations to Channel 7 and the news. She figured she might as well find out why they'd been at the hospital. The cheery cohosts, male and female anchors, said a few remarks and then went straight to their reporter, the woman Rory had seen outside the hospital: Pauline Kirby.

"We are at Laurelton General Hospital where we may finally learn what happened to Liam Bastian's runaway bride, Aurora Abernathy Bastian, who has been missing for five years. You may remember five years ago when a gunman opened fire on a Seattle open-air wedding, killing Ms. Bastian's stepbrother, Aaron Stemple. The bride, Ms. Bastian, who'd married Liam Bastian in a civil ceremony earlier that year, disappeared before her walk down the aisle that fateful day. Ms. Bastian never resurfaced throughout the police investigation that followed. Former Seattle PD Detective Roger Mickelson was convinced the shooter was one Peter DeGrere, who, after serving time for an unrelated crime, was recently released from prison and, just this week, on his first day out, was brutally murdered behind the Nile, a Seattle area nightclub. That homicide was two days ago, and now Ms. Bastian has suddenly appeared here in Portland, in Liam Bastian's backyard with a child in tow, a little girl who's being treated at this hospital."

"Oh . . . no," Rory moaned.

Pauline went on. "Before we could interview Ms. Bastian, she ran away from our cameras . . ."

Ran away? Rory drew a sharp breath when the camera moved off Pauline to close in on Rory standing in front of the doors of the hospital, her face drawn and white, her clothes wrinkled, looking for all the world ready to rabbit again. And then, yes, of course, she saw herself retreat back into the hospital and hurry away.

"Members of Seattle PD are anxious to meet with Ms. Bastian," Kirby went on, "and interview her to find out what she knows about that brutal massacre at her aborted wedding ceremony. Sources close to Ms. Bastian say that the reason she ran from the wedding was that she was attacked by a masked assailant in her hotel room, and that she feared for her life and that of her unborn child."

"Who said that?" Rory cried. Didn't matter that it was mostly the truth. Someone had given the press an earful.

Liam. Her mouth set in a thin line. *Who else? And yet . . .*

Kirby asked, "Was she involved somehow in the tragedy that occurred? Her stepbrother lay dead at the scene. The groom, Liam Bastian, suffered bullet wounds, but recovered. Liam's father, business tycoon Geoffrey Bastian, was struck down by the shooter as well. He has been confined to a wheelchair ever since." Pauline consulted her notes and added, "Ms. Bastian has a lot to answer for, and the Bastians are anxious to find out the extent of her involvement in this terrible tragedy. Does she know more than she's saying?"

Rory swallowed in shock, glued to the set.

"Liam Bastian was surprised to learn that his wayward wife

had returned with a four-year-old child, and the questions about the girl's parentage are on everyone's mind. Ms. Bastian is claiming—"

No! Don't talk about Charlotte!

"—the child is Liam's, and the Bastians are understandably requesting a DNA test to establish paternity."

Requesting? *Demanding* would be a better word.

"We understand the little girl in the hospital is suffering from this darned summer flu that's been running rampant." She looked up. "My usual cameraman, Darrell, has fallen victim to it. Hi, Darrell." She smiled and lifted a hand to the camera. "Come back soon. We miss you." She blew him a kiss, then grew serious once more. "There are so many moving pieces to this story, we haven't gotten a complete report at this time, but this is a story that's breaking, and be assured, we're on it. The police have been notified and—"

Rory jumped up and switched off the set. She couldn't stand to hear it. Kirby's reporting leaned toward the salacious and it all just made Rory feel dirty. Who had told the press about Charlotte? Couldn't be Liam. He wouldn't talk to the press about Charlotte. He wouldn't expose her this way. He couldn't. That wasn't the Liam Bastian she'd fallen in love with. He just . . . couldn't.

The police have been notified . . .

Well, she'd known she would be facing them very soon. Someone from the Bastian camp would alert them. She shook her head. Liam wouldn't sell her and his daughter out. She wouldn't believe that.

But what do you really know about him, Rory?

She couldn't answer her own question. Apart from those few wild and reckless months of crazy love, he was a virtual stranger. Had what they'd had even been real? She'd thought so at the time, believed it with all her heart.

Maybe not Liam . . . but who, then—Stella? Did Liam's mother hate her that much?

Of course she does. You know she does!

And it probably only made matters worse that she'd taken off, fleeing from her own damned wedding. Stella must have been mortified. Liam's mother would never understand that Rory had left to save her unborn child.

You'll never get away, and that baby of yours will die.

In hindsight, she could have handled it all so much better. She'd run because she didn't know what else to do. From the beginning she'd suspected that she could never meld her family with the Bastians, yet she'd gone ahead and fallen for the fairy tale, all the while knowing in the back of her head that it wouldn't work. But she'd wanted it so much! The proverbial house with the picket fence. A man who loved her with all his heart. A perfect baby to add to their happiness.

If she'd stayed . . . would things have been better? If she'd stayed, would she have been gunned down on the bridal path like Aaron, losing Charlotte's life as well as her own?

Shivering inside, she forced her thoughts away from the "wedding" that had never come off. As ever, it didn't bear thinking about.

After taking a moment to stop and peek through the curtains to make certain she was alone, she grabbed her purse from the bed, then looked again. There was no one waiting for her as far as she could tell. Even the dog had left.

She stepped outside to the upper gallery and hurried to the stairs. Tired as she was, she needed to return to the hospital. She couldn't stand being away. Not while the Bastians and Bethany were anywhere near her daughter.

Ten minutes later she parked in a hospital lot on the lowest side of the building. Laurelton General had been built on a steep lot and this parking area on the north side of the lowest tier was half-full, a smattering of cars baking in the evening heat. As she slipped her keys into her purse, she heard the distinctive rumble of a motorcycle. Shutting the Honda's driver's door, she saw a shiny bike wheel into a spot a few yards away. The driver, clad in black leather, a dark helmet shielding his face, killed the engine. She turned from him to make a cursory search of the lot, her gaze sweeping the asphalt as she looked for Pauline Kirby and her entourage, but thankfully there was no sign of Channel 7 news team . . . yet.

Taking a quick breath, she hurried toward the door on the north side of the building just as the man climbed off his motorcycle and, unstrapping his helmet, loped toward the door ahead of her.

Rory slowed as she grew near, keeping space between them, letting him enter the hospital ahead of her, but he hesitated near the door. Something about his body type, the width of his shoulders, the way his neck turned, sent all her nerves screaming.

Oh, shit! *Everett!*

She backed up rapidly, nearly falling over her feet as his helmet came off and she stared straight at him, damn near hyperventilating.

No, no, not Everett, but . . .

Hand over her heart, she whispered, "Sweet Jesus . . . *Cal?*"

"Rory." He gazed at her as if he were seeing a ghost, which was exactly the same way she felt.

His hair was longer and wilder, and the full motorcycle leathers, gloves, and boots and all, made him look mean and dangerous. At least that was her first impression. After her first words she found she couldn't speak.

"Don't look at me that way," he said, his familiar voice causing her knees to tremble.

It was *Cal*. Not Everett. Had he been the person she'd felt was following her, watching her? The back of her throat went dry with a new kind of apprehension.

"What are you doing here?" she asked.

"Well, I, I live here now. In Laurelton."

"You do? I mean, what are you doing at the hospital?"

He shrugged sheepishly. "I saw you on the news and . . . well, I wanted to see you again."

She felt herself start to sway. Alarmed, he reached out a hand to her, but she backed up, pulling herself together.

"On the broadcast, they said you were at this hospital, had some footage of it, so I came back here. I was cruising the upper lot, then came over to this one and decided you might be inside. Instead you're here . . ." He half laughed. "Didn't really believe it would be that easy."

"Cal." It felt like all her muscles were liquid. The aftermath of pure fear.

"That Kirby woman—the reporter? She's kind of a bitch, huh? The way she talked about you? I really thought she could use a punch in the face—" He stopped, hearing himself. "Not really, but you know what I mean."

Her head was buzzing. She felt like she was in some kind of alternate reality. Memories picked at her brain. The last time she saw him . . . Oh. God. "I . . . I thought I saw you . . . at the wedding."

He eyed her closely. "Whoa. You look like you're gonna pass out. You're not gonna pass out, are ya? Don't . . ."

"No, I'm fine. I'm fine." She was starting to recover herself, but she was far from fine. Seeing him was a shock.

"Okay." There was strained silence between them. "I just wanted to say, you know . . . I'm sorry. Sorry I was such a fuck-up back then, you know."

He was talking about when she'd left him . . . because of his temper and his thievery. After the miscarriage there'd been no reason to stay and so many to leave. All she said now was, "A lot of water under the bridge."

"Yeah . . ."

"So, you're here now? Permanently?" she asked, wishing she could just sweep past him and get to Charlotte.

"I guess. Me and Nona, we've got a catering business. She does the cooking and I'm the muscle." He smiled faintly, but it didn't quite reach his eyes.

"Excuse me." A woman in her forties bustled past them without so much as a glance at Rory. She disappeared into the hospital and Rory found Cal studying her.

He had been hurt when they'd broken up, but had pretended to not let it bother him, although at the time Aaron had confided in her he wasn't handling it well.

"Watch your back, Rory," Aaron had warned, his face etched in concern.

She'd run from Cal. Changed her phone and moved apartments, though he'd known where she worked. But he'd kept his distance, hadn't bothered her. She'd heard from Aaron that he knew about her engagement to Liam, but he'd never challenged it. Everett was the one who'd jeered about her marrying a rich man for his money. "Were you there? At the wedding?" she asked again, not really expecting an answer.

Cal made a face, then lowered his head and looked up at her from the tops of his eyes, puppy-dog fashion. "Well, yeah . . . the police took my name, so I guess you're the only one who doesn't really know. I was working in the kitchen. I mean, it's what I do, right?"

Even though it confirmed what she'd thought, it still surprised her. "You knew it was *my* wedding?"

"Well, yeah, but honestly, it wasn't about that. I'd kinda gotten in trouble . . . you know . . . with taking a few things . . ."

"I remember."

"And I was working my way back in. Aaron got me the job."

"Aaron?" she repeated in disbelief but remembered her step-brother had worked in some restaurants in the Seattle area.

"Okay, I begged him. I'm not proud of it, but he told me about it and got me on with the catering staff. They were pretty well-known and I worked my butt off. After everything that went down, a lot of people quit. There was one gal on the wait-staff who kinda got PTSD. She was going to go outside, but then she changed her mind and *blam, blam, blam, blam!* It was scary as shit and she kinda collapsed. Really screwed her up, for a while at least. Been a while since I've seen her."

"You gave your name to the police?" Rory asked, a hot breeze touching the back of her neck.

"Well, yeah. I had to. They just came through and started asking questions. I told 'em I knew you. They were looking for you by then, but I didn't know where you were. But mostly they were chasing the shooter. Knew he was on the rooftop, but he was fast. They asked me tons of questions afterwards, but I didn't know where the hell you were."

"So, it wasn't a coincidence." She wasn't certain.

"I just needed a job." He seemed sincere.

She nodded, not knowing whether to completely believe him. "So, now you're in the catering business with your girl-friend."

"Yeah, Nona. She's . . ." He smiled, and this time it did reach his eyes. "I think you'd like her."

"Well, good for you, Cal," she said.

"Yeah?" he asked seriously.

"Yeah."

He cleared his throat. "Glad to hear you say that. I'm in this program, y'know? Not the whole seven steps or whatever the hell it is, but something kinda like it. My own version. I was really pissed when you dumped me for Bastian, and I had a lot of bad thoughts. I'm working through it all, now. Making amends. Telling people I'm sorry, and all that."

"Well, okay," she said, surprised. "But for the record, I didn't dump you for Liam."

"Maybe. You did break up with me, though. It was a bitch. Took me a while to get over it. I can admit that. Here, let me help you."

Rory hadn't realized she'd locked her knees, and when she finally moved she stumbled a little. She reluctantly accepted his gloved hand, wishing she could find a good way to exit.

"I was still a little pissed at you at the wedding," he admitted as shadows stretched across the sidewalks. "I was sorry I'd taken the job at first. But I didn't want to let Aaron down. And then, holy shit, Rory. They killed *him*!"

"They?"

"Well, whoever. The guy that musta done it. The one that Kirby bitch mentioned. DeGrere? He killed Aaron." His face clouded. "I'm glad that DeGrere's dead. I was just shit-shocked when everything went down, you know, at the wedding, and so was Everett."

Rory had started to lose focus, but now she gave him her full attention. "You talked to Everett about it?"

"Well, yeah. And about you just taking off. We talked a lot about it and the shooter. We wanted to kill that fucker, whoever he was. And then you were gone and . . . they found that bloody dress . . . man, what a freak show." He shook his head. "But like I said, I'm sorry. Where were you all this time? Why did you leave?"

She'd told her story already today and knew she would be telling it again to the police, but she answered, "The guy that attacked me threatened my baby."

He blinked. "Baby?"

"My daughter, Charlotte, who's here at the hospital. That's why I'm here. I'm just going in to see her."

"Oh. The one that has the flu."

"Right."

They gazed at each other awkwardly, then Cal shrugged. "So, are we cool? You and me?"

"We're cool."

He relaxed a little and she saw a brief glimpse of the boy she'd fallen for years before. "Are you sticking around, or what's your story?"

"I just want Charlotte well, and we'll see. I don't have a story."

He paused and out of the corner of her eye she saw another car, a white four-door, roll into the parking lot and take a spot. An elderly couple slowly emerged. Cal asked, "Those Bastians have as much money as they say?"

"I don't know, Cal. I've been gone awhile."

"They seem to have a lot." He moved away from her. "You be careful with them."

Like Aaron had warned her about him.

"Okay," she said.

"If you do stick around, and they need a caterer . . . tell 'em Nona's Catering. Google it."

Then he was putting his helmet back on as the woman in the white sedan pulled a walker from the back seat of her car.

Finally, Rory pushed her way through the door and headed straight for the elevators. Her pulse was running light and fast. The encounter with Cal had scared her weariness away, at least temporarily, making her feel sharp and alert, though she sensed she was running on the very last of her energy.

She called for the elevator, tapping a hand against one thigh. She was anxious as hell to see Charlotte again, assure herself that her daughter was okay. The day had been a nightmare from start to finish, the only good part being that Charlotte was on the mend.

The elevator doors opened and Rory stepped inside to hover near the back of the car just in case Pauline Kirby or one of her cohorts was hanging around the front desk.

Rory was crowded to the rear, which suited her just fine. She squeezed through a knot of riders to step off the elevator into the hallway leading to Pediatrics.

She rounded a corner to stop short.

Two men in suits were standing outside the entrance.

Police . . . detectives, she would bet.

Oh . . . shit . . .

Her heart sank, but the men caught sight of her coming to a halt and regarded her soberly. One of them stepped forward and said, "Ms. Bastian?"

Her head was swimming. Her gut was icy. Her silence was apparently affirmation enough as they came toward her. They were a matched set in height, about five-ten, and weight, somewhere around two fifty, she guessed, but one had a mustache and he was the one who asked, "Are you Aurora Abernathy Bastian?"

She nodded. What could she do? She needed to be here, near Charlotte.

They introduced themselves as Detectives Grant and Susskind of the Portland Police Department; Grant was the one with the mustache. "We would like to ask you a few questions, down at the station. Would you be willing to go with us?"

No. Never. I can't leave my daughter.

But what came out of her mouth was a shaky, "Okay. But not this second, not until I check on my daughter. Charlotte. I need to see that, that she's okay."

They both nodded and she swiveled toward the doors to Pediatrics, hurried down the hallway, and stopped at the nurses' station to flag down the first nurse she saw, a lanky blonde with short hair and a quick smile. "I'm Charlotte Johnson's mother," she said, her voice catching on the name that she'd created, one more lie in the web she'd spun. "I'd like to know how she's doing." She threw a glance at the door to Charlotte's room, not fifteen feet away. Maybe she should have checked on her daughter first.

"Much better," the nurse said and walked with Rory to Charlotte's room. "She was awake a little bit ago," the nurse said, "but she's sleeping again." With a wink, the nurse concluded, "She's an imp, that one, I can tell."

"Yes. Yes, she is. Thank you," Rory said, walking on wooden legs. The police were here. They wanted to talk to her . . . oh, Lord. Would they keep her, interrogate her for hours, even arrest her for whatever they thought they had on her for leaving the wedding? Would she be considered an accomplice?

With the nurse in attendance, the detectives standing less than ten feet from her, she peeked through the open door and saw Charlotte sleeping on the hospital bed, her color normal, her eyelashes brushing the tops of her cheeks. Rory watched as she let out a little sigh.

Tears sprang to Rory's eyes. Her heart twisted. Would she be pulled away from her child?

"Mrs. Bastian?" the mustached detective said.

Turning, she saw Liam coming off the elevator, stalking straight for her.

Her heart ached upon seeing him. She felt a well of emotion fill her chest, turn her throat hot, her eyes burning. The police . . . She wanted to throw herself into Liam's arms and cry.

Chapter 17

Detective Grant saw Liam and nodded at him and smiled. What was this? Rory watched in silence as the two men shook hands and remarked about the passing years. High school classmates, she realized, uncertain how this would affect her.

Grant grew serious and turned to Rory. "If you'll come with us . . . ?"

"No, I'll drive myself. But this can't take too long. I have a sick daughter and I'm not going to leave her for hours on end."

"Okay," he said, shooting a glance at Liam. Rory suspected what he was thinking: that she was a flight risk.

"I'll be there," she insisted, turning to the older detective, Susskind.

"Want me to take you?" Liam asked her.

"I can handle this."

None of the men responded and she realized she probably looked like she was about to pass out. She'd been worried out of her mind about her kid, had barely slept in forty-eight hours, hadn't eaten since she could remember, never even con-

sidered a lick of lipstick or touch of makeup. She'd been ha-
rassed by about everyone she met.

A bit of humor touched Liam's eyes. "There's the girl I remember."

"Not a girl," she said. She stepped away from the knot of
men, avoided a teenager plugged into his phone, and slapped
the button to call the elevator. "Not anymore." Despite the recent feeling that she could crumple into his arms, she shook her
head, her hair brushing the back of her shoulders. "I got this,
Liam. I can handle it." Could she? God, she doubted it. To the
detectives she said, "What's the address?"

Susskind rattled it off and added, "We'll follow you."

A warning. Of course. Perfect.

Don't get any ideas of running away again.

"You're sure about this?" Liam asked her. "You know a
lawyer might be a good—"

"I *don't* need an attorney." The doors to the elevator car
opened and she, along with the cops, Liam, and a middle-aged
couple all crowded inside. It was a struggle to breathe. As soon
as the car landed, she muscled her way into the hallway and
through the doors to the lower parking area. The sun was settling lower in the western sky, and she spied Liam's Tahoe
parked one aisle over from her vehicle.

As she yanked her keys from her purse and stalked toward
her car, Liam caught up with her and fell into step. "I'm coming
with you."

"So you can be with your cop buddy."

"No."

She unlocked her Honda on the fly.

The little car chirped in response, its lights flickering.

Yanking the door open, she noticed the two cops climbing
into a nondescript sedan parked in the shade of a struggling

sapling, one of several trees planted in an effort to break up the acres of asphalt.

"I want to help. Come on, Rory."

Help. She didn't trust his kind of help. "No, thanks." She slid into the warm interior of her Honda and slammed the door shut. Her heart was hammering and it was all she could do to keep from breaking down. She was going to the police station, a place she'd avoided like the plague all these years, to tell the story she'd kept secret for five years. Everything in her life would change and there was a chance she would be arrested, that . . . that . . . oh, damn.

She opened the door again as Liam was walking back toward his vehicle. "Just . . . if something happens . . ." she called. "If the cops, I don't know . . . if they keep me too long? Come back here for Charlotte."

"They won't."

God, I hope. But who knows?

"Liam?"

"Yes. Of course."

She wanted to cry again, but pulled the door shut and plunged her key into the ignition. A grinding noise ensued and she tapped the gas. "Oh . . . God . . . come on!"

The engine coughed, but wouldn't turn over.

She stopped turning the key, took a deep breath and gave it another go. Then another.

The ignition ground as it struggled and failed to spark. Her left hand held the steering wheel in a death grip. The engine struggled. More coughing, then nothing. Rapidly, she stepped on the accelerator three times, then switched on the engine again.

Click, click, click! No spark. No ignition. No damned thing.

The starter, she thought. Or, the battery. She should have waited for The Magician to look at it.

She wanted to scream. Drawing a breath, she sent up a prayer.

Give me strength. Through the bug-spattered windshield, she spied the detectives waiting in their own car. and Liam now at the wheel of his Tahoe. *Great. Just . . . great.*

Hot, tired, and hungry, she swore pungently inside her mind, then counted to ten. Why? Why now? With everything else, now was not the time for her little car to give up the ghost. She tried once more, already assuming failure. *Click, click, click.* The starter. Definitely.

Snapping the keys from the car, she scooped up her purse, flung open the door, and stepped outside. Liam had rolled down the window of his rig. "Problems?"

She fought back the desire to kick one of the Honda's tires. "Looks like I need that ride after all."

"Hop in."

She was already rounding the SUV and reaching for the passenger door. As she settled into the seat, she slid a pair of sunglasses onto the bridge of her nose and said, "Let's get this over with."

Several hours later, Rory sat staring at the smooth, windowless walls of the interrogation room. She knew she was being filmed, assumed she was being watched and really didn't care. The two detectives were in the room: Liam's classmate, Grant, the younger guy with the mustache, at the small table across from her; and Susskind, standing, his graying hair falling over his eyes, one beefy shoulder propped against the door frame.

She'd told them her story, going over it three times, starting with the assault at the wedding by the masked man and finishing by explaining how she'd ended up at Laurelton General Hospital and the Lamplighter Inn. She'd taken a lie detector test and given a DNA sample and even written down Kent Daley and Maude Sutter's names, addresses, and phone numbers.

Had she sold them out?

Probably.

Right now, dead tired, her stomach rumbling, she didn't care. She'd told the authorities the truth, every bit of it, and now the cops could do with it what they would. All that mattered to Rory was Charlotte.

When they'd asked her about Teri Mulvaney, she'd been shocked. How in the world did they expect her to know anything about the dead woman?

It's because you're back and the last time you were with the Bastians, people died.

Still . . .

Though they were noncommittal, it was clear to Rory that the two detectives were skeptical. She believed they still thought she might take off at a moment's notice. While Grant had asked questions, Susskind had been the gofer and, she supposed, the good cop. He'd listened for the most part, but had left several times to bring her a bottle of water and later, a Diet Coke. Lubrication, she'd thought, to avoid a dry throat and keep her talking, which she had.

Did she know who attacked her?

No.

Was she wounded?

No, not really. She'd given as good as she got, stabbing her attacker in the back of the hand.

Did she have any idea who the shooter could be?

No, but wasn't it someone named Pete DeGrere? That's what she'd heard.

Did she know DeGrere?

No!

Did anyone in her extended family know him? Anyone, like Harold Stemple?

They would have to ask him, and since he was in prison, that shouldn't be too tough.

Who would want DeGrere dead?

She couldn't answer that because she didn't know him. Weren't they listening?

Why did she run? Where did she go? Who did she contact? Why did she change her name? Who would want her dead? Who would attack people at her wedding? Who was the real target? Was she the target? Or Liam? Or Aaron? Why didn't she contact the police? Why didn't she contact her husband? Why didn't she tell Liam Bastian that he was a father? Could that child be anyone else's? Who, did she think, would want her and her child dead?

"I don't know," she repeated to the questions that just kept coming.

On and on it went, over and over again, as the minutes and hours ticked away and she thought she'd go mad. Susskind had spoken to some detective at the Seattle PD and come back with some new questions, which, again, she couldn't answer because she didn't know.

The afternoon had bled to evening when she finally said, "I've told you everything. Absolutely everything. You've asked me the same questions over and over. I fled the wedding to save my life and that of my unborn daughter, and I stayed hidden because we were threatened. I've always been scared, okay? Scared out of my mind, afraid someone was following me, afraid they would try again, afraid for my little girl, and . . ." She stopped, aware she was rambling, and added, "Well, you know it all."

Grant nodded, apparently finally satisfied, but Susskind wasn't looking quite as convinced. He opened his mouth to ask another question, but Rory cut him off.

"If you're going to stop me, arrest me, then do it. Otherwise I need to go. You took my cell phone information, texts, messages, recent calls, whatever, as well as the license plate of my car and my driver's license—"

"—in the name of Heather Johnson." Susskind broke in. No more good cop, apparently.

"But you know who I am," she said evenly. She scraped back the uncomfortable molded plastic chair where she'd sat for the past four hours. They'd given her her phone back and it was tucked safely in her purse, so there was nothing holding her here. "Charge me, or let me go."

Grant rubbed the corner of his mustache. "We're good for now. But don't go anywhere."

Susskind opened the door and escorted Rory through a series of hallways and elevators to the rear parking lot. "I can give you a lift back to the hospital," the detective offered, but she was having none of it, and fortunately she spied Liam, standing near his Tahoe, cell phone in hand.

For a second a whisper of déjà vu floated through her brain. How she'd first seen him on a rain-slick Seattle sidewalk. He looked up and the ice around her heart cracked, just a little. "Thought you could use another ride," he said.

"You waited all this time?"

"I told Grant I would come by the station and go over the death of the woman whose body was found at our construction site. We're not really old friends. That's how we reconnected. "

"Teri Mulvaney," she said. "They asked me about her, too."

"Really." He was surprised.

"They asked me pretty much everything they could think of, and I answered every single question. Did you talk to Susskind? Because Grant was with me most of the time."

He nodded. "It was just routine. I don't know what they think you could know about Teri Mulvaney."

"I'm a master criminal, didn't you know?" Her belligerence actually scared a faint smile out of him, which hadn't been her intention. He was entirely too attractive when he smiled, so she looked away and said, "That interview couldn't have taken that long."

"I wanted to wait for you anyway," he said. "And I checked on Charlotte. She's fine. She asked about you, so the nurse—"

"Karin with an I?"

"Yes, she told her you'd be by in the morning. Darlene's already at the hospital."

"But I have to go to see Charlotte now." She was already climbing into his rig.

"Rory, you're dead on your feet."

"She's only four."

"And she'll be all right for a few more hours. The last I heard she was sleeping again." He started the Tahoe, then pulled out his cell phone and speed-dialed a number. "Pediatrics, please. Nurse Karin White. Yeah . . . I'll hold." To Rory, he said, "Talk to the nurse. Maybe she can fill you in better than I can and she'll let you talk to Charlotte." He handed her the phone before wheeling out of the lot and heading west, where the sun had set and the lights of the city winked to the rim of mountains, barely visible in the twilight.

"This is Nurse Karin White," a cheery voice on the other end of the connection said. Rory identified herself as Charlotte's mother and launched into all of her questions. The nurse listened, then gave her an update on Charlotte's condition. "She's alert, stable, and her temp's normal. Her appetite's back and I'd guess that she'll be released tomorrow."

"I'm on my way."

"She's sleeping now. I don't think she'll wake until morning. Maybe early, but who knows."

Rory hung up and handed the phone back to Liam. Sagging against the seat, the exhaustion Liam had mentioned stealing over her, she said, "I have to go back to the hospital anyway. I guess Charlotte's sleeping, but I still need to get my car somehow."

"We'll deal with it in the morning."

"Just leave it at the hospital?" she asked as the streetlights

306 Lisa Jackson and Nancy Bush

sped by and a sports car passed them as if they were standing still.

"The police already know why it's there."

That much was true. "I still need . . ."

He shot her a look and she let the sentence die. "Okay. Fine. Take me to the Lamplighter."

"The what?"

"Where I'm staying."

One dark eyebrow cocked. She saw the movement as the headlight beams from cars moving in the opposite direction washed over the interior. "I think you're staying at my place."

She shook her head. That was not a good idea. Staying at his place, seeing where he lived, the intimacy of it? No way. At least not tonight. "No, I need to be close to the hospital and . . ." She yawned. "I . . . I need to think about things." Then the penny dropped. "You're afraid I'm going to leave, even with my child in the hospital!"

"Of course not." His lips twisted. "Kind of hard now, right? No car."

"Right." Her voice was tight.

When he veered off the highway, she thought for a second that he might be taking her to his place after all, damn near abducting her, but she was wrong. Instead he drove her into the line to the drive-up window of a hamburger stand, and when she heard a cheery voice say, "Welcome to Brenda's Burgers, what can I get for you?" she was transported back to her own job at the Point Bob Buzz. She'd worked there so recently, just earlier in the week, and yet it already felt like a lifetime ago.

Liam ordered two cheeseburgers, French fries, onion rings, a Diet Coke, and a vanilla milkshake, which were bagged and ready in the five minutes it took to crawl to the window. A tattooed waitress with a nose ring and neon pink smile greeted them, took their money, and handed them their dinner.

"Next time it will be more elegant," Liam promised as he engaged the Tahoe again and drove unerringly toward Laurelton General. The odors of charred beef, dill pickles, and grease from a fresh batch of French fries mingled and teased at Rory's nostrils and it was all she could do to leave her burger wrapped in its cocoon of paper, though she did find herself picking at the hot fries. Just before they reached the entrance to the hospital, Rory pointed out the turnoff to the motel.

Liam turned into the access road leading to the motel with its glowing gaslights and aging façade. "Don't say it," she warned as Liam eased the Tahoe into an empty space delineated by faded stripes marking the pavement in front of the units.

"Say what?"

"It's cheap, doesn't require a credit card, and is close to the hospital. Everything I need." She was out of the door and heading up the stairs to her room as he cut the engine.

She heard him behind her, packing their white sacks, taking the steps two at a time, and it crossed Rory's mind that this was a mistake as well, that never in her wildest imaginings would she think that she'd be here, at a cheesy motel . . . with her husband.

What a difference a week had made.

Within minutes, they were seated at the small table, Liam in the only chair, she perched on a corner of the bed and devouring her burger. She had to force herself to take sips from her drink rather than bolt down every last onion ring and French fry, but slowly, her hunger was sated to the point that she didn't finish the last bit of bun, just couldn't do it.

"Better?" he asked.

"Yes. Lots. Thank you."

"*De nada.*"

She eyed the detritus of the meal—wrinkled sacks, globs of catsup from used, open packets congealing on the paper that had wrapped their burgers, empty cups and straws. She couldn't stifle the yawn that overtook her. "Look, I think I have to lie down. Do you mind . . . ?" She began picking up the trash.

"I'll leave," he said, helping her stuff the remainders into an empty sack.

"Thanks."

"I'll be back," he said, and walked to the door with the trash. "I'll take this with me since you may not want to wake up to the smell of old grease and onions."

"Is it worse than stale air, dust, and some kind of air freshener?"

"Slightly."

She watched him walk outside and shut the door behind him. She instantly felt bereft, alone, and it kind of pissed her off. She slipped between the covers and stretched, sighing. Her muscles instantly started to relax. It was heaven, even in the Lamplighter's too-hard bed with its faded coverlet that matched the long, blue curtains framing the window.

She'd just let her eyelids droop closed when she heard the door open again, and the sounds of the night—a dog barking, traffic rumbling on the highway, a car's radio blasting heavy-metal as it passed—reached her ears over the steady hum of the air-conditioning unit rattling beneath the room's single window. As he closed the door again, she listened to the whine of a motorcycle accelerating through its gears. "That reminds me," she said, the sound fading.

"What? What reminds you?"

"The motorcycle that just passed. Earlier today I ran into Cal. On a bike. Dressed head to toe in leathers."

Liam paused. "Redmond?" he asked, surprised.

"He was actually looking for me." Forcing herself up, she propped herself on her elbows as Liam stood at the door. She quickly told him about Cal and his need to unburden himself in his own version of a twelve-step program. Seven, in Cal's case.

"I never liked the guy," Liam stated flatly. "Never trusted him."

Liam had known Cal more from pictures and what Rory had told him rather than direct contact. She said, "That was probably a good idea, but he seems to have turned over a new leaf."

"If you believe in that kind of thing." He fiddled with the blinds, drawing the curtains over them, blocking out any chance of light entering or, she thought, unwanted eyes peering through.

"You obviously don't."

"No." He twisted around the chair he'd been sitting in, straddling the back and facing the bed.

"He seemed sincere, but . . ." She shrugged. "I don't know. I was glad when it was over."

Liam nodded, his hair seeming darker in the dim room illuminated only by the bedside lamp. "What happened with the cops?"

"I told them everything I knew." She gave him a quick recap of those hours of interrogation, finishing with, "I half expected Pauline Kirby to be waiting for me when I got back here, that she'd found out where I was staying."

"She's known for her deep 'investigative reporting.'"

"Right." She shook her head. "Your cop friend asked me about everything and everyone, Pete DeGrere, Everett, Harold, and, of course, Aaron, like I said."

"What did you tell them about your family?"

"Stepfamily. That Aaron was a pretty good guy, that Everett wasn't, and that I wasn't surprised Harold was in prison. I also told them I didn't know Pete DeGrere, and that I ran because I was attacked and scared."

"Derek blames Everett for the sabotage at the Hallifax project."

"I know. He brought it up earlier."

Liam got up from the chair to sit on the edge of the bed. "Scoot over a bit."

Rory eyed him speculatively. Did he think she would just

throw open the covers and let him slide in beside her? To take up where they'd left off, or to start up again? Is that what he wanted? What she wanted?

But he only sat on the edge of the bed, the old mattress sagging beneath him.

"What do you think?"

"About Everett? He's sure capable of it, but I don't know. I did think he's been following me."

"Here?"

"And in Point Roberts, and Vancouver. Like I said, I don't know." Yawning again, she stretched one arm over her head. "It's just a feeling I've had and I'm not sure."

"I don't like it."

"You had someone follow me," she pointed out.

"To find you."

"Still, it's scary."

He nodded. "Sorry."

"It's okay . . . well, it's not, but I get it. I can't blame you for that," she admitted. "And you want a divorce?"

He was silent a moment, then admitted, "That's why I was looking for you."

"So you can marry Bethany."

"That part," he said slowly, "I'm not so sure about."

She felt a small flare of hope and tried to crush it back down. They might still be husband and wife, but there was no "them" any longer. She had to remember that. "But you are all about the divorce."

A beat.

Another.

She held her breath, counting her heartbeats.

"I think we have a lot to discuss, Rory," he said, and she knew he was talking about her daughter, his daughter, *their* daughter. "But not now. Tomorrow . . ."

"Okay."

It was all she could do to get those two syllables out. Their relationship of husband and wife could never be the same. It hadn't even been a marriage that had the time to mellow and age, and their child . . . she didn't know him. Would it be so hard for Charlotte to accept she had a father that she saw only part of the time? It wasn't as if she'd lost anything. She'd never even known about him.

Unless, of course, he tried to take Charlotte from her.

No . . . no . . . the Liam she knew wouldn't do that.

And if he tried, she'd fight him with every breath in her body.

"We'll figure it out," he said, reassuring her, though she understood the words were spoken to placate her, to table the discussion, to put off the inevitable battle, but she couldn't fight, not tonight, at least not now. "Sleep now," he said, then added, "I could stay—"

Yes! No! God.

"—or not."

She felt the bed shift and hadn't realized she'd closed her eyes for a second. He was right about her being dead on her feet.

"I'll see you in the morning. With coffee."

"Gallons," she murmured into her pillow. She felt the warmth of his lips brush against her cheek . . . didn't she? She was drifting.

"Get up and throw the bolt," his voice ordered from a long way away as he snapped off the light.

"Uh-hmmm."

"Rory, I'm serious."

She heard him twist the lock in the knob, then the soft thud of the door closing behind him, but she couldn't move . . .

He'd kissed her . . . hadn't he? Something soft and warm. She wanted him to kiss her more . . . She wanted . . .

Bam! Bam! Bam!

The sudden noise jolted Rory into wakefulness. She blinked awake. Where was she? The room was dark. Pitch dark. Oh, God, she was at the motel, and Charlotte was at the hospital and Liam . . . he'd just left. He must've forgotten something . . . Bleary. She was bleary and it was with an effort that she threw back the covers, her fingers searching for the light switch. She stumbled through the coverlet as the sorry little room was flooded with illumination.

She was reaching for the doorknob when she stopped, some of the fuzziness in her mind clearing. Maybe whoever was banging on the door wasn't Liam. Maybe she'd been asleep longer than it seemed. She peered through the peephole to the darkness beyond. Nothing. "Liam?" she called, still trying to chase the cobwebs from her mind. "What?" She slipped the chain through its lock, then opened the door a crack, peering out to the poorly illuminated porch.

No one . . . just the still night. Cars parked in the lot. The smell of alcohol? Maybe the faint tinge of cigarette smoke?

Her skin crawled.

"Don't shut the door, Rory," he warned.

Not Liam . . . *not Liam*!

Before she could slam it shut, the door smashed against the chain, straining. She scrabbled with it, trying to close it, opened her mouth to scream—

Wham!

The door flew open with a sickening splintering of wood as the screws holding the chain gave way. *Craaack!*

Rory saw stars. Stumbled back. Pain behind her eyes, nearly blinding her. Blood pouring from her nose.

"Get out!" she cried.

What the hell was happening? Dazed, she focused on the intruder, trying to think, to seek a way of escape, or a weapon to defend herself. Half her face throbbed and she reached up to her cheek, her hand sticky with blood.

She blinked, fighting her dizziness, focused.

She knew him, knew his build.

As her foggy mind cleared, her heart froze in her chest.

Cal Redmond, dressed in his black leathers, his face twisted into an angry grimace, grabbed her by the throat and stared at her with hot hatred. He kicked at the door, which shuddered against its splintered frame.

"Cal?" she squeaked out, backing up. She couldn't believe it. *Cal? Cal was here? Infuriated?*

"I think," he said in a barely audible whisper, "we should clear the air."

He smelled of whiskey. Was clearly drunk. "What are you talking about?" She could barely get the words out, he was squeezing so tight. As if realizing it, he slowly released her throat.

Rory's knees hit the edge of the bed and nearly knocked her off her feet, but she stayed upright. Needed to stay upright. Run, if she could.

"Unfinished business." He pulled a pocketknife from his jacket and clicked it open.

Zzzip!

A switchblade.

He waggled it dangerously under her dripping nose.

Sweet. Jesus.

"I don't . . . I don't . . . you said we were okay!" she whispered, her eyes focused on the evil, glinting blade. Her mind searched for a means of escape or a weapon of some kind, *any* kind, because the malicious glint in his eyes was unmistakable.

He was here to do damage.

To her.

With his free hand, he pointed a finger at her. "You lied to me, Rory."

"No—I—"

"You're still lying."

"I don't know what you're talking about!" She had to get

out of here. Get away. She noticed for the first time that he wasn't wearing gloves. His bare hands were exposed, the scar visible on the back of one. Oh. Jesus. She'd made that jagged rough line just before she was set to walk down the aisle of her wedding ceremony. She'd plunged a knife into the back of his hand before running out of the hotel room. Cal was the man who had attacked her! The assailant who'd disguised his voice with helium, the madman who had guessed she was pregnant and vowed to kill her and her child.

"Why are you doing this?" she said on a sob.

"Because you destroyed our baby and kept his."

"What?" *The miscarriage, he is bringing up the miscarriage?*

"You didn't want my baby, but you sure wanted that rich fucker's. I tried to forgive you. I tried really hard. But I can't."

She gasped as she backed away from him. If she could just ease into the bathroom and lock the door, call the police or Liam or someone. Her phone . . . where the hell was her phone? She searched the room in her peripheral vision, her gaze still centered on the deadly knife.

"You murdered our kid. Couldn't be with someone as worthless as me. Nona . . . Nona knows I'm worth something, but not you. You never did. I was never good enough for Rory Abernathy." Anguish and fury twisted his features.

"No, Cal. That's just not true. I lost the baby. It just happened." She remembered the cramping, the spotting. "I wanted—"

"Shut up!" he shouted, spittle spraying, the reek of whiskey surrounding him.

Where the hell is the phone?

Sweating, heart trip-hammering, she caught a glimpse of her phone on the edge of the nightstand. Too far. If she leaped for it, he'd be on her, on the bed and . . . he'd kill her. She saw the murderous intent swimming in his eyes.

"I don't know why you're here, but you need to leave," she said, hoping to reason with him as she stepped around the chair that Liam had pulled from the small table. Lord, that seemed like a lifetime ago. She nearly tripped over the coverlet that had pooled on the stained carpet, but she kept moving. Backing away. Ever away. The bathroom was only five feet away now . . .

"You got pregnant and married that son of a bitch." His voice was low and accusatory, judge and jury all rolled into one low growl.

How did he know this? "No one knew I was pregnant." *Not even Liam.*

"I was watching you." He poked the knife closer toward her.

A chill ran down her spine. Could she make it to the bathroom?

"Saw you go to the drug store."

"What?"

"Pick up that little kit . . . the same kind you used when you found out about our baby."

The pregnancy test. "I didn't kill our baby, Cal," she pleaded.

"You shut your lying mouth," he warned.

He was crazy. Wasted. She had to calm him down "What—what about your program? Twelve steps . . . or you said, seven?"

The bathroom was only a few feet away.

If she could launch herself, fling her body through the open door, slam it shut, lock it, and scream bloody murder, maybe she could scare him off, get someone to come or call the cops. But she was still stunned from the door smashing into her face, her nose and mouth throbbing, the taste of blood on her lips. She backed up slowly, one step at a time. "So you came to my wedding on purpose. To what, kill me?"

"Teach you a lesson."

"And you killed Aaron in the process!" She could feel her fear changing to anger. Good. She wanted to be mad!

"That wasn't me. I just wanted to talk to you, reason with you, make you admit what you did. I saw the balloons, and I had the mask, and I knew which room you were in. I saw you go in. You . . . you *stabbed* me!"

Rory edged backwards. *Keep him talking. Just keep him talking.* "You attacked me, Cal! I just wanted to get away!"

"I had to wrap my hand in my black apron to hide where you stabbed me when the police showed up!" He shook his fist at her, the scar white against his skin. "They weren't looking for a knife wound, and all of us in the kitchen vouched for each other anyway. No one knew I was even gone for a while. Thought I was serving."

He was rounding the chair, his black boots on the quilt, his eyes shining with bloodlust, the edges of his teeth visible between his thin lips. "Part of me will always love you," he whispered, the knife inches from her, the roar in her ears pulsing with fear, "But you need to pay for killing our baby . . ."

Chapter 18

Liam blinked awake. Found himself seated in his darkened truck. For a second he was discombobulated, lost about where he was. He rubbed a kink from his neck. Where was he and what the hell was he doing here? Why was he—?

In a flash, he remembered. He was parked on the far side of Lamplighter's lot, backed into a space, the nose of his truck facing the building, giving him a view of the front façade of the motel. He glanced at Rory's second-floor room. There was a sliver of light around the door frame, as if it wasn't completely shut.

He saw movement behind the curtained window. Rory? *Someone else?*

Oh, shit.

Liam threw open the Tahoe's driver's door. Leaping from the cab, Liam kept his eyes focused on Rory's windows. Two figures.

Could be anyone, he told himself.

But he had a bad feeling.

Liam raced up the stairs, taking them two at a time. He heard Rory's tense voice, a man's answering growl. What the hell?

He pushed open the door just as the man lunged forward, a knife in his hand, swinging at a dazed-looking Rory. Without thinking he hurled himself forward. At the same moment Rory bent over, grabbed a wad of bedding that had puddled on the floor, and yanked.

The assailant's booted feet slipped. He tried to recover his balance as Liam slammed into him, driving both their bodies to the floor in a tangle of the bedding. "Get out!" Liam yelled at Rory as he struggled to subdue the assailant. But the attacker was a wild man. Though facedown in the coverlet, the assailant, all sinew and muscle beneath his slippery leather outfit, squirmed and slashed, making quick wide arcs behind him, a sharp blade slicing wildly through the air, intent on finding a mark.

Liam grabbed at the deadly arm, but his grip slid and he was forced to dodge and weave, holding the growling, wriggling thug down while trying to avoid being sliced to ribbons.

Somewhere, Liam thought, he heard sirens.

Get here! Get here fast!

The guy must've been a wrestler because he moved suddenly, feinting right, throwing Liam's weight to one side, then gathering himself and arching, moving left, reversing the situation so he, red-faced and angry, was on top. Liam's grip slipped as he jerked his arm away. "You sick son of a bitch," the attacker spewed, raising his arm, intent on ramming his knife into Liam's face.

Liam bucked just as Rory came into view near the door. The room went suddenly dark.

Crash!

The attacker's body jerked and he yowled as something heavy collided with him. He slumped against Liam, who struggled out from under him and then climbed atop the son of a bitch. He didn't know what had happened, but he wasn't taking any chances. The guy was dazed and Liam took advantage of it.

"You bastard!" Rory gritted out, her voice shaking. Footsteps sounded through the open doorway.

"What's going on?" a woman's shrill voice demanded. "I called 911 on you!"

Thank, God, Liam thought as the sirens screamed closer.

"You called the cops?" a gravelly voiced man asked in shock.

"Jesus, Warren, yes! Did you hear them?" the woman answered back.

The overhead light snapped on and Liam saw Rory, still holding the lamp she'd used as a weapon, braced against the wall near the windows. Blood crusted her nostrils and her skin was white as chalk. "Cal," she whispered, staring. "It was Cal. All along. He tried to kill me then . . . at the wedding, and he tried to kill me now."

"Redmond?"

She was nodding as the footsteps clambered on the porch outside. A second later a police officer stood in the doorway, weapon drawn. "Police!" he ordered. "Get down! Now!" He caught a glimpse of Rory. "You, too." Another officer appeared behind the first. Her sidearm was in her hand.

Liam lifted his palms. "I'm Liam Bastian and this is my wife—"

"Do it!" the female cop ordered, her anxiety evident in her strangled tone. "Hands over your head. Get on the floor. Now!"

Liam placed his hands over his head and lay on the floor. Rory slithered down the wall, then did the same. He felt his wallet being tugged from the back pocket of his jeans, allowed his hands to be cuffed behind his back.

He didn't care. The police could restrain him all they liked. As long as Rory was safe. It would all be sorted out soon enough anyway. At least the madman, now, finally, was being handcuffed.

Now, maybe the nightmare of the last five years was finally over.

Bethany was waiting.

And she was the last person Liam expected to find at the Laurelton police station when their story was told and he was finally released. But there she was, sitting ramrod stiff on a bench in a brightly lit, austere area of the department where family members were allowed to wait for their loved ones. Two others were in the room as well, an African American kid of about nineteen, earplugs connected to his cell phone. He barely glanced up as Liam walked out. The other was a worried pregnant woman whose face dropped in disappointment at the sight of Liam. Through the glass partition separating this waiting area from the rest of the department, he saw an officer seated at a desk.

Beth's mouth dropped open at the sight of him. "For the love of God, Liam! What the . . . what's going on? You were arrested?" She stared at Liam as if he'd sprouted horns from his head.

"I was questioned. But yeah, I took a ride in a cruiser." Actually he and Rory had been forced into the back of a police vehicle and driven here to be questioned for over two hours about the attack by Cal Redmond. The police had been suspicious and had called Portland PD as he'd given his story. That had alerted the homicide detectives who'd grilled Rory earlier, and Detective Grant had interviewed Liam as well, wondering if there was some kind of link between the Cal Redmond attack, the assault at the wedding, and Teri Mulvaney's murder. Both he and Susskind seemed to believe Liam was holding out on them. Apparently, the detectives had brushed up against him too often in the last few days for them to think it was coincidental.

But the truth of the matter was, Liam didn't know.

Finally, he'd been allowed to leave. Rory was with another officer and he knew it was going to take longer for her to be released. Cal had attacked her twice, and Liam had been informed that the police wanted full statements. He would have to come back for her, so he'd called Derek, explained the situation, saying he would need him later for a ride back to the Lamplighter to retrieve his Tahoe.

But here was Beth.

"How'd you know I was here?"

"You were with Rory," Beth accused in disbelief. She was nearly shivering in some kind of pent-up rage. Devoid of make-up, her hair pulled back and clipped away from her face, she was hurt and upset, arms folded under her chest beneath the too-bright lights of this small area.

"Who told you?"

"Does it matter?"

"Hell, yeah, it matters."

"The bigger question is why were you and Rory attacked in a motel room? Jesus, Liam, you'll never get over her, will you?"

So like Beth to go straight there. No concern for him. Not, *How are you doing?* Not, *Is Rory okay?* Not even, *Who was the assailant and what did he want?* Nope. The burning question in Bethany's mind was: *You'll never get over her, will you?* And she was right. He knew that now; he'd known it from the moment he'd seen his runaway bride again.

"Let's get coffee," he suggested as he looked through the sidelights to the exterior door and saw a fast food place on the other side of a wide parking strip.

She eyed the all-night diner, glowing bright in the night, a few cars parked nearby. "I think we should just go home."

He cocked an eyebrow. Home?

"I'll take you to your place," she clarified tightly.

"Seriously?"

She nodded. Vigorously.

"I'm coming back for Rory, so you'd better take me to my car."

She seemed to tighten all over. Lips, corners of the eyes, neck muscles, shoulders. "Of course."

He said, "But first, coffee. I'll tell you how I ended up in police custody and you tell me how you knew I was at the Laurelton police station. Deal?" he asked, holding the door for her.

Without answering, she walked stiffly through. As the door swung shut, she muttered, "What's taking so long with her?"

"They have more questions for her."

"What does that tell you, Liam? Huh? That she comes back into town and almost immediately all hell breaks loose?"

They were walking across the nearly empty parking lot where Bethany's white Lexus gleamed pearlescent beneath a security lamp. With Bethany a few steps behind, Liam stepped over the curb to a short path cutting between struggling boxwood plants in the strip of landscaped earth between the two buildings. The path was wide and littered, created by thousands of feet that had made the trek between the all-night diner and the station.

Inside, the restaurant was nearly empty, one tired waitress manning the cash register, a sprinkling of night-owls tucked in worn booths and huddled over coffee or sodas in the middle of the night. Though not lit as harshly as the waiting area of the Laurelton PD, the restaurant was hardly intimate.

Liam slid into a booth near the window with a view of the police station.

"You can't go on living your life for a woman who comes and goes as she pleases, who's apt to disappear and reappear on a whim."

"She's my wife, Beth. And Charlotte's my kid."

"You *think*."

"Pretty sure."

"Until there's a DNA test."

"It's happening. Should get the results soon. Private lab with a rush order, but I know."

Beth was about to say something else when a thin, fiftyish waitress with bags under her eyes and a weary smile stopped at their table. She was holding a coffeepot and turned over the cups already set on the booth's battle-worn table. "Breakfast?" she asked, and Bethany gave an almost imperceptible shake of her head, her lips knotted.

"Just coffee. Thanks. And black is fine," he added, anticipating her request.

"Cream and sugar on the table anyway." She pointed a long, gnarled finger tipped in red toward the condiments and napkin holder pressed against the far end of the booth near the window. "How about you, honey?" She eyed Bethany, who visibly bristled.

"Nothing. Oh. Maybe sparkling water. With a slice of lemon."

The waitress, whose name tag read Nora, nodded. "Okay. Let me know if you change your mind about breakfast. The special today is a Belgian waffle with fresh strawberries and a side of bacon."

"Will do," Liam promised, and she returned quickly with the water glass, complete with lemon, then made the rounds with her coffeepot, stopping at the next booth where two teenagers, dressed in hoodies and ripped jeans, drinking sodas, were plugged into their cell phones. Liam looked at the time and saw it was after midnight.

He took a swallow of coffee.

"How can you be so damned calm?" Bethany asked once the waitress was out of earshot. "You've been up half the night, assaulted by a deranged ex, dragged down to the police station, for God's sake . . . All I'm saying, Liam, is that Rory is trouble. Real trouble. Her mother is a wacko, her stepfather's in jail, and her brothers are petty crooks at the very least."

"Stepbrothers. And Aaron is—"

"Yes, I know he's gone. Caught in the crossfire at *your* wedding to *her.* You got hurt yourself. I know."

Her words made him want to rub his thigh, but he stopped himself. A habit he needed to break.

"And your father?" Her eyes were ice-cold. "Because of Rory, Geoff is in a wheelchair."

"What happened at the wedding wasn't her fault," he argued, starting to lose his cool. He was tired, angry, and he didn't need a fight with Bethany. Not now. Well, not ever.

"You don't know that. My God, Liam. Why do you defend her? She's dangerous." Her eyes narrowed and she swirled her straw in her untouched water glass, making the slice of lemon dance and swirl within the tiny cubes.

"I just don't blame her for what happened."

"A few days ago, not even a week, you were going to divorce her." She raised her eyes, pinned him in her gaze. "Now—?"

"I don't know."

She made a sound of disbelief. "Fine. I tried, you know, to be more like her. God, it was so obvious you were in love with her! I really tried. Even colored my hair a more reddish shade of blond. How stupid is that?" She laughed bitterly. "You never even noticed."

He hadn't really. Her hair had always been pale, but now, yeah, it was redder.

"What a fool I've been." Sighing, she suddenly realized she was fiddling with the straw and let go of it. Her big eyes were hurt, wounded. "Do you know how hard it is to compete with a ghost? You didn't know if she was alive or dead and somehow she became this . . . this angel. And look, will you? She actually left you high and dry, bleeding at your own damned wedding ceremony. What does that tell you about her?" She glared at him as if she wanted to kill him. "She hid out for nearly five years in that stupid little rinky-dink town as far north as she could flee, never letting you know where she was, keeping her daughter secret, living under an alias, probably . . . oh, I don't know . . . making up a story about a pretend ex-husband who was abusive or running from the law or whatever. She's shady, that's all I'm saying, a liar and an escape artist. Open your eyes and take a look at who she really is."

"How do you know so much about her?" he asked slowly, taking in everything she'd said.

"From *you*. Come on, Liam. She's all you ever talked about."

He didn't think so, and yet Beth was firm, her lips knife-blade thin, her French-tipped nails digging into her palms. "I never had a chance. The ghost of Rory has always been between us, even though she was alive and well and she could have returned to you anytime she wanted, but she just let you twist in the wind while she was hiding in Point Roberts making Frappuccinos for tourists!" She threw a glance at the ceiling, tears standing in her eyes. "God, I've been a fool."

"I haven't talked about her," Liam said. He'd been careful about Rory with Beth. Always very careful. "And I didn't know she was in Point Roberts until just recently."

"It's common knowledge now."

"But it hasn't been. And I didn't talk about it with you."

"Well, I heard it. No big deal." She gave him the look, leaning back in the booth, eyebrows faintly arching. Almost daring him to figure it out. And he did.

"You knew," he said.

"Knew what?"

"Where she was."

"Who? Rory? You've got to be kidding. How would I—"

"Someone told you. Who?" It hit him like a punch in the gut as soon as he asked the question. "Jacoby," he said. Hadn't Liam asked the Van Hornes if they'd ever used a private investigator? Hadn't it been Beth herself who said her father worked with Brian Jacoby? Now it was his turn to feel the fool. "He told you where she was."

"No . . . why would he?"

But she was lying. He could tell. "He told you where she was at the same time he told me."

"No."

And then he knew something else, the realization coming to him with icy clarity. "You hired him to find her before I did. You didn't want me hiring him to find Rory. You wanted to find her."

She didn't deny it, just glared at him with such hatred he hardly recognized her. He realized Jacoby had been playing both ends against the middle. Collecting fees from both him and Beth. Suddenly, he asked, "Did you know where she was before I did?"

She didn't answer for a second, weighing her options: truth against the lie.

"Beth," he warned.

"Why would I look for her?" she blustered. "What good would that have done me?"

"How long have you known where she was?"

She let out a huff of disgust. Her silence was as much a deception as an outright lie.

"I love you," she said as if it were a defense, then, gauging his reaction, she suddenly reached into her purse and retrieved the Yoda ring. "Talk about stupid." Angrily she flicked the bit of plastic away as if she were a frat boy flipping beer bottle caps at his friends. The green ring skidded over the worn tile floor to settle against the edge of another booth. "It was a dumb thing. Almost as dumb as waiting for a real engagement ring from a man who was still hung up on his first wife. You were—are—still married to her, and I wanted you to get that divorce!" Her anger was palpable. "Whether you admit it to yourself or not, you're still in love with her."

Before he could respond, she stood abruptly and, either by intent or accident, he couldn't tell which, knocked over the water glass, sending ice cubes and the lemon slice skittering across the table in a splash of icy water that landed in his lap. Muttering under her breath, she breezed past the teenagers, who didn't so much as look up from their devices, then turned abruptly around and stormed back to him.

"There's something I've been meaning to tell you. Wasn't sure I was going to, but . . ."

Liam waited. She was clearly struggling with herself.

"Your family has secrets," she finally said. "And I know about them. And they know I know about them."

"Okay."

"Oh, don't be so smug!" she hissed.

"I'm not smug. I'm just waiting for you to tell me what you think you know about my family."

His choice of words was wrong. He knew it immediately, but it was too late. She straightened up as if pulled by a string.

"To hell with you, Liam," she choked out before stalking through the restaurant and across the parking lot to the well-worn path to the police station. Seconds later he saw her white Lexus tear out of the station's lot to speed down a side street.

"Uh-oh," the waitress said, showing up with a towel and mop. "Trouble in paradise?" she asked as Liam swiped at his pants with napkins.

He found his wallet and dropped a twenty on the table. "Trust me, it was never paradise."

Rory couldn't get out of the police station fast enough. They were decent to her, offering medical care, photographing her injuries for future documentation, bringing her water and asking her if she wanted anything else, but all she desired was to get back to Charlotte. She said as much as she told her story of the attack to a woman officer with the Laurelton Police Department who wrote everything down. In turn Rory learned that Liam had talked to the Portland detectives, alerting them to the fact that Cal Redmond was the would-be killer who'd attacked her at the wedding, that his motivation was his belief that she'd aborted his child and that his assault on her, then and now, apparently had nothing to do with the assassination at the wedding.

When she was finished, she walked outside and her knees nearly went weak when she saw Liam was waiting for her by his Tahoe. "Derek picked me up and took me to my car," he explained as she climbed inside. "He had a million questions about Cal and he asked about you, too."

"I've had enough explaining."

"Yep. Finally talked him into leaving." Liam put the vehicle in gear just as a police cruiser drove into the lot, the beams of headlights splashing against the side of the building. "Let's get out of here."

"To the hospital."

"It's the middle of the night and Charlotte's sleeping. I just checked and I called Darlene. She's already there."

Rory felt her muscles relax.

"You," he said in a surprisingly tender voice, "need to get some more sleep. I hate to say it, but you look like hell."

He flipped down the passenger visor so she could see for herself the bruising that was already visible around her eyes. Her hair was a wild red mess, her pallor ghostly, her nose swollen. "I look like I've been in a bar fight," she grumbled, as he started the SUV.

"Not quite that bad. But if you want to see a doctor—"

"No. No doctor. The only reason I want to go to the hospital is to see Charlotte."

"Here." He handed her his phone. "The last number dialed goes directly to the nurses' station at Pediatrics."

"I've got my phone," she said, but memorized the number from his before making the call. She learned from one of the nurses that, as he'd said, not only was Charlotte still sleeping, but yes, Darlene had arrived. She next placed a call to her mother, but before she could say anything, Darlene jumped in with, "Oh, my God, Rory! Are you all right? Liam said you were attacked by Cal. I never liked him, you know. Untrustworthy. You could see it in his face!"

This from the woman who had tied the knot with Harold Stemple, a thief who lately had spent more time behind bars than as a free man. But at least Darlene was concerned and willing to stay with Charlotte until Rory could pull herself together. "If Charlotte's sleeping, I think I'll go back to my motel and do the same."

"Oh, absolutely, honey. I'm here. For as long as you need me."

"Thanks, Mom," Rory said, heartfelt. She was suddenly close to tears. She clicked off and closed her eyes, fighting a hot wave of emotion. As soon as the emotion passed, she reopened them and for the first time noted that they were heading east, toward Portland and away from the center of Laurelton. "Where are we going?" she asked. Street lamps glowed, offering watery blue light against the dark sky.

"My place."

"Wait. What?" Liam's home? "No. I have a motel room."

"That's currently a crime scene," he pointed out as he merged onto Highway 26.

"But my things? I don't have—"

"I do."

"What?"

"Some of your stuff." He cast a glance at her in the darkened

SUV and she saw the self-deprecating turn of his lips. "Never got rid of it."

"Oh . . ." She didn't know how to feel about that. Glad that he'd kept reminders of her or sad that he hadn't let go. Hadn't he said he wanted a divorce? Then, why? *Because he didn't believe you were dead. He hoped you were coming back, that he would see you again, if only for a final showdown, a prelude to the divorce.* "I don't know about being at your place."

He didn't change course.

"What about Bethany?"

"It's over."

She cast him a disbelieving look.

"She's out of my life."

"Since when?" she asked.

"Since earlier this evening. We had a break up, ring and all."

Ring? "I didn't think you were engaged already," she said, processing.

"We weren't. I'll explain later."

"Okay."

Again there was silence, the interior of the Tahoe illuminating in flashes as they passed streetlights and oncoming cars. Finally Liam said, "I know you're sick to the back teeth of talking, but I'd like to know about Cal, when you're ready."

"He thought I killed our baby. His and mine."

Liam's head swiveled quickly her way, so she launched into the story, what she knew of it, of her miscarriage and Cal's subsequent belief that she'd aborted the child, of his jealousy and obsession with her, how he'd gotten the catering job at the wedding, how he'd hidden his injury from the police. "He says he didn't know the suspected shooter, DeGrere, that he had nothing to do with what happened at the wedding."

"Do you believe him?"

Rory shrugged. "I don't know."

They were silent again for a while, but the silence was becoming more companionable. "Were you coming to Portland when Charlotte got sick?" he asked.

"No." She felt guilty admitting the truth. "I was heading south. As far as I could get. I figured everyone would think I'd go to Canada, I mean it was so close to Point Roberts and all. And I did for a while . . . you know."

"With Kent Daley and his friend Maude."

"Right. I thought driving as far as I could in the opposite direction would be a smart idea. LA or Phoenix, maybe. But then Charlotte got sick, so . . ." She cast him a look. "I ended up in your backyard."

"The place you wanted to avoid."

They crested a final hill before dropping through the canyon cutting into the center of the city, streetlights blurring past. Liam maneuvered through the one-way streets on the west side of the river and into the parking garage of a high-rise located in the Pearl District. A converted warehouse, the brick-and-concrete structure still held on to some of its authentic nineteenth-century charm, while equipped with the latest conveniences and finishes. When Rory walked out of the elevator and into Liam's penthouse, she found herself in a huge, nearly cavernous room with floor-to-ceiling windows and a view of the city lights and one of the bridges crossing the dark Willamette River.

The living room area opened to a roof-top deck. "Nice," she said, eyeing the shimmering stainless steel-and-white kitchen equipped with all the bells and whistles. A far cry from the apartment they had shared in Seattle.

"One of the first projects I worked on when I took over the company," he said, but didn't add, *After the sniper attack on the wedding. After you disappeared. After I recovered from gunshot wounds that nearly took my life.* "Hungry?" he asked, and she shook her head.

"No." Her stomach grumbled loudly at that moment. "Okay, changed my mind. Make that ravenous."

"Sit." He pointed to a long couch backing the kitchen area and she didn't argue, just dropped onto the plush cushions as he rattled around in his bachelor pad. There was no sign of Bethany that she could see. No earrings left on the table, no pictures of her on the mantel of a tiled fireplace, no lingering scent of her perfume. Not that it was any of her concern, she reminded herself as she closed her eyes and listened to the sound of bacon sizzling on the stove. Nudging off her shoes, she told herself to still the questions that spun crazily through her mind and just relax. She smelled the warm scent of coffee and was aware of the familiar sounds of a coffeepot gurgling and hissing. Once more her stomach responded noisily.

She'd thought she'd barely closed her eyes when she felt a hand on her shoulder. Blinking, she found Liam in front of her. On the glass-topped coffee table was a plate of scrambled eggs, toast, and bacon, and beside the platter sat a cup of steaming coffee, cream clouding the dark liquid. "Eat first. Then sleep."

"Mmm, so now you're a chef?" she asked, yawning and stretching.

He grinned. "An apprentice fry cook at best."

She swung into a sitting position and Liam joined her.

"We made the news," he said as she took a swallow from her cup and felt the warmth of the coffee slide down her throat.

A television, mounted over the fireplace, was turned on but muted, closed-captioning running along the bottom of the screen. "Oh, God." The coffee that had tasted so wonderful a moment earlier suddenly curdled in her stomach as she saw Pauline Kirby's intense face on the screen and noted that she was standing, microphone in hand, in front of the Lamplighter Inn. "Turn on the volume."

"You're sure?"

"Better the devil you know than the devil you don't."

He touched the remote and Pauline's voice was suddenly filling the room.

"... details are incomplete at this time, but we do know that Liam Bastian and his wife, Aurora, known as Rory, the runaway bride, were questioned and released about an hour ago. Calvin Redmond, an ex-boyfriend of Aurora's, is being held, charged with assault against her at the Lamplighter Inn late last night. There is speculation, as yet unconfirmed, that Redmond might have had a part in the shooting at the wedding ceremony of Liam and Aurora Bastian in Seattle five years ago. That attack left one man dead and several others wounded—"

Liam clicked off the set. "Okay?" he asked her.

She nodded. She'd had enough as well.

He plunged a bite of eggs into his mouth, then when he noticed Rory hadn't taken a bite, pointed at her plate with his fork. "Eat."

She did. At first mechanically, and then with more gusto as the food hit her stomach. Very little was said as they ate their meal, and as she took the last slice of bacon from the plate, Rory felt her limbs go liquid as her tension subsided. It was all she could do to follow Liam to the bathroom while he sorted through his meager medical supplies. The bruises beneath her eyes were more pronounced and the cut on her chin had healed to a small scrape. Her nose looked like she'd run into a door, which, well . . . she had.

She cleaned up as best she could, and as she turned off the faucets she caught Liam's gaze in the mirror. He was leaning in the doorway, faintly smiling. "Good as new?"

"More like 'as good as it gets.'"

She turned around to find his gaze moving slowly up her body. "Pretty damned good, I'd say."

"You must be blind," she accused.

"Come here."

"No."

"Just come here."

"That is not a good idea."

"Yes, it is."

She could feel the sexual tension rising between them. Heart beginning to pound, she stepped closer to him, knowing she shouldn't, unable to stop herself. He reached forward, clasped her by the shoulders, the pressure points of his fingers warm enough to permeate her top and heat her muscles.

He's going to kiss me.

Her pulse skyrocketed as he leaned in close, his coffee-laced breath whispering across her skin. His face was so near that she noticed the changing color of his eyes, the way his whiskers were starting to appear. Panic and a little bit of anticipation surged through her. "Come on," he said in a low voice and applied a little pressure, pulling her forward until she was in the bedroom—*his* bedroom—as he guided her toward the bed.

I can't, she thought wildly.

I can't stop was the quickly following thought.

He gave her the slightest of pushes toward the bed and then said, "Now. You. Sleep." And then he was backing out of the room and closing the door and she wanted to cry out and call him back, to close her mind to the world and tangle in the cool sheets and his warm arms.

But she didn't.

Instead she dropped onto the mattress, snuggled under the covers, closed her eyes and fell into a deep, dreamless sleep.

Chapter 19

Charlotte!

Rory's eyes flew open.

Charlotte was in the hospital and she was . . . Oh, Lord, she was lying in Liam's bed, in his penthouse and . . . he was sleeping beside her. As if the last five years hadn't existed.

"Hey," he said as she stirred.

"What're you doing here?"

"This is my bed."

"Clearly, but . . ."

He levered himself up on an elbow, his dark hair falling over his forehead, his eyes full of lazy amusement.

He thought this . . . situation was *funny*?

"I have to get to the hospital."

"It's the dead of night. When I called them, they said Charlotte's going to be released, but the doctor has to sign the forms and she won't be there until around eleven. We've got hours. Might as well use them."

"Meaning?"

He didn't answer but she could see his expression in the strip of moonlight that penetrated his bedroom window shades. She recognized the look in his eye, even felt a ridiculous sense of anticipation deep inside. "You're insane."

"Nah . . ." He reached over to clasp a warm hand around her wrist.

"Liam," she protested as he tugged her toward him and she slid across the small expanse of sheets. "I'm not sure this is a good idea."

"Probably not." he agreed pleasantly, then lowered his head and kissed her, his lips warm and pliant and oh, so familiar, a sweet pressure that brought tender memories to the fore. She'd always looked forward to making love with him. One arch of his eyebrow in the right situation, a suggestion that he wanted to take her to bed, could cause her to melt inside. She'd thought she was long over those feelings, but not so.

"Cal?" she asked.

"In custody. I double-checked."

"My car—"

"Already towed to a mechanic. My mechanic."

"And I need a place to stay."

"Here works."

"Here? With you?" The idea had its allure. "And Charlotte . . ."

"Will come here, too. First, though, she's going to be with Darlene at my folks' house."

"Your *folks*?" The term was almost comical, thinking of stolid, unbending Geoffrey Bastian, his icy wife, and the way they'd treated her, how they'd insisted that she was only a gold digger, how they'd sneered at Rory and her family . . . Nothing folksy about them. "That's wrong on so many levels, starting with I can't see Darlene anywhere near your parents."

"It's all arranged. There's a guest apartment on the grounds, where Darlene can stay with Charlotte. Everyone agrees."

"Really."

He nodded, though Rory doubted his assessment. She didn't think Stella Bastian would ever accept Rory, or probably Charlotte either. She was just that cold. "Your mother, too?"

"In the loop," he said, satisfied with himself. "You can change everything later. Make other arrangements, once you know what you want to do. I just wanted a stable, safe place for Charlotte, considering how things have been going."

She thought about Cal bursting into the cheap motel so easily and with murderous intent. For the moment, Liam was right, and even though Cal was behind bars, he could have had an accomplice. Liam would not rest until the shooting incident had been solved, the culprits locked up.

He leaned in ever so close and she caught her breath as he brushed his lips across hers, lazily, as if they had all the time in the world.

For once she decided not to worry, and as his arms pulled her closer and the kiss deepened, she let herself get lost in this man, her husband. With a moan, she opened her mouth and felt his tongue slide through her lips.

A frisson of desire slid into her core, and her blood heated.

How long had it been? Years. The last time they'd made love had been the night before the day they were to recite their vows at the hotel in front of all the guests. She'd already been pregnant with Charlotte.

It had been five long years.

There was no reason to wait a second longer. When he started tugging at her clothes, she helped, kicking off her jeans, pulling at her T-shirt, feeling the heat of his fingertips brush her back as he unhooked her bra.

"You're beautiful," he breathed against her skin, his lips scraping her neck.

She actually laughed as she remembered her visage in the Tahoe's visor mirror: bruises and scrapes, a knot on her forehead, a fat nose.

He ignored her amusement, kissing the scratch on her chin before sliding lower. A pulsing warmth invaded her, caused her to ache deep inside. She cradled his head, and her fingers caught in his hair as he found her breast and began to suckle.

"Oh," she gasped reflexively, and as she arched upward, he slid one hand under the small of her back, dragging her closer still, until their abdomens seemed to meld and the room spun away.

"Rory," he whispered into her skin, pressing his knees between hers, pulling her upward as he nudged into her, waiting just a second before plunging into her depths.

Her breath caught in her throat, a strangled cry.

Three quick thrusts and her body strained with desire as if it had just been waiting for this moment. She clung to him, moving with him, catching his rhythm, closing her eyes against tears of relief and joy, teetering on the edge of true passion. Carried away, her thoughts spinning, she kissed him wildly, frantically. His tempo increased and she cried out with the first convulsion. The world shattered with each spasm, pleasure erupting, her thoughts centered only on him, just Liam, the man she still loved.

His climax came with a primal cry, his body jerking, his hips colliding with hers in a long, sweet moment before he collapsed atop her and let out a long breath. His heart was pounding, thudding in rapid counterpoint to her own, and she fought tears as, holding him close to her, she floated back to the stark reality that this couldn't last, couldn't be. It was just for the moment. He'd flat out told her he'd chased her down to end their marriage.

"Well, Mrs. Bastian," he said, levering onto one elbow to stare down at her. "It's been a while, but I gotta say, it was worth the wait."

"Yeah?" She was still collecting her breath.

"Yeah." A slow, sexy smile crawled across his jaw and he whispered, "Let's do it again . . ."

"I—"

He didn't wait for her to finish. Just began kissing her mouth and throat and lower, in a line down her center, not stopping . . .

With a strangled sound, she gave in, squeezing her eyes closed as she threw her head back, forgetting everything. *Tomorrow*, was the ragged thought that pierced her consciousness. She would think about what to do tomorrow.

Liam's cell rang at seven thirty a.m.

Groaning and wiping a hand over his face to wake up, he snatched the damned phone off his nightstand so as not to wake his wife, who, all curves and warmth, was nestled against him. Why, he wondered, did it feel so right to be in bed with her, after all of her lies, all of her deception, all of her need to get as far away from him as possible?

Without an answer, he checked his cell's screen and saw the caller was Lester Steele, his foreman.

Now what? he thought, shooting a look toward Rory, who was stirring. He wanted to enfold her into his arms, forget about all the questions and problems facing them and make love to her again.

"Yeah?" he answered, throwing his legs over the side of the bed to the spot on the floor where his jeans had landed after he'd so eagerly kicked them off. Dragging his attention back to the phone, he said a bit shortly, "What's up?"

"Hate to tell you this, but there's been more sabotage," Steele informed him, and Liam's heart sank. "This time at the Flavel Apartments."

Liam swore softly, snagged his jeans, then padded quietly into the bathroom so as not to disturb Rory. "What happened?" he asked, shutting the door.

"Same thing. Broken windows . . . some graffiti. Might be the homeless, or maybe . . . I don't know . . ."

"Flavel's been boarded up for months."

"They broke in. Smashed what wasn't already smashed. Wrote some stuff that seemed kind of personal."

"How do you mean?" He caught a glimpse of himself in the mirror—unshaven and naked, his hair tousled.

"The graffiti. Slurs against your family . . . and their business dealings." He cleared his throat.

"Against the family?" So not just teenagers with a spray can, no curfew and hours to kill by getting into trouble.

"Yeah," Steele said. "I've been thinkin' about that."

"And?"

"Well, I know Barlow tried to buy the building from your dad back in the day, even went to Flavel himself, but it was too late. By that time Flavel had sold everything lock, stock, and barrel to your dad when their partnership split up, and that included the Flavel apartment building."

Barlow Industries was Steele's old company, the one from which Bastian-Flavel Construction had hired him. Ned Barlow was reportedly still bitter about losing Steele and Jarrod Uller, and blamed Geoff entirely, though it had been Liam's idea to hire the men, not his father's. But Barlow didn't know that, obviously, or that Geoff had railed against the hirings. Barlow was also purportedly upset about several other projects that the Bastians had won by outbidding their competitors, especially the ones "taken" from Barlow Industries. However, in the case of the Flavel building, which Barlow had offered good money for once upon a time and James Flavel had accepted, the deal had gone south through no fault of Barlow's.

Geoff Bastian, then Flavel's partner, had nixed that deal, refusing to sign when the contracts were presented to him. Barlow had called foul and threatened to sue. In fact the entire mishandled real estate negotiation had been one of the deciding factors in the breakup of the Flavel-Bastian partnership. Geoff had bought out Flavel, thus owning the company in its entirety, while Flavel, nest egg securely pocketed, had sailed off into the sunset.

But the legal threats and reshuffling of the company had happened years earlier. Hiring Steele and Jarrod Uller away from Barlow had been recent.

"Ned Barlow wouldn't stoop to sabotage," Liam said.

"Yeah? You're probably right. But he'd look the other way if someone wanted to help him."

"You know him better than I do."

Steele sighed. "I've already called Uller and he's going to get someone over to Flavel and assess the damage."

"Might not matter. That building will be more of a gut job than Hallifax."

"Okay," Les agreed. "Just thought you oughta know."

"Thanks. Can you send me some pictures of the graffiti? Just message them to me."

"Will do."

"I'll be there as soon as I can," Liam promised, then hung up, thinking about the Flavel apartment building, which wasn't in the best part of town and was less centrally located than the Hallifax building.

Slurs against the Bastians . . .

It felt like he was being attacked from all sides.

Though he didn't think Ned Barlow was behind the sabotage, he didn't believe it was a homeless person, either. He agreed with Lester that the destruction seemed more pointed.

But then who? Who had a grudge against his family?

He thought back to the wedding. Pete DeGrere? Or De-Grere's unknown accomplice? Or whoever hired him, if indeed, he was the assassin? And what was their gripe against the Bastians?

Or was he making a leap that didn't exist? Maybe the assault at the wedding and the vandalism were unrelated.

Then what about Teri Mulvaney's death?

Without any answers, he looked in on Rory, saw the tumble of red hair above the covers and almost stalked across the room to wake her up and make love to her again, see what the tenor of their relationship was this morning.

Call it crazy, he'd never gotten over her. If anything, his feelings had grown, and he wasn't sorry that it was over with Bethany. That never would have worked, with or without Rory.

He took a quick shower and by the time he was toweling off, Rory stumbled into the bathroom herself.

"I should have gone back to the hospital and stayed with Charlotte," Rory fretted, sweeping back her mane of hair. Beyond the scrape on her chin, she had a line of bruises down the left side of her face and a knot on her forehead, the aftereffects of Cal's attack. Even so she was more beautiful than he remembered.

You got it bad, pal.

"Call her. She's probably up."

"Let's just get there."

"Okay." He glanced at her body and kicked himself mentally for thinking of making love to her again.

"You said you had some of my things?"

"Right." With a towel wrapped around his hips, he led her

ONE LAST BREATH 343

back to the bedroom, then rifled in the extra closet, pushing aside several jackets. "In here."

"Amazing." She pulled out one dress or blouse after another, then found a pair of jeans and a boat-necked T-shirt sitting atop a manila envelope. "I haven't seen these chothes . . ."

"I know."

"It's okay if I run through the shower?"

He swallowed a wolfish grin and looked away, nodding. "Sure." *Just like the old days.* "Just get a move on."

As if she needed more incentive.

She dashed into the bathroom and he heard the shower spray, but within minutes she was back in the bedroom, dressed, her hair a mass of wet curls, digging through her purse for a compact, then scurrying back to the bathroom. A few minutes later, she returned, her scrapes and bruises covered by concealer.

"You look good," he told her.

"At least the size of my nose has gone down." She touched it carefully. "Sore, but okay. As long as I don't get black eyes."

"You would know by now if that was going to happen."

She gave him a quick smile and asked, "Ready?"

"Yes, ma'am."

He locked the condo behind them and guided her to the elevator to the parking garage. On the way down, he said, "We had some more sabotage last night. A different building that's not as close in as Hallifax, the one where Teri Mulvaney was found."

"Oh, no."

"The building might be razed anyway, but I've got to check it out."

"Okay, but I need to go be with Charlotte—make sure my mom's on board to stay up here. At your folks' house. It still feels wrong."

"Got a better idea?"

"Not yet."

"Let's pick up your car on the way. I had it sent to an all-night service and the mechanic texted me that it was just a loose wire."

"Really?"

"That's what he said. We'll find out. Never used them before."

"I hope he's right."

"I'll drive you, and then I'll meet you at the house." He'd given her the address, which she'd entered into her phone.

"I thought you had to be at the job site."

"It can wait."

"That's ridiculous. You go. I'll be fine."

He arched a brow.

"Mom and Charlotte will be with me," she insisted.

"I know."

"I can handle your family, Liam." That was probably a lie, but it wasn't as if she were a child. "If things get hairy, I'll—"

"Leave?" he asked.

She flushed. "No, I'll call you."

He hesitated a moment, then said, "Okay. I'll be there as soon as I can."

They reached the parking garage and Liam's Tahoe. Rory climbed in, and as Liam slid behind the wheel he warned himself not to fall into the trap of believing that everything was as it should be, that his wife was home and he had a daughter and they would be together every day and make love every night. A nice pipe dream. They still had a lot of hurdles to leap before they could repair their marriage, if Rory was even so inclined.

And what about you? Are you ready to forgive and forget?

He didn't have an answer to that one.

＊ ＊ ＊

Just as they arrived at the repair shop Liam got another call. "Derek," he muttered.

He seemed about to click off, but Rory said, "Take it. I've got this."

"Sure?"

"Yes." She almost added, "I've been on my own a long time," but hurried inside the building. No need to point out the obvious.

She was starting to feel anxious about her daughter. In the light of day she wasn't sure why she'd agreed to let Charlotte be under Liam's family's care. It was going to be a problem, even with Darlene on her side.

But you wanted to be with Liam.

Well, fine, yes. She'd wanted to be with him. Her mind touched on their lovemaking and she almost blushed. Five years hadn't diminished how wonderful it was, how familiar. And oh, God, what did it say about them that they hadn't used protection? Rory knew she wasn't anywhere near a conception date, but Liam didn't. She wondered what that meant, given his recent relationship with Bethany. What form of contraception had they used?

She heard Liam answer slightly impatiently, "Yeah?" to his brother as she walked through the open door of the repair shop. Gauging from its construction, it had once been a gas station, now converted into car repair, the smells of oil, dust, and cleanser tickling her nose as she told the one guy working, a mechanic wearing dreads pulled into a ponytail and a full beard covering the bottom half of his face, that her car had been picked up the night before.

He nodded. "The Honda. With all the stuff in it?"

"That's the one."

When she tried to pay, Stu, if the name embroidered on his gray jumpsuit was any indication, waved her off. "No worries. The man who called gave a credit card number. All taken care of."

She wanted to argue, but he was already handing her the key and pointing to a gravel parking lot surrounded by a mesh fence topped with razor wire, as if the place were some kind of minimum security prison. If he noticed her scrapes and bruises, he was polite enough not to say so and for that, she supposed, she was thankful.

The car started with a flick of her wrist, the engine sparking easily, which was encouraging. She'd bought it used from Mr. Wharton in Point Roberts. She grimaced, realized she should probably text or call Connie again, but couldn't face all the questions right now. Instead, she drove straight to the hospital. She looked to the road behind, half expecting some vehicle to be following her. Old habits died hard and she'd been hiding out for years, feeling as if she was being followed. Now, she should feel safe. Cal was in custody and the private detective, Jacoby, was no longer tailing her. So why did she still feel as if she was being watched, her every move recorded?

"Paranoia, that's why," she muttered. She flipped on the radio, heard static, and fiddled with the dial, trying to locate a Portland station, only to give up. Following the street signs to Laurelton, she tried to keep her mind off Liam, their lovemaking, and thoughts of being with him again. "One day at a time . . . actually, more like one minute at a time," she told herself as she parked in the lower lot of Laurelton General and made her way to Charlotte's room in Pediatrics. Charlotte was up and dressed, her hair pulled into pigtails, as she sat on her grandma's lap watching a video playing on Darlene's phone.

"Mommy!" she squealed, happily sliding off her grandmother's lap and crossing the room in three bounds to land in Rory's open arms. "I misses you!"

"Me, too, bug," Rory said, her heart lighter. She had to rub her tender nose to stop it from burning.

"We gets to go home!" she said.

"Well, close to it," Rory equivocated. She held the little girl until Charlotte couldn't stand it another second and wriggled away. She was so relieved that her daughter was, indeed, well, that she felt near collapse. She caught Darlene's eye and asked, "Are you okay with all of this?" as Darlene shoved the phone into the pocket of an oversized cardigan.

"I should be asking you that. Goodness, your face!"

"Does it look that bad?" she asked anxiously. "My nose isn't swollen as much."

"No, no, you're fine. I'm just your mother. Terrible, what happened. Cal ..." She clucked her tongue. "Liam told me what happened."

"I never dreamed it was Cal who attacked me at the wedding."

"I know, dear. Neither did I."

"How do you feel about taking care of Charlotte at the Bastians'?" Rory asked in an undertone.

Darlene glanced at Charlotte, who was peering out the doorway to the hall, apparently uninterested in the adults' conversation. "It's only temporary and anything can be endured for a short while. This way I get a chance to know my granddaughter better."

"Yeah, but ..."

"I'm just glad you and Liam are getting along." She slid Rory a knowing look, which made Rory groan inside. "And anyway, what doesn't kill us makes us stronger, or something like that. Who said that?" She whipped out her phone again, quickly poking at buttons. "Let's Google it, shall we? Sounds like some statesman, like Churchill or ... Oh, yes. Here it is: 'That which does not kill us, makes us stronger.' Nietzsche!" She let out a short sigh. "Well, of course." As if she'd known it all along.

"I just hope he's right," Rory said dryly.

"He is, dear, you'll see." She nodded as if with an inner knowledge of all things philosophical. At least she wasn't going into her psychic stuff . . . yet. And beyond that, Rory wasn't certain Nietzsche's observation was even true. She was pretty sure that if anyone could zap someone's strength, it was Stella Bastian.

"Besides, I called Stella," Darlene announced.

"What? You called her?"

"Didn't want to walk in there cold, and I wasn't sure if Liam would be with us or not, so we . . . discussed the situation and I think you'll find she's amenable."

"Amenable . . . really." Rory shook her head. "What did you tell her?"

"That if she ever wanted to have a decent relationship with her granddaughter, she'd better start now. For all her faults, I think Stella is all about her kids and grandkids. So, maybe this isn't exactly what she had in mind for Liam, but there it is." She offered a beatific smile. "We'll be fine, honey."

Dr. McMannis hurried in, to Charlotte's delight; the little girl had truly bonded with the warm physician. McMannis gave out the familiar instructions to Rory about rest and hydration. "Just keep an eye on her, okay? The last thing we need is a relapse." She flashed a smile, winked at Charlotte, then signed the release forms, and she was out the door again, walking briskly, lab coat billowing behind her, to leave Rory to sign the same forms and pocket her copy.

"Okay, we're outta here," she said to her daughter.

"Yesss!" Charlotte yelled. It was so good to see her usual, curious, almost hyper girl again, but Rory wondered how all of that would work with the Bastians. Darlene gathered a bag of her granddaughter's belongings while Rory struggled to keep up with her four-year-old as she tore down the hallway to the elevators.

In separate cars, they drove to a local fast food restaurant, where Charlotte sucked the catsup from her fries and ate less than a third of her portion of chicken nuggets. Rory wasn't all that hungry, but managed to chase around leaves of a Caesar salad as Darlene tore into a turkey sandwich and side of fries. When Rory was nervous, she couldn't eat, but when Darlene experienced even the slightest anxiety, she could mow through a seven-course meal, and that apparently hadn't changed over the past five years Rory had lived in Point Roberts.

Once the meal was over, Rory hauled Charlotte into her car seat, checked the address and route on her phone to remind herself where the Bastians lived (she'd been there exactly once before the wedding debacle), then drove to the Bastian home in the West Hills. On the way, Rory kept one eye on the rearview mirror, making certain Darlene, in her ancient Toyota, was following. The Camry was easy to spot as it was decorated with bumper stickers, and a crystal swung from the interior mirror, catching the light and casting colored beams to the rest of the traffic.

Give me strength, she thought, pulling through open gates and parking in the circular drive. Darlene, crystal swinging with the wide turn, did the same. Liam's Tahoe was nowhere to be seen—probably still dealing with this newest sabotage at the job site—but a Mercedes SUV squatted near the front door, blocking the drive. Rory parked behind the sleek white rig and braced herself.

Stomach knotted, she managed to get Charlotte out of the car and corral her to the front door. Darlene joined them just as Rory poked the doorbell. *Here goes nothing.*

A few seconds later she heard footsteps and then the door swung open. It was Liam's sister, Vivian, dressed in a khaki skirt and white blouse, her hair twisted into a messy bun, earrings sparkling in the sunlight. Her gaze swung from Rory to

Darlene, to Charlotte, and finally back to Rory. "The miracles of modern cosmetics," she said dryly.

"You heard what happened?" Rory asked.

"Liam talked to Derek and he let us all know. Come on in."

As they stepped inside, Rory shuddered inwardly as the memory of Cal's face, twisted in rage, the switchblade inches from her nose, skidded through her brain.

"I hope that's the end of it," Vivian said. "Maybe now we can get some peace."

Rory realized she thought Cal was behind the shooting at the wedding. Maybe he was.

"Well, Charlotte," Vivian said, leaning down to the girl. "Looks like I'm going to be your Aunt Viv." She straightened up and added, "I'm just about to head back to the office. Mom took my kids to the park and Dad's in his den. I just stopped by for a sec—but let me show you to . . . the guest house. It's not really a house, more like an apartment, but come on."

"Where do you work?" Rory asked, more to make conversation than anything else as Vivian led them through the house to a back hallway.

"For Bastian-Flavel. First day," she said dryly as she opened the door to a carpeted staircase, complete with windowed landing, that wound upward to a second-story apartment. An exterior door led to the backyard, and Rory made note of the pool as Vivian led the way up the stairs. "Once Dad thought this would be his home office, I think," Vivian explained, "but . . . that was before . . . you know. Now he'd need an elevator, so Mom converted the space into guest quarters. So, here you are. Make yourselves comfortable. There are drinks, soft drinks and beer, in the fridge and whatever else is stocked in the shelves. Towels in the bathroom and . . . oh, keys in this drawer." She pulled open a kitchen drawer nearest the staircase. "If you need anything, just ask. If Mom or Dad can't help you, there's always me or the babysitter . . ." And she was off, hurrying down the stairs, footsteps fading, the door at the ground level closing with a soft thud. Less than half a minute later a smooth engine roared to life.

"This is nice," Darlene said, looking around. "And see? All that angst for nothing, and what a great place. It's like brand-new." She ran her fingers over the marble counter, then she, with Rory and Charlotte following behind, checked out the open living quarters. In the wide living area, two chairs and a low-slung couch clustered around a credenza and flat-screen TV. The kitchen was fully equipped and separated from the living room by a marble-topped island. French doors opened to a Juliet balcony overlooking the pool area. The bedroom was airy, and large enough for a king-sized bed and another oversized television.

Charlotte was in heaven. "Can we go swimming?" she demanded, pushing her nose to the glass and looking down at the aquamarine water. Sunlight glinted on the surface.

"Yeah, but not now. You just got out of the hospital," she reminded her, though of course no one would know it. When Charlotte looked as if she might argue, Rory added, "Soon, I promise. But right now, I've got to run out for groceries and to try and wrestle our clothes and things from the police."

"Wrestle?"

"I mean it might take a while. Wanna come?" she asked, and Charlotte started to say yes, but Darlene, standing behind her granddaughter, was shaking her head, and Rory was reminded that the rambunctious four-year-old was supposed to be taking it easy and resting.

"Why don't you stay with me and we'll explore," Darlene suggested. "It could be fun. Who knows what we'll find? You've got cousins here and I just bet there are some toys and books if we hunt for them."

"I don't know—" Rory said, but Charlotte's curiosity was piqued, so Rory decided to take advantage of it. She didn't really want to drag her kid to the police station, if it came to that.

"You need some money?" Darlene asked.

"No, I've got this. I won't be long and you have my number." She bussed Charlotte on the top of her head. "Be back in a flash."

Chapter 20

Rory was wrong on that score. It took her nearly three hours with first a stop at the Laurelton Police Department (she'd wanted to get an update on Cal, if she could, find out if they'd learned anything new, but they were politely uninformative), then she'd had to wrangle with the manager of the Lamplighter in order to gather her belongings. She also stopped at an all-in-one store and bought some water toys, floaties, and a swimming suit for Charlotte she found on sale.

As she picked up essentials of peanut butter, jelly, bread, cereal, fruit, and the like, she wondered just how long they would be staying with Liam's family. Not long, she told herself as she placed her items on the checkout counter, refusing to look too far into a future that was murky at best. One night in Liam's bed and a couple of days of being with him did not a lifetime make, she reminded herself as she hauled her purchases to her car where it sat baking in the sun.

Liam seemed to get it that she wasn't involved in the attack at the wedding and had forgiven her for fleeing and hiding out, at least temporarily, but there was still the matter of the mystery surrounding the shooting. On that issue she wasn't completely in the clear with Seattle PD, but at least no one was trying to arrest her.

Yet.

She drove with the windows down, and worried her lower lip as she tried to piece together what had happened that awful day. Again. How many times had she wondered who had attacked the wedding party and why? Now that she knew about Cal, she considered if he'd been involved in the shooting, too. Or, maybe it was someone he knew? A partner in crime? She slowed for a red light, once again coming up with no answers. Cal was in custody, so maybe he'd break, come completely clean, give up whoever was working with him, if that was the way it had gone down.

If he had a partner. But what if, as Cal claims, the shooter— DeGrere, the police thought—had been hired by someone else?

A horn blasted behind her and Rory realized the light had changed while she was lost in thought. Shooting a quick glimpse into her mirror, she saw the driver of a silver SUV holding up his hands, fingers spread in a *what the hell are you doing, lady?* gesture of complete frustration. "Sorry," she said aloud and hit the gas, but she wasn't fast enough for him. He sped around her in the intersection, a flash of silver glinting in the sunlight . . .

Her heart lurched as a memory assailed her. The wedding day. Running. Escaping. Confused. A silver SUV barreling in and spiraling toward the upper levels of a parking garage, nearly hitting her. Maybe gray? Not clean and shining like the one that just zoomed past her, but dirty. Had it been DeGrere's? Racing to the scene of his crime? Or had it been someone else's vehicle?

Turning the fragment of recall over in her mind, she drove onward, and by the time she'd returned to the Bastian estate the July sun had reached its apex and was slowly starting its descent. She carried several bags up the stairs into the apartment, found it empty, and looked out to the pool. No one there. Fighting back a burst of panic that something had gone wrong, she remembered that she'd seen Darlene's distinctive Toyota parked near the garage.

"Everything's cool," she said, taking a breath, annoyed at her rollicking pulse. She hastened down the stairs to the main house and stepped into the back hallway. She was about to call out when Stella suddenly appeared.

"Oh, hi," Rory said awkwardly.

Her mother-in-law . . . hard to believe they still shared that connection . . . looked her up and down, not mentioning her scrapes and bruises, though her gaze lingered on the left side of Rory's face. Before anything more could be said, Charlotte came sliding around the corner, looking flushed.

"You all right?" Rory asked, worried. She could feel the animosity radiating off Stella in waves. Well, Rory was pissed right back. No one ever said you had to like your in-laws. Though her relationship with Liam was tenuous, she was still married to him, and Stella could just chew on that.

Darlene was right on Charlotte's heels. "Oh, she's fine. Just running around like a monkey, even though I try to tell her to take it easy like the doctor ordered."

Stella said coolly, "I'll be in my rooms if anyone needs me."

A clamor of noise, and then Vivian's two children came bursting into view as well, nearly running into their grandmother. "Charlotte!" the little girl squealed.

"Mommy, they like to chase me!" Charlotte said, delighted.

Stella tip-tapped away on heels, her blond hair swept into a chignon, her black sundress showing off toned calves and arms. A young woman came into view and attempted to shoo the children back toward the kitchen—the babysitter, Rory realized.

Charlotte turned to follow after the children, but Rory

grabbed her. "Hey, wait a minute." Charlotte skidded to a stop and regarded her mother impatiently. "A hello kiss?" Rory asked.

Charlotte's face cleared and she hurried back, slid a kiss across Rory's lips, then skittered after her newfound friends.

"Been like that all morning," Darlene said. "She's really bounced back."

"I'm really glad you're here. I don't know what I would have done . . ."

"Hey, she's mine, too. She's got a great aura. Reminds me of you, when you were little."

Rory nodded but didn't respond. She owed her mother for stepping up and helping her. And even though she understood Darlene's last observation was a positive one, she never liked tempting fate; continuing that kind of dialogue might set off a groundswell of pseudo-psychic comments and catchphrases.

Darlene touched Rory's arm in a conspiratorial way and jerked her head to indicate to follow her back through the door and up the carpeted stairway.

"Now that we're finally alone. Tell me, how was last night?"

"How do you mean?"

"Well, you stayed with Liam. Is everything all right?"

"Yes," Rory answered cautiously.

"Everyone thinks it's because of you that Liam broke up with Bethany."

"For God's sake. I wasn't the reason."

"You sure about that?"

"Yes." Rory then launched into Liam's distrust of the private detective, Jacoby, and his relationship to the Van Hornes, but Darlene had already ceased listening.

"It's just wonderful that the two of you have found your way back to each other."

"We're a long way from that," Rory protested.

"Oh, I don't know. You're still married, a family now. He sees that, I'm sure. You were never supposed to be apart."

"Mom . . ."

"I'm not blaming you for cutting out. Cal was stalking you. He attacked you! You had to do something. I see that, but now that we know who's at fault here . . ." She broke off on a sigh and looked around, as if expecting someone to be listening. "I have something to tell you, and I don't want you to get upset."

"I don't like the sound of that. What?"

"No, no. It's fine. It's just that . . . well, Everett contacted me."

"*What?*"

"Shhh. He wasn't the one following you. That was Cal. And Everett's changed, I've told you he's changed."

"Mom, I don't know for sure if Cal was following me. I never thought I saw him."

"Just hear me out. Everett's coming down to Portland to clear the air. He's hurt that you think he has any involvement in the shooting. We can talk to him together, if you like."

"I don't want to talk to him at all"—she flashed back to the nights as a teenager and her fear that her oldest stepbrother would sneak into her room—"ever."

"I hear you. I just know that Liam wants to get to the bottom of what happened at the wedding, and I thought you did, too."

"Of course I do!"

"We don't know for sure who the shooter was. You remember, Harold, Everett, and I all took lie detector tests and we all passed, because we had *nothing to do* with the shooting."

"Yes, Mom. I know."

"Just talk to Everett. You'll see. And you can eliminate him as a suspect."

Rory shuddered inwardly at the thought of seeing her stepbrother again. She hated that her mother was actually making sense about this. Trying to be rational, she said, "I need to talk to Liam about this."

"Great idea. Call him." Darlene nodded her agreement. "He should meet with Everett, too."

"He's working. I . . ." She didn't know how to say that she didn't want to bother him, that their relationship was too new once again, too fragile. She didn't even know if they had a relationship. Maybe last night was just a one-night stand, a good-bye, or a response to high emotion after the fight in the motel room where lives were at stake. She didn't want to be a pest, and she definitely didn't want to see Everett. "When is he coming?"

"He's going to call me when he gets to Portland."

"*Today?*"

"Well, I think so, I—"

"Aurora?" Geoff Bastian's distinctive voice shut Darlene off as if someone had cut off her tongue.

Rory froze. "Yes?"

She heard the squeak of his wheelchair, and a few moments later he appeared at the end of the hallway. His hair was a little grayer, his countenance stern, and, of course, he was seated in the chair, his legs useless though his upper body appeared strong and his eyes, as they drilled into her, looked sharp as ever. His mouth was a thin line, bespeaking his foul mood.

Rory held her breath, wondering what this was all about. Nothing good.

"That guy roughed you up a little," he observed.

"I'm okay."

His eyebrows tweaked a bit and she wondered if she should start wearing sunglasses and a baseball cap.

"Would you mind following me to my den? There are some things I'd like to discuss with you."

"Should I come?" Darlene asked, but the dark look Liam's father sent her made his feelings known. She shrank away.

With a last look back at her mother, Rory trailed after Geoffrey Bastian, who'd done a police U-turn in his wheelchair and was moving into the main body of the house, turning down a hallway lined with pictures of the family, everyone included, Rory noted, except for her.

No surprise there.

That morning Liam had had to make a quick detour on his way to the Flavel job site after a call from Jarrod Uller, the fore-man under Steele who'd reported a water main had been clipped with a backhoe at the Hallifax building. The driver of the equipment had been beside himself, claiming it wasn't his fault, so Uller had called in Liam. By the time he made it to Hallifax, the operator, a tobacco-chewing twentysomething, had calmed down some, saying it was lucky it was a water line he'd hit, not gas—and amen to that. The plumber blamed the backhoe oper-ator, and there was a bit of a glaring standoff before the pipe was fixed and work resumed. Afterwards Uller had walked Liam to his SUV and said, "Children," in his supercilious way, before heading to his own truck.

Uller was a proficient foreman, but the man was a little too slick for his own good. Liam preferred the older, no-nonsense Steele to the handsome fortysomething Uller.

Now Liam pulled out his cell as he climbed into his rig. True to his word, Les Steele had sent pictures of the vandalism in a series of text messages. Ugly stuff. Angry and personal. Di-rected at his family. *Bastian Pigs* and *Rich Bastards* were scrawled along the walls with the usual four-letter words used to de-scribe, in graphic terms, what should be done to anyone named Bastian.

Not teenagers. Someone with a grudge, someone who had it in for the family and the company. Who? Why? Were they seri-ously dangerous? Or were they just cowards with extra cans of spray paint stacking up in their garages and basements? One culprit? Or more?

His Tahoe was parked on the street, in the shade of a nearby, mainly vacant, two-storied office building, which boasted a commercial Realtor's FOR SALE sign in several of the windows. Before heading out, he called Derek, who picked up on the second ring. "Yo, little bro," Derek greeted him.

"On my way to Flavel," Liam told him. "More broken windows, vandalism."

"Huh. Maybe we should thank them for doing the demolition for us."

"Let's meet over there."

"You got it."

"I'll call Dad."

He heard Derek suck in his breath. "You think that's a good idea?"

Liam grimaced, watching a plastic bag caught in the wind float past his car. "He'll be pissed if we don't keep him in the loop."

"It's your funeral."

"Yep." He started the engine of his rig. "Okay, see ya there."

"How'd it go with Rory last night?" Derek asked.

"Well enough." He wasn't going to elaborate, though of course his brother probably wanted to know if they'd spent the night together. Let him figure it out for himself.

"Just like old times?"

"She's my wife, Derek." Liam couldn't keep the bite out of his words. He didn't want to discuss Rory with anyone, least of all his brother.

"No details?"

"How old are you? Twelve? Just meet me at Flavel."

"Ever figure out what Beth meant about knowing something about your family?"

"Haven't really had time to think about it."

"That good last night, huh?"

"I'll be at Flavel in twenty." Liam cut the connection, then pulled away from the curb. Why was it his brother could so easily get under his skin?

Because you let him and because he's still a little pissed that you're higher up in the company than he is. Dad did that. Favored you, at least in Derek's opinion. Never mind that you went to college, graduated in business, and worked your way up in the company. From Derek's view, you're still the "little bro."

As his vehicle melded with traffic, he called his father via voice activation of his Bluetooth connection. But his call went unanswered. Pulling into the right lane, he tried again, this time calling the house, letting it ring until, surprisingly, Vivian answered.

"Thought this was your first day," Liam said.

"Yeah, well, I'm trying to get back there. Got the babysitter here, and what do you know, she suddenly has to leave. Some problem with her ailing mother, which I think is bullshit, but okay. I had to whip back here, and now I'm trying to leave again."

"The office can wait, Viv," Liam said. They were basically making a job for her anyway, so there was no rush. But she was testy about it, so he added, "Aren't Rory and Darlene there?"

"Yes, and Charlotte, but it's not like . . . I don't know . . . I can just dump my children on them. We really hardly know each other, and what are you doing with her, anyway?"

"With Rory?"

"Is everything cool now? With you and your better half? You just going to forgive and forget?"

"Where's Mom?" Liam asked, fighting annoyance.

"In her rooms. She's not sharing any space with Rory, or Darlene, or anyone else. You know how she gets." She let out a huff. "As if Mom would be any real help anyway."

A guy in a white BMW swung into his lane, nearly clipping the front panel of his Tahoe, and Liam slammed on his brakes, biting back a curse.

Vivian was rambling on. "It's summer and my kids are running in and out of the house and jumping in the pool and screaming their bloody heads off. Charlotte's there, too, as much as Darlene and your little wifey will let her be, since she just got out of the hospital. Big fight about going in the pool. Everyone's afraid Charlotte's going to die or something if she gets wet."

Though he loved Viv, sometimes she could be a pain in the neck. "I'll bring them back to my place."

"Oh, don't be pissy, for God's sake. I'm just joking. Everyone's so fucking touchy."

Sensing she was about to hang up on him, he said, "Wait, I want to talk to Dad."

"He's in a meeting with your little wifey."

"What? Why?"

"Ask them. They just went in his den together," she snapped, then mused, "Maybe he's rewriting his will as we speak."

"Unlikely." The truth was, Liam didn't know what to think, but he sensed that Geoff wouldn't be welcoming her back to the family. "Tell him to call me."

"If I see him, I will. Gotta go." And she disconnected.

Liam almost turned around, worry stirring in his gut. But Steele was waiting for him, Derek was meeting them at the job site, and he couldn't rationally see how a conversation between Rory and his father would be truly harmful. Maybe it would even clear the air. Geoff had a tendency to fall into black moods, before and after the shooting, but he'd always managed to rally for company.

Arriving at the Flavel building and seeing the neon green and orange paint sprayed so ineloquently across the new stone façade, he set his jaw. He eyed the vandalism as he climbed from his rig to meet Steele, who, in a safety vest and hard hat, was striding across a gravel access road. He was pointing to his head and Liam nodded before reaching into the back seat and pulling

out his white hard hat with the BASTIAN-FLAVEL CONSTRUC-
TION logo.

Somebody's got it in for us, he thought.

Derek's Ford truck wheeled into the lot in a spray of gravel
and cloud of dust. He climbed out and stalked toward them,
then stopped short and glowered at the graffiti. "This shit never
ends. First a chick kills herself on our property and now this?"

Les said, "We'll get it cleaned up pronto."

"Yeah. No shit. Do that. Don't we have security cams?"
Derek asked, searching the surrounding area, shading his eyes
as he stared first at the dilapidated building, then farther afield,
toward distant buildings screened by overgrown brush that
was working its way to the Flavel building's front door.

Steele said, "Not yet. Gettin' them soon." His fingers
searched beneath his safety vest to a pocket beneath, liberating
a pack of cigarettes. "There's no homeless to root out, at least.
Some were here, but we had a sweep about three weeks ago. Either Uller or I make it a point to check on the place every
morning."

"You trust him?" Derek questioned.

"Uller? Yes." Lester lit up, drew hard, blew smoke in a
geyser from the side of his mouth and gazed hard at Derek.
"That's not where I'd look."

"Where would you look?" Derek asked with a trace of belligerence.

"Derek . . ." Liam had already had enough drama for one
day and it wasn't even noon.

"Barlow Construction. Ned Barlow," the foreman said.

"Ned Barlow?" Derek blinked. "You gotta be kidding."

"Nope."

Liam said, "Barlow might still be upset that Lester and Jarrod came to work for us."

"You believe that?" Derek asked Liam curiously.

"It's possible," Liam answered.

Steele put in, "There's not a lot of love lost between him and your old man. That's all I'm sayin'."

Derek frowned at the building again. "Let's not mention this to Dad. Not until we know something more. It could set him off." He looked at each of the other men. "Nobody wants that."

For once Liam agreed with his brother. They talked for a few more minutes, and Les left to check out other jobs. Liam did a quick tour of the building's five floors, a walk-up with no elevator. Nothing but broken glass, dust, and bits of trash from earlier homeless encampments greeted him.

He returned to his SUV where Derek was lounging against the back bumper. Good ol' Derek. He never wanted to do more than he felt he was getting paid for.

Derek asked, "You believe that shit about Barlow?"

Liam shrugged. "Not really. He and Dad had their moments, but that . . ."

He hitched a thumb toward the crude, scrawled message. "Not really his style."

"Maybe it's Uller, or even Steele himself."

Liam's head snapped up. "What?"

"I'm not paranoid, bro. Both worked for Barlow, and Les just said it, there's still bad blood between Barlow and Dad."

"Steele's one of the best foremen we've had in a long while," Liam snapped back, forgetting in the moment that Derek had been one of those less than worthy ones.

But Derek didn't take offense. "I didn't tell you this because you were all caught up in the Rory thing, but Uller's come to me a couple of times, wanting to borrow money. He lives a little fast and rich, y'know? When I didn't loan him the money, he went to the accountant and tried to get an advance on his paycheck." He looked at Liam. "Again, no go. And he's tried more than once."

"How come I didn't know this?" Liam demanded.

"Not for publication, apparently. I only know because I was there at the time, at the office, and I overheard the conversation. After Uller left I asked the bookkeeper about it, and he said it had happened a couple of times before, but Uller was always given a turndown. He never mentioned it to me, but he could have talked to Dad."

Liam was pretty sure if anything had gone on in the company like that and Geoff found out, he'd be calling Liam on the carpet as fast as possible.

"And he's got paint. Saw a couple of cans in his truck. Uses it to mark stuff on the buildings, lets the other subs know where he's plannin' to run wires or notch out boxes and switches. Whatever."

"Everyone on the job has access to paint."

"Okay, maybe I'm wrong." He lifted his hands. "Just don't want us to look bad, in case it comes down that way." His cell phone beeped and he pulled it from his pocket, started walking backwards to his Ford truck. "We done here?" he asked Liam.

Liam glanced again at the ugly words splayed across the building. "For now."

Rory sat in the chair opposite Geoff's desk in a room that was all dark wood, leather-bound editions, and crystal decanters of what looked to be whiskey. A cupboard held scrolled blueprints, their neatly wound ends visible. French doors led to the covered patio outside, and the pool beyond. The hint of a recently smoked cigar lingered in the air.

The whole effect was designed to portend wealth, power, and probably intimidation.

Geoff had deftly maneuvered his wheelchair into position on the opposite side of what seemed to be acres of walnut, and now he was staring at her, wheels turning silently in his mind. If this was intimidation, it was working, and Rory stiffened her spine and forced herself to stare back at him. This was, after all, a meeting he'd asked for. Was he just playing with her, or did he really have something to say?

After a long minute of scrutiny, he finally said, "Do you think I was the target of the attack at your wedding?"

Rory was a bit surprised. "It's one theory," she said slowly, wondering where this was going. "No one's said for sure that you were the intended victim, just that . . . somehow you were hit."

"I know all the theories. What I asked is what *you* think."

"As I said, I'm not sure. The police are working on it."

"Are they?" His eyes flashed, his temper and patience snapping in an instant. "They've been 'working on it' for five years and still don't have answers." His face, suffused with blood, turned a dull red. "When I find out who put me in this cage, let me tell you, they're going to pay." He slammed his hands down on the arms of the wheelchair. "I don't care who it is, you understand?"

She nearly jumped. "Yes."

"Even if it's your brother."

So there it was. He thought Everett was behind the attack. Everett, who was on his way to Portland. Funny how his name kept coming up.

"You understand?"

"My stepbrother," she corrected carefully, aware he was working himself up to a full-blown fury. "And yes."

"Or anyone in your family. Anyone," he said pointedly, his gaze drilling into her.

Did he think she was behind the assault? A part of it? The mastermind? When she'd been running for her life?

She slowly rose from her chair and leaned across the desk. "If you're insinuating that I was behind . . . this," she said, pointing at his chair, "you're sadly mistaken. I was attacked as well."

"And disappeared. Conveniently. You think we're all going to believe that you had nothing to do with that bloodbath?"

She could feel her own temper hitting the stratosphere, but was saved from answering when there was a tap on the door.

"What?" Geoff demanded.

Vivian poked her head in. "I'm leaving. Just wanted Rory to know because of the kids. I don't know where Darlene is, at the moment. The sitter's gone on another emergency, but Mom's in her rooms. She'll watch Landon and Estella." Then, as if sensing the tension in the room, the barely repressed anger, she just lifted a hand and stepped back out.

"Where are you going?" her father barked.

"Back to work, Dad." She looked from him to Rory with a *what the hell's going on here?* expression.

He snorted derisively and waved a dismissing hand at her. "Go."

Viv sent one last glance at Rory, a silent question. Rory said, "I'm right behind you," and followed her out. She wasn't about to take Geoff's accusations any longer. Yes, she and Charlotte were guests in his house, but if he threw her out, so be it.

As she started out after Vivian, Geoff's hard voice followed her: "I may be stuck in this chair, but I know men who can get things done. Anything for a price. When the truth comes out, you'd better hope you're on the right side of this!"

Shanice stared through the windshield of her Ford Escape, her gaze focused on the straight stretch of I-5 in front of her. She and Mick were heading steadily south from Seattle. Since DeGrere's death there had been renewed interest in the shooting and assassination at the Bastian wedding, and Mick had been fielding calls from Seattle PD and several reporters. He'd been offered a job to learn the truth, and he and Shanice had been on the road for nearly three hours, heading to Oregon, determined to talk to Rory Abernathy Bastian aka Heather Johnson and get some answers.

Mick was just pocketing his phone after a long, mostly one-sided conversation with a friend in the police department. He cracked the window, then thought better of it with the rush of wind and traffic noise and closed it again.

"So," she said, nudging Mick to share. "What are they saying now? Does Seattle PD think Abernathy's involved in Pete's death?"

He gave a quick shake of his head. "Pretty tight-lipped about all that. They want to take and not give. You know how it goes."

"Yeah, I know."

"Still won't say if they've pegged Pete as the shooter at the wedding."

She snorted. "You mean they don't want to admit you were right."

"They're already getting shit about not finding Abernathy for five years and then all hell breaks loose at once: Pete De-Grere gets out, hardly has time to drink a beer and get a hard-on at a strip club before he's murdered. And it happened at the time Abernathy shows up in Portland with a sick kid. But that's not the end of it. Last night Seattle PD gets a call, and guess what? Abernathy was attacked by Cal Redmond, an ex who's holding a grudge. A big one. According to Abernathy he's the one who attacked her at the wedding."

"But DeGrere's the shooter."

"I haven't changed my mind."

She pulled into the slower lane. Her cell phone rang, she saw it was Deon and didn't pick up. Their relationship had been on its last gasp for too long. The man just didn't understand the phrase, "It's over." Letting the phone go to voice mail, she turned her attention back to Mick. "You think Redmond was in cahoots with DeGrere? They were partners?"

Mick glanced at the phone. "You wanna get that?"

"Uh-uh. Redmond and DeGrere?"

"Unknown. Redmond is claiming he wasn't involved in the shooting. Didn't have any idea it was going down, is completely innocent of that crime. He was just there to break up the wedding, I guess, maybe slice up his ex—scare her or kill her, still unclear—but mess up everything. Don't know if he knew she was already legally married to Liam Bastian. If he did, it was all for show."

"And vengeance."

"Yeah." Mick rubbed his neck in frustration. "Redmond's in custody now. Clammed up. Demanded a lawyer, but so far, his story checks out. Once they compare his blood to the sample on the wedding dress that Abernathy ditched, we'll know."

Shanice took a quick check over her shoulder, then switched lanes to pass a semi even though it was barreling down the freeway at a few miles over the speed limit. She eased off on the accelerator but hated slowing down, even a few miles an hour. The trip was long, three to four hours depending on traffic, and she had the feeling that time was of the essence, that she was in some kind of race with an invisible enemy. She couldn't hide her anticipation that she was going to finally meet the disappearing Abernathy and be able to ask her the questions that had kept her awake for the past five years. And finally, maybe Aaron would get some justice. "Hard to believe that the two attacks that day were completely separate and unrelated."

"Stranger things have happened, I suppose," Mick said, not sounding convinced. They talked it out a bit, going around in circles just as the tires of her little car kept spinning down the freeway.

Finally, Shanice posed, "What are the chances that Redmond's lying and he was the one who killed DeGrere?"

"Police are checking his alibi now. He claims he was at work when Pete was offed. He works with his girlfriend in a catering business. She says he was around, but maybe she's covering for him. He could've driven up to the Nile, killed Pete, and driven back without raising notice if she wasn't paying attention or is covering for him now."

"And somewhere in there an Abernathy look-alike falls off a building at one of Bastian-Flavel real estate deals," she reminded him.

"Look-alike?" he repeated. "The leaper?"

"Red hair. Same kind of body type. That was your description of her. What's her name?"

"McVaney . . . no, Mulvaney. Teri. No one knows if she fell, jumped, or was pushed."

"Don't tell me it hasn't crossed your mind that there might be some connection. She dies soon after DeGrere is killed, when Rory Abernathy reappears, *before* the latest attack on her."

"Look-alike," he said again. He could admit the resemblance between Aurora Abernathy and Teri Mulvaney was uncanny. Shanice had hit on it the second she saw the photo on the driver's license of the dead woman. "They're not dead ringers, but . . ."

"Red hair, fine features, about the same build . . . they could be sisters, if not twins." She slid him another glance.

"She could have just fallen. Someone gets drunk, decides to climb to the upper story and slips and falls. Not often, but it does happen."

"Why not go up to one of the restaurants with elevators and a view, then? Nah, she was up there for a reason," Shanice said. "Maybe with someone."

"She had sex with someone shortly before her death."

"The guy who gave her a little push?" Shanice suggested, then, "Damn! Watch out!" She slammed on her brakes, holding tight to the wheel. The little car slewed sideways but stayed in the lane as she hit the brakes.

A motorcycle cut through the space between her Escape and

the pickup she was following, then hit the gas in the slow lane, accelerating and whining to whip around a slower vehicle. The bike wove in and out of traffic doing eighty-five or ninety. "Where the hell is a cop when you need one?" she asked rhetorically before picking up the conversation again. "So, what— Seattle PD thinks Rory Abernathy's reappearance is all a coincidence?"

"They're not saying. Ex-cops aren't on the need to know list."

"Hey, we're the ones who finally got through to DeGrere's sister. Being an ex-cop helped you. *Ex* being the word."

Pete DeGrere's sister, Sally, had no use for the authorities, and only by promises and pleas that no, he was no longer with the police department or any other law enforcement agency had she agreed to see them. Just yesterday they'd driven to Sally DeGrere Brown's house, a mobile home set on a brick foundation in a park. She'd been upset and red-eyed, weeping and smoking, carrying on about her brother. She'd clearly wanted to talk to someone, but had adamantly refused to speak to the police, saying she knew nothing about her brother, and that was that.

However, with Shanice, an understanding woman, paving the way, Sally had reluctantly opened her door to them. "He wasn't all bad," she'd said, dabbing at her eyes as her three cats eyed Mick and Shanice with unblinking suspicion. A calico was hidden under the couch, peering fearfully from beneath the frayed and sparse fringe; a tuxedo sat on a window ledge eyeing a bird feeder with lust, his long, black tail twitching, his white whiskers shivering as he studied the sparrows flitting around the strewn seeds; and a big gray tabby watched the intruders with disdain from its spot on the dining room table, right on top of a lacy cloth.

Sally, her frosted, thinning hair pulled into a ponytail, had beseeched them. "He didn't do it. I've said it over and over. He wouldn't shoot anybody . . . kill anybody. I just don't understand."

Mick wanted to remind her that her brother had been a marksman in the service, but that would have gotten him nowhere. Instead, he and Shanice nodded sympathetically and she'd finally allowed them into the room she'd set up for him, a paneled eight-by-ten bedroom with a twin bed, sleeping bag, and narrow plastic dresser. On the dresser stood a bowling trophy, a framed high school graduation diploma, and a sharpshooter award from a local range.

Shanice had casually asked about it, and Sally had nodded so fast her ponytail had quivered. "Oh, yes, he was a good shot. Learned hunting from Dad. He got his first rifle, a twenty-two if I remember correctly, probably by the time he was eight, maybe nine. Loved to hunt. Anything—birds, squirrels, deer, you name it. He'd draw a bead on it and . . ." She seemed to finally hear herself and broke off . . . switching to, "Petey had his faults, you know. Couldn't pass a bar without going in, but he was a good man, good brother."

Mick thought about where Pete DeGrere had been found, behind a pussy parlor called the Nile, but he kept listening earnestly. Sally's thoughts apparently were traveling down the same path, because she said, "That Nile place . . . that was his downfall. Girls. Well, and booze." She'd walked them back to the main living area where a fourth cat, this one orange and skittish, had dived under the table occupied by the fat gray one, then hopped up on a chair, eyeing Shanice through the draped lace. When it hissed loudly, Sally giggled and said, "Oh, Dizzy, you stop that," temporarily drawn from her grief. "Don't worry about her, she's all talk, that one. Wouldn't hurt a flea and I should know. I've been fighting *that* battle for a long time now. Once those things get into the rug you can never get them out."

Shanice had eyed the brown shag rug, matted in some places,

with newfound concern. The cats hadn't bothered her in the least, not even with the acrid aroma of a hidden litter box filtering through the room, but she didn't like the idea of fleas.

They'd stayed another fifteen minutes and listened to Sally's reminiscences. The only glimmer of information had been her contention that DeGrere had a thing against rich people. "He was always looking for a get-rich-quick scheme," she said. "Had all kinds of ideas that would've panned out if he'd gotten a break, but things didn't work out for Petey. He always got caught doing something, and it wasn't always his fault. He just couldn't catch a break," she repeated, a phrase that sounded like a theme song for the hapless Pete DeGrere. "Those people on TV with all the money? Lots of cars and houses . . . he just felt like that should've been him. Maybe we all feel that way."

They'd left soon after, promising to let Sally know if they found anything. Hours later, upon hearing that Aurora Abernathy Bastian had appeared within days of Pete DeGrere's release from prison and subsequent murder, they'd decided to meet with the runaway bride face-to-face.

If they could.

That was still in question.

They hadn't talked to Abernathy herself, and so far, the once-jilted husband was putting up roadblocks.

Now, Mick said, "There's one guy I know. Worked with him before he transferred south to the Portland PD. Owes me a favor for taking over a couple of his shifts when his kid was having drug/detox problems. Zach Pitman."

"Think he'll give you some information on Abernathy?"

"I'll try to locate him, call in my marks." He was already checking his phone for the number. He grunted when he found it and placed the call, only to run into the man's voice mail. He left his name and a request that Zach call him, then clicked off, hoping Pitman would follow up.

Shanice said, "I'm thinking Everett Stemple killed Pete De-Grere for taking the life of his brother."

Mick grunted. This was old territory.

"It just makes sense. Everett's old man, Harold, knew when Pete was getting out and he probably knew where he was going. Pete didn't keep his fondness for strip clubs a secret. So Harold tipped Everett off and he did the job. Both Harold and Everett wanted revenge."

"We think," he reminded her. They'd theorized the same thing a number of times before. "But where's the proof?" he grumbled. "Did Everett know DeGrere?"

"DeGrere knew his old man."

"Again, that's conjecture. Emphasis on *con*."

"I wish they'd given you more information than they did," Shanice said on a sigh.

"Cons will tell you anything you want to hear. You just gotta sort through all the bullshit."

As soon as he learned of DeGrere's murder, Mick had set up interviews with a couple of the felons who'd known Pete before and after he was incarcerated. Both men had said what he already knew: Pete was a blowhard. You couldn't trust anything he said. He was a braggart and kind of a pain in the ass. Mick had even been granted a visit to Harold Stemple, who'd acted like he barely knew Pete DeGrere existed, which Mick knew was a full-out lie by the smile on the man's ruggedly handsome face as he made his denial. But there was no making him talk. He was already in prison, and though Mick had brought up his son Everett's name, hoping for a reaction, Harold had just shrugged and said, "My son didn't kill his own brother."

"Maybe Aaron got in the way."

"Of what? Eh? Who would my son want dead?"

"I was hoping you'd tell me," Mick had told the con, who'd snorted and said, "Ask him yourself, but you'll have to stand in line. The police are trying to frame him, too, but he didn't do it. Has an iron-clad alibi."

"He could have paid DeGrere."

"So could a lot of guys."

He'd been right about that, Mick thought now. But Shanice hadn't given up on the idea.

"Everett was probably Harold Stemple's outside man during that botched home invasion. He owed his dad for keeping quiet about him, and he wanted to get payback for Aaron's death, so he took Pete out."

Shanice was verbalizing Mick's own version of the crime, but it felt like there were big missing pieces. Maybe Liam Bastian or his wife could fill them in.

They rode in silence for the next twenty miles and slowed as traffic became congested as they passed through Vancouver, Washington, and inched their way across the I-5 bridge spanning the Columbia River. As they drove under a sign that read ENTERING OREGON, Shanice felt more than a little tingle of anticipation tinged with a taste of revenge. The truth was she'd never been much of a fan of the cowardly runaway bride. She'd told herself it was because she wanted justice for Aaron, but it sure tasted good. She couldn't wait to finally meet the woman who had somehow escaped the carnage of her own damned wedding.

Chapter 21

By the time Liam returned to his parents' house it was afternoon. He'd texted Rory, explaining, and she'd texted back that she was handling things. How, he didn't know, but the thought made him smile as he parked in the circular drive and noted that Rory's car was angled near an older model Toyota plastered with bumper stickers. Darlene, he guessed. Good. He only hoped that when he walked inside, all hell hadn't broken loose. His parents weren't exactly models of temperance, and the house had sometimes been more like a war zone than a haven when he was growing up. That's why he'd lammed out as early as possible, finding refuge in college and his own independence. And yet . . . he'd returned, not to live under the same roof as Stella and Geoff, but to work for the company.

You sold out. As did Derek, and now even Viv wants to be part of the Bastian fold.

The thought tightened his stomach a little as he climbed from the Tahoe. He'd barely put one foot out when Derek wheeled up in a shiny black sports car. He climbed out and glanced at the house. For a second his face was severe as he stared at the stone-and-cedar walls, and Liam remembered his half brother as a younger man, full of piss and vinegar, as they say, a young buck always battling the old man. Derek had fought with Geoff long and often, though those fights had abated after Geoff had been confined to a wheelchair. Before Geoff's injury, Geoff and Derek had almost always been at odds. In those days Geoffrey had been fit, worked out at a gym, even taken on younger men as sparring partners and boxed for sport. He and Derek had come to physical blows more than once, and even the week before Liam's wedding had gone at it so hard, wrestling in the den and rolling against a table leg, that it caused one of Stella's treasures, a crystal vase, to roll and crash to the floor. Derek had ended up with glass in the heel of his hand, and when Stella, hearing the smash of glass, had run to the den and seen them lying on the floor, breathing hard, their clothes disheveled and torn, blood smearing the hardwood, she'd snarled, "You're barbarians! Both of you! Clean up yourselves and this mess right now!"

Liam had heard about the battle later that day when Derek had called him and confessed, "He's such an asshole, you know. Our old man. Only out for number one. I hate him."

Liam had only said, "You might try to avoid him, or at least not provoke him."

"*He* provokes *me*. Hell, he provokes *every*one. Including Stella."

"They're married."

"And so are you, bro. You should take a good look at what it's all about. Shit. And now this farce of a wedding when you've already tied the knot."

"Mom's idea."

"Well, it's a piss-poor one, and the fact that you agreed to go along with it only shows what a wimp you are." He'd hung up then.

Liam hadn't called him back.

For the most part, these days, everyone got along—at least on the surface—but remembering the days when father and son had gone at it brought the bile up the back of Liam's throat to burn in his mouth.

Lifting a hand, sun at his back, Derek yelled, "Hey, bro!"

Bro.

His brother's name for him. As if they'd always had each other's back, but both of Geoffrey Bastian's sons had been hellions, just as the old man had probably been. That's why they'd always been at loggerheads, always spoiling for a fight. In Derek's case, he'd felt the back of the old man's hand and his wrath more often than not.

"When'd you get the Corvette?" Liam asked.

Derek grinned like a devil. "Think the old man'll finally loosen the purse strings and help me pay for it? Or maybe, like Uller, I'll ask for a loan from the company. Whad'ya say, Mr. CEO?"

"You'd have a better chance with the old man."

Derek laughed, made a gun out of his hand, and pointed it at him. "What I figured."

They headed toward the house together. The acid in Liam's gut roiled at a particular memory, one he'd forgotten, or more likely buried, from long ago. He'd been fourteen at the time and it was summer. He and his friends had planned an overnight by the river on property belonging to the Bastians. Somehow everyone's parents had agreed to the campout, mainly because Derek, older, had promised to look in on the younger boys. Of course the whole plot had been a recipe for disaster, but even Geoff and Stella had given Derek and Liam the green light as long as they "were responsible" and "made good choices." This was in a time when cell phones weren't as prevalent by any means, but Stella had offered hers up to Derek, "in case of an emergency, which, by the way, I don't think there will be." She'd leveled her most don't-disappoint-me glare at both boys, and dropped the massive phone into Derek's outstretched palm.

They'd been home free.

But Liam hadn't left it at that and had decided it would be an awesome idea to pour a mixture of his father's whiskey from the decanters on his desk into a flask he'd found in Geoff's hunting gear. He thought about telling Derek what he'd done, then decided against it. Derek didn't know how to keep his mouth shut. Where Liam had chosen a select few times to test the boundaries, Derek was always on the wrong side of something.

Late that afternoon, Liam had taken his pilfered treasures, rolled up in his sleeping bag, to a spot by the Willamette's shore. A few boats were speeding across the clear water, pulling skiers, while fishermen, mostly drinking beer, were lazily trolling, their poles visible, lines disappearing into the river's uneven surface.

A hawk circled above the water, wings spread against a blue sky, where gauzy clouds slowly scudded. The summer sun hung low, casting ever-longer shadows onto the shallows as Liam stashed his booty into the root hole of a huge fir tree standing guard on the crumbling bank. A rocky beach stretched out below the ridge and the fresh, wet smell of the river filled his nostrils as a gust of wind toyed with his hair, which was "far too shaggy" to meet Stella's standard. Well, tough, it was summer, he was free except for the hours he helped out at his old man's job sites—too young to officially be on the payroll but old enough to help load trash and scraps into a Dumpster. He considered taking a pull on the flask, just for the hell of it— after all, he'd taken all the risks that day and he owed himself a swallow of the booze.

He only had a few hours to wait.

He found a smooth stone on the rocky beach and, flipping his wrist, flung it into the river, watching it skip, creating wavering pools on the slow-moving river. Yeah, he loved summer.

He glanced back at the fir tree and headed back to the deep hollow in the bank. It still looked a little weird, like he was hiding something, which he was, the exposed dirt between the tangled roots too fresh, so he covered the area with a piece of driftwood and littered it with dry needles and cones, effectively, he hoped, hiding the burrow. He was dusting his hands when he heard a commotion—shouting and cursing—coming from the winding path leading up the short rise to the house.

"You goddamned thief!" Geoffrey roared over the buzz of motor craft on the river. "What the hell do you think you're doing? Stealing from me? *Me?*"

Liam flattened himself against the bank. What the hell had Derek done?

"I didn't take anything!" his brother threw back at the old man.

"I marked those bottles, Derek. I *know* just how much was in each one," the old man roared, infuriated.

Oh, shit! His dad had figured out that some of the booze was missing. Already. As if he'd been lying in wait. And he blamed Derek for the crime. Of course he did. Derek was always in trouble, and Geoffrey Bastian had a dark side, a cruel side that he tried and failed to keep at bay. It didn't help that Derek couldn't keep from yanking the old man's chain.

"But I didn't, Dad. I didn't take *anything*. Swear to God!" Derek sounded frantic and angry.

"Like you didn't take the Porsche out? Like you didn't bring some girl into the house when we were gone? And she was barely sixteen! You're so lucky—"

"Am I?" Derek threw back at him.

Thwack! The sound of a fist hitting something hard.

"OWW! Jesus, Dad, why did you—?"

Thwack! Another hard smack and this time Derek groaned.
Shit! Shit! Shit!

"You're a bastard, you know that, don't you?" Derek groaned.
"A sick, old bastard."

"And you're a privileged, snot-nosed thief who would steal
from his old man and lie about it. My own damned kid! You're
lucky I don't beat you within an inch of your life."

"I'll call 9-1-1!" Derek snarled. "Tell them, social services or
whatever, that you beat me."

"Go ahead. Let's see how that turns out."

Dad was beating the living shit out of his brother for a crime
Liam had committed. No! God, no! Liam had to stop it.

"Think about it, son. Think real hard about what you did,"
Geoff spit out with sheer malice.

Then there was silence, oppressive, horrifying silence. Scared
to death, sweating wildly, his damned heart beating like it
would jump from his rib cage, Liam forced himself away from
the bank just as he heard his brother growl, "You'll get yours.
Just you wait!"

Thump! The sound of a boot or shoe thudding against flesh,
then Derek roared. "What do you want to do? Kill me?" His
voice was in the stratosphere, filled with pain, a shriek of agony.

Liam couldn't just let this kind of brutality happen to his
brother, especially when he was the one who'd stolen his dad's
whiskey. If Derek could take blows from the old man, then so
could he, damn it. He thrashed out of his position under the
bank and started up the path, only to find Derek half lying in
the bent grass and holding a hand to his nose. Blood dripped
between his fingers and stained his T-shirt. "What're you
lookin' at?" he snarled, fighting tears and blinking up at Liam.
There was no sign of their father.

"Are you—?"

"Shit, I'm okay." Derek let out his breath and pulled his hand from his face. The blood flow had stanched to a trickle, but he looked bad. A cut above his eyes, his nose probably broken, bruises appearing. He was shaken up. Even scared. And mad, too. He rolled to a sitting position and with his wrists propped on his knees, looked down at the water. "That old fart can't beat me up like that and get away with it."

"Call the police," Liam urged.

"Are you out of your mind?"

"Then tell Mom."

"She'll only back him up," Derek growled, sniffing. "Fat old cocksucker!" He stood and winced, then suddenly realized, as if for the first time, that Liam had appeared out of nowhere. "What are you doin' down here?"

"Getting ready, y'know. For tonight." He hesitated to add anything else as Derek, muscles coiled, was still furious and dangerous.

"What do you mean?" One of Derek's eyes was swelling shut, but still he managed to narrow his gaze suspiciously on his brother.

In a split second Liam realized there was no way out of this. Sooner or later Derek would figure it out, that he'd just taken the beating of his life because of his younger brother. "It was me, okay? I took the old man's booze and . . . and some of Mom's smokes."

"You?"

"Yeah. I . . . I should have . . . I'm sorry."

"I bet you are," Derek said, spitting a globule of spittle mixed with blood onto the sparse grass. "You did it and you let me . . . let him . . . oh, fuck . . . you little shit!" Derek didn't wait, just sprang, rounding on Liam and landing a punch that sent him sprawling, his back hitting a stick, his shoulders slamming into the hardpan beneath the grass.

"I'm sorry! I'm sorry."

"I just bet you are, you little bitch." Derek sprang just as Liam started to scuttle away. "Ooof!" The older boy landed on Liam, knocking the breath out of him, pounding wildly with his fists as Liam, wriggling like a worm on a hook, tried to get away.

Bam! A fist connected with his jaw. Pain exploded behind his eyes.

Thud! Another jab hit him hard in the ribs.

Liam cried out, "Stop! Derek!"

"Dickhead!" Derek hissed, bringing his head low so spittle rained on Liam. "Do you want the old man to come back?"

"No! Stop!"

Derek hauled back to hit him again and Liam threw himself upward, head-butting his older sibling. *Crack!* Agony ripped through his skull and Derek slumped over, rolling off him. On his back, Liam crab-scuttled away. His head throbbed and his stomach heaved. He turned to one side and threw up all over the long grass.

"Damn you . . . you're a dead man!" Derek spat out, then groaned loudly, writhing and holding his head. "I'm going to beat the living hell out of you. Right after I make the old man pay."

Now, years later, as Derek realized Liam was lost in thought, he asked, "What?" with a shrug.

"Nothing. Just thinking. Come on."

They walked inside to a complete madhouse. The kids were chasing each other, running in and out of the open door to the pool area. Through the windows Liam caught sight of a twentysomething girl, the errant babysitter having returned, he presumed. She was lounging in one of the deck chairs, soaking up rays, and paying more attention to her cell phone and a bevy of text messages than she was to her charges. Dressed in a flamingo-pink bikini, her blond hair twisted into two little knots on her head, she looked up, frowned, and said, "Hey, be careful. Landon, Estella, no running!" then glanced back at her phone again.

Rory and Darlene were in attendance, too, seated together around a small table in the shade of its umbrella, so at least Charlotte and her cousins were being supervised. As he walked through the family room, Rory caught sight of him and the smile that curved her lips made his heart leap. She was wearing sunglasses, and, with the concealer, she almost looked as if nothing had happened. He could see the scratch on her chin, mostly because he knew it was there, but with her hair down, red curls swinging around her face, it was almost impossible to discern.

Darlene, gray hair braided down her back, granny sunglasses propped on her nose, a lacy caftan covering her body, lay back in a lounge chair, bare toes visible. She visibly brightened at the sight of Liam.

"How're you doing?" he asked as he crossed to the outside table.

"Surviving," Rory said.

"Great!" Darlene responded.

"Hey!" Charlotte careened across the patio and looked up at him with big eyes. "We are going to swim," she announced, waving a floatie-clad arm at the pool.

"I see that." He knelt so that he could look her in the eyes. She looked so much like Rory, but again, he saw a bit of his sister, or maybe himself. Wishful thinking? He didn't believe it. In his heart he knew this little girl belonged to him.

"You can, too."

"Maybe I will."

"Mommy can, too!"

"Yeah . . ." His gaze caught Rory's and his heart twisted. If only they could turn back the clock, he thought, knowing he was being ridiculous, wanting it anyway.

"Come on!" Charlotte insisted and tugged at his hand.

"I, uh, think maybe I should find a suit."

"Charlotte, Liam will swim with you later," Rory said.

"You, too, Mommy," she said, then giggled, let go of him, and took off.

"Don't run!" Rory called, looking away from him, her shaded gaze following Charlotte as the little girl struggled to keep from racing to the pool.

If only things were simpler, but, of course, they weren't, he thought, straightening.

The babysitter echoed Rory, calling distractedly, "No running," and waved her hand in the general direction of the pool. Liam's cell phone vibrated in his pocket and he saw that Mick Mickelson, the detective from the Seattle area, was calling. Again. So far he'd ignored the man, but he'd have to call him back soon. Just not at the moment.

Charlotte was on the first step of the shallow end, water lapping around her. Swinging her legs and splashing, she chortled in sheer delight as her cousins swam around her.

As if none of them had a care in the world.

The way it should be, and Liam wished, not for the first time, that the cloud of mystery, the ever-present sense that there was danger lurking around every dark corner or in any dark crack, would evaporate.

"Where's Viv?" Derek asked as he stopped by the refrigerator in the kitchen and grabbed a beer before sauntering onto the patio.

"Who knows?" Stella asked as she appeared, the sharp slap of her sandals against tile heralding her arrival. "She's in and out, leaving us with"—she sent a disapproving look at the babysitter—"Candace."

The sitter twisted her head when she heard her name. "What?"

Stella's smile was brittle. "Nothing, dear," she said, giving a little wave of her hand, her French manicured nails catching in the sunlight. "Go back to your little friends on your phone."

Candace hesitated, then decided she'd better show some interest or she might lose her cushy job with all its tanning benefits. "Okay, kids," she said, setting aside her phone by placing it on a small table near her lounge chair. "Do you know how to play Marco Polo?"

Stella heaved a long-suffering sigh and slid her designer shades over the bridge of her nose. Derek flopped into a lounge chair not far from Candace. If possible, Stella's lips twisted into deeper disapproval. She said to the group in general, "Vivian should be home soon, I would think, though heaven knows where she goes."

Liam said, "To the office."

Stella just laughed.

"She started today."

"Well, where's she been going all this time? Never here. Always has somewhere else to be." Stella glanced at the pool, where the kids were splashing and laughing. "She has children, you know." She threw a pointed glance at the lazing Candace. "And I've already raised mine. Which reminds me, I'd better check on your father." She got up from the chair and slapped away.

He met Rory's eyes, but was unprepared for her next words, "Mom says Everett wants to meet with me today."

"*What?*"

Darlene hurriedly put in, "I think you should both meet him."

"Oh, there's a good idea. Meet with the guy who killed Pete DeGrere," Derek drawled.

Liam said, "Just because Cal Redmond is in custody and Pete DeGrere is dead, doesn't mean this is over. Whoever hired DeGrere, if he was the actual shooter, is probably still around. Still willing to do damage."

"But Everett took a lie detector test, and nothing's happened for five years," Darlene pointed out.

"I bet you can lie to those things," Derek said.

"Everett's changed," Darlene insisted.

"This is my family," Liam stated firmly. "I don't like it that Everett's suddenly showing up."

"It's because Rory's come back," Darlene said. "It's been on the news."

Derek lifted his brows over his sunglasses. "He wants to see Rory after all this time?"

"You didn't say anything to him?" Rory asked her mother.

"Of course not. You swore me to secrecy and I . . ." She gestured with her finger and thumb pressed together, sliding them over her closed mouth, effectively miming zipping her lips.

"I'm not meeting him, Mom."

Darlene glanced to one side, avoiding Rory's gaze. "You've always said you want answers. Well, here's your chance to get answers."

Rory gazed at her mother with dawning horror. "Where are we supposed to meet? You didn't tell him I was here, did you? You wouldn't tell him where I am."

"I may have said we were staying here for a few days."

Derek whistled under his breath. Rory looked apoplectic and Liam wanted to throttle Darlene. "I don't want him here," Liam said through his teeth.

"Neither do I," Rory seconded.

Again Darlene pulled a face and Derek muttered under his breath, "Wow. This should be interesting."

Liam had a picture in his head of this moment in time: the

kids in the pool, the disinterested babysitter, he and his brother, his wife, her mother . . . And a shadow passed over it, the threat of the unknown danger sliding over this innocent group.

Darlene cleared her throat. "He might be on his way."

"No," Liam said as Rory stared at her mother, aghast.

"I don't know how many times I have to say it. He's changed. Really changed. Believe me, I've talked to him and I . . . I even talked to Laurie about him. She says it's more than possible that he's turned over a new leaf, a better one, he's found—"

"It's not happening here," Liam cut in just as the sounds of chimes from the front doorbell rang through the house, tinkling through outside speakers.

"Oh, bro, I think it is," Derek said as the *slap, slap, slap* of Stella's sandals could be heard as she made her way to the foyer.

All of Rory's feelings of safety shattered in an instant. The specter of Everett Stemple loomed behind her eyes. Tall, muscular, with a voice like sandpaper whispering in her ear. *It's okay, baby, just relax . . .*

Rory flew to her feet, nearly knocking over the table. Ready to scoop Charlotte out of the pool and start running, she took two steps toward her daughter and stopped dead in her tracks.

Where? Where are you going? He's here. It's too late!

But panic overtook her and her heart thudded crazily, fear pulsing wildly through her veins. The world seemed to spin faster on its axis. Everett was the person who had followed her, frightened her, threatened her . . . in one insane instant she was certain of it.

"I'll take care of this," Liam said, suddenly beside her, one hand gripping her forearm, his face inches from hers. Strong. Determined. Fiercely protective. "Don't worry."

God, she wanted to believe him. But the wedding. Cal's attack. The madman who had rained bullets on the assemblage. The sound of balloons popping. *Do as I say, or you both die. I'll slit your throat and then I'll slit his.* Yes, that threat had been Cal's, but deep inside she'd thought he'd been working with the shooter and in her gut she'd believed, if not the gunman himself, Everett was somehow behind the shooting.

Would he kill his own brother? No. That had been an error. The rifleman—DeGrere—had made a mistake and killed Aaron by accident.

Maybe.

And when DeGrere had gotten out of prison Everett had killed him, *slit his throat.*

Her terror must've shown on her face because Liam's fingers tightened over her arm a bit. And his voice was calm as he said, "Trust me. I've got this." He waited until she nodded and let out her breath, then asked, "Okay?"

"Okay," she agreed with forced calm.

"Good. Hang in there."

"But Charlotte—"

"I won't let anything happen to her." His face was a mask of determination. "And neither will you."

"Yes . . . right."

"Good."

He released her arm, then strode to the patio door, where Stella, slightly bewildered for once, was now standing to one side. Beside her was a tall man, a *big* man, with long hair starting to turn prematurely gray. His face was fleshy, his waistline enormous, his features nearly unrecognizable.

"Rory," Everett said with the hint of a smile. "I'm so glad to see you again." His voice was still gravelly, and as he stepped onto the patio she braced herself. "I have something for you."

"Stop right there." Liam blocked the bigger man's path.

Everett held up both of his meaty hands and Rory flinched when she spied something black in one hand.

Until she recognized it as a book . . . no, not just a book, a Bible.

"I came to apologize, for every wrong I did you." Again the peaceful smile, so out of place on the man she remembered. "I've taken Jesus into my heart." Here he paused. Even the kids playing in the pool seemed to quiet. Rory couldn't believe what she was hearing, but Everett was staring past Liam, his strong gaze holding hers. "I'd like to talk to you and ask your forgiveness."

Chapter 22

"... and so, if you can find it in your heart to forgive me, I would be forever grateful," Everett said. He'd taken a seat at the table next to Darlene and across from Rory and had opened his Bible to a marked section. After quoting a passage on forgiveness, he'd explained that he'd straightened out his life, had become the manager of a local plumbing store by day and, in his free time, a youth minister. He owed his transformation from criminal and thug to finding Jesus through the love of a good woman, his wife, Mary-Catherine. Named after two saints, she was the most loving woman Everett had ever met.

Liam stood inches from Rory, just out of the shade of the umbrella but listening to all of the conversation, his gaze razor-sharp on the heavier man. Thankfully, Derek and Stella were standing near the mobile bar, next to the French doors, talking to each other and shooting looks at the small gathering. For once Candace was actually in the pool with the kids.

And Everett was begging Rory to let bygones be bygones. "... but I don't think I can live with myself if I don't right the wrongs I've dealt, and one of them is you, Aurora." He tried to take her hand, but she drew away from his touch. She hadn't trusted him as a teenager and she wasn't going to start now. "Mary-Catherine says it's important to face those you've wronged, admit your sins against them, to them and to God, through Jesus."

He appeared sincere, but Rory remembered him as a teenager, the barely repressed anger, the hot eyes that scoured her body. Still, he wasn't the person who'd been following her; this Everett was too bulky, far different from the slender man of his youth. Not the person she'd seen from afar.

"You're trying to convince me that you weren't part of the attack at the wedding," she said, clarifying, though he'd gone around that subject, never really addressing it.

He blinked at her. "You don't think . . . I mean, surely you know I would never hurt Aaron."

Well, when was this miraculous change? She let the thought cross her mind, but she kept it to herself.

He held her gaze. "No, no . . . I've told the police all about where I was that day, and it wasn't anywhere near the wedding."

"But you could have hired DeGrere."

"Is that what you think?" For the first time it seemed his denials weren't staged. "No." He shook his head, ponytail sliding across his shoulders, reminding her of a serpent. "Dear Lord, Father in Heaven, I swear to you on this"—he thumped a finger on the Bible splayed open between them—"the Word of the Holy Father, that I wasn't involved in any way in that attack." He flattened his hand over his heart. "No, Rory. Never."

He was either a better liar than even she knew, or he was telling the truth. The hint of deception had disappeared from his eyes, but it was going to take more to convince her than one staged appearance. He went on, "So now, Rory, can you find it in your heart to forgive me for any time that I . . . that I made you uncomfortable . . ."

"Uncomfortable?" she repeated dryly, realizing the times he'd tried to sexually assault her.

Darlene interjected, "Just hear him out."

"I think I've got the gist," she said.

"Rory." His voice had the same smooth quality she'd heard in her darkened bedroom when he'd closed the door and spoken to her.

Her flesh crawled. *No, no, no.*

She didn't trust him, would never, and she wanted him gone. Away from her. Away from her child.

She had trouble keeping her quavering voice steady, but she wasn't going to hold back. "You scared me . . ." She glanced at her mother. "And you didn't come to my rescue."

"Nothing happened," Darlene protested.

"Something happened." Rory rounded on her. "He made it impossible for me to trust for a long time." She leveled her gaze at the man she'd feared for half of her years and decided, if nothing else, that fear was gone. "If you want forgiveness, take it up with God."

"Who do you think sent me here?"

"Not your wife? Who said you have to face those you've wronged?" she challenged.

"You should leave," Liam told him. He'd been standing behind Rory throughout Everett's unburdening, but now he moved forward. From the sound of it, he was having as much trouble believing Everett's bid for atonement as Rory was herself. Maybe he'd found the Lord, maybe he would never hurt anyone again, maybe she should forgive him and move on.

Or, maybe this was an act, a phase, a way to assuage guilt. Whatever his truth, she didn't want to be involved in it.

"Rory, please . . ." he tried.

"I'm sorry, Everett, but I've got nothing to say to you. I hope you're sincere. I really do. But—"

"I am."

"Liam's right. You need to go." From the corner of her eye, she saw Charlotte climb out of the pool and start tippy-toeing toward her, trying to heed her mother's warning not to run as she left a trail of small wet footprints across the cement. Rory didn't want Everett Stemple anywhere near her child.

"I've come a long way, and I'm not talking about physical miles," he said.

"Good. Just keep on that journey."

"If I could just hear the words—"

"What words?" Charlotte asked as she climbed, wet and dripping, onto Rory's lap.

"Nothing, sweetheart." Rory held her daughter close. To Everett, she said, "I appreciate that you came all the way here, now—"

"Rory, honey!" Darlene broke in. "Don't you think—?"

Rory swiftly cut her off. "No, Mom."

"This is your child?" Everett asked, and Rory, Charlotte tight in her arms, rose so abruptly that her chair squeaked as it scraped against the concrete. She didn't like the way his gaze appraised her daughter.

"She's beautiful."

Rory's stomach convulsed. She'd heard that comment on his lips too many times. A wheedling plea for her to allow him in.

Her heart was thudding in that same horrendous panic she'd felt years before. "Thank you for apologizing." Her voice was brittle. "But don't ever try to contact me or my family again."

"Time to leave." Liam's voice was steel as he escorted Rory and Charlotte around Everett, keeping his body between them.

Rory took Charlotte toward the gate to the pool area. "Let's get you dried off," she said into her daughter's wet curls as she snatched a towel hanging from a hook on the fence. She swept through the gate and Liam closed it behind her. She set Charlotte down inside the doorway leading to the upper unit and rubbed her down with the towel. Her skin was still crawling at the site of her stepbrother. She never, *never* wanted to see him again, God or no God. She hadn't liked the way he looked at either her or her daughter. The man was a wolf in sheep's clothing.

They climbed up the stairs and Rory found a dry set of shorts and T-shirt for Charlotte, then combed her daughter's wild, wet hair into a curly ponytail.

Within minutes Darlene had climbed up the stairs, padded into the bathroom, and found Charlotte sitting on the counter, Rory standing in front of the mirror, putting clips into the little girl's hair to keep the stragglers out of her face. The reproachful look in Darlene's eyes portended an argument—or at least a discussion—and Rory wasn't in the mood. She didn't want to hear about Everett's new life with God, nor the pious Mary-Catherine, whoever the hell she was, nor Laurie's predictions of a happy, flowers-and-sunshine future for all of them.

"Don't, Mom," she warned. "If you want a relationship with Harold and Everett, then fine, but I'm not going to. Nor is my daughter." Then realizing Charlotte was staring at her with worried eyes, added, "You know what you need?"

"Ice cream?"

"Well, yeah, probably that, too, but I was thinking of—let's see if you've got one." She dug in Charlotte's backpack, found an aqua ribbon that she quickly wrapped around the band holding the ponytail in place. "What d'ya say?" Using a hand mirror, she showed her daughter her work, and while Charlotte was surveying the back of her head, Rory sent Darlene a *don't even think about crossing me* look in the larger mirror's reflection.

"I don't think he was following you," her mother said.

"I don't, either. I think it was that private investigator that Liam hired."

Darlene brightened, then her face clouded over.

"What?" Rory asked.

"You're not going to like it."

Rory groaned, "Oh, Mom."

"I've gotten a couple of calls. One was from a reporter. A woman."

Rory silently swore inside her head. "Pauline Kirby?"

"Why, yes. Channel 7."

"I'm telling you right now, I'm not talking to her. And you'd better not, either." Rory picked up Charlotte and put her on the floor, and the little girl ran off to the living area.

"Well . . . I believe she's on her way over . . ."

"*Mom!*"

"Well, I didn't *ask* her to come," Darlene retorted. "She just is."

Rory drew a breath. "I almost don't want to ask what the other call was."

"It was a detective."

Rory's heart clutched. "Grant . . . or Susskind?"

She paused, slowly shook her head. "No . . . He was with the police in Seattle. He said he wanted to talk to you. He's on his way."

"To *Portland*? The *Seattle* police?"

"His name is Mike. Or was that his last name? Michaelson? I have his number on my phone." She dug in the pocket of her caftan, and if Rory's heart had sunk a second ago, it was now in free fall.

"Mick," Rory corrected. She'd read everything she could about the investigation into the assault on the wedding once she'd learned what happened. She knew the name of the lead homicide investigator. "Mick Mickelson. Surely you talked to him after Aaron was killed."

"Oh, that's right. That's who he is."

"What did you tell him?" she asked, then she heard a loud noise from the other room. A braying noise, a donkey? Peeking into the living room, she saw that Charlotte was on the couch, a blanket wrapped around her, her stuffed animal tucked under her arm as she stared at the giant screen where some cartoon was playing. Satisfied her daughter was safe, Rory turned to Darlene again. Her mother was eyeing her own image in the mirror and slicking back a few hairs that had escaped her braid.

Rory said, "I thought he quit the department."

"All I know is he wants to meet you here."

"Here in Portland . . . or here at the Bastians'?" She stared at her mother in dawning horror. "I can't meet him here!"

"Them. He's with an associate. Well, I wasn't sure what to tell them," she said defensively.

"Tell them I'll call them."

"Rory, they're on their way over," she admitted. "And celestially it's a really good time for you to take care of old business."

Liam checked on Rory and Charlotte to find his daughter asleep on the couch, wound tight in a blanket, a plate with the remains of toast and pieces of banana sitting on the coffee table next to a half-drunk glass of milk. Darlene, feet tucked under the folds of her caftan, was propped by an array of pillows on the other end of the couch and she, too, seemed to be dozing.

Rory appeared from the stairway and held a finger to her lips, then, seeing that he'd gotten the message, went back to her task of sweeping crumbs from the counter into a waiting waste bin.

"Everett's gone." He hesitated only briefly before folding her into his arms and kissing the top of her head.

"Good," she stated flatly.

"Something else . . . ?"

Pulling him into the hallway, she related the conversation with her mother and the impending visits from Pauline Kirby and two investigators from Seattle, one of them being Mick Mickelson. She ended with, "We've got to get out of here. It isn't good for Charlotte or me. Your mother makes no bones about how she feels, and your father believes I'm somehow responsible for the shooting. All we are is trouble, so . . . we're going to have to go."

"My father doesn't think you're responsible."

"Coulda fooled me."

He'd made a mistake not circling back immediately and breaking up his father's meeting with Rory. "You could live with me," he said.

She sighed. "We're moving fast. Maybe too fast."

He wanted to deny it, but just last week he'd been hell-bent on divorcing her. That was a fact. "Mickelson's been calling me and I've ignored him. Maybe seeing him and his partner is a good start to . . . the rest of our lives."

"You and my mother."

"What?"

"What about Pauline Kirby?"

He smiled. "We'll take care of her, too."

Rory made a strangled sound.

"Be strong," he said and kissed her warmly.

She leaned into him, soft and pliant. He remembered making love to her long before, at the beach, in a room where they could hear the roar of the ocean and the pounding of the rain on the roof, and again, in the apartment they'd briefly shared, when the neighbor cat slipped in through an open window and scared the life out of Rory. The black tomcat had hopped onto the bed, causing her to shriek and him to laugh. And then they'd shooed the little beast back outside and collapsed on the bed and made love all over again.

God, he'd lost her once, he couldn't bear the thought of it again.

She lifted her head and stared into his eyes. "Okay. But now, to be strong, and not in the aromatic sense of the word, I'm just gonna hop into the shower. Wanna join?"

More than anything.

But he thought of Charlotte on the couch . . . or Darlene with her lack of boundaries . . . "How about a rain check," he said, "when we're alone or Charlotte's in bed for the night."

"Deal," she said. "Give me twenty minutes and I'll find you."

He closed his mind to the erection that had started to rise and headed back to his family. By the time he'd reached the bottom step he'd decided that the first order of business was to move Rory and Charlotte to his town house. Though he appreciated her being there for Charlotte, Darlene was not invited. He wanted it to be him and Rory and Charlotte looking to the future as a family.

Still a lot of unanswered questions, he reminded himself.

He walked through the gate to the pool area, but no one was lingering on the patio, the tables and chairs were empty, only a forgotten orange flip-flop and a wadded-up towel evidence that anyone had been outside recently. The water in the pool was calm and quiet, shadows stretching across the surface. A few filmy clouds stretched over the horizon and the sun was lowering over the forested slopes, a warm evening on a bit of breeze, bees still buzzing over Stella's pots of jasmine and lavender.

He entered the family room through the open patio door. Candace and the kids were situated around the TV, Estella and Landon watching some cartoon show he didn't recognize, the sitter lounging on the couch near the children, but, of course, paying more attention to her cell phone than her charges. They had, though, changed into shorts and tops and were picking at what looked to be microwaved Tater Tots and pizza.

"When's Viv coming back?" he asked Candace. She didn't remove her attention from her cell phone, but she cocked her head his way, as if listening. "Has she called?" he questioned when she didn't respond.

"Uh . . . yeah, I think. Yeah. She's, um, like, coming back soon." She finally blinked up at him and Liam made a mental note to tell his sister to find someone a little more interested in her kids. He heard raised voices from the hallway and followed the sound.

His parents. At it again. He probably should let things be. But they should know that the investigators and reporter were coming. "You might want to take it down a notch," he said, pushing open the doorway to Geoff's office. His father was scowling and red faced, seated behind his desk in his wheelchair, Stella was standing to one side of his desk, while Derek sat in a chair near the window, drink in hand.

"Why?" Geoff demanded.

"Hey, Mr. CEO. Right on time." Derek hoisted his glass in a mock toast, then took a long pull from what Liam assumed was some of their father's whiskey.

"For what?" Liam asked.

Stella turned, her expression pinched, and in that instant Liam wondered when he'd last seen his mother smiling or laughing. Not that Stella had ever been lighthearted, but somehow, over the years, she'd become as bitter as her husband. Had it been since the assault and Geoffrey's confinement to the chair? Or had it occurred earlier, when the marriage and her dreams had begun to sour, when the gilt of being Mrs. Geoffrey Bastian had worn thin and maybe even become a burden?

"It's Viv," Derek said, and Stella shot him a warning glance. "She's up to something."

Liam closed the door behind him, didn't want the kids hearing. "Like what?"

Geoffrey snorted. "Derek's got it in his mind that your sister might be in some kind of . . . trouble."

"With Javier?" Liam asked, trying to follow.

"He thinks she's gotten herself into some kind of money problem or dire financial straits. That's what all the talk was about the job."

"She's sneaking around," Stella said through tight lips.

"Actually, I think she might be involved in what happened at the wedding," Derek admitted carefully, eyeing first Stella and then his father.

"No." Liam shook his head.

"I told him the same thing," Stella snapped.

"There's no way." Liam faced his brother, flabbergasted. "You're talking about Viv. *Viv?*"

"You think I like saying that?" Derek flushed.

"She was at the wedding."

"But you were the one who got hit, and Dad. And if Rory was taken out, who would inherit?"

"Mom." Where the hell was this going?

"Oh, for God's sake!" His mother gazed at Derek with pure hatred.

Derek lifted his hands. "Your mother first, Liam, then her heirs. We all know where I stand in this family."

"You aren't cut completely out of the will." Geoff's remark seemed pulled out of his gut. He glared at his oldest son.

"That's a drastic way to get an inheritance," Liam said angrily. "No one would—"

"Kill a family member for money? It's a time-honored tradition, bro."

"You're full of shit, Derek."

"We all know she needs money."

"Her marriage may be falling apart, but she's not destitute." Liam couldn't buy this. It was crazy. Off the charts.

Only his mother and father weren't saying anything.

"You're not listening to this," he declared, looking from his mother to his father.

"Maybe Viv meant to kill Rory and got her stepbrother instead. Rory was supposed to be with Aaron, coming down that aisle. Viv couldn't know that she was going to run out on you."

"This is crazy," said Liam.

"You think I don't love my sister? You think I haven't run all this around my head?" Derek demanded.

"I don't think it's Vivian," Stella snapped. "Rory's the one who had the most to gain. That's why she didn't walk down the aisle."

"She was in on it," Geoff agreed.

"I checked with our lawyer about the lab results," Stella said tightly to Liam. "DNA proves Charlotte's yours. A Bastian."

"I don't think it's Rory," Derek said, taking a long sip from his drink.

"You'd rather believe it's your own sister?" Stella's voice dripped acid.

"Well, where the hell's she been going?" Derek asked her. "You said yourself she's been sneaking out, never saying what she's doing. I called the office, by the way." He turned to Liam. "She showed up and left, and never returned. She's meeting someone, that's what I think. Our sister has demanded a job, for money, but maybe to get the hell out of the house without anyone knowing where she is."

"She moved in here by choice," Liam reminded him.

"Or, did Javier kick her out?"

"Enough speculation. Call her up! Ask her where she is," Geoff growled.

"Good idea." Liam's voice was harsh.

"You know I hope I'm wrong," Derek said, his lips turning down. "It's just when you lay it all out . . ."

"Where is everybody?" Vivian's voice rang out from the foyer.

Derek spread his hands. Looked at his father.

"We're in the den," Geoff called harshly.

Liam heard her footsteps head their way, then she was standing in the doorway. She looked haggard and worn in a way he'd never seen.

"What are you talking about?" she asked them.

Liam spoke before anyone else could. "They're questioning your loyalty to the family," he bit out. "Think maybe you're after Dad's money. Maybe even were involved in the shooting."

Vivian's mouth dropped open in horror.

"I never said that!" Stella cried.

"Where have you been going, sister, dear?" Derek drawled. "Who've you been meeting?"

Vivian stared at him as if she'd never seen him before. She turned to Liam, then her mother, and finally her father.

And burst into tears.

"Tell me," Shanice insisted as Mick clicked off his phone. After Liam Bastian had ignored his calls and they had struck out at Liam Bastian's penthouse apartment as well as the Bastian-Flavel Construction offices, they'd finally gotten a break with Darlene Stemple and learned where Aurora Abernathy was. They were just finishing up an early dinner at a Mexican food cart in downtown Portland when Mick got the word, and almost immediately afterward, Mick's buddy, Zach Pitman, got back to him.

Wadding up the paper wrapper of his quesadilla, Mick marched toward the car, Shanice right behind him. "Let's roll. I'll tell you on the way to the Bastians'."

They climbed into her car and she eased into traffic, nearly striking a bicyclist who'd wooshed by on his way to trying to beat a red light. "Son of a—"

"This is a bike town," he reminded her. She could see that. Bike lanes were marked in paint and bicycles flitted the core of the city.

Carefully, she melded into traffic and told Mick to punch Geoffrey's address into her GPS.

"Pitman had some good info. They've come to the conclusion that Teri Mulvaney, the woman who took a leap from the

Bastian-Flavel Construction site, the one we drove to earlier today?"

"Hallifax."

"Yeah, well, they think it was more likely murder than suicide or an accident, mainly because Ms. Mulvaney was seen with a guy earlier that night at the bar. The forensics team is still working on the physics of it, but preliminarily it looks like she was pushed. Portland PD is working on the homicide theory. They checked with her roommate and friends and anyone she had been seeing, to find out who was accounted for, had an alibi. But a local bartender who saw a guy buying her drinks is coming up with a composite sketch with an artist. Sounds like a hook-up at a bar."

"Teri Mulvaney's lucky night," Shanice said with a grimace. She slowed as the cars in front of her were piling up, waiting for a traffic light to change. "Why take her to a construction site to kill her?"

"It was nearby. Convenient. Empty."

"But how did he know that?" She squinted against the sunlight bouncing off the hoods and mirrors of the surrounding vehicles. They were heading into the setting sun, where the hills flanked the west side of the city, traffic crawling in a thick, slow stream out of the downtown area. "Do you think he'd already scouted out the Bastian building?"

"Maybe he worked there. One of the guys on the construction team? One thing: unprotected sex was involved."

"DNA," she said with satisfaction, easing on the gas again, the line of cars starting to edge forward.

"They're hoping to get a hit. Match the DNA to someone already in the data banks. And they're sorting through footage from a couple of street cameras that might have caught an image nearby. Too bad the construction site didn't have any. This guy's sloppy. No condom, so maybe a camera caught him."

"We should be so lucky. But how does that connect with what happened at the wedding?"

"Might not. Just the latest crime connected to the Bastians . . . and it happened about the same time as Liam Bastian's runaway bride returned."

"Correlation isn't causation," she said, repeating a line Mick said often himself.

He frowned and nodded. His need to solve the Bastian shooting was his great white whale, the one that got away, the case that had kept him awake at night long after he'd retired from the force.

Shanice's motives were different. She wanted justice for Aaron. Right now her jaw was clenched so hard it ached, and she forced herself to calm down. They were getting closer, she knew it. She just hoped they would get a break. And she felt Rory Abernathy was the key.

Mick's phone rang again as Shanice exited the highway and headed down winding streets where trees guarded gated estates. Stately manors, built near the turn of the last century, stood next to modern homes, all built into the hillside with expansive views of the city. Nice neighborhood.

She heard him grunt a hello into the phone as she drew up near their destination. Geoffrey Bastian's home was much like his neighbors', hidden from the street by a tall fence and trees, a circular drive leading to the home itself. Thankfully, the gate was open, the drive filled with a bevy of vehicles, from an older, silver Honda—presumably not a Bastian vehicle—to a sleek black Corvette and another black vehicle, a Tahoe. She pulled in behind a green Mercedes SUV parked haphazardly and taking up too much space. The whole aura of the home and its surroundings oozed money. Expensive. Grand.

She'd had some experience with the extremely wealthy. Within their walls were secrets, dark and dirty, the same dirt hidden behind every damned wall in the world. Didn't matter if those walls were constructed of marble and gold, or tar paper and tin, they were often also constructed of lies and deception. If they were lucky, she and Mick were about to lay bare a few of those well-hidden lies. She glanced at the glove box, where she'd locked her sidearm.

"Who was that?" she asked Mick as she popped the box and pulled out her gun.

Sounding satisfied, Mick said, "Hal at Seattle PD came through. They've got video from different angles about three blocks around the Nile and have been checking out the vehicles. He's sharing with me."

She knew he was referring to a deputy he'd once worked with at Seattle PD. "He's taking a chance."

"If we learn anything, he wants first crack. I'm happy to oblige. Anything to solve this thing." He looked over the front of the house. "All right, let's go."

Chapter 23

Beth finished her third glass of wine—or was it the fourth?—and who the hell cared anyway? Five years of her life, gone. *Snap!* Just because Rory Abernathy *Bastian* reappeared as if she'd been gone overnight instead of . . . how many days was it? Like eighteen hundred? Beth should know because she'd spent twenty-four hours of every day thinking of Liam Bastian, hoping to marry him.

She took a long swallow and fought tears, while having a private pity party for herself in the living room of her apartment, nice though it was. She'd turned on the gas fire and the place was warm, probably too warm, but she didn't care. She'd expected to move in with Liam and now it was over. Her future. Her whole life. At least as Mrs. Liam Bastian. Turns out there was already someone filling that role and that's the way Liam, the idiot, wanted it. She had to face facts. She wouldn't have him back now if he came crawling back to her on his hands and knees, a five-carat diamond ring in one hand.

Oh, yes you would.

She swore softly, more than a little buzzy. She was holding

her phone in one hand and systematically, as she spied a picture of Liam, took a drink, then deleted the photo. She'd already taken down all the photos she'd put on display as part of the apartment's decoration. They were in the garbage, their frames broken, the glass shattered as she'd smashed them all.

Now, it was time to delete the memories captured on her phone. There was one by the lion exhibit at the zoo. *Click!* Gone. Oh, another favorite, a selfie with Liam as they were hiking at Multnomah Falls, the water cascading behind them. *Click!* And poof! it was no more. Oh, and this one, at a concert out at Edgefield. *Click!* Just like that, history.

God, this was depressing. He'd been her whole life for so long, even before that wretched wedding, though she'd pretended not to care. Now nothing mattered. Not even the job she'd liked so well, working at a boutique art gallery. She couldn't work up any enthusiasm. The friends they'd shared were mostly coupled up, engaged, married, or at least dating *seriously*, and she couldn't face them. She started to cry but blinked back tears and reminded herself she at least would no longer have to deal with his family: Stella, with her sneers, Vivian, never realizing how great her life was, Derek with his quick, sharp tongue, and Geoffrey, who had never been a barrel of laughs to begin with, but after the shooting had become utterly joyless.

Like you. Now.

She took another gulp of wine and staggered to her feet. The sun was setting outside the window. She was done thinking about those damned Bastians. She wobbled to the slider door and her private patio, just big enough for two chairs and a small table. How many times had she'd shared a bottle of wine with Liam right here, from the eighth floor with its peekaboo view of the Hawthorne Bridge? Yes, another high-rise blocked most of the view, but still, it was pretty nice here. Or had been. And now? Now what? Start over? Date some stranger on the Internet? Ask her friends if they know anyone? Start taking up golf or tennis or attend church? Forget five damned years? When she thought of the hours she'd sat at his hospital bedside as he'd gone through the operations that had put him back together again after the attack at the wedding, she wanted to scream! Why couldn't the assailant have killed Rory instead? That would have solved all her problems!

Problems...

Liam had other problems he didn't even know about yet.

A burning anger swept through her like wildfire and she swept up her phone again. Liam was number one on her contact list and she pressed the button, waiting for him to answer. When the call went to voice mail, his cool voice telling her to leave a message, she almost threw her phone over the edge of the balcony.

Instead, she did just as he suggested. Telling him just enough to assure he would call her back.

Immediately afterward she fell into a dark funk. Head lolling back, she cried silent tears, distantly aware of the city far below, the rumble of vehicle engines occasionally interrupted by a shout or a honk, bits of conversation floating upward, the heat of the day still rising from the streets.

He's going to be real sorry, she thought. *I'll make sure of it.*

Rory heard the sobbing even before she hit the bottom step to the back hallway. It was coming from the wing housing the den, and the tortured sobs were followed by shouting and questions and a general scramble emanating from Geoff's den.

Rory froze, not sure whether she wanted to step into this family drama, but at that moment Vivian burst from the room, her face twisted in some kind of agony or anger. Immediately she dashed for the front of the house. Behind Vivian, his strides longer, Liam was half running to catch up to her and didn't notice Rory in the intersecting corridor. His eyes were trained on his sister.

Stella's voice echoed down the hallway—"For God's sake!"— as Derek, hot on his brother's heels, burst from the room. As if sensing Rory, he glanced back at her, shaking his head, seemed about to say something, then moved on quickly, the leaves of a potted plant shivering as he passed.

Rory started to take after them all, when Stella stepped into the hallway, and Geoff's wheelchair nearly bumped into his wife as he followed as well. "Well, get out of the way," he barked, the wheels of his chair skidding a bit.

Stella whipped around, looked like she wanted to slap him, saw Rory, and turned her fury on her daughter-in-law. "Stop skulking around!" And she took off after their children with Geoff rolling behind her, strong shoulders and arms pushing the wheelchair forward.

Well, hell.

Rory wasn't about to stand there, frozen to the damned spot in their house. No way. This was her family, too. She strode after them to the front door, which was standing wide-open to an orange sunset, a soft summer breeze with the scents of roses riding on it wafted into the foyer. Outside, in the driveway, Vivian was trying to get into her car, the Mercedes's driver's door open, she struggling with her seat belt, the car alarm dinging softly. Liam was attempting to reason with her, but she was beyond reason, and she rounded on Derek when he stopped short at the end of the porch. "You bastard. You . . . you fucking bastard!" she screamed, angry and hurt and looking as if she wanted to murder him.

"I'm sorry." Derek was short.

"How could you? I love my family. I love all of you." Furiously, her face red, tear tracks visible, she swept an arm out. "All of you, damn it!" All trace of the Vivian of old, the contained woman with the sly smile, drawling and cool manner, was gone. "And while I'm trying to put my marriage back together! Doing everything I can to hold on to my . . . future with the man I love . . . you stab me in the back! Accuse me of unthinkable crimes? It's . . . unbelievable." Fighting sobs, she yelled, "Horrible, horrible stuff. How *dare* you!"

"I didn't know you were following Javier," Derek said stiffly as the incessant seat belt alarm kept chiming. "Sneaking around after him, stalking him. I had no idea you were that pathetic!"

She launched from her SUV, suddenly abandoning her car and, face contorted in rage, charged Derek.

"Whoa," Liam said, grabbing Vivian around the waist as she flew at her half brother like a virago.

In that second, Rory realized they weren't alone. There was another car wedged between Vivian's and the curve in the driveway, a small SUV. A man and a woman climbed out of the Ford Escape that had been sitting at the end of the drive.

Mick Mickelson, she'd bet.

Vivian was still screaming at Derek, who did look a bit sheepish and had taken two steps backward. Liam hadn't yet let go his grip on his sister, and about that time Stella spied the approaching couple and straightened as if shot by a cattle prod. "Uh-oh," she said under her breath while her husband stared at them as well, his jaw rock hard.

Liam followed their gazes, looking behind him, slowly releasing his grip on Vivian, who woke up slowly to the fact that something momentous had taken the focus away from her and her tirade. She glanced back, her face red and puffy, her mouth quivering. Upon seeing the man who radiated "the law," even if he was maybe retired, and his female partner, who appeared to have a gun on her hip, Vivian took a step away from Liam and tried to bring her breathing, which was practically a pant at this point, under control.

"Mickelson," Liam said, and the man and woman looked at him.

"Who?" Vivian asked, shuddering a little and swiping at her face to brush away tears or hair that had fallen over her cheeks.

Stella's hand had flown to her chest. "Oh, my God. What's happened?"

"Liam Bastian?" the man asked, and Liam nodded curtly.

"You were expecting them?" Derek asked in disbelief.

"I'll tell you all about it when we're inside," Liam said, making ushering motions to his entire family. His eyes met Rory's, but before anyone could take more than a few steps, a news van approached. White and gleaming in the dying sun, the station's call sign emblazoned across the side, a satellite dish visible, it rumbled to the open gates. Liam saw Rory's gaze shift and glance back. "Everyone inside," he barked, "unless you want to be on the Channel 7 news."

Liam wanted to meet with Mickelson and his partner alone, but as soon as his father understood who they were, Geoff refused anything but a full-on family meeting in the living room. "Everyone's got something to say," he practically roared. "Just say it!"

Stella, with a hard glance at her husband, went out to make sure Candace was still entertaining the children. She returned moments later and retook her seat on the couch near the bay window, where she crossed her legs and somehow managed to look perturbed.

Liam had forgotten that his father had actually liked the retired police detective. He'd had faith in Mickelson for a long while, until he'd retired from the police department—or been put out to pasture, Geoff's real belief in how the detective had been removed from the job.

Mickelson introduced his partner as Shanice Clayburgh. She was younger, with darker skin, her hair pulled into a tight bun

at her nape, but she possessed the same take-no-prisoners attitude as he did. Mickelson himself seemed disinclined to talk to
them as a group, but it was clear those were Geoffrey Bastian's
rules, so he launched into why he'd shown up in Portland.

"We would like to talk to you," he said, directing his attention to Rory. "We've talked to the local PD and know about the
attack last night, as well as the one at the wedding, both perpe-
trated by Cal Redmond. And we also know what he's said the
reasons are. We would like to hear the chain of events the night
of the wedding."

Liam's cell phone rang, and everyone's eyes swung his way.
He saw it was Beth and let it go to voice mail.

"Who was that?" Stella asked, squinting. As if she didn't
trust him.

"Beth. I'll call her back."

"Do," Stella instructed.

Rory ignored her mother-in-law and answered the detective.
"I've said everything, absolutely everything, I can. Over and
over again. Everything I can remember, to the police, both
Portland and Laurelton, who talked with Seattle PD." She was
getting angry again. "I'm sorry my mother thought it would be
a good idea to tell you how to find me, because it's a big waste
of time." She leveled her gaze at the big man. "You can ask me
a million questions, go at it different ways, but really, there's
just nothing more I can come up with."

"Your mother invited these . . . people?" Stella asked in that
sneering tone Liam detested.

Liam forced himself to ignore her and asked Mickelson,
"You're investigating the wedding shooting, privately? You're
not associated with the police?" His phone beeped faintly, a
voice mail message from Beth.

Geoffrey snapped, "I hired them. I want to know who hired
DeGrere to shoot up your wedding and put me in this chair."

All heads turned to look at him.

Mickelson spoke into the stunned moment, "Shanice and I never really gave up on the case. DeGrere's homicide put it back on a front burner."

"You mean, Geoff hiring you put it on a front burner," Stella corrected, looking at her husband. "You couldn't have told me?"

"I'm telling you now," Geoff said gruffly. "Damn case had gone cold."

Liam stared at his father. "You wanted to surprise us?"

"Just Dad's way," Derek drawled with a touch of anger.

"I want answers, God damn it!" He rapped his fist on the arm of his wheelchair. "It's been five years and—"

The door chimes pealed, interrupting him, and seconds later there was a sharp *rap, rap, rap* of impatient knuckles on the front door.

"Oh, hell. It's that Pauline Kirby," Vivian growled as she peered through the half-closed blinds. She sat on the far end of the same couch occupied by her mother, but Viv's arms hugged her chest tightly as if she couldn't bear the thought of touching Stella, or probably anyone in the room, for that matter.

"I'll take care of this," Derek said, getting up and stalking to the door. In a pleasant voice he told whoever was on the other side to go fuck themselves.

"Derek!" Stella cried and dropped her forehead to one hand. "Oh. God. You'll be on the news saying that!"

"They'll bleep me out." Shrugging, he slid back into the armchair he'd recently vacated and seemed almost pleased with himself.

Stella drilled him with her eyes. "They'll probably camp out there, you know, at the edge of the driveway. With others. It's like they breed, you know. One comes up then another, then another . . ." She shivered at the thought. "I've seen it on the news." Glancing to the window, she said, "We should call the police."

Derek gave a little snort. "Oh, right. Now there's a great idea."

"Got a better one?" she countered.

"Mother!" Liam cut in, tired of Stella's theatrics.

"Mrs. Bastian?" Mickelson inquired, seeming unruffled by the display.

Stella turned sharply toward him, but the detective was looking at Rory. The *other* Mrs. Bastian. "Would you mind going over it one more time?" When he saw that Rory was about to protest, he held up a hand. "I know. I heard you. You're sick of telling the story. But, please. Just one more time. I'd like to hear your take on the events of the wedding day and what you did, where you were, what you thought."

Liam thought Rory was going to tell Mickelson to beat it and leave her alone as she looked tired and beyond stressed. The makeup on her face was fading and the dark bruising and swelling was apparent now. She didn't need this.

He started to step in and cut Mickelson off. "Maybe another time would be better—"

"No. If I'm going to do this at all, it may as well be now. And here." Somehow Rory seemed to marshal her strength and gamely did as the ex-detective had requested, answering his questions truthfully. She sat perched on the edge of an ottoman, with Mickelson and his partner occupying two matching chairs near the foyer. Derek leaned against the fireplace and Geoffrey positioned himself near the coffee table, his chair out of any walking path. Standing next to the chair Rory had taken, Liam glanced at the phone that had been vibrating in his pocket. The call identified as being from a news station. Sick of reporters, he clicked his phone off. They could wait.

She was saying, "So I was getting ready, had my dress on and was kind of freaking out because I was already late . . ." She explained once again about the knock on the door, the helium balloons, and the weird, high-pitched voice threatening her.

When she mentioned Cal, Liam saw his mother roll her eyes. God, she could be a bitch, and Vivian had a weird expression on her face. Was she even listening?

Rory went on to explain about the knife attack, the blood, and the fear that propelled her to race out the door and down the hall of the unfamiliar hotel. She'd ended up in the basement and then up the ramp to the exit. "I didn't know what was happening, why anyone would want to kill me, and I heard the music from the wedding . . . and . . . and . . ."

Her words faded, her story interrupted, and she stared through the window, not seeing the manicured grounds of the Bastian home but something else, another panorama seen only in her mind's eye. "Oh." She swallowed. Lost in thought. "But there was . . . Oh, God," she whispered and the ensuing silence was deafening.

"What?" Mickelson asked softly.

"I think . . . I mean . . ." Biting her lip, she thought, her eyes narrowing as if she were focusing on an object just out of view. "There was a silver car. I was running in the parking structure, trying to get out, but . . . but it was racing, almost careening into the lot. It headed up the ramp and I could hear the tires squealing. It was going fast and I remember thinking he should be careful, he could hurt someone . . ." She gazed at Mickelson and her expression turned to one of regret. "I didn't think about it again. It was like not even in my memory. And at the time I didn't know what happened at the wedding, not till later." She bit her lip. "It's probably nothing."

"Maybe not," Mickelson encouraged, his voice low.

She swallowed. Hard. "Could . . . do you think that the driver may have been the shooter?" All the color had drained from her face at the thought.

Mickelson had gone still, as if afraid to move. "It was a silver car?"

"Or gray . . . maybe?"

"Do you know what make it was?"

Rory shook her head slowly, her eyebrows drawn in concentration. "Oh, I'm . . . I'm just so bad about cars. I don't know."

"Okay. How about this," Mickelson said. "Was it a sedan, or an SUV, or a truck?"

"No. Not a truck. Yeah, just a car—a sedan."

"Four door?" he asked. "Two?"

"I don't know." Her brow furrowed even further. "He went by in a blur."

"He?" Mickelson waited.

"I mean. It."

"Did you see the driver?"

"No—uh, no." She was shaking her head.

The partner, Shanice, asked, "What about a passenger?" and when Rory responded negatively, she asked about license plates, or dents, or parking permits, or bumper stickers, or anything that would make identifying the vehicle easier. Each time she struck out.

"I'm sorry. I don't know why I even remember that, about the car, now. All of a sudden."

"But you're sure it was gray."

"Yes. Uh-huh."

There was a moment of silence, and then, as if he couldn't stand the suspense, Derek blurted out, "What?"

It was their father who answered. Geoff's voice was hard, the words brittle. "Pete DeGrere's car was a gray sedan. It was found abandoned miles from the hotel. No gun. He was either aided and abetted by someone or dropped the rifle somewhere, though it was never found."

Shanice said, "Good memory."

Geoff looked at her coolly and rapped his fingers on his wheelchair. "I've had a lot of time to go over that day and everything that's happened since." His lips turned downward. "You know, I think I was the target."

Mickelson's head jerked as he turned to face the old man. "You?"

Shanice asked, "Why?"

"Just a gut feeling, I guess you'd say," Geoff said, but his brittle joke fell flat. "I don't have any proof, if that's what you mean, but . . . you're talking about a real marksman in De-Grere. Would he make such a mistake?"

"He could have been distracted. His timing off," Derek said.

Vivian glared at her father. "Oh, so that's it now? DeGrere for sure? Well, I didn't have anything to do with it!" Vivian said through her teeth, her eyes shooting daggers at both Derek and Geoff.

"You think it was Pete DeGrere that I saw, then? In the car?" Rory asked, still piecing it together. There had been speculation, of course. DeGrere had been a "person of interest" in the unsolved case.

Mickelson was nodding. "I've always felt it was DeGrere. The hotel had one camera on that exit ramp, and it wasn't working. The whole place was being retrofitted, but it hadn't happened by the time of the shooting. DeGrere probably knew that. During the search we found his car, abandoned. He said it was because he'd been drinking and he didn't want to get picked up, so he got out and started walking. It was on a side street. Older industrial. No cameras there, either. He couldn't ever explain what he was doing in that area besides that he'd gotten lost. We searched the surrounding warehouses. No gun. Then Pete, being Pete, tried holding up a convenience store, waving a handgun around, and got himself a prison sentence. We had no corroboration that Pete's car was at the hotel that day. We just knew he'd been in the area. He frequented a bar a few blocks from the hotel. More upscale than his usual haunts, but he was sweet on one of the bartenders, who we believe was involved in some minor prostitution with the occasional cus-

tomer to make ends meet. Possibly Pete was one of those customers. She was fired soon after Pete's incarceration."

"She picked him up that day," Geoff said with certainty.

"No," Shanice answered. "She was at the bar during the entire wedding ceremony. She's the one who first fingered De-
Grere. Said he was talking a big score. Taking out one of those
fat cats who had too much money."

"You see!" Geoff said. "I knew it! That low-life bastard."

It was Mickelson's turn to disagree. "DeGrere talked like
that a lot, even in prison. He claimed other jobs that he couldn't
have done, all because 'those fat cats had too much money.' He
bragged about a lot of things. He had grandiose ideas about
himself."

"He was crazy," Stella stated flatly.

"Come on, Mom," Viv said with an expressive roll of her
eyes. "Like you knew him. Like you'd ever know anyone like
him. Give me a break!"

"More accurately," Shanice said, "I'd say Pete DeGrere was
someone who occasionally broke with reality."

Mickelson added, "DeGrere was paid for the job. He didn't
just act on impulse. Someone knew he was a marksman, although they may not have known he was unstable. He took the
job and maybe, Geoff, because you're wealthy, you were on his
radar, too. Could be. He was a real nutcase. Or, someone knew
that about him and appealed to his prejudice, the icing on the
cake to perform the job." He cleared his throat. "There is a
chance he was hired to simply create chaos."

"Would someone in your family actually kill your stepbrother Aaron?" Shanice asked Rory in an icy voice.

Liam wasn't sure what that was about, but it felt personal, as
if the woman PI had a personal grudge against Rory, but his
wife, if she sensed there was anything but professionalism in
the question, didn't show it. Rory just shook her head, and

tears glistened in her eyes. She sniffed, swatted away any tears, then said, "No." Clearing her throat she repeated, "No. Of course not. Everyone . . . we all . . . loved Aaron."

"Let's go at this from a different direction," Mickelson suggested as the rest of the room had gone deathly still.

Liam watched his family members as they were all focused on the private investigator, and he wondered what each of them was thinking. Vivian, calmer now, but still wary. Stella haughty as ever, but lines of strain around her mouth. Derek, ever the rogue, still appearing bored. And Geoff, agitated as always, needing answers, needing control. A sorry lot, this, his family.

Mickelson said, "I've been going over my notes from five years ago. Reexamining information. Talking to both Seattle PD and the Portland police."

Did Vivian's eyes widen?

Did his mother wince just a bit?

Was he imagining things?

Mickelson went on, "I've learned that you've had some sabotage on your job sites recently, and a homicide."

"Homicide?" Derek repeated.

"Teri Mulvaney's death was a homicide?" Liam asked at the same time.

"That's how it's been ruled. So, in the last two weeks, less really, there have been two deaths related to your family, De-Grere's and Mulvaney's, and you've had the reappearance of a missing person."

Rory.

She stiffened a bit and he knew she felt the weight of everyone's eyes in the room boring into her.

Shanice said, "We believe there's a connection. Whoever killed Teri Mulvaney was sloppy, left his semen and therefore DNA. If he's in the system, he'll be found. The Portland police are working on it. If he's not, DNA samples will be requested from anyone associated with Mulvaney or the Bastians."

"The women, too?" Stella said with distaste.

"It's strictly voluntary," she answered.

"Leaving DNA behind is more than sloppy," Derek observed.

Shanice answered, "Maybe the condom broke. Maybe he never intended it to go that far."

"Maybe he wants to be caught," Mickelson said.

Vivian finally spoke up. "I don't understand what this Teri Mulvaney could have to do with the wedding shooting." She'd recovered her composure somewhat, but now looked pale and sober.

"Maybe nothing," Shanice said.

Except she looked a lot like my wife and her hair was almost the exact same shade as Rory's. Liam caught his brother glancing at Rory, then when he looked away, Liam wondered if Derek had been thinking the very same thing.

"Hey!" a voice called from the other side of one of the doors to the living room, and Candace, wearing shorts and a T-shirt over her swimsuit, stepped into the room, then paused as she saw everyone. "Oh, whoa. Sorry. Um." She zeroed in on Vivian and pulled a face. "I uh, need to get going and, you know, need to be paid."

"Oh, right! Uh—just a sec," Vivian said, forcing herself from the couch. "Of course."

With a sigh, Stella said, "Let me get my purse."

"Really, Mom?" Vivian shot her mother a withering glance. "I can take care of it. Come on, come on, let's go," she said to Candace, ushering the babysitter to the door.

"Fine." Stella threw up a hand. "I was just trying to help. You're the one always complaining about money, you know," Stella called after her daughter, then, staring at the detective, added, "If you'll excuse me, I have things to do. We all do. I think we've helped you as much as we can." Her smile held no warmth.

"I think we're done here," Mickelson said. Though he didn't seem satisfied, both he and his partner got to their feet. Geoff waited until the two private detectives were securely out the door behind Vivian, then muttered that he was going to his den to have a drink.

"Helluva day," he said to no one in particular as he rolled along the corridor. "Helluva day."

"Can't argue with that," Derek said, rubbing the back of his neck and staring after his old man. "Can you believe that?"

"What?"

"About the shooter? That it was that DeGrere character all along? Come on, I'll buy you a drink." Derek started into the family room and, realizing that Estella and Landon had fallen asleep on the couch, motioned for Rory and Liam to wend their way past the couch to the door leading outside to the patio, where he found the drink cart. He uncorked a bottle of whiskey. "So," he said, pouring a glass and offering it to Rory, who shook her head, then to Liam, who accepted it, "you buying the DeGrere theory?"

"How about wine?" he said to Rory.

"I'm good." Again she shook her head. "No, thanks."

Liam took a swallow of the whiskey, tasted the smoky flavor and gazed at the pool, now calm and dark. Though small lamps hidden within the shrubbery gave off warm illumination and the lights of the city twinkled in the distance, the water of the pool was nearly black.

"You didn't answer my question."

"About DeGrere? I've always thought he was involved."

"What about Dad being the target?" Derek asked.

"I don't know. Could be, I suppose, but hell, I don't know." He saw something in his brother's eyes. "You think DeGrere intended to shoot Dad?"

"I just thought . . ." A shrug. Derek took a sip of whiskey. "Who the hell knows?"

"No. Wait." Something was going on here. "You still think Vivian's behind it? That she would go to those extremes to inherit? She would hire someone to kill her own—our own—father?" Liam wasn't buying it. "No way. She and Javier were fine five years ago. There were no money problems between them. And Dad's still here, so if she really wants to take him out, she's sure playing the long game."

"Okay." Derek glanced at the patio door, as if expecting Vivian to come barreling through. "Okay, fine. It's just that she's been acting weird lately." He turned to Rory, who'd remained silent throughout their exchange and was taking it all in. "What do you think?"

"About?"

"Everything."

"It doesn't matter what I think. The police seem to think it was DeGrere. Look, I've been over this a million times. I'm done."

"Yeah, agreed. It's been a long one." Liam set his unfinished drink on the cart. "Come on," he said to Rory, reaching for her hand. "Let's go."

"Go?"

"Let's get you out of here and into bed."

"Subtle, bro." Derek sniggered and tossed back his drink.

She shot her brother-in-law a glare that said silently *Grow up*, then turned to Liam. "I can't leave. Not right now. Charlotte's upstairs and I've got to make sure she's had a decent meal and getting ready for bed."

He hesitated, thought about going to tuck in his kid himself, and vowed that he would. Soon. Every night. "Just let Darlene know you're coming with me. She'll be okay with it. She likes me."

Derek made a deprecating noise.

"I'll see," Rory said, but headed for the guest quarters. Liam watched her go and felt a little tingle of anticipation at the coming night.

"Man, you've got it bad," Derek said, shaking his head.

"Yep." That he did.

His brother sighed through his nose. "You might want to slow it down a bit. You know, be a little more careful."

"That so?" Liam wasn't interested in Derek's older-brother advice. Or anyone's, for that matter. He'd waited five years as it was.

"Yeah, it is. Look, I hate to be the one to burst your sexual bubble, here, but if you haven't noticed, things started going bad, I mean real bad, just about the minute your wife decided to show up again."

Liam couldn't believe it. "What is it with you, man? First Vivian, now Rory?" Liam could feel the tight rein he'd had on his emotions over Derek's wild accusations start to slip again.

"Get real, Liam," he said, with sudden seriousness. The night seemed suddenly close. "Somebody's playing us. All of us. We need to know who it is, and you getting in deep with Rory again isn't helping things."

Before Liam could respond, footsteps pounded through the kitchen and family area and Vivian flew onto the patio. "Jesus, they're still there. I could barely get Candace out of here without her giving them an interview!"

"Who?" Liam asked.

"Pauline Kirby or whatever her name is."

"Guess she didn't take my hint," Derek said, and picked up Liam's unfinished drink.

"I guess not." Viv was in a full-blown rage again. "And that Candace? She's starstruck, that's what she is! Loved the idea of being on TV, even though she doesn't know a goddamn thing about us. Wouldn't put it past her to make up something, the little bitch."

"Ouch!" Derek said.

"Oh, bite me, Derek. I haven't forgotten what you tried to do to me. Un-be-lieve-able." Vivian looked as if she wanted to throttle her brother right then and there, but somehow pulled herself together. "I'm not done with this," she warned, "but . . . damn, sometimes it sucks being an adult. Excuse me while I put my kids to bed." She started to step inside again, then said, "You might want to make a note that I'm in the house, with the kids." She threw Derek an icy look as she slipped back through the still open door, then added, "Just in case you need to know where I am and what I'm doing."

"You see?" Derek said when Vivian was out of earshot.

"That she's mad at you? Blindingly clear."

"That she's not herself. Crying, then mad, then cold as the Arctic. I'm telling you, something's going on with her."

Javier had said something along the same lines, but Liam wasn't buying it. "She's going through a possible divorce and you accused her of trying to kill our father. That tends to make a person a little testy."

"I was just pointing out she needs money."

"You were doing a helluva lot more than that . . . bro."

"Fine. Don't believe me," Derek said, his face flushed with fury. "You know, why don't you ignore what's happening around here. Good idea. Just take your damned wife to your place and screw all night long. Live in your own reality, like Pete DeGrere. Things are falling apart, Liam. If you haven't noticed, the sky is falling!"

Derek finished Liam's drink in one swallow, slamming down the glass so that it fell off the drink cart and cracked as it hit the concrete. He strode across the patio and through the house.

"Derek," Liam said, following him.

"Fuck off." Derek strode out of the house and slammed the door behind him.

Liam watched through the sidelights as Derek, still visibly furious, half jogged to his car. A team of newshounds headed toward him, though Pauline Kirby had apparently given up the siege for the night as the van for Channel 7 was driving away from the estate. One of the remaining reporters recognized Derek and yelled a question at him. "No comment," Derek clipped out. "Now get the hell off of my family's property or we'll call the police. Now!"

The reporter said something to a cameraman, then backed off as Derek slid behind the wheel of his car. The engine fired and with a squeal of tires, he backed around Darlene's car, did a three-point turn. Then, to circumvent some of the other vehicles clogging the drive, he drove partially on the lawn and nearly clipped a fast escaping reporter on the way.

What was wrong with him? Liam wondered.

With all of them?

Every member of Liam's family seemed on the verge of a nervous breakdown, and the visit from Mickelson and his partner coupled with the appearance of the reporters hadn't helped. It was as if a fine piece of porcelain with a few old cracks that had been barely visible was now beginning to shatter.

All because Rory returned.

Derek's theory was a crock. Just another way to blame someone else for dysfunctions that had been festering in their family for years. But one thing Derek was right about—they had to figure out who had a vendetta against the Bastians. The wedding attack and now vandalism and murder at their properties . . . This had to stop.

He didn't have long to contemplate it, though, because Rory returned a few minutes later. She'd taken the time to brush her hair and change her clothes and she was carrying the smallest of her bags. "You were right," she admitted. "Mom said she'd stay with Charlotte, but I have to be back early in the morning. Early. I can't just keep depending on Mom as a babysitter."

"Okay. We'll take them both to breakfast. Deal?"

"Deal. If you're up to it."

"Oh, lady—be careful."

She winked at him and he caught the glint in her eye, the sensual way she raised one eyebrow. Just like she had in the past, playing the part of the tease. He grabbed her then and kissed her hard, feeling her bones melt against him.

"Come on, let's go," he said, breaking the embrace reluctantly. But they needed privacy. And fast. "When we go past the reporters, let me do the talking."

"You got it."

He opened the door, and taking her hand, they ran the gauntlet to his Tahoe.

Beth slowly woke up to a crick in her neck and a foul taste in her mouth. She looked around, blinking to focus. The glass she'd set on the deck beside her chair had tipped over but hadn't broken. It was full-on dark now, the only illumination coming from the city lights below her and a weak light shimmering from inside her apartment, the under-counter kitchen lights, which she'd left on.

What time is it?

She found her phone, also on the deck. Thank God she hadn't thrown it over the rail.

Almost one? She'd been out for hours.

And Liam hadn't called back.

Bastard!

She was angry, then overwhelmingly sad. She choked back a sob, and standing, found she was a little unsteady as she headed inside. On the kitchen counter was the near-empty bottle of rosé she'd been drinking, the one that Liam had bought for her birthday during their last trip to Sonoma. The idiot. Wouldn't go with her this time. Had to go chase after Rory and *find her.*

She poured the rest of the bottle into her glass and gulped it down all at once. She wanted to be drunk. To not care. To never think of Liam Bastian again. Ever.

She searched for another bottle in the wine refrigerator, her hand hovering over the most expensive bottle she owned. Over two hundred of Liam's dollars. Well, yeah, sure. Might as well drink it tonight. She was cutting the foil when she heard a tap at her door. At this time of night?

Liam.

There'd been times when they'd fought and he'd come to her in the middle of the night. Okay, she'd begged him to come over, but he'd always shown up. Her heart soared as she hurried, almost stumbling to the door.

She peered through the peephole, but there was no one there. Had she imagined it?

"Liam?" she asked, standing on her side of the door, counting her heartbeats.

She felt faintly dizzy from the full glass of wine she'd chugged down. *It's not Liam. It's your imagination.* "Are you out there? Don't tease me."

Nothing.

"Did you listen to my voice mail?" she asked.

"Yes."

It *was* Liam.

Carefully, she opened the door a crack, and then a little bit wider.

No one.

Where was he?

And then the door slammed into her face. *Bam!* Pain ricocheted through her brain. She stumbled backward, the world spinning, her legs too unsteady to break her fall. She landed on her butt with a sharp cry and tried like hell to see straight, but her vision was blurred. Dear God, was he wearing a mask?

Before she could gather her wits, he was on her. Kicking the door shut and tackling her, one gloved hand over her mouth as her head banged into the floor. *No! Oh, God, no!* She twisted and writhed against the carpet. Panic surged through her. Fear gripped her heart.

Who are you? she wanted to scream, but he had her completely pinned down, her mouth covered.

Her head throbbed.

No, no, no!

It's a dream. A really bad dream.

But the pain in her face told her differently and when she saw him rear back, his fist curled, she wriggled with all her strength. Kicking, flailing, struggling to get free.

He wore a Spider-Man mask.

I'm kind of a Spider-Man fan myself . . .

Not Liam, but someone who knows him, she finally thought clearly. He pressed against her, pinning her against the floor, and she felt his erection. Hard. As if he was really getting off on this.

He's going to rape you, Beth. Rape you and possibly kill you. Don't let the mask fool you.

No, God, no!

From the corner of her eye she saw the fist slam down at her. *Crack!* Her cheek seemed to implode with the force. Red lights flashed in front of her eyes. She went suddenly limp and her eyes rolled up in her head.

The pain began to recede.

Darkness plucked at her consciousness.

Barely aware of being lifted from the floor, she embraced the numbness. She heard a low sound and realized it was her own voice, moaning. He was carrying her now and she should be worried, frantic, but she couldn't get her body to move. Maybe he'd take her to the bedroom . . . or somewhere else?

Open your eyes, Beth. Somewhere deep in her brain she knew she should fight, but she just . . . couldn't.

Vaguely she heard the sounds of the city, smelled fresh air, and she was outside as he hoisted her up . . . Dear God. She blinked at the rush of adrenaline and she saw the brick exterior of her apartment building, the darkened windows and—

He let go.

Noooo!

Suddenly she was falling into the Portland night.

She was shivering all over. All this time . . . *all this time!* And here they were. Back to square one, or maybe reversed even further, in the negatives.

She turned her face toward the warm night breeze and looked up at the sky. The moon was waning, working its way back to a thin smile before total darkness again. Had it only been a few days since she'd met him at that hotel? It felt like a lifetime or two ago.

Her cell phone was in her hand. She dialed his number. It rang and rang and then went to voice mail. She immediately called him back. She didn't care where he was, what he was doing or whom he was with, he'd better damn well take her call this time.

On her fourth try he picked up. "Hello, you horny bitch," he greeted her. She could hear the grin in his voice and imagined him leering like a jack-o'-lantern. "Come on over and let me take care of that itch for you."

"They're getting too close. Do you hear me? They're getting too close."

"You worry too much."

"You don't worry enough! What are you doing? Trying to get caught? You're not taking me with you!" She really hated him. The only part she liked was his cock. Sometimes that was all she thought about, his hard dick and what it could do for her. He knew her weakness and used it to his advantage. It killed her to admit it, but even now there was a part of herself that wanted to do exactly as he suggested, run over to his place and squiggle down on his cock, sliding it in and out until she was wet and soppy and climaxing in a wild scream.

But right now that would be suicide.

"We have to be extremely careful."

"Well, we don't have to worry about Bethany Van Horne anymore."

"What do you mean?" she asked sharply.

"She took a little leap, like that other redheaded whore."

"What? What?" She thought she might faint. Then, "Other? Bethany's not a redhead."

"She kinda got that way, didn't she? Trying to impress Liam."

Her hand was slick with sweat on her phone. Nerves. "Did you have sex with her?"

"No."

"You're lying. Again. Oh, God. You can't leave redheads alone, and you're going to get us caught!"

He laughed. "No worries. You keep reminding me that De-Grere didn't know about you, so you're safe."

"I don't trust *you*," she snapped. "You'll give me up in seconds flat. I know you will."

"Oh, babe, I love you too much," he said with a sneer.

"Fuck you."

"Come on over and make that a reality."

She wanted to. How she wanted to. She could feel every cell in her body turn toward the phone, like a plant to the sun, pulled by an inexorable force. But she had to tamp down that desire. Squash it. She was in self-preservation mode now, and she couldn't be derailed.

"It's over. You understand? It's over!"

"I told you, I didn't touch her."

"Lies. You sure *touched* Teri Mulvaney. And then you pushed her off the building so she would never be able to tell! And now *Beth*! The Van Hornes will throw all their money at this. You stupid, stupid man!"

"Mountains again."

"*What?*" she practically screeched.

"You're making mountains out of molehills."

"You call what you did a *molehill*. You have to do something, or we're both going to be found out. You left your DNA in her, didn't you? They're going to find you!"

"I leave it in you, too, sweetheart."

"That doesn't matter, unless you're planning to kill me, too."

"Now, there's an idea," he drawled.

His insouciance nearly drove her mad. Why did she put up with him? Why did she care?

"We need a plan," she said, calming herself down with an effort. "We've been afraid something was going to happen, and now it has. Not the way we wanted, but people are putting answers together! You're going to be found out. I can feel it. But I'm not going down with you. You need to do something!"

Finally it felt like he was listening to her. She could hear him breathing on the other end of the line. He could be so charming, urbane, smart. But it felt like that persona was dying, buried under an avalanche of mediocrity.

If it wasn't for his cock she would have bailed years earlier.

"I'll take care of it," he said.

"How? Don't you dare get caught! I won't go down for this. I won't."

"You won't," he agreed, finally sounding full of the steel resolve that had drawn her to him in the first place. "I won't, either. But I'll make sure someone else does." A smile entered his
voice. "I'm licking the phone and thinking of you." She could
hear the *scritch* of his tongue on the cell. "My tongue is inside
you and you're hot and wet . . ."

She clicked off, furious. Nope. She wasn't going to let him
get to her. Not now, when the stakes were so high. Oh, Lord,
Bethany.

Drawing a breath, she threw a last glance at the fading moon
and set her jaw. She'd known it from the beginning. She was
going to have to kill him.

Chapter 24

Rory awakened to morning sunshine streaming through Liam's bedroom window and the faint intermittent buzz of a number of texts showing up in her phone. She checked her cell and saw the messages were from Charlotte, clearly with Darlene's help:

Good morning Mommy!!!! the first one read, along with a string of emojis.

The second was, **I love YOU!!!!**, more emojis.

And the third was simply: **Come home soon**

She checked the time and saw it was almost eight, then looked over at Liam, who was still sound asleep. No wonder. Tired as she was, they'd made love twice before she'd fallen asleep, and then once more right before dawn, where she'd initiated it by running her fingers along his jawline, reveling in the stubble, waking him up. In the glow of city lights through his window, his lazy smile had brought one to her lips as well. After that, they'd come together with kisses and touches and slow-building desire.

But now they had to go.

Duty and reality called.

"Wake up," she whispered in his ear.

One of his eyes opened and then, as the second lid raised and he focused on her, he grinned. Over a yawn he asked, "What time is it?" and stretched, dragging the covers from her.

"Eight. Well, actually eight-oh-seven if you want to be precise."

"Are you always this sassy in the morning?"

"Precise. I'm just precise."

"Yeah, right." Another yawn. "I turned my phone off." He rubbed a hand over his face, waking. "Didn't think I'd sleep this late." He glanced at her again, as if finally realizing that they were together in his bed after a night of lovemaking. He grinned wickedly, then reached out and caught one of her curls, smoothing it between his finger and thumb. "Good morning," he said.

"Good morning to you." Then seeing a glint of desire in his eyes, she eased off the bed and headed to the shower. She really didn't have time for anything . . . but she glanced over her shoulder, caught him watching her naked backside, and couldn't help herself. She gave a quick lift of her brows and it was all the encouragement he needed. He bounded out of bed to join her.

Half an hour later, shaved, showered, and dressed, Liam joined her in the bedroom, where she was searching through her suitcase, pushing clothes aside. "I'm sure I packed my makeup. I wouldn't have left it."

"You don't need it."

"I think I should maybe try to cover the bruises."

"You're beautiful the way you are."

"And you're full of it. I could scare someone with the way I look. Aha! There you are." She set the makeup kit aside and, rocking back on her heels, eyed his extra closet where'd he kept her clothes. "You got room? For . . . y'know, a few more of my things?"

Sitting on the end of the bed, tying on a shoe, he nodded. "Yeah. Sure. Do it."

She grinned at him, walked to the closet, reached in and moved a couple of pairs of jeans to one side, then stopped to pull out the letter-size manila envelope she'd seen the first time she'd rifled through her own clothes. "What's this? I noticed it the other day."

Liam drew a sharp breath, finished tying his shoes and said, "Wedding pictures."

"You mean, from the day—" She dropped them onto the floor as if they burned her.

"Yeah. The photographer captured the moments right before the shooting while we were all waiting for you . . . and a few afterward, I think, before he knew what was happening. I gave copies to the police, but those are mine . . . ours."

Her eyes rounded. "Do they show . . . Aaron?"

"I haven't looked at them in years, but yeah. Afraid so. I think there's one or two of him. On the ground. Already hit. My father falling. The photographer quit taking pictures almost immediately, so they're not . . . visually horrific. They're just . . . knowing how it all turned out, they're hard to look at."

"Okay." She couldn't take her eyes off the envelope, now that she knew what was inside.

"Here," he said, walking over to her. He picked up the envelope and slid the photos out onto the top of the dresser, glossy photographs catching that fateful moment in time. Rory stood rooted to the spot, forcing herself, though her body wanted to recoil. Carefully, she reached a hand out and moved aside the top picture: one of Liam, Derek, and the minister waiting at the end of the petal-strewn aisle. The photographer was at the opposite end of the aisle from the would-be altar, and the next photo encompassed all of the crowd. Vivian in her yellow dress and hat. His father moving down his row toward the aisle. Then Geoff in the aisle, talking to Liam. The next was of Aaron's back, and another shot of him, but farther away as he'd traveled down the aisle.

Rory paused, her stomach tight. In the next photograph, Aaron had dropped to the petal-strewn ground and Geoff was standing with a surprised look on his face, his mouth an O. The next two pictures caught the father of the groom falling while the crowd looked around frantically, heads turned in different directions.

"My God," Rory whispered. She took several steps backward and sank onto the end of the bed, collapsing as if her bones had melted.

"I know."

Tears filled her eyes, but the images remained burned into her brain. She couldn't speak for a second, but then felt some relief, that finally she'd been able to glimpse those frantic, mad moments that had changed the course of their lives forever. "I'm glad I saw them," she said, as he quickly scooped them up and put them back in the envelope.

"Yeah?"

She nodded and swiped at her tears. "I needed to see. I just . . . I don't get why it happened."

"Pete DeGrere did it for money."

"But whose money?"

Liam shook his head. "The police have been working on that for years. They checked all our bank accounts, but nothing. No big withdrawals."

"They checked my mother's, too."

He swept up his phone from the nightstand. "So, unless someone took out smaller bills over a long time, it wasn't anyone we're related to."

So there they were, back to the beginning again with all the same unanswered questions. "Who then? Cal? It just doesn't—"

"Holy Mother of God," Liam whispered, cutting her off as he stared at his phone's screen.

"What?" Rory's head snapped up. She was on her feet in an instant, trying to see what had caused the cords on the back of his neck to appear and his color to drain. "Liam?"

Scrolling through his texts, he let out his breath. As he turned on the ringer, his cell rang in his hand. Clicking on, he said in a shaking voice, "Derek? God, what the hell happened?"

Though Liam was holding his phone to his ear, she heard the rumbling, excited tone of his brother's voice, though she couldn't make out what he was saying. "Slow down," Liam said, his voice a harsh whisper, his jaw set as he pressed "speaker" and then:

". . . trying to get hold of you! Police are going to be at your door! Van Horne's on the news, blaming you! Says you killed her!"

"What?" Rory whispered, clasping her hand over her chest. "Who?" Then she knew. "Bethany?"

Liam was struggling to process. "When—did this—"

"Middle of the night. Threw herself off her balcony. Just like our jumper!"

Liam was shaking his head in denial, staring at the phone as if he didn't believe the words his brother was speaking. "But that Teri Mulvaney, her death was a homicide. You heard Mickelson. Forensics said—"

"Hell, Liam, who knows? They could be wrong! Or not. I don't know. None of us even knew the woman at the construction site. But Beth is different. We all know—er, knew—her."

"Amen to that," Liam said.

"Look, you and I both know that Beth was distraught over Rory showing up again. And about you breaking up with her. Man, she thought she was going to marry you."

Rory cringed at the words, the thought that Bethany had actually been so morose as to take her own life.

"She wasn't suicidal." Liam was pacing the length of the bedroom, the cell phone held in front of him.

"I don't know that. *You* don't know that. Maybe she did do it. Her father thinks so."

"He thinks she committed suicide? I thought you said—"

"He blames you for breaking it off with her! Says that's the reason she killed herself!"

"Oh, God. My God." Rory's knees would barely hold her. She sank onto the bed again and cursed herself for ever running from the wedding or returning. Whatever she did turned out badly and someone died. But Beth?

"She was angry when I last saw her. Not distraught . . . Beth's not like that. She's—"

Bang, bang, bang.

Rory jumped at the sound of a fist hitting the door of the penthouse. "The police," she said aloud.

"That your door?" Derek asked.

"Yeah." Liam was already out of the bedroom and Rory was on his heels. Derek said, "Get that. Whoever it is. Call me back. Jesus Christ . . ."

Liam clicked the off button and headed for the front door. He could scarcely think. He peered through the peephole, then said to Rory, "Brace yourself. Derek was right." He opened the door and Detectives Grant and Susskind filled the outer hallway. Homicide detectives.

"I just heard about Beth," he said. His voice sounded strange, even to his own ears. "Derek called. My brother said it was suicide."

His phone rang in his hand again. He recognized Mick Mickelson's number.

"We'd like to talk to you about Ms. Van Horne's death. Can we come inside?" Grant asked. There was no trace of comraderie in his manner any longer.

Liam shook the cobwebs from his mind. "Sure, yes, but . . ." He looked back at Rory. "I need to run an errand. Take my wife back to relieve the babysitter and take care of our daughter. Can I meet you at the station in . . . about an hour?"

Grant nodded and Susskind said, "Since you already know that Ms. Van Horne is deceased, can you tell me where you were last night?"

"Here. First at my parents' house with all of my family, and then Rory and I came back here."

Susskind's eyes slid to Rory. "We came right here after the meeting."

"And what time was that?"

"I don't know, but it was dark. After nine," Liam said. "Look, just give me a little time and I'll come to the department."

"Fine," Grant said. "An hour." Liam wondered if the two men were going to tail him, if they seriously thought he would have had anything to do with Beth's death.

Grabbing his keys off a nearby table, Liam couldn't help but ask, "You're with the homicide department. I thought it was . . . my brother said it was suicide."

Susskind answered, "We'll go over it all at the station."

"Okay."

Liam shut the door behind the detectives as they left, and stood in shock for a moment. Rory was holding herself up by one hand on the edge of the kitchen counter. "What's going on?" she asked. She looked as if she might crumple. "Beth? Oh, God, why Beth?"

"I don't know." He crossed the area between the hallway and kitchen and wrapped his arms around her. "But we'll get through this."

"Are you sure? I mean suicide? Because of you and me? Or else she might have been murdered? You're right. They were homicide detectives."

"Shh. It'll be okay," he said, knowing he was lying. "Maybe this is all wrong. Maybe it was just a horrible, unfortunate accident."

"You don't believe that," she said, her breath hot through his shirt.

She was right; he didn't believe it for a second.

"Call him again," Shanice said. They'd taken separate rooms at a local Holiday Inn and were sharing coffee and croissants at another food cart. Mick had been on the phone with Zach Pitman about Bethany Van Horne's gruesome death, which was all over the news. He'd gotten as many details as his friend could supply. Now he was trying to reach Liam Bastian.

"He's not picking up." He finished his coffee and crumpled the cup in a fist. "Bet Homicide's with him."

"Zach said it was definitely a homicide."

"Zach said nobody knew jack shit yet, but Van Horne's father is a man possessed. He blames Liam Bastian, alternately wants the police to arrest him, and then wants to talk to him himself. He's at St. Vincent's. Heart palpitations."

"Call Bastian again," she repeated, tossing her empty coffee cup into a nearby receptacle.

Mick did as she suggested, and once again got Liam Bastian's voice mail. "I'm not leaving another message."

"What do you think about her death?" This was also a question Shanice had voiced several times.

"What I don't think it is, is suicide. Pitman said Van Horne was upset about her breakup with Bastian, but he didn't see any signs that she was going to do anything drastic. Neither did her mother, who is at the hospital with Mr. Van Horne, barely holding it together herself. Bethany was their only child."

Shanice shook her head. "So, if it's homicide, who did it?"

"Well, let's figure that out. First, I want to go down to the station and make a pest of myself. Get Homicide to listen to me. You with me?"

"Mick, being a pain in the ass is what I live for."

"We might get thrown out."

She offered up a thin smile, showing a bit of even white teeth. "Gotta be more than that to scare me."

At the Bastian estate, Charlotte rushed out to meet their car and her unbridled joy brought tears to Rory's eyes again. She brushed them away and put on a bright smile—well, it was a weak smile but she gave it her all. Darlene, in flowing pants and an orange peasant blouse was right behind her granddaughter, making sure of her safety.

"Hey, bug," Rory said, sweeping the little girl into her arms, squeezing her and laying a big kiss on her cheek.

Charlotte wriggled in her mom's arms. "We have breckfuss. Come on!" She wanted down immediately, so Rory put her back on the ground and Liam walked up to her. "Hey, Char," he said, half kneeling to look the little girl in her face.

"My name's not Char!" She glared at him as if he'd grown horns.

"Not into shortening her name," Rory explained.

"Charlotte it is," Liam said, and the little girl narrowed her eyes at him, taking stock because he'd been with her mother.

"We have breckfuss!" she announced, then shot back toward the house, past an older car with a missing bumper. Candace's, Rory surmised as Darlene hurried after the disappearing child.

"She's precocious," Rory explained.

"Don't know where she gets that," he said, trying to lighten the mood when they both were preoccupied with Beth's death. Standing on tiptoe, she kissed him on his cheek. "Hang in there."

"You, too. I'll see you later. I don't know how long it'll take, but I'll be in touch."

"Looks like I'm getting breckfuss and you're not."

He managed a faint smile. "I'll find something."

He kissed her on the lips, a long one, then slid into the open door of his Tahoe, closed his door and took off. Trying not to dwell on Beth's death or the pictures she'd seen of Aaron's murder on the day of her wedding, Rory followed Charlotte and Darlene inside. At the kitchen door, Darlene suddenly hesitated.

"Grandma? Grandma!" Charlotte called.

"Be right there, honey," Darlene yelled back.

She grabbed Rory by the arm and pulled her into an alcove near the dining room, but Rory said, "I know about Beth, Mom. Derek called Liam."

"It's been terrible. Stella and Vivian, and Geoff, too. We're all stunned. Can't believe it."

Rory heard Candace's voice from the kitchen and asked, "When did Candace get here?"

"Almost from the moment we heard. Vivian left in a panic to see Javier. She uses every opportunity to throw herself at him, apparently, though she can never take those children with her anywhere." She heard herself and pressed a hand to her mouth. "That was mean. I think I must be channeling Stella. She's in a state, too."

"Where is she?"

"In her rooms. She's actually going to see her doctor, who seems to have open office hours when it comes to the Bastians. But, oh, maybe that's for the best," she said, checking over her shoulder, peering through the open door to the kitchen but finding no prying eyes. In a lowered voice she said, "I think she needs some medication. Something to calm her down. She and Geoff, they just don't seem to ever communicate or get along."

This, from the wife of Harold Stemple, Rory thought ungraciously.

"And right now . . . Geoff's in his den, at least I think he's still there. He went into his study early and hasn't come out." She drew a shaky breath. "My Lord, the tragedies that surround this family! Rory, there's an aura here that I haven't felt before. And it's not good. Not good."

"It's called grief, Mom."

"No, it's something more. Seriously, Rory, I'm worried. I think we should take Charlotte and leave as soon as possible."

"Leave this house?"

"Yes!" Darlene looked over her shoulder again.

"Well, I'm with you there. I don't really want to stay here. You were the one that wanted me to reconnect with Liam."

"Was that a bad idea?" she challenged.

"No. It was a good idea, actually," Rory said. "It's just, I'd like to be out from under their . . ."

"Thumbs?"

"Watchful eyes."

"Then let's make plans. I really think we need to leave today. Soon. I'm just feeling . . . uncomfortable."

"Liam's heading to the police station now to go over Bethany's death. I don't think they suspect he's involved, but he's as eager to talk to them as they are to him. When he gets back, we'll go. Maybe to his place, I don't know . . ."

"Well, he's not going to want me there." Her face pulled into a puckering pout, but only for a second. "No, no, that's fine. Fine. I'll go back to my house in Salem. It will be better there. Away from all this—" She waved a hand to encompass the entire house. "But I really think you and Charlotte should come with me."

"Grandma! Mommmmiiiiieee!"

"Just a minute, bug!" Rory hollered. To Darlene, she whispered, "I'm with Liam again. He's my husband and I think, I mean I hope, we can work things out." Neither one of them had really broached the subject of getting back together, but they were working toward it, both of them. She looked into Darlene's worried eyes. "It's what you wanted. Me and Liam together. And so far, it's wonderful. So, I'm not leaving him, if that's what you're getting at."

"No, no! But. Maybe. Just temporarily. You need to get away from—" She hesitated, and then said, "Well, you know. Them." Meaning the Bastians. All of them. Except, of course, Liam.

"We are on the same page, Mom."

"Mommmmmmmm . . . !"

"I gotta answer the call." She bypassed Darlene and headed for the kitchen, glancing back once to see her mother frowning down at her phone. *Probably a tarot card app*, Rory thought, before her mind went to a mental picture of Beth's body crashed and bloody upon a Portland city street.

Her stomach lurched and she forcefully pushed the image aside. She didn't want to think about Beth, or the other woman who'd swan-dived to her death from one of the Bastian-Flavel construction sites. *No, not a dive. She was pushed. Homicide. Remember?*

Rory shivered and turned back to the kitchen. Aura or no aura, her mother was right. It was time to leave.

Liam was a little surprised to find Mick Mickelson and Shanice Clayburgh waiting inside the station when he arrived. A dark-haired, fiftyish, uniformed officer was with them, and he introduced himself as Zach Pitman.

"Zach and I've known each other awhile," Mick said.

"You're meeting with Detectives Grant and Susskind about Ms. Van Horne's death?" Shanice asked.

Liam nodded curtly. The thought of Beth's tragic demise soured his stomach. "They want to go over it, and so do I."

Mickelson said, "I don't think they'd appreciate us in the meeting, but I'd like to talk to them, too. Zach's letting them know, and if you have no objection . . . ?"

And then it hit him. The reason Mickelson was here. His personal great white whale: the person behind the carnage at his wedding. "So. Wait a sec. You think Bethany's death is connected to what happened five years ago? In Seattle?" Liam asked him. He was just surfacing enough to start wondering himself. He didn't believe Beth's death was suicide, it wasn't in her psyche, or so he thought, and apparently the police were on the same wavelength.

"Maybe. Maybe not." Mickelson was grim. "But it's a lot of crimes and tragedies around your family. I left you a voice mail. I'd just like to compare notes."

"Fine with me," Liam said. He didn't care whom he spoke with, just as long as there was some conclusion to the mystery surrounding the attack at his wedding, and if Bethany was really murdered, that sick son of a bitch brought to justice. He put his cards on the table. "Sure. Let's talk. I just want answers. I want to know who hired Pete DeGrere, and who killed Teri Mulvaney and Bethany. That's what I want." His throat closed for a moment.

Zach said, "I've talked to Susskind. He's usually more amenable to talking to retired cops. He said they want to speak to Mr. Bastian alone, first."

"I understand," Mickelson said.

But Shanice piped up as Liam was being led through a door to the inner offices by a uniformed cop. "If they start pushing you, call for us."

Long-sufferingly, Mick said, "Shanice." The old cop versus the young private investigator.

Here we go, Liam thought, walking into the same airless interrogation room he'd been in earlier.

Susskind and Grant were both seated at a table and Susskind asked Liam to take the remaining empty chair.

As soon as Liam was seated, Grant asked, "Can you tell us where you were between eleven p.m. and four a.m. last night?"

"We went over this before. At my house."

Susskind's smile was easy, affable. "Indulge us. This is for the record." Meaning they were filming the interview, and others were watching from behind the mirror running along one side of the room. They sure as hell didn't waste any time. And he was going to be nothing but cooperative. "I was sleeping at my place."

"Alone?"

They'd seen Rory there, but he answered them for the record. "No. My wife spent the night with me."

"Aurora Abernathy Bastian."

"Correct."

They ran him through the usual questions about the events of the evening before he'd gone to bed, what his relationship with the victim was, what had caused their breakup. Finally, it was Liam's turn to ask a question.

"You think it's homicide?"

Grant said, "The physical evidence suggests she invited someone in. One of her shoes was just inside the door, the other was near her foot after she fell. There may have been a struggle, some reason the shoe was removed."

Susskind added, "A neighbor heard a scream that sounded like, 'Stop.'"

Liam's empty stomach felt like it flipped over.

"She'd been drinking wine," Grant went on. "Alone. She was in the process of opening a new bottle, when she stopped. We think she may have heard whoever was at the door. It looks like she opened the door to whoever was on the other side."

Liam had a sudden memory of going to her house at night. She'd called to him, saying his name, and when he'd answered, "Yes," she'd opened the door. "Almost didn't sound like you," she'd said, laughing, because she'd already been into the wine.

"We understand from David Van Horne that you and she had both hired a private investigator to find your wife."

"Yes." Liam's throat was dry.

"But that you were unaware that Ms. Van Horne had hired him as well."

"That's right." He'd been furious at the time, but now . . . Jesus.

Susskind put in, "We've asked Mr. Jacoby to come in today as well. Your wife intimated that she felt someone was always following her while she was out of the country or in Point Roberts, Washington, and she identified this man as Mr. Brian Jacoby."

"Yes. Though she thought it was someone else for a long time—her stepbrother, Everett Stemple."

"You agree that Mr. Jacoby was following her, per your agreement with him?" Grant asked.

Liam nodded.

"You've given us a lot of background on your relationship with your wife, and you and your wife both believe that Mr. Pete DeGrere was the man who opened fire on your wedding ceremony five years ago," Grant said.

"Isn't that what you or the Seattle cops think?"

A pause.

The detectives eyed each other, then Susskind nodded. "We're trying to get to the bottom of this by any means necessary. Mr. Mickelson and Ms. Clayburgh have asked if they could be part of this exchange of information," Susskind said.

"I told them that would be fine with me," Liam said. "Mickelson's never let go of the wedding shooting."

"Bring them in," Grant told Susskind, who left the room and returned a few moments later with Mickelson and Shanice. Mickelson had a file tucked under his arm.

"What is that?" Grant asked him.

"My notes. On the wedding shooting. I've been in contact with the Seattle Police Department, where I was employed at the time of the shooting."

"Personal copies?" Grant asked.

"I've cleared this with Seattle PD." Mickelson didn't back down.

"He did," Grant said.

With a faint curving of his lips, as if it was almost possible for his mouth to fully engage in a smile, Susskind said, "You've never let this one go."

"No, I haven't," Mickelson said honestly.

"All right, what have you got?" Grant asked. "And tell me how it ties into the death of two Portland women."

"Anybody want coffee and doughnuts before we start?" Susskind wondered, looking around the table.

Liam nodded, checking his watch. He wanted to get this over with as fast as possible and get back to Rory and Charlotte.

Rory packed up Charlotte and her meager belongings, thinking everything they owned wouldn't take up that much space at Liam's place. Could they move in with him? Should they? Especially now, with Bethany's death. Just thinking about it made goose bumps pop out on her flesh.

She headed out to the car with her bags, put them inside, then sat down behind the steering wheel, her mind splintered with thoughts of life and death, weddings and funerals, her life and how it changed. Looking at the stately house, she felt cold inside and couldn't wait to leave. Maybe Darlene had infected her, but she definitely had the heebie-jeebies. She suddenly wanted to be at the police station with Liam, hearing everything he was hearing, being beside him. Maybe she would tell Darlene to take Charlotte now and head to Salem.

Was that crazy paranoid? Yes.

Was it part of her own MO she couldn't seem to shake? Also, yes.

Darlene suddenly opened the front door and stepped into the morning sunshine. "Where are you going?" she called as bees buzzed near a row of lavender near the front gates.

Rory rolled down her window to release some of the heat.

Felt like it was going to be a scorcher today. "Nowhere yet. I'd like to meet Liam at the police station. I just feel I should be with him. I've got all our stuff in the car, so we leave later today."

"Good."

"Or, maybe now."

As they were talking, Derek's green truck rumbled into the drive. He pulled up and got out, looking grim and tired as he slammed the Ford F1's door. He hadn't bothered to shave and he was dressed in jeans and a work shirt, as if making a quick detour on his way to one of Bastian's construction sites.

"You're working today?" Rory asked him.

"Wasn't going to. But with the news . . ." He shook his head and made a face. "Can't just sit around and think about it."

"I know. I feel exactly the same way. I'm heading out right now." She looked over at her mother, silently asking if they were on the same page with that.

Darlene nodded, waved her away, and headed for the house. "I'll get us both ready while you're gone," she called over her shoulder. "Don't be long."

"Ready for what?" Derek asked without much interest. He, too, was starting to saunter to the house.

"We're leaving, Mom, Charlotte, and I."

He stopped short. "Leaving? Does Liam know?"

"I think we've overstayed our welcome here. I'm on my way to the police station to tell Liam now. Darlene's taking Charlotte to her home in Salem, and I don't know until I talk to Liam exactly what my plans are."

"I get it," he said and raked a hand through his hair just as she switched on the ignition. The starter ground, then caught for a second, only to die. "Oh, no, not now," she said, and tried again. A grinding sound, another attempt at ignition, but the little car choked and coughed. "Damn it." Counting to ten, more for herself than the car, she gave it another go, but this time there was just a sickening ticking noise.

The little Honda wasn't going anywhere.

She slapped the steering wheel, then decided she'd have to rely on Darlene. Oh, great. "For God's sake," she muttered.

Derek came back and stood outside her window. "Didn't you get this thing fixed?"

"I thought so. But . . . maybe not."

She tried again and swore inside her head. She felt hot, tired, and sick over what had happened to Beth.

"Come on, I'll give you a ride to the station." He waved for her to get out of the car and follow him to his truck. "If I'd known, I woulda brought the Corvette."

Rory wanted to bang her fist on the car's hood. It always failed her at the worst times.

Stuffing her phone into her back pocket, she grabbed her purse, got out of the car, mentally cursing its undependability, then slid into the passenger seat of his truck, which was pushed so far forward that her knees nearly banged into the glove box.

"Sorry," Derek said, putting an arm over the back of the vehicle, preparing to back up.

"I've got it." She pushed the seat back and reached for the seat belt that was tangled beneath it. "Come on," she said, jerking on the belt.

"Sorry. It's a little jacked. But it should work."

She yanked again and the seat belt snapped back as if whatever had wedged it had released. She started to strap in when she noticed a red plastic cap that rolled from beneath the seat. No wonder the belt was jacked. The pickup was a mess. Not only was the cap littering the floor, but she also found a crumpled coffee cup and an empty beer can.

"I didn't drink it while I was driving," Derek said.

"I didn't say you did."

They smiled at each other. Derek's gaze touched on the left side of her face and she asked, "Are my bruises still bad? Geez. I tried to cover them up."

"Nah, they're fine."

He pulled out onto the road and started heading down into the city. They drove for several minutes and Rory's gaze landed on the red plastic cap. It looked like it belonged on a can of window cleaner, or a spray can of paint.

Derek saw her looking at it and, as if of their own volition, his eyes moved from the cap to the crumpled coffee cup. As if in a dream Rory bent down and picked up the paper cup, unfolding it.

Her heart nearly stopped as she read the label.

THE POINT BOB BUZZ stood out in its all too familiar script.

"Well, well," Derek drawled. "Would you look at that."

Chapter 25

"We're going to have to make a detour, I'm afraid," Derek said as Rory's heart pounded.

Derek had been to the Buzz? He'd been the one who had been following her. Oh, holy . . .

"Excuse me." He reached across Rory, popped open the glove box, pulled out a handgun, set it gingerly in the side pocket beside him as he drove with one hand down the twisting roads of the West Hills. "It's loaded. Yes, I know it's unsafe, but I'm pretty careful . . . usually."

Rory stared at him. The crumpled cup was still in her hands. The red cap was by her feet. Her mind was racing. So many thoughts. So many connections. She couldn't *think*! "You're the saboteur," was what came out of her mouth, sounding as poleaxed as she felt.

"Yes."

"Why? Why are you doing this?"

Run, Rory. Get out! Jump out of the truck before it picks up any more speed. This isn't right.

He shrugged. Hit the gas. The truck sped around a corner and Rory's seat belt snapped to attention. Held her in place. There was something about him not only vile, but also careless and wild and oh, so dangerous.

"What do you think's going to happen?" she asked.

"Dunno, really. I thought my life was going to be one way, and then it wasn't, and now it's something else."

"But . . . that sabotage . . . Liam told me what awful things you wrote . . . against your family."

"My family?" He made a deprecating noise as he took another corner. A Volkswagen van had to veer to the side of the road as Derek swung into the oncoming lane. The driver laid on his horn then flipped Derek off.

"Fuck you, too," Derek yelled, as if the guy could hear him. Then, back to Rory. "I'm not a part of that family. You know that. You know what it's like not to be part of a family. You're not a Stemple."

"Of course not."

"Well, there you go. I never wanted to be a Bastian. You know how my father is. Dear old Dad. He divorced my mother for Stella. And you know what? My mom? She was more than happy to leave him and me. Get that. She left me with that miserable dickwad, left me in his care. And he cared for me, all right," he said bitterly.

Rory felt herself go cold. She glanced out the window. They were traveling fast, but these were city streets. There was bound to be a stoplight, a traffic jam, a blockade of road construction. He wouldn't shoot her. He wasn't a killer, he was just a deeply angry man.

Except Teri Mulvaney was there during some of the sabotage.

No. No, no, no. "How did Teri Mulvaney die?" she whispered.

"What? You think I killed her?" he asked in horror.

Rory stared at him, her heart pounding so hard it hurt her chest. There was a little smile on his lips and they twitched a bit, proving that his horror was fake. His eyes darkened evilly.

"I didn't know her last name until after she was dead and everyone was talking about her. I only knew her as Teri."

"You did kill her." She could barely get the words out. She reached for the door handle, but if she opened it now, at the speed they were going, she would be thrown out, down the hillside, surely breaking her neck. *Think, Rory, think. Find a way to escape. You can . . . just try.* "Why did you do it?"

"I just wanted to," he said easily. "She was too easy. Wanted to have sex with me, no matter what I did. I took her to the top of Hallifax and showed her how to break out windows with a hammer. Then I swung it at her head and threw her over. I don't know if the police even know I bludgeoned her first. I like that word, bludgeoned. You can *feel* it, y'know?"

"You're lying!" she blurted out, hoping against hope. "You're not this unfeeling. This cruel. Derek, my God. This isn't real!" This madman, this homicidal maniac, if he was to be believed, was her brother-in-law, a man she'd known nearly as long as she'd known Liam.

He shot her an affectionate look. "Want to know why I picked her out? Little Teri who was panting for me?"

His eyes seemed to caress her and she thought she might be sick. What had she heard, that the dead woman had resembled Rory? Her skin crawled. No . . . it had nothing to do with her. Surely not. "No," she whispered aloud and felt the crumpled cup in her hand. She was crushing it so hard it dug into her flesh. "You were there," she realized, her brain engaging again. "You followed me to Point Roberts. You were the one stalking me. It was you!"

"Nah. Jacoby was following you. You were right on that.

What a joke that Beth hired him first, then didn't tell Liam what she'd done. Thought I would die when I heard. Had to pretend for my bro that I was as surprised as he was. Hah!"

She opened her hand. The crushed cup opened like a flower. "But you were there . . ."

"Just once. Okay? Yeah, guilty as charged. But only to see if you really were there. Everyone was so upset about you. I gotta admit, I wondered where you'd gone to. Didn't know about Cal."

They were slowing for a light and Rory gathered herself. She could get out of the truck. She could run. They weren't anywhere near the route to the police station. He was taking her somewhere else.

"Don't do anything," Derek warned. He'd slipped the gun into his left hand and was pointing it at her, across his body. "I really don't want to use this, but I will if you try to get away."

"They'll catch you . . . see you . . . if you fire it . . . they'll get you!" Fear was making her nearly incoherent.

"If that happens I'll kill myself, too," he said matter-of-factly. "But you really should think about that. For your daughter. You don't want to leave her."

Charlotte. Her perfect baby. Who depended on her. "Don't bring her into this."

"Just reminding you that you're a mother."

"I *know* that." The gun. If she could somehow get the gun and turn it on him. Could she? Would she have the nerve to shoot him? *Think of Charlotte.* "What are you going to do?" she asked, a catch in her throat. She stared at the gun, its barrel like a dark, soulless eye staring at her.

"You mean right now? Good question."

They passed through the light. Rory was frozen. She believed him now. Believed he meant to do exactly what he said.

"You kind of caught me unawares, so I'm winging it. Not how I thought this would end between us."

Between us . . . was there meaning there?

As if he read her mind, he said, "Go on. Ask me." He wiggled the gun and every muscle in her body contracted as more cars surrounded them and he actually managed to merge onto the freeway.

Rory's thoughts were moving at warp speed. She had to get away. Had to. She could barely follow the conversation. "Ask you what?"

"Why I chose Teri."

"Didn't you say because she was easy?"

"No, that's why I *killed* her. That's not why I *picked* her." He was irritated now, driving faster again.

"Okay. Yeah. Why . . . why did you choose Teri?"

Another indulgent look her way, his gaze cresting to the top of her crown. "Because she had red hair . . ."

"We have video from a camera down the street from the Hallifax building the night Teri Mulvaney was killed," Detective Grant was saying. "Here are stills from that video. You can see that we captured a number of vehicles that were parked in the area." He laid the black-and-white photos in front of Liam. "We checked out the ones we had full license numbers for. Nearby residents. A couple we don't have the full plate. This one . . ." He pointed to the tail end of a dark sports car with no license plate on the back. A Corvette.

Liam felt himself go cold inside. A Corvette? Like the one Derek drove? Still . . . it was nothing. Just a coincidence.

Mick Mickelson said, "Do you mind if I take a look at those?"

Grant looked at him askance and he explained, "Seattle PD's got pictures of vehicles around the Nile the day DeGrere was murdered. I just want to compare."

Shanice said, "Want me to call? And see if they'll release them? If not, maybe we can upload these pictures to them."

"There's no connection between Teri Mulvaney and Pete DeGrere," Liam heard himself say. He felt like he was in a vacuum. His voice sounded tinny and far away as if it belonged to someone else.

Mickelson turned to regard him soberly. "I just want to gather all material related to your family in one place. See what crops up."

Your family has secrets . . . And I know about them.

Beth . . . Beth had thrown those words in his face.

And they know I know about them . . .

The detectives were talking all around him, buzzing, a hive of voices.

It's not Derek, he told himself. *It's not. Can't be. There are lots of Corvettes. This city, this* state *is crawling with them, and when you add in Washington . . .*

One question kept scraping at his brain:

How long has he had that car?

"I liked Beth better when she became a redhead," he said as they turned off the freeway to a surface street that wound east, away from the city center.

Beth? What does Beth have to do with . . . Her heart clutched. Beth was dead, too. "What do you mean? About Beth?"

"You know, don't you?" he teased, then concentrated on the drive, as if he had the streetlights timed in his head. As luck would have it, he never had to stop for a red light. Not that she could have escaped anyway. The barrel of his pistol was too close.

Beth. Oh, God, did he kill her?

Through the dusty, bug-smeared windshield she looked for her chance of escape, prayed for it. But the opportunities were less as he drove expertly through a residential area that bled into suburbia and to a commercial section where there was more land between the buildings. Bigger lots. Older plots of land that had once been rural and were slowly becoming developed. She didn't know the area well, but knew she was on the east side of the Willamette, far from the heart of the city.

"Where are we going?" she demanded. "Liam's waiting for me."

"He'll just have to wait a little longer, won't he?" Derek said as he slowed for a turnoff and Rory reached again for the door handle.

"Uh-uh-uh," he said in a soft voice that was threaded with steel, as hard and cold as the barrel of the gun pointed on her. He drove down a winding drive to an older building surrounded by trees, a once-grand, multi-story home now in ruin, the roof collapsing, the siding rotting, decaying within a small copse of trees and brambles that separated it from other properties. Despite the heat of the summer and the fact that it was still morning, the day new, there was a darkness here, a sinister malevolence that seemed to emanate from the old house with its broken windows and teetering porch.

Who had lived here?

That thought was chased away quickly with another.

Who had died here?

She licked her lips. There had to be a way. Some way to get out of this. She stared at the house as if within its decrepit hallways she might find an answer. There were signs that someone had been here recently.

Graffiti in bright neon yellow and blood red had been scrawled across the mouldering walls, the same ugly phrases that had been sprayed on other buildings owned by the Bastians, though some of the vile words aimed at the Bastians had been painted over.

The graffiti had been painted by Derek. And aimed at his own family.

Why?

As if reading her mind, he said, "I blamed it all on your step-brother, you know. Everett was such an easy target, and so I managed to lay the blame at his feet for years, for everything." He chuckled. Satisfied and proud of himself. "But hell, it only works so long, right? Who would guess that he'd show up . . . a damned Bible thumper! And you looked so scared to meet him." He was amused by how it had all worked out. The man was sick.

Still, she attempted to reason with him, all the while trying to plot her escape. If she could just reach her phone, tucked into her pocket, and call 9-1-1 or Liam or . . . first she had to get away. "Derek, you have to let me go. You're right. I have a daughter. Your niece. I need to be with her."

"And Liam? You need to be with Liam, too?"

Oh, God, yes!

He drove around to the back of the dilapidated house, then suddenly stood on the brakes. This was her chance! She reached for the door handle, pulled it back, but the damned seat belt.

"Shit!" he growled at the sight of another car parked in the sparse, weed-choked gravel.

Rory's heart soared. Someone was here. He wouldn't shoot her in front of whoever—

Oh, Lord. She recognized the white Lexus, dappled by sunlight, its engine running, that filled the space in front of a listing garage.

"Damn," he said, then shook his head and began chuckling, slowly at first, then laughing hysterically, as Stella stepped out of the car.

"What? What's she doing here?"

"Exactly."

Stella was shading her eyes, squinting at them.

"Fuckin' A. We've been caught!"

* * *

You should tell them. Tell them about Derek's car.

How long has he had that car? Liam couldn't remember. The interrogation room suddenly seemed airless. Confining.

Shanice was looking at him hard, taking the decision from him when she asked, "What kind of vehicle does your brother drive?"

She saw it in the driveway. Was that just yesterday?

"He has a Ford truck . . . and . . ."

All of their attention was on him. He was under the microscope, but it was a mistake. A coincidence.

"He has a new Corvette," Liam admitted. "I'd never seen it before yesterday."

"Does it have a plate on the back?" Grant asked him.

"I don't know," Liam admitted.

"Did he know Teri Mulvaney?" the mustached detective then posed.

"No!" Liam said quickly, defensively, then said, "I-I don't know."

"Does he have a beef against your family?" That was from Mickelson.

He's thinking about the wedding shooting. That's his deal. He wants to pin the wedding shooting on my brother!

"Mr. Bastian?" Shanice's gaze was boring into him.

"It's his family, too," Liam said, but his mind caught on something that felt out of place. What was it? He thought, then twigged to it: the wedding photos that he'd stashed away but never been able to throw away. He'd just looked at them again with Rory this morning. Something about the wedding photos.

He looked at Mickelson. "I gave the police the pictures the photographer took at the wedding."

"I have copies," Mickelson admitted, pointing to the thick file he carried with him.

Liam felt as if he couldn't breathe, but he managed to ask, "Could I see them?"

The two Portland detectives looked at each other, but neither stopped Mickelson from pulling out the photos and handing them over to Liam. Once again, there was Vivian in her bright yellow dress. Once again there was his father, moving down his row, intending to take matters into his own hands, angry at the delay. And once again there he was himself, hit by bullets, starting to fall.

And Derek was way off to the right side. Moments before he'd been standing by Liam. Now he was nearly to the edge of the seats, as far from the aisle as he could probably be in those few seconds.

"What are you doing here, Mommie dearest?" Derek asked Stella as he swung out of his truck. He was still training the gun on Rory, keeping the driver's door of his truck open. "This is your stop," he told Rory. "The Flavel apartments. Aren't they nice?"

Why wasn't Stella doing something? Why the hell was she here? Did she have any idea? Surely she could see the gun in her stepson's hand, the way he was brandishing it.

When Rory didn't move, he waggled the gun at her and she stiffly released the seat belt and opened the passenger door. Thinking about fleeing somehow, some way, she climbed out of the car.

"What is going on?" she asked her mother-in-law.

Stella was utterly rigid. She stared in disbelief at Rory. "What . . . what are you doing here?" Then pointing to the pistol, "For the love of God, Derek, are you out of your mind?"

"Don't panic. Everything's under control," he said.

"What? Don't panic? Is that what you said? Seriously. And everything's under control? What planet do you live on?"

Rory took a step and Derek spun, aimed the gun straight at her face. "Don't fuckin' move. And if you scream, I'll drop you, like that!" He snapped his fingers and she froze. Believed him. There was nothing between her and the madman with the gun.

He was nuts. Certifiable. And he would kill her in an instant, she knew it. And Stella . . . what was her part in all of this? But there was no time for conjecture. Not now. She forced her eyes on Derek, on the damned gun, but in her peripheral vision she was taking stock of her surroundings. Trees . . . bushes . . . cover, if she could get there. But Stella . . . could she just leave her with Derek?

"What are you doing here?" Derek asked her again, then inched up his chin a bit. "Ahh, you were looking for me. I said I was going to be here, didn't I? Want a little quick one at the scene of my latest crime. That it?"

Latest crime? Did he kill someone else here? Rape them? What? Or was he talking about her?

"Oh, my God. You're crazy!" Stella cried.

Derek's smile was almost a rictus as he turned to Rory. "It's all gone to shit, you know. Too bad. But to be truthful, it wasn't a good plan to begin with. Not well thought out. I didn't see it, you know. About Pete. Thought I'd just wind him up about fucking rich people. Get him to shoot dear old Dad. Saved a lot of little dollars over the years, didn't we, lover?" This he threw at Stella, who had drained of all color.

She seemed about to faint, but caught herself. "You stupid, stupid, stupid boy . . ." She choked.

He laughed. "I wasn't much more than a boy when we started. Well, okay, you didn't make your move till I was of age. I'll give you that."

Stella moaned and covered her face with her hands.

Derek and Stella? Lovers?

Rory thought she'd be sick. Her stomach turned over and she had to fight the urge to wretch as she began to understand what had happened, how cruel the world had turned.

"Hate to break it to you, Aurora. But Mommie dearest never liked you."

Rory didn't respond. Didn't care how Stella had felt about her. Right now, she had to think. To ignore anything other than to find a way to escape. He was a killer. Derek Bastian was a killer. He'd hired Pete DeGrere. And murdered Teri Mulvaney . . . oh, dear God. How many others? Beth? Panic grabbed her by the throat.

She moved ever so slightly away from him, inching her way, feeling sweat collect on her scalp and run down her back. All the while she focused on the gun. The damned gun.

"She wanted to take you out, too, you know. At the wedding? But you wouldn't come down the aisle. And then De-Grere must've thought he had a good shot, and *bam*. Pulled the trigger and down goes Geoffrey Bastian. Stella wanted the money and to be rid of the bastard, and well, so did I. But she wanted you dead, too, and I guess Pete just thought, fuck it, might as well kill all the rich people I can."

"Derek!" Stella yelled.

Rory inched a little closer to the bushes. Oh, Lord, could she get away with it? A few more feet and she could spring to scramble away. And go where? Two of them, one with a gun, would hunt her down like a wounded fawn.

Derek added to Rory in an aside, "Old Petey. He wasn't the most stable, you know."

"You were supposed to take care of this!" Stella's fury increased to a fever pitch, but it only seemed to amuse Derek as he went on with his story.

"But dear old Dad *didn't die*, did he? And then, Mommie

dearest gets cold feet. Afraid we'll be found out if there's another attempt on his life."

"You shot Liam, too!" Stella shrieked, her eyes wild.

"Not me." He held up both his hands in a plea for amnesty. The pistol shifted a little. "Pete. I got nothing against my brother. Except maybe that he scored all the beautiful women." His gaze caressed Rory as it took her in.

"Enough with all this ancient history," Stella said, approaching her stepson finally. "What are we gonna do now? What's your latest and greatest brilliant idea?"

"Well, we'll have to get rid of her," Derek said reasonably as a hot wind scattered some dry leaves across the ground. "She figured out it was me, and I had to bring her here before she told Liam."

"She figured out it was you? What did you do! You're such a careless fool. You want to get caught!"

"I took care of Beth, didn't I?"

So it was confirmed—what Rory had suspected. She fought to keep her voice from quivering as she asked, "You killed Bethany?"

"She saw me with Stella. Caught us having a quick one in the back hallway of the house."

Stella shrieked and grabbed her hair. "You pushed me up against the wall and I didn't want it!"

"Oh, yes, you did. You were hot and wet as a sauna. You just didn't want to get caught."

"Now look what you've done!" She waved her arms at Rory as if she wanted to make her disappear.

"Fine! Let's take care of it." He leaped across the patchy dry grass separating himself from Rory and as she turned to run, he grabbed her, and holding her tight, jammed the barrel of the gun against her temple. "Want me to do it now?" he asked Stella silkily.

"What? God, no!" All of the starch left her and suddenly Liam's mother sank onto her knees in the dry weeds and gravel. "No . . . no . . ."

"Maybe after Rory and I have a little time together . . . ?" he added.

With the gun pressed hard to her head, Derek leaned in and licked her face.

Beth . . . Beth . . . Someone killed Beth.
Derek killed Beth . . .

Liam felt like he was living in a dream. A nightmare.

Dully, he remembered, *She called you . . . you didn't pick up.*

He pulled out his cell phone, stared at it, said to the room at large, "I think Beth left me a message."

He pressed the buttons to access voice mail. Mickelson's message was first, which he deleted. Then Beth's voice: "Your brother sexually attacked your mother. I saw them in the back hallway of your parents' house. I didn't say anything because both of them begged me not to, especially Stella. Your brother's sick, Liam. *Sick.* Maybe your whole family's sick! I'm glad to be out of it!"

Liam's stomach curled in a knot. All that he'd denied came crashing in on him as the truth was laid bare.

"We need to pick up Derek Bastian," Grant stated firmly.

"I've got to call Rory," Liam said, dazed.

Rory's phone rang in her pocket.

Derek immediately whipped the gun away and patted her down, digging into her pockets. "Which one?" he demanded. "Where is it?"

"My . . . back pocket . . ."

He was frantic. He knocked Rory off her feet in his attempts to get it, and by the time he'd ripped the phone from her jeans she was scrambling backward on her hands and feet. Fast. Toward the woods.

Move, move, move!

"It's Liam!" Derek shrieked almost gleefully, staring at the screen. "Should we answer, let him know what we're doing?"

"You're out of your mind," Stella said in horror.

Derek laughed and threw down the phone. With his heavy construction boots, he stomped up and down, grinding the cell into the dust and pebbles. "Maybe I will have to kill him next, Mommie dearest," he said, breathing hard from excitement.

"Over my dead body."

He turned his razor-sharp attention on Stella. "You're getting me hard."

"Fuck you," she said, daring him in a sexual way

Rory turned away from the perverse chemistry to find her cell. Her phone was there, inches from her hand. All he had to do was move a few feet toward Stella, and she could grab it, pray that it still worked.

"I'm leaving," Stella rasped.

She turned toward her Lexus and Derek jumped forward, intent on stopping her. This was her chance. Sliding across the ground, Rory reached over and snatched up the phone, then she vaulted to her feet. Up and running, she took off for the thicket of trees—her only chance of escape.

Run, run, run! Faster, Rory, move it!

She was flying and heard Stella shriek, "Let go of me! Let go of me! Oh, hell, she's getting away!"

Derek let out an echoing, furious roar.

Rory sped up. Adrenaline fired her blood, fear propelled her.

Bang!

Zzzpt! The bullet zipped past her. Rory stumbled, kept moving, fighting tears and fear. She zigged to the left, scrambling into berry vines.

Bang!

Another shot.

Another miss.

She pressed redial. Her arms and legs were on fire as thorns sliced into her exposed skin. She kept moving and rolled out of the blackberries, though their leafy vines clawed after her.

"Shit! What the hell?" Derek, too, had landed in the brambles.

Liam answered, sounding strange. "Rory, I—"

"I'm at Flavel! Derek's trying to kill me. Your mother—"

Bang!

Rory screamed as the bullet zinged into the tree just to her right. She dived left and landed in bushes at the edge of the small grouping of Douglas firs. She scrambled quickly behind the trees, hazarding a glance backwards. Stella was clinging to Derek's arm, making it difficult for him to aim.

Rory took off, charging into the trees, branches catching at her hair, as she hoped against hope that the copse was larger than it looked and that she wouldn't be running into an open area. Pausing behind a tree, she realized the cell phone was still in her hand, but Liam was no longer there. With shaking fingers, she tried to call him back. Failed twice. Sobbed. It wouldn't turn on. No lights, no apps. Derek's stomping must have killed it.

Liam was at his Tahoe. The cops were behind him, yelling at him. He'd run out of the room and through the station. "Wait!" someone had yelled. Maybe Mickelson.

"Derek's at the Flavel building with Rory!" he screamed. If they tried to stop him he didn't know what he'd do. Fight them. Wrestle them all.

He drove fast with fierce concentration, trying repeatedly to call Rory back but she wasn't answering. *God, oh, God. Let her be all right.*

His brother. His older brother.

It wasn't real. None of this was real.

He heard sirens in the distance behind him.

The cavalry.

He couldn't wait for them. He gripped the wheel, pressed his toe to the accelerator and swerved around a sedan moving at a snail's pace.

"Rory?"

Derek's voice, trying to soothe, too high with excitement to get the job done.

The bole of a tree was at her back. Ahead of her, thinning trees. Nowhere to go. If she ran he would shoot her in the back. No Stella to distract him.

"Aurora?" he said softly.

She tried to still her breathing.

"You know I don't want to hurt you. I've always liked you. Saw you in Point Roberts that time, and well, I've had a few dreams about you since then. Good dreams."

He was growing closer. Thirty feet behind her? Twenty? Was the fir really hiding her? Could he see something? A scrap of her blue shirt? Her jeans?

"It's that red hair. When I saw Teri, I saw you. You know what I mean?"

There was a fallen branch on the ground in front of her. Looked about the right circumference for her hand. Where was he? Ten feet?

She started counting in her head.

Traffic. Liam blasted his horn, running a red light. A chorus of angry horns blasted right back at him, but he made it through.

How far was he? How much time?

At least ten minutes.

"Shit!"

Rory stared at the branch. One, two—

"Gotcha!" Derek declared, jumping from behind the tree, gun leveled at her.

Rory emitted an aborted scream and then he was pinning her to the tree, rubbing up against her.

"Where's . . . Stella?" she gasped. She needed time. Time for Liam to get here. If he got the message . . . If he heard her before the phone gave out.

"You shouldn't care about her. She's the one who wanted you dead. DeGrere was supposed to wait for you, then kill you, then dear old Dad. Stella signed off on that."

"You killed DeGrere?"

"Had to. He was just too damn untrustworthy. Beth, too, as it turned out."

"But Teri was because she had red hair."

He picked up one of her curls, moving it between his fingers as somewhere overhead a crow let out an unworldly cackle. "True," he said meditatively. "Didn't know how much I liked it till Liam took up with you. It just seemed to grab me, you know? Recognizing those times in life when you're made for something . . . you know what I mean?"

She shook her head.

"Those moments that matter. I knew I was supposed to be with someone like you. But Liam got there first. He was always the good boy. Always knew how to play that role. But did he ever tell you about the time he got me in trouble? Stole Dad's liquor and I took the beating. Didn't tell you, did he?"

"No."

"I want you to kiss me. Do it like you mean it."

"What about Stella?"

He sighed. "I think it might be over with Mommie dearest now. What do you think?"

"I—don't know."

"We stayed away from each other after the wedding. Really difficult for her. But it started up again, about the time Jacoby found you. Couldn't keep my hands off her, and she's just the same. Don't let her fool you. But I wanted more."

"What about—"

"Shhh." He put his finger over her mouth. "You're stalling."

"No, I'm—"

He ground his mouth down on hers and pressed her into the tree, the bark hard against her. "Kiss me back, or pay the price," he warned.

She didn't have to ask what the price was. It was her life.

Liam bumped down the drive to Flavel with its traces of graffitti and broken windows. He drove around the back and there was his mother's car. Stella was on the ground, kneeling forward, sobbing.

When she saw him she stared at him with a tearstained face. "It's not my fault. I tried to save you."

"Where's Rory?" he clipped out.

She looked toward the stand of Douglas firs. "He's got a gun," she called after him as Liam raced away.

Derek pulled back, cocked his head. "Someone's here."

Rory saw her chance. Her subdued urge exploded and she let it rip, gouging and clawing and screaming. Her knee slammed into his crotch.

Derek howled and staggered and she pushed him away. In

one swift movement she swept up the branch, leveled it at his head. He feinted at the last second and she got his shoulder, knocking the gun. They both reached for it. Rory got there first but he pulled it from her grasp.

He held it on her as they heard pounding footsteps and Liam yelling, "Derek! No! Derek!"

Then he turned the gun on himself and fired.

Epilogue

Rory sat by the pool, watching Charlotte, Landon, and Estella, her thoughts far away. Her mother sat beside her, a solid presence. Darlene was constantly grabbing Rory's hand and patting it, watching her with worried eyes.

The police had questioned her and Liam and Stella throughout the past few days, and Pauline Kirby had worked a deal with Candace, who knew enough to be dangerous. It was Geoff who'd finally met with the reporter and set her straight. Learning that Derek and Stella had plotted his death had had a profound effect on him. He was now grayer, quieter, even seemed thinner, though it had been less than a week since Derek's death.

Vivian stood at the edge of the pool near the children. She'd been quieter, too. Tears came and went as she processed. She was keeping her children as close to her as possible. Javier had been around almost constantly. Maybe they would reconcile again. Maybe they wouldn't.

Liam walked out to the pool. He was looking more haggard as well, but it did nothing to curb his appeal. She loved him. Always had. It was just a shock to learn how his mother and brother had plotted so viciously against them.

"How's your mother?" Darlene asked as he came near.

"Still professing her innocence. Still having no one believe her." He looked over at Charlotte, his expression softening.

"Her lawyer will help her," Darlene said.

"Maybe."

Rory knew Liam didn't know what to think about his mother. Didn't know what to wish for her.

"I spoke with another lawyer in their firm who's going to help straighten out all our legal problems."

Charlotte's citizenship . . . Rory's use of fake identification. Rory gazed at him gratefully.

"You okay?" he asked. Like he always asked since Derek had kidnapped her.

"Doing better," she answered, like she always did when he asked. Only this time she smiled.

He smiled back.

"You know I talked to Laurie, and she said that you would both rise from the ashes together," Darlene said. "Like the phoenix that—"

"Mom!" Rory cried.

Darlene grinned at her. "Well, am I wrong?"